MW01470643

Atlantis

Like you've never imagined it before !

Warrior women,

Ten times stronger than men
in one corner.

Military Men

With high technology and low morals
in the other.

The Ultimate
Battle of the Sexes

These two parts of Atlantis come in contact like a
spark and an open tank of gasoline
and the conflagratiosn destroys civilization
at tthe dawn of time, 15,000 years ago.

Master Storyteller Neil Thompsett takes a totally
original look at this lost civilization and brings it to life
in such detail and color, that you will never be able to
think of Atlantis again without thinking of the
characters, the cultures and the conflicts he has created
in this remarkable saga.

Other novels by Neil Thompsett

Becoming
Human

(Written at 13)

Only Human
Martian Independence

(Written at 15)

Neil has a serious Learning Disability
He can't read and he can't write.
Yet, at 17, he's already published 3 novels !

Neil is a Gifted Visual Spatial Learner. He sees and learns and understands things in a very different way than the rest of us do. He has great difficulty reading and his handwriting is virtually illegible. This makes school work very difficult for him. Yet that disability turns into a special ability when it comes to his writing. It gives him special powers and turns everything into magic, somehow.

He brings an exciting freshness and an original twist to even everyday things. His books are complex, thought-provoking and unique, yet they are still full of action and remain very easy to read. Consequently, Neil's books are truly like no books you've ever come across before.

One New York reviewer wrote: *"Congratulations Mr Thompsett; you have devised a new style; crisp short images like comic book panels, with just as much action."* Famed deli man and author Murray "Boy" Maltin said *"All I can say is that if this is the kind of performance you get with a learning disability - give me one just like it !"* Psychologist Lee Travathan, in her book *"Rebel Writer"*, called Neil a *"young genius"* and said about him *"One more Rebel Writer hits the deck running, and we are all the better for it."* And Mr Sci Fi himself, Forrest J Ackerman, wrote: *"In my 85 years, I've only come across his like two or three times. Neil is one of those rare fellows who comes along only once or twice in a generation - a natural sotryteller - an untaught spellbinder."*

Suddenly, in Neil's hands, English is a whole new language

Since Neil doesn't read very much, when he sits down to write, he can't depend on using the phrases and words of other writers. He almost has to make up the language anew, for every sentence. He performs a sort of mental jiu jitsu on words and makes them sit up, roll over and do tricks that you never thought possible before. And, if he can't think of a word to express what he wants to say; well, he just invents one. Yet, no matter how original the phrasing, or how creative the word, you know exacty what he means.

So fasten your safety belt and take a deep breath - you're about to go on a reading adventure like none you've ever been on before.

(Unless you've read Neil's other books)

What this means for other kids with reading problems

Neil has a lot of trouble reading, so when he writes, he throws out all the difficult stuff and keeps in all the exciting stuff. As a result his books are remarkably easy to read - especially for kids, like Neil himself, who have problems with reading. For many of these kids, Neil's books are the first books they've ever read all the way through.

Neil speaks at local schools to help motivate kids with learning disabilities and he donates his books to schools, learning centres and even to Juvenile Hall to help kids with reading difficulties.

Here's a quick smapling of the kind sof responses he gets:

"Dear Neil; Thank you for your gift of books to the Barry J Nixdorf Juvenile Hall. These books will be an inspiration to the kids. To know that they can use their imagination, as the author has done, to bring entertainment and information to others will be a wonderful lesson. "

Juanita Stanley,
Program Manager, Operation Read LA Coutnry Parole Department;

Dear Neil; I passed both of your books on to a specialist who deals with children with learnign and behavioural problems. They ahve put ina budget request to roder a number of copies for use as examples and as a workbook of sorts. You will be hearing from them as soon as they get budget approval.
Ross McKay; New Brunswick, Canada.

Hey Neil; - *Just to tell you - my English teacher may use your book 'Becoming Human' in her class next semester or next year. My friend is hooked so I might have problems getting my book back.*
Michelle Monk - Ontario Canada

I recently received your books as a gift. I am a teacher and tutor and would like to give a few of my students a copy of your book. Good luck in your future endeavors and your studies.
Jerry L Clark- Bellflower California

Praise for Neil's work

Neil's first book was published when he was 13 and his second when he was 14. Since then, his books have been selling all over the world. He's been written up in newspapers from Beverly Hills to Hong Kong, he's been on TV talk shows and he's even been written up in a book by a psychologist. Here's what people are saying about Neil and his work:

About three bloody bodies per page . . . but somehow the piece is irritatingly compelling -Paul McGuire/South China Morning Post (Hong Kong)

The turn of nearly every page brings a fresh carcass or obliterated city . . . a diverting Sci-Fi thriller from, the visceral imaginings of Beverly Hills' own Neil Lee Thompsett - Ben Davidson/Beverly Hills Courier

Congratulations Mr. Thompsett upon an extraordinary novel. You have devised a new style: crisp, short images like panels in a comic book, with just as much action. Keep writing. Best of luck - A Walker Bingham IV/NYC

Dear Neil; Forry Ackerman sent me a copy of your novel: Becoming Human. Reading it had been an enjoyable experience. It reminds me very much of the rip-roaring space stories that used to appear in the pulp magazines in the years when space travel was just a dream.This is a remarkable creation for a person of your age. I hope it turns out to be just the first in a constantly improving succession of books from you.
Harry Warner Jr / Hagerstown MD

Dear Neil - I am a 61 year old grandmother who ahd never read science fiction until I got your book Becoming Human. Now I am an SF fan.
Suzy Tse /Porto Alegre, Brazil

Neil - I must admit: Becoming Human must be the most insightful work ever written by a 13 year old. The aliens in your story had to become warriors to survive. Maybe war is a virus or a pathology as you describe it, or maybe the terms human and violent are synonymous.
Thanks for the great read. - Jim Starkloff

To the Publishers of Neil Thompsett:
We just can't get enough of him down here
Marshall Corozza / Auckland, New Zealand

No Man's Land

The Warrior Women of Atlantis

Book One in the Atlantis Trilogy
by
Neil Lee Thompsett

noggin
FICTION

No Man's Land
The Warrior Women of Atlantis

ISBN 1-892412-38-1

FIRST EDITION
APRIL 2002

Published by
noggin
Galactic Headquarters
289 South Robertson Blvd, PMB Penthouse Suite 880
Beverly Hills California, CA 90211

To order
Copies of this book are available for US$ 13.00
(plus US$2.00 for shipping and handling in USA).
Write to the above address and include payment in full.
(Don't forget this last part).
Make out cheques to: Noggin
or visit our website at:
www.nogginshop.com
(Prices subject to change without warning)

Warning

Weasel words
This is a work of fiction.
Any resemblance to any person, living, dead or unborn,
or any locale or event in the past, present or future
is entirely coincidental.
And any attempt to claim otherwise is just plain stupid.

*I dedicate this book to my father
-the Raggedy Old Man-
The most mysterious Atlantean of them all*

Acknowledgements

I'd like to give thanks

To all my friends who were my dearest friends
To all my friends who feigned friendship
To all the girls who helped me up
To all the girls who turned me down
To all the teachers who tried their best
To al the teachers who did their worst
To all those who lived
To all those who died

May you all have as much fun as I am having
on your journey to Becoming Human

I'd also like to thank my mom, my dad and
my brother for all their help and support

Neil Lee Thompsett
Beverly Hills, 2002

Cover illustrations and all interior illustrations
by Neil Lee Thompsett

It takes a lifetime
to find a simple life

You are here

15,000 years ago, long before the mud-cities of Erech or Ur were built and long before recorded human history began, there was a great civilization, with electricity, radio, writing and high technology, It was called Atlantis. But it didn't sink into the ocean, as all the rumors imply. In fact, it's still there. Fabled Atlantis was actually in both North and South America.

In the Sud, there was a mighty technical society which had mastered medicine, engineering, architecture and flight. They powered their machines by breaking the molecular bonds of crystals. So they ended up scouring the world for more and more diamonds and gems. (Which explains why there aren't any left in Europe, North Africa and South America). They built pyramids, (half-diamond shapes), so their flying machines could find the diamond collection points in the heavy jungles and forests of the time and, when the diamonds ran out, they simply left. They had the technology to get to Europe. The European natives did not have the technology to follow them back to Atlantis. So when the Atlanteans stopped coming, the natives simply said that Atlantis sank into the sea. And that's the truth of the matter. But not the whole truth.

For in North Atlantis, in a forgotten land between the glaciers of the retreating Ice Age, there was another part of Atlantis. An Empire ruled by warrior women, who were ten times stronger than any man. Their entire culture was built on the idea that women were superior in all things and men were only toys or slaves.

Here is the true story of how these two halves of Atlantis discovered each other and what eventually happened because of it:

II

A glimpse
of the future,
written
slightly differently
than it
actually
happened.

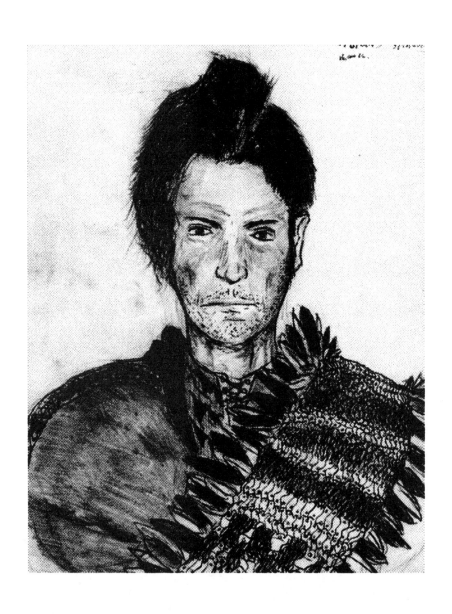

Kline - Leader of the Lost Expedition

Boys meet girl in Atlantis

I was sitting high in a tree when they found a woman to rape.

It was late afternoon and I'd climbed up there to get dry. Me and my little band of ruffians had crossed the barren miles of ice and finally found the fabled lands of the North Continent. As promised, they were lush and fertile, with endless grass and greenery. But, this close to the ever-melting ice, they were soggy and humid. I wanted a chance to write up our adventure in my journal and dry out at the same time. But if truth be told, I was happy to get well above the stink of my men. After three weeks in the same clothes, none of them were fit company.

And then, of course, there were the diamonds.

Four full bags of huge uncut stones that one of them had picked up right off the ground. The possibilities for mining and endless power were unlimited. I wanted to look at the diamonds, by myself, without thought of my thuggish crew slinking around and trying to steal some for themselves. As the other bags were passed around, no doubt they had pocketed many and kept them - but this bag was all I needed to present to investors to make the entire expedition a success - and we'd only just arrived.

I heard the yell - "Woman in the woods" and looked up. It was a cry I'd heard before on this journey. The men I'd managed to get on my crew to undertake a journey onto the endless ice, in a fool's quest for new diamonds, were not the sensitive poetic type of men. Most were on the run from jailers or the families of innocent people they had victimized or were just too stupid to realize the foolhardy mission we were on. So if they caught a woman alone, they showed no mercy.

"Surround her!" I heard, along with great stomping of boots and rustling of bushes.

Before they'd reached the glacier ice, they had also found women alone; one at their training camp and another before they went out on the ice.

They'd tracked them, surrounded them, gang raped them and then killed them. It wasn't an uncommon fate for women. Women in the Sudutan lands were viewed as property of their fathers, then of their husbands, then of their sons. But there were some rules: for example - if my group were to come across an ox or a pig, they would kill and eat it. And the lawful thing to do would be to pay the owner a fair price for the consumed beast.

The same applied to women. If you killed one, by law, you had to pay her family a certain price - determined by her age and physical beauty. That's the way it had always been done. That's the way my crew did it before they went onto the ice. Twice - that I knew of.

"What are you doing out in the woods alone, my pretty," I heard one of the men start the game.

I had heard it before and didn't much like it. They taunted the women they found. Humiliated them and had fun with them.

Then, suddenly, the games would end.

I had played similar games when I was a young man, but I no longer liked to play. Not since Ennis.

I had been thinking a lot about Ennis ever since we began this expedition. She'd financed it, in a way. She was my lover. I'd promised her I would care for her - and bring her along on this expedition - but then I'd let the a powerful man have her in return for financing the expedition and furthering my own career - 'Marsolla forgive me,' I often said to myself - but there was no forgiveness there.

The man had financed this trip but what I'd profited in sponsorship, I was now paying back in guilt. I just couldn't get her out of my mind. Especially after watching how my men treated other women.

For I'd sold my sweet Ennis to the most degenerate of men - the Emperor-King himself - who made my rough crew seem like Sudutan gentlemen.

He had probably used her far worse than my men would ever use women - and tossed her broken body away like trash - just an afternoon's diversion.

I hadn't given it a second thought at the time. You buy and sell possessions all your life. Everyone does. Yet you don't stay up nights thinking about the fate of that knife you sold. Or that dog. Yet I could not get her out of my mind.

VI

And when my men had killed the other two girls and paid off their families, the only tears that were shed by anyone were my own. And even I didn't know why.

I looked down.

They had surrounded the woman in the clearing almost directly below me. They were taking turns talking to her and teasing her - working up their nerve.

Although I was their leader, I didn't want to try and stop them now. I hadn't stopped them before because it was an accepted custom in Sudutan lands. Everyone knew to keep their women inside. There were consequences for letting women roam about alone - the masters of the women and the women themselves knew those consequences. Just as all people know the consequences of getting between a mother bear and her cub or between a wolf-pack and its kill. Nature will take its course. And, following their three weeks on the ice, I didn't want to try and curb their hungers. After all, I still depended on them to get me back.So I made no effort to stop what was going on. But I made no effort to look away, either.

And yet . . . the woman didn't seem to be cowering in terror, like the others had. She seemed to feel as if she had been stopped by a group of children who wanted to play.

'Been gok, feem of your T'hrist, Mistress ?" she said.

The men laughed.

I frowned. It sounded familiar.

They had her completely surrounded now and she had stopped walking.

Suddenly it hit me - it was the old language. She spoke the way we all spoke 1000 years ago. I had studied the old form of speech for years to do my research work, but I had never heard it spoken.

"Men-things, " she had said, using the insulting term; "Where goes your Mistress ?"

Maybe I had it wrong, I thought. It seemed a silly thing to say, under the circumstances. But it was definitely the old language. I was delighted. Here was another treasure of my first expedition. I had discovered that there were people in the North Continent and that they were related to the Sudutans. 1000 years ago they must have broken away from civilization and settled up here int he land between the ice.

VII

What I thought was some trick or art of self-defense, I now saw was a terrible strength. The strength of ten strong men in the body of one small woman. Like a full grown warrior fighting with toddlers.

VIII

I thought I would really be famous now. I would go down in history for this discovery alone, whether we found another full throat of diamonds or not. I was in heaven, imagining my fame.

"She speaks nonsense" said one of the men

"Maybe she's an idiot" said another.

"You don't screw her brain" said a third.

They all laughed.

"*Tusave n'aow must'y Ik'n-Streys ?*" she said loudly, turning slowly and looking around the circle.

"You poor men look terrible - are you lost or are you strays ?" she had said. I was understanding every word now.

"There she goes again with the gibberish" one of the men shook his head.

"I like my women quiet - no matter what they speak" said one pulling out a knife. "Let me cut her tongue out first and shut her up."

The woman turned to this one. "Your Mistress allows you to carry weapons ?" she asked arrogantly. "I'll have her up on charges."

The man walked closer to her.

"Careful there - her tongue is sharp," someone yelled out.

The others laughed.

The woman looked at him curiously. She was a smallish woman and the man towered over her, even though he was one of the shortest of the group. He held the knife low in one hand and reached down with the other to grab her by the neck.

"You dare touch me, uninvited, man ?" she said contemptuously as she grabbed his outstretched arm and snapped it like a twig.

The man roared like a wounded bear and tried to ram her with the knife. She caught his arm easily, and put her other hand on the back of his neck. Then she turned the knife inward and slowly, as he watched in horror, she forced his own hand to push the knife between his own ribs and into his heart. Blood spurted. She held him up off the ground by the back of the neck, as one would hold a dead rabbit, and turned, displaying his dying to the circle.

"Never get above yourselves." she said. "The price, as you can see, is death !"

The men still didn't understand her, so when they got over their shock they attacked altogether, like a pack of wolves.

IX

Yet she seemed unconcerned.

What I thought was some trick or art of self-defense, I now saw was a terrible strength. The strength of ten strong men in the body of one small woman. Like a full grown warrior fighting with toddlers.

She had no weapon, yet she ripped the arm completely off one man and the head off another. One large man she tossed through the air over twenty feet and his skull was stove in on the trunk of the tree where I hid. Yet another she simply hit in the chest and stopped his heart.

Within seconds she had despatched all of the armed men, and then came over to stand under my tree.

I held my breath, beginning to cry in terror as she walked closer. She looked up at me with her terrible gaze. She pointed to the man with the knife; the first she had killed, and held up her arm with one finger raised.

She swept her arm around at all the others she had killed, and held up her arm with two fingers raised. She pointed at me next, cowering up my tree. She raised three fingers, then she simply shook her head, wiped her hands together and continued on her way, humming away, as if she had just paused to step on a few ants.

As for me, I held my breath until I was sure that she was well and truly gone.

- From Kline's Journal: ' The Lost Expeditioneers'

X

The best stories
always
start
at the end.

The Mediterranean coast of Spain
on a warm Tuesday evening,
13,000 B.C.

The end of this story was quite undramatic.

Two old men were sitting and talking and drinking. One got up and left. The other stayed.

It was near the shore, by a the fisherman's wooden docking port, at an open pub with no walls but only four poles holding up the thatched roof. The air was humid and warm.

There, in the middle of the room, drinking wheat alcohol, sat the Old Man, who had stayed. But he was not alone for long. He was soon surrounded by bigger, stronger fishermen who came over only listen to him. They always listened to his tales - it was the best entertainment they ever had. It was also the only entertainment they ever had.

They knew that he was old and foreign but they still listened to him as he told each story with just as much drama as the last, only resulting in everyone wanting him to go on.

He was mesmerizing.

His stories were interesting and so described in detail that some even thought that his stories might have actually happened.

Whenever someone asked him to tell a grand story, the whole room would go silent waiting for him to project his voice.

He then would look at all the eager faces and begin:

"Although none of you have ever left this place, tonight I will tell you how you first came to be here. Tonight, I will tell you the story of the great battle which brought the end to Marsolla - the world where all life began.

At the peak of civilization, on Marsolla, our great ancestors were like gods. They rode nothing but their mighty thoughts, and went anywhere they wanted. They thought 'I want to go over there.'

1

And instantly - they were there"

There was an amused laugh from the fishermen.

"They were able to survive under water without the fear of drowning, they went into the sky past the blue and they travelled to the very stars. All on the power of their thoughts alone.

They were magnificent. But they became arrogant. They searched across the great ocean of stars, and found a doorway into heaven. What they found there were the ones who formed Marsolla before anyone lived there. And our ancestors arrogantly thought that these powerful Gods were now keeping secrets from them. So they invaded heaven, mocked the Gods, and finally, they actually killed some of the Gods.

To kill your keepers. To kill your Gods. There is always shock and trauma at first, but then you get an unquenchable thirst for it.

And so the blood frenzy was upon them.

Our ancestors killed millions of the Gods - often just for the sport and thrill. They killed not because they had to, but only because they could. Then, after much patience, the Gods struck back. And did so with no mercy. To be pushed that far could only in return bring a push beyond imagining. The lives of our powerful ancestors were now endangered, for now they dealt with vengeful Gods. The ancestors were forced into a self inflicted war. The war took years, and many more of our ancestors died, still showing no end to their arrogance.

Finally at the turning point of the war, our home of paradise, Marsolla was cursed and plagued by the angry Gods. Thousands of their chariots and ships closed up, sailing fast through the sea of stars, ending all life there.

They finished it off totally , killing every man, woman and child and placing death dealing demons to kill any who still survived their wrath. Marsolla was blasted to desert, and the mind of Marsolla, who had been in all our thoughts for thousands of years, spoke to us no longer. But when the Gods left, they did not realize that the remnants of Marsolla's warriors, along with a large group of children had been told to flee by Marsolla, to find a new home and become a new, better people. And so the lesson is, don't be too arrogant . . . to buy an Old Man a drink.."

The spell was broken. The fishermen laughed and coughed and bought the Old Man his drink.

2

" You have told us the story of the great battle, the tales of the exodus from the cold world, and the tale of the wrath of the Gods. These are mighty tales indeed. But do you have any other stories to tell us, Old Man?" asked an eager fisherman.

The Old Man smiled and laughed through his nose as his wrinkled face showed his own joy in telling them. "I'm sorry, there isn't a single ordinary person who is worth a story. I don't know any more stories that I could tell you. You all know most of them by heart now. After all, I am an Old Man. I've been all over the world and seen everything there is to see. And have told all of it to you - who have never gone anywhere, nor seen anything. The telling is over."

All the fishermen started to grumble, feeling sad that he had no more stories to tell. He had told these stories ever since he had arrived a few months ago. He himself was a fisherman and, although he was new here, they respected him because he knew the sea better than anyone else in the world. As he sighed and sipped from his wooden cup he heard everyone go back to talking amongst themselves.

" What about Atlantis? What about the great civilization that once dominated us and all other lands of our fathers' fathers ?" shouted a large man. "If you've seen anything, you must have seen that ?"

The Old Man paid no attention to him and still took another drink from his cup.

The large man, grinning at the look of disgust the fishermen showed, came over uninvited.

He sat near the Old Man and gave a slight grin then quickly slapped the drink from the Old Man's hand. The Old Man still did nothing as he grabbed his fallen wooden cup again.

The big man then grabbed the Old Man with one hand. All the others backed away, knowing then who this was. This large man was a murderer, a crazed lunatic, a pirate looking for treasures to melt, and jewels to sell.

The Old Man turned and looked at him.

" Well Old Man, I have heard all sorts of stories of Atlantis in the bars and ports all across the seas. Are you the only storyteller who has no story about it ? Is it not past the pillars of stone out of the small sea and far into the large one ?

3

Is there not a three-ringed city in the capital of it ? Is it true that it's people use diamonds and gold for every thing?"

The Old Man looked at him, " You are a stupid one, aren't you ?"

" Do you know who I am, Old Man ?"

" Oh, yes I do. You are the sad little pirate who has killed many men, wanting something that none of them could give you. What is it you want ? The location of Atlantis ? It's that way. Good luck, "he pointed out to sea.

"You lie !" shouted the pirate.

The Old Man smiled as he gazed into the murderer's eyes, showing no fear to the large sea pirate.

" Atlantis is a myth you stupid piece of shit!" the Old Man shouted.

Everyone began to get frightened.

The pirate grinned as he spat on the Old Man.

" Are you choosing to be the next man to die then, Old Man ?" he said.

The Old Man's smile quickly turned into a frown. "I never die," he said quietly

Suddenly, as the pirate was going to punch, the Old Man swung his heavy wooden cup, breaking the pirate's nose. The pirate yelled in agony and as he bent over, howling, the Old Man calmly kicked him in the balls and watched him fall to the floor. He jumped on the big man's back, twisting the pirate's arm high on his back.

" Give me a fork!" shouted the Old Man.

A fisherman handed him a long-tined fork.

He stabbed the fork into the pirate's back, deep between two ribs. The fork held the twisted arm behind the pirate's back and the pressure of the twisted arm held the fork in place.

The pirate screamed.

The Old Man bent down to his ear.

"Here is a lesson from Atlantis that you can easily understand. What I did to you is a common slave-hold. It is woman's work."

The men at the bar, stupefied, began to laugh.

"You are one stupid ass, thinking that you could hurt even an Old Man like me. If you want some wisdom, here's some for you to remember: Never underestimate the old who have seen the heat of battle many more times than the young who have only heard it in boasts and rants and dreams of glory. Being old, they don't give a damn for dying. And it is those who don't give a damn that always win. "

The Old Man twisted the fork a little, hearing the pirate scream in agony, then left him on the dirt floor.

The Old Man stood up, grabbing his cup which was slightly cracked. He walked over to the bartender and held up his cup as he turned and faced the fishermen.

"And that's the only story of Atlantis you're going to get out of me !" he said as he began to laugh. The fishermen cheered him on.

He sat back down, handing the wooden cup to the bartender, " May I have one more drink?" he said.

The bartender smiled and poured him another cup from a pot filled with strong drink.

" This one's on me." the bartender said.

The Old Man drank it quickly as it leaked out of the cracks in his cup. All over the room, the fishermen were clapping and coming over to him, praising him like a hero.

They then started to kick the pirate and threw him out of the bar.

The Old Man went back to sitting and became a sweet Old Man once more, drunk and mumbling.

The fishermen didn't questioned why he never wanted to tell stories of Atlantis. The way it sounded, the island must have existed because he seemed to feel sad when they mentioned the name, but that was all they knew and they respected his silence.

Later that night, the Old Man started to get drunker than usual.

He was singing folk songs with the other fishermen and was sinking deeper into mumblings and ramblings instead of actual words, Then everyone began to get tired and started to head home. The Old Man was quite sick and weak. As he made his way home, he began to feel dizzy. His vision was blurred and spinning. As he mumbled the songs and doddled down the wooden roads, leading to his small shack, he fell to the ground.

" What?" he mumbled, confused, drunk and furious at something. As he tried to stand up again, he began to look around.

" What you want, you can't have, pirate!" he shouted to the darkness all around him. All that echoed back to his yells were splashes of the water to the sand and the creaking of boats.

Nothing else shouted back at him.

"Atlantis is no more !" he bellowed.

A few torches, which were burning their wax slowly, glowed on the path to his shack. The Old Man started to breath deeply, still feeling scared and walking briskly now.

" Leave me in peace!" shouted the Old Man.

He began to feel something catching up with him, so he began to run and try to get to safety . But the sounds of footsteps were stronger, faster, and greater in mass than the Old Man. Suddenly the Old Man stopped to turn around, drawing a knife.

There was no one there.

The Old Man began to get nervous, anxiously moving around, trying to be quick and alert.

" I may be drunk, pirate, but I am still a skilled swordsman." shouted the Old Man trying not to blink. He looked side to side, trying to catch some movement in action.

Suddenly in a flash, a group of pirates rushed the Old Man. Drunk as he was, he began a strange, graceful dance with hands and feet and knife flashing out almost too fast to see. In an instant, his attackers were all cut and bleeding. Even barely able to stand, the Old Man dispensed with all who came within the reach of his hands or feet. His attackers lay about the path, groaning and moaning and bleeding. The Old Man turned slowly around, looking for more attackers.

Suddenly the pirate king, whose nose was broken and whose arm was wrapped in a cloth came out of the darkness. As one of the attackers groggily rose from the ground and the Old Man turned to face him, the pirate threw a large rock and hit the Old Man on the back of the head. Then the pirate, holding a stout stick, ran to where the Old Man lay. swinging it powerfully in a quick blow to the Old Man's head, knocking him out   The Old Man lay on the floor, completely unconscious from the blow. The pirate grinned as he directed some men to pick the Old Man up and then he walked to his boat with his limping, groaning crew.

It was pitch dark, and his main crew were preparing the supplies, walking up the plank and placing barrels all over the deck. The pirate walked up the plank, pointing the way for the others who were carrying up the torches.

He showed them where to throw the Old Man to the floor as the others sealed up the boat and got ready for sailing.

" Found your new crew member, Likooshas?" asked one of the crewmen.

The pirate grinned at him. " No, but I have found the key to our locked door." Likooshas said. "The locked door to Atlantis."" Greko, take him in and tie him to the mast." Likooshas shouted at me.

I was 13 and sort of the cabin boy and adopted son of the crew, so I got to do all the horrible jobs. "And tie him well, he is a holy terror, even dead drunk."

Others in the crew told me the story of the Old Maninthe tavern when he stabbed Likooshas and on the pathway, where he fought them off so well, but this was where I first saw the Old Man, for myself.

I was scared to look at our Pirate chieftain. He was a strong man of uncertain temper and could kill me if he felt like it. I nodded to him, saying nothing, for fear that he would get furious and try to hurt me.

I looked to the unconsious Old Man and grabbed him by the waist then threw him over my shoulder. He was frail and light. How could this old grandpa be a threat, I thought. Nevertheless, I slowly walked to the bottom rowing deck and tied him tightly to the mast. The bruise on his head was swelling and looked rather discolored.

" Let's set sail now!" shouted Likooshas as he stepped to the rudder of the long boat. Men started to jump to the bottom deck, getting to a seat and grabbing the giant paddles. I went to a bench too, beginning to row with the others.

We made a quiet getaway from the fishermen's village long before dawn. Where we were going was along the edge of the Inland Sea, then from there, we would make our final stop at the Gates of Stone before heading to Atlantis - and glory.

After a while, when the sun was just begiinging to come up, we stopped rowing and pulled down the sail. The night man took control of steering the rudder of the ship and the rest of us slept like dogs in the sun. All together we got six hours of sleep before waking and rowing into land and docking at the next safe port.

It was early evening and the others had wandered off to get their last drinks, their last pleasures, and their last-minute supplies, knowing that they would be gone for a long time.

I stayed behind. I never liked traveling with the others in port, especially at night. Since I was short, I was afraid that I would get robbed or even killed at these sorts of markets after dark.

Although I seldom got to see the darker side of these ports, nor seldom wanted to, I always went to the market places in daylight if I could. I loved the waves and tides of people who would wash through a good market square over the course of a day. And I loved the stories people would tell me about their lives and their families and the histories of their countries and cities. I would be rewarded with the sound of the crashing waves of history and the greenish blue depths of their triumphs and miseries - as much as I was by the waves and colors and tides of the ocean.

I was born to sail the seas - so said the soothsayers - and I took that to mean the oceans of water and those of human affairs and there was nothing that was going to stop me.That was why I chose to join these pirates. To see the ports and parts of the ocean where the fishers and traders never go. Just to sail virgin ocean and feel the thrill of discovery. I stayed with them, not because of the treasures of Atlantis. I had no use for treasure. But the tale of Atlantis - now that was a story worth hearing.

I was looking out at the view of the port, seeing the other boats docked and the people coming off of them. I hadn't noticed many things that day, so excited was I about the upcoming voyage. One of the things I did notice, however, was that the Old Man had come to.

" Where - Who ?" he mumbled.

He was confused and unsure of himself.

I turned to him, he saw me and became startled.

" Get me out of this, boy !" he shouted, beginning to fight and move up and down, trying to loosen the ropes tied around him.

I said nothing to him, slowly coming closer.

" What are you doing ? Help me get loose !" he shouted. He started to growl, still fighting and moving around, trying to get loose. I came nearer and sat close to him, feeling scared.

" Is it true ?" I asked him nervously.

He looked at me with concern, " Are you bloody stupid and deaf? I told you to release me and now you are asking me a question which seems to be gibberish."

I only looked at him.

" I'm sorry, I cannot release you."

He looked at me,

" Why not?"

"Direct commands of Likooshas." I replied to him.

"Are you telling me that you cannot save a sweet Old Man like me but you can listen to a pigshit pirate who seems to spend more time on the floor drunk than sailing? You must be mentally ill if you are going to listen to a grunt like him."

I looked at him,

" You're wrong ! He provides for us. He got us this boat which was considered the best for sailing long distance."

" This boat ? What long distance could ape men like you hope to go in a jumped up rowboat like this ?"

"We sail for Atlantis, with the tide "

"You all plan to go to Atlantis in this? This couldn't handle a change in the tide. Believe me, the sea gets much more rough than this little puddle - your Inland Sea. You really have no idea, boy. The sea is too large and this boat is too small to get there or anywhere near. " he said.

"Then there really is an Atlantis ? And you have really sailed there?"

"I do not speak of Atlantis."

" Why is it that you won't talk about Atlantis, Old Man?" I asked him, trying to get some info. Even if you do not know much, I value stories of all types. I save them up. I am a collector. Please tell me any stories of Atlantis that you've heard. Anything at all."

To me this was fascinating. I never really believed in the place - any more than I believed in Marsolla - although I thought the search would be magnificent in itself.

" Why don't I speak of Atlantis, you ask? Because it doesn't exist, boy. Your grunt thinks that it does but it doesn't. Not any more. Please let me go. All of you are sailing straight to death and I have no wish to keep you company on that journey."

" But there is too much evidence that it does exist, Old Man."

" What if I was to tell you that it did exist but not in the way that all of you imagined it to be?"

" So you do say that it does exists?"

" Yes, I mean that it exists as. . ." The Old Man looked to the side, hearing someone stepping up the plank. He quickly turned to me and looked extremely concerned, "Time is running out boy, please, if there is any sense in you, let me go and try to forget that any of this actually happened."

I was scared. If I let him go, Likooshas would of killed me.

Likooshas started to walk over to me,

" Good work Greko, you are a good guard."

The Old Man became frisky again, frantically trying to jump up, growling and cursing.

Likooshas turned to the Old Man, "Well, well, Old Man, I would have thought that you'd of escaped by now. You were quick to throw me onto the floor and stab me in the back, and just as quick to pummel my men about. Why is it that you do not try to escape now that you are sober? Have you finally decided to accept your fate ?"

The Old Man stopped struggling immediately. He first looked to me, then he turned to Likooshas. The Old Man looked directly into the pirate's pupils, almost as if he was reading him, then he slowly began to grin.

" What do you know of fate and destiny, whore-dripping ?"

" I know nothing of your fancy philosophies, Old Man, but this much I do know - every man and woman under heaven has a job to do - and fight though he may to shirk that job, it will be thrust upon him in the end, in one form or another - and if forced, will not be as much to his liking as if he volunteered to do it freely."

"Well said and well aimed. You wanted to see Atlantis ? Well then I have a deal for you, you loutish young Sea Pup. If you want me to bring you to Atlantis then you must be prepared to expect everything that you thought was a myth as real and that sometimes what you expect to find is not quite the thing you're looking for. If you want me to lead you willingly to the continent of Atlantis, you must all listen to me without questioning me. You must give me a quarter of every type booty you collect on the way and you must be prepared to fight anything that could come along including horrors that you cannot even begin to imagine now.

Not only that, but you must promise me that I will be returned to my home after you have what you are looking for."

Likooshas grinned, showing his sharp, tattered teeth.

"Your word on peace"

"My word"

" Greko, cut this man loose." he said to me.

I quickly ran over to the Old Man, untying the knots.

" What are you doing Old Man?" I whispered.

" He has tamed me with his destiny talk. It is a mission that was given to me by another, long ago, and that I have been covering over with drink and stories for 30 years around these backward colonies here.

My rest is over. I must take up my load again and return. It took a complete fool to remind me of that.

Besides - and let this be a life lesson to you, young Greko - the best deal is one in which everybody gets pretty well what he wants. I am giving the pirate what he wants, although he has no idea what he will be getting. And I get a ride back to fulfill my ancient fate, which I must do before I die.

Also, you'll get what you want too. If I am to die on this boat, which seems very likely, I want all of my memories to be transferred to you, so that they can be preserved. If I cannot do what my fate calls me to do, then I charge you with the mission of fulfilling my destiny. I do not want to be the only one burdened with what I know." answered the Old Man closely.

I looked to his grin and was confused by his logic. Last night he had laid low almost the entire crew, and somehow cut a hole in the back of Likooshas and broken his nose. And up to a second ago he was struggling to escape. Now he was civil and was going to be our guide.

I got the knot loose and pulled it apart. As I did, he slowly stood up, rubbing his hands and stretching his legs.

Likooshas walked over to the Old Man, but remembered to keep his distance.

The Old Man paid no attention to Likooshas. He looked around, seeing the crew of thirty returning to the boat, the single mast, and the single white sail wrapped around the stem seeming barely able to handle a day out at sea.

"I see you are admiring this magnificent ship. It's the best that you could find, I stole it myself." Likooshas said.

The Old Man looked at Likooshas and seemed to be disgusted. " If you plan to go with this ship, I recommend that you let me kill you all now and save all the hardship and pain that will occur between now and our eventual end."

" What ? Why do you underestimate this prized ship ?"asked Likooshas.

The Old Man looked at him with anger. He then began to point outwards."See the mast ?" the Old Man shouted.

" Yes ?" answered Likooshas.

" There's only one mast. That'll take you as far as the next port. Where we're going, there will be no next port."

" Well, it's a minor problem. After all, we have thirty good sturdy men who could row this boat whenever the wind gives out." Likooshas argued.

" Men can't paddle that far."

" We have supplies that could last us."

" How much worth ?"

" One month's worth, maybe more."

The Old Man nodded. " Alright, water?"

" About seven barrels."

" Not enough."

" Not enough? Fine, water will be a costless supply to stock up on." What about the design of the ship? We have two levels instead of one like the usual boats."

" The first level is sturdy but the second is open, it has to be sealed up. A good wave could fill us and swamp the boat. A decent storm could just wipe it out and sink it."

Likooshas began to get frustrated, He ground his teeth," Is there anything else you need to nit-pick about?" he asked.

The Old Man began to scald loudly, frowning and looking sharply. " Remember that you are the one who wants to sacrifice everyone here to go to the wretched land called Atlantis, so I expect you to not give me any quarrel, understand ?"

Likooshas grinned." Fine, what can we do to make this boat sailible ?"

The Old Man looked at the boat, stomping on the deck to see how weak it was, he then looked at the oars that stuck out of the sides of the boat.

" Is there any shallow water close by?" he asked.

" Yes, why?" replied Likooshas.

" If we're going to make this ship sailible then we're going to have to make a few major adjustments without losing any more money."

Likooshas looked to the man who held the handle of the rudder, then at the men getting ready to start rowing.

" Set sail, we need to stop up the shore a ways to make some adjustments" shouted Likooshas.

I walked over to the Old Man behind Likooshas' back and began to whisper to him. " What just happened? I thought that you wanted to get to Atlantis quickly now?" I whispered to him.

He grinned, " And I thought that you wanted to survive to know about Atlantis?" The Old Man answered.

"What?"

" Well, there is no sense transferring my knowledge and my fate to a dead man, is there? And that's what you'll be unless we can make this boat seaworthy. And convincing all of you that I am right by sailing now and dying, is not the type of convincing I want to do."

" Why do you want to convince any of us?" I whispered.

He only looked at me.

The boat began to move slowly from the port and was moving west .

Likooshas walked over to see the view of the beach, not looking back at us. "I hope you're right about this deal, Old Man." he said.

" You know I'm right, pirate. If I wasn't, you would have tried to kill me right away." said the Old Man.

Likooshas turned his head to look at the Old Man, seemingly proving that he was wise and logical. He only grinned, lowering his brows and not showing his smile. The Old Man looked back at him not showing any of the laughter that he seemed to be feeling.

Likooshas turned his head to look once more on the shore line.

" Well then Old Man, I hope you survive." he said.

Three days had gone by. They had made stops along the shores to buy sails, lumber, axes, and many more barrels of water to get ready. The Old Man had made them buy strange foods like corn and flour, raisins and oranges.

They had landed on shallow water, pushing the boat onto the soft beach. There they unloaded their supplies and waited for the Old Man to tell them what to do.

The Old Man inspected the boat, this time from the bottom up. Still not sure where to start first, he sighed.

" Well Old Man, we have the tools and the resources, now you must tell us what to do." said Likooshas.

First, the time will be at least two months on the water, even with the South Winds. You will need much more food and much more water. Have half your men hunt a dozen deer and cut the meat into thin strips - this big - and leave them hanging in the sun to dry like the horsemen of the Mongol plains do. And have some other men take the corn and grind it into mealy pap like the dark Mhazis of Africa do. Seal the flour in watertight barrels and have at least 10 barrels of raisins and dried oranges sealed in the same manner.

Likooshas listened to what he said and sent men scurrying away to do his bidding.

The Old Man looked at the sails they had, which were thick, brightly colored and long.

" Greko, come here. I need your assistance," the Old Man shouted.

I ran over to him. " Yes sir?"

" Hold the other side of this sail."

I nodded, strutting over to the other side and picking up the sail.

Three more men came over, holding the long sail by its corners.

The Old Man backed away, looking at it.

He took out his dagger and suddenly stabbed a side of the sail that one of the men were holding on to.

The man was startled,

" Don't let go." the Old Man shouted.

He then slowly began to move the blade diagonally, cutting the long, rectangular sail into two triangles.

" Let go of them now!" said the Old Man.

He walked over to one of the men.

" Stitch up the edges and then, for one fourth of the sails we have, I want you to do this same thing."

The man was puzzled. " What will this do?"

The Old Man acidicly grinned as he looked at him.

" This will save your life."

Likooshas came over to him.

" First you tell us our supplies are no good, now you cut our sails up? What are you trying to do Old Man?"

The Old Man paid no attention as he began to look at the length of the ship.

"I'm trying to preserve my life - and yours along with it. I need you to cut down a big tree, smoothen them out, and fasten onto the ship." the Old Man ordered.

" What?" asked Likooshas.

" You heard me, it has to be big enough to reach three quarters the size of this ship" replied the Old Man.

Likooshas was puzzled but still grabbed his axe.

The Old Man turned around and was now furious." Well, what are you waiting for?"

Likooshas frowned as he grumbled. He turned around, walking up the beach.

"I need four strong men to go with me, we'll be getting some lumber!" he shouted.

Likooshas pointed at the Old Man." You better be right about this Old Man, because if you're not "

"Trust me, I'm right. You'll kiss me on the lips for doing this !" the Old Man shouted in retaliation and showed his snaggly teeth.

Likooshas turned and started to walk again with the others.

All day, the crew were working frantically to the measurements, the accuracy, and the instructions that the Old Man gave.

I was aiding the Old Man, giving him suggestions and a cup of water every now and then. Likooshas and his men returned, dragging a giant tree with them. The four men struggled, pulling the fastened rope on their backs as they dragged the tree onto the beach. The Old Man came up to the tree trunk, he looked at it and grinned.

" Good, all you need is to smoothen it all out and I'll show you how to fasten it onto the boat;" he said.

Likooshas grumbled, calling his men to go back into the forest.

I followed the Old Man as he went to sit down.

" Old Man, what do you expect to accomplish with these adjustments onto our boat?" I asked.

" I don't understand, boy." he asked.

" I mean . . . " I stopped, wanting to ask him the question about the adjustments but my intriguement with Atlantis kept coming up every time I tried to talk to him.

The Old Man grinned as I tried to arrange what I wanted to say.

" Well, if you can't talk straight then may I ask you a question?"

I was bewildered, raising one brow to his question.my paranoia was eating me but my curiosity was stronger.

" Yes, you may" I said.

He took a deep breath, closing his eyes and beginning to talk a little softer. " Do you really want to hear the forgotten tale of Atlantis?"

I was shocked, my nervousness started to overact with intensity. " Yes, yes. More than anything. I think that I am ready to hear it." I said anxiously.

He then looked at me with his dark eyes, I could feel his sharply pointed nose breathing on me. " Keep in mind that the tale I have, you must keep it as a secret. What I know could change everything and lead to chaos."

I was still anxious, paying no attention to his warning at all.

" Yes Old Man, tell me the story. I will not repeat it. I am a collector of tales, not a teller. And above all, I want to collect the true story of Atlantis." I said.

The Old Man began to lay back and take a deep breath. He wiped his brow with his fingers and got comfortable .

I sat down, thinking that it was going to be long, then he began...

"This is the story of us. The true story of where we came from. It is not the story I usually tell. Nor is it a story that you have ever heard before. But it is the true story.

Everyone beleives that Marsolla helped our ancestors get away to settle here. That is a lie. There are gods all around us.They do no look like us, but they created us. And we just never turned out right. Everytimethey create a new place for us, we revolt and try to escape. But they are wise and loving, and they never completely kill us all off. They take our children and try to make them grow up diffferently.

That's what they did with us.

They, not Marsolla, but the gods who fought and defeatede our ancestors, brought children to this world.

They put ten groups of children all over the world, with guards to protect and advise them.

Two groups were put in Atlantis. One in the South, where the land was warm and fertile. One in the North, between great walls of ice. They did not know about one another.

The Guardians died out of left to go back home and both groups were left on t heir own. The Northern group grew strangely. The women became stronger than the men. Much stronger. And their culture grew up based on that fact. Which made it very strange.

Perhaps it was something in the ice, for the group in the South had moved away from the ice, settling throughout the southern continent. They flourished and learned things beyond what others in Europe and Asia and Africa knew. They had become a technical civilization and required almost limitless energy to power their many machines. They discovered a way to extract that power from diamonds, crystals, and gems. So, to keep their power going, these southern Atlanteans began to explore the world they lived in.

In time, they conquered most places in the world, like your Europe, like Africa and Asia - not to expand their empire, but to search for more and more diamonds and crystals to keep their civilization going. They ravaged and mined most of the civilized world and when the diamonds ran out, they left, leaving the natives to fend for themselves. Still, even after travelling over much of the world, they knew nothing of the other civilization above them, for they believed it was totally covered with ice.

Most story tellers had come in contact with these miners and engineers from the South, or stories about them, that is why you hear so many magical versions of Atlantis. Simple things that the miners had, the natives saw as magical. Firestarters, flying machines, ocean going sailing ships and simple crystal technology. They were amazed and the stories reflect this. But you will find that all Atlantis stories end the same way. Atlantis sinks into the sea.

Well - not really, if you think about it - - for few natives ever saw Atlantis. All they saw were the Atlanteans. And when the diamonds were mined out, the Atlanteans left - in their great sailing ships - and sank into the sea. Atlantis had the technology to come to Europe, but Europe did not have the technology to go to Atlantis - and still doesn't

17

if this piece-of-crap ship is any indication. But believe me - Atlantis is still there - two huge continents - not two islands - and nothing has sunk - except ape-men Europeans trying to get there in ships like this.So that's the background you need to understand Atlantis. Now, for the story.

Unfortunately the story that I am going to tell you doesn't begin where most would.

Unlike other stories, I will not begin with the glory or downfall of Atlantis. The story that I remember begins deep in the North continent of Atlantis, in the wilderness where men are men - and women are 10 times stronger. Where these strong armed women rule like savage barbarian princesses and keep their men as property and slaves and where the silence is your only true companion.

This part of the story begins in the cold of a stormy night. In a winter storm amongst the greatest winter storms which had blown in over one thousand years of recorded history.

This story begins in one of the most frightening places in the world - in the deep, dark territory of Makaitia in North Atlantis.

It was late and the storm was dying down. In the great distance walked a tired horse, carrying a Buushu woman. She was skinny, bony and frostbitten, yet she seemed to hold onto something tenderly.

As she neared the village, she took hold of her wooly longcoat and began to unbutton it, uncovering the baby that she held. The infant cried for food, but the Buushu paid no attention to its cries.

As her horse stomped through the snow, she could smell the cattle meat that was being cooked in the town's eating house.

She gulped as she licked her lips. She got anxious to hurry up and wrapped her scarf tighter around her mouth. She then looked at the child, feeling mournful for it, feeling a warrior mother's love yet trying to keep her emotions shallow in front of it.

She then gave the horse two kicks, moving into a trot and then to a gallop towards the inn.

As she came to its crudely made gate, she stopped the horse, unwrapping her scarf and pushing back her long hood from her face.

She called out for the guard to come down from the gate and let her in.

A guardwoman slowly walked over to look down at her. The guard wore battle-torn armor which was loosely tied on. She carried a spear on her left arm, held with the right.

"I am rogue Buushu, killer of many and welcome everywhere. I have a baby boy to sell to you. That is if you open the gates." she replied to the Guard. "Otherwise the damn thing will freeze and you will pay for it."

" What do you want Buushu ?"asked the Guard. "Your kind is not welcomed here."

The Buushu woman looked up at her. "I am rogue Buushu, killer of many and welcome everywhere. I have a baby boy to sell to you. That is if you open the gates." she replied to the Guard. "Otherwise the damn thing will freeze and you will pay for it."

The guard looked at her, twitching with suspicion to her reply.

" Show me the boy!" shouted the guard.

She took out the baby from her unbuttoned coat and raised him.

" Open the gates, Makaiton fool, before the cold kills us both." shouted the Buushu.

The guard ran over to open the doors. She began to turn the cranes, opening the doors, As they creaked open, the Buushu slowly trotted her horse into the gated courtyard of the inn.

She saw that most of the houses in the compound were closed up, all except for the food house and the stable.

As she got off the horse, she grabbed her saddle bags and gave the horse to the stable keeper. She then walked over to the food house, smelling the cattle meat, almost tasting it.

She opened the doors, seeing a few women farmers and other merchants socializing.

She slowly walked in seeing everyone staring at her but used to it in this enemy territory. As she went to ask for a piece of meat, her infant boy started to cry, calling attention from the others. She grabbed the piece of meat roughly and took it to a table where she sat down, placing the infant on the table as well.

The baby cried but the woman ignored its call as she stuffed her face with the meat; swallowing it all down and savoring the taste of it.

A merchant woman came to sit next to her. The Buushu woman looked at the merchant's unusual tattoo which covered her left eye and cheek. It was the symbol of a wolf, thinly lined and dotted with embedded ink which made the outline stand out.

It was an old custom - one in which the first born of Makaiton women get tattooed.

The Buushu instantly knew that this was no ordinary merchant but was a believer of the Marsollan religion

A High Makaiton Clan member.

The merchant looked at the baby, not realizing that it was a boy. As she stroked its head, she uncovered a small tattoo on the back of it's neck. Even though it was small, it was very complicated and finely drawn - showing the child to be Oxna Buushu - the Royal clan, protectors of the Prophet of Tierra.

Tierra, the Goddess of all Buushu.

She smiled at it.

" How old is she?" asked the merchant.

The Buushu wiped her mouth and grabbed the baby,

" It's a he. If you want to buy him, he's twenty gold pieces."

The merchant looked at the child.

"For sale?" asked the merchant.

The woman grinned.

" Yes, he's good for training. I know that because he is my... son. A full blood Buushu, might I add." she said.

" Your son ? Why don't you arrange for him to get married to a wealthy woman ?"

" Believe me, if I had enough money, I would get arrangements for it. My family is poor, and I was given rogue status in the clan for insulting the Prophet and even though it doesn't fall on the children - no woman wants the son of a rogue to be a concubine. I have a promising daughter but there can only be room for one child. I cannot afford to feed the son. That is why I want to sell him, to feed the rest of my family." she said.

"But you do merchant work like me. Times are good. You should be making a lot , enough to support a small family."

" I am a warrior, trained and tested in the eyes of the Goddess Tierra. Good times means peaceful times. No one needs a rogue warrior. When they fight at all they hire loyal clan women.

Not defiant armies of one."

" I see." the merchant said, looking at the child and glimpsing at its frail features and runty size.

The Buushu looked to the Merchant.

" I didn't catch your name, Makaiton." the mother said.

The Makaiton merchant gave a fierce smile.

" My name is Cruce', Cruce'-Fix."

The woman holding the baby gave a polite nod, thanking the prospective buyer for telling her name.

Cruce'-Fix looked at the child. She saw the poor thing, still crying from hunger. It was so young, probably not old enough to even feed on solid foods. It needed to be breast fed. " Twenty gold pieces?" she said, taking out her bag and getting ready to go into Merchant battle-mode.

The woman holding the baby grinned aesthetically at her. " Yes, twenty."

She held out her hand ,waiting to receive the gold.

The Merchant held the pieces of gold tightly,

" He is too runty for twenty. He is likely dying from lack of food and the cold. Four."

"Nineteen and you must promise to raise him well."

" Pah. Five and I promise nothing. But you must tit-feed him before you go"

"Sixteen and you buy me a bottle and a bigger meal here"

"Ha ! I thought you were a warrior - not a robber. Six and a weapon like none you have ever seen before."

"Show me the weapon."

" Feed the child first."

The desperate woman quickly freed a breast from her unbuttoned coat and let the child suck until he was full and sleepy.

"The weapon ?"

Cruce' bent to her bag and took out some sort of weapon, never before seen by the eyes of the Buushu woman.

It looked to have the smooth and odd shape of a handle, sticking out at a 145 degree angle, while the top of it had three thick lead pipes sticking out of the front. The parts seemed to be made out of all sorts of things; wood covering, steel pipes from thick spears, and three triangular triggers on each side of the three pipes.

The merchant explained: " It's called a Mammoth musket. These three pipes are the barrel. It shoots out spear capsules like those you find in Buushu hunting spears. You point and aim with the barrels - like this - and then you squeeze the trigger - one for each barrel. Thus the target you're aiming at is shot and dies."

The woman looked at it in amazement.

" Where did you get such an advanced hunting tool ?"
" One of the smithwomen near the Eastern borders Makatia de-
signed them. They're expensive and extremely rare out here." She said
as she handed it to the Buushu.
" This plus six for the boy ?"
" Done."
"What is his name ?"
"He is only trade goods. He has no name. Call him Six—Piece to
remind you of his low value.
Now tell me about the weapon. It is too much and too powerful.
And you would give it to a Buushu warrior ? " the woman
chuckled. "You know well as I do, Makaiton. Buushu and Makaiton
are age old enemies. What is the catch ?"she finished.
"I have need of friends among worthy women on the frontier - I
have a plan to unite all the Clans." the merchant said. "I want you to
bring this back to your settlement, province, wherever you came from
and I want you to say that it was a gift from the Makaiton. Use it to buy
your way back into good grace and give your daughter an even better
future." She finished, with a grin. "Keep it yourself or give it to your
Mufta. It is more a symbol than a weapon - but it is a mighty weapon
too."
"For Mammoth ?"
"For the two legged she-mammoth"
The woman looked at the gun and grabbed it.
" Once you have had your three shots, what do you do with it -
use it as a club?"
"Load it with three more" said the Merchant, giving the Buushu a
bag of pellets and shot.
"I will do as you say and speak of Makaiton generosity " said the
Buushu warrior , "but I will keep the weapon rather than use it to buy
my way home."
Then she handed over the child.
Cruce' smiled, caressing the child in her arms. She then looked up
at the mother. She threw the pieces to her and motioned to the inn-
keeper to feed the woman and quench her thirst.
The Buushu began to giggle and laugh in happiness as she ate
and drank a full meal.

" You are so kind, merchant. I hope he becomes a good slave for you." she said when she finished.

As she began to stand up the merchant holding the child looked at her and asked: " Where are you going?"

The woman quickly picked up her saddle bags and buttoned up her armored coat.

She looked at the merchant." I'm leaving. You know that there are pickpockets all over. I must go back."

" Are you insane? It's dangerous out there, you might not be able to survive with the nocturnal hunters out there."

" Believe me, Makaiton. It is more so dangerous here in the company of your kind than anything I will run into out there." "Don't worry, my horse could outrun anything;" the woman said. "And I have my new weapon. Speaking of which, why is it that you Makaitons are not bringing this new device to the Imperial council ?" she asked.

The Imperial Council of the Arkaiton Empire was the dominant clan nation had occupied every region of the North for hundreds of years.

" Because we want to overthrow the Empire..." The merchant said with a sly tongue.

The woman looked at her, not sure if she was joking or not. "It is death to say so"

Cruce' grinned.

The woman grinned along with her, but still wasn't sure if she was joking. She then left the food house, frightened to spend more time with the merchant, and walked to the stable and got her horse.

As she rode to the gate she could hear her baby crying frantically to his mother leaving him. She covered her emotions by thinking of the money she had received for the child. Her breasts were full and her heart was heavy.

The gates opened and she trotted out, still having the cries of the baby echoing through her head. She trotted the horse further into the woods, taking the shortcut that she remembered. For hours she went deeper and deeper, into the woods, still hearing the cries in her head.

" Was it right that I traded my son for a few pieces of gold ?" she thought. " I shouldn't think of it, besides, what could my son have benefitted me with? A good marriage?

I doubt that he would have lived past six years.

I should not have guilt, besides, he's at a better place now, with that high caste slave merchant." she finished.

Although, she tried to clear her conscience, she still felt the throbbing feeling in her heart, a feeling that was almost as powerful as her horse. She felt the pain grow intensely the more she rode, so painful that her face began to show grief and sorrow.

She immediately felt that it was wrong after convincing herself that it was right. She began to hear smaller patters of feet coming up in tremendous speed but at first thought it was her imagination - her baby chasing after.

She looked back and saw nothing but glowing eyes and heard nothing but pants and growls. Hungry dire wolves had caught her scent.

She got scared, kicking the horse to go faster but the gigantic wolves began to catch up.

Suddenly a wolf jumped out in front of the horse, biting its neck and trying to bring it down. The tremendous weight of the pony-sized wolf, which was over 300 pounds, threw the horse off balance and within a few steps, it fell.

The woman rolled free and, seeing the wolves coming up, she began to run, digging her feet into the snow. She realized she could never outrun them. She stopped and turned anxious to fight with her spear at the ready. Then she took out her new pistol.

Most of the pack stayed with the horse to feed, but a few followed on tracking the woman.

The first wolf reached her quickly and lunged for her throat. She had no time to use her spear. It was too close. She pulled the trigger. Sparks and smoke puffed powerfully out of the barrel.

Her arm jumped back with the recoil as the lead pellet hit the wolf in the chest and turned him right over in the air. Two more were coming , she pulled the trigger twice more, killing both and turned to run for the trees. She was now hearing more behind her but was not sure if they were chasing her or feasting on her horse.

She realized she had no shots left and no idea how to reload. As she ran, she heard something else. She could hear the cry of her child loudly - not sure if it was real or in her mind.

The Old Man had stopped telling his story once the evening came. " Why can't you continue the story Old Man?" I frustratedly asked, thinking that, like most stories, it would come to an end soon and tie up all the loose pieces that the Old Man had left dangling.

He only looked at me, patting me on the head.

The noises of hammerings and sawing filled the evening. Sawdust was so thick in the air that it made some of the men sneeze.

" This story is too long to tell in an evening." he said.

" It's probably too long only because you won't finish it. No story is too long to tell in an evening. You're just torturing me. Now finish it !" I shouted.

He gave a mild chuckle at my comment. "It's good that you are the sophist type, selfish and shallow, but you can't argue with the Master of Argument. Trust me, you'll hear the rest of the story, just not all at once."

I wanted to say something but I couldn't think of anything to say.

" Old Man, where do we move the barrels ?" asked a crewman, trying to figure out a space problem.

The Old Man began to walk over and I followed him, curious to know what was going on.

The Old Man looked to the barrels which were fastened onto the boat. "Unload them, the construction will take a little longer than Likooshas expects."

The man looked at the barrels, " Likooshas expects to have this boat done by morning." he said.

" Well Likooshas expects a lot of things and will be disappointed in most. He's going to have to learn that patience is the key to everything." the Old Man replied.

The man sighed and called for help in unloading the barrels. The Old Man then looked at the shore line, then at the evening sky. I looked at him, " What's wrong Old Man?" I asked.

"There's a storm coming," he said. He then shouted out; " Tie down the boat! Get all the supplies into the ship, there's a storm coming over!"

The men were puzzled, "Don't be silly. There's no storm coming!" shouted one of them.

Suddenly it started to rain.

The Old Man looked up at the unconvinced man, " Satisfied ? I am always right. You are always wrong. Don't question my orders again. Now do as I say before the storm gets worse." he shouted. "And it will."

The others grumbled once more as they were proved wrong and the Old Man was proved right.

I began to get curious. He seemed to be taking charge of a plan which he dreaded. All of it was rather unusual. He had finally started talking about the stories of Atlantis and didn't mind. To me that was a great leap - from a man who wanted to escape Likooshas to a man who insisted in not only going - but leading us all to the Lost Island.

As the rain got much more intense, I shielded my eyes with my hands and I walked closer to the Old Man.

"All right Old Man, if you do not want to finish the story now then when do you plan to?" I shouted to him.

He only grinned.

" Why, this story will take longer than you think. It took a lifetime of 60 years for me to hear, translate, and fully understand it, so I guarantee you that it will be a long time from now before we're done with it.

Trust me when I say this, young Greko; when you asked me to tell you my story of Atlantis, you thought that it was going to be a short fable or a poem written by some sophist or anchorite of some sort.

After you hear the rest of it, and the telling will take weeks, it's going to take another entire lifetime for you to fully understand it." He then turned around and headed to his loosely built shelter, I ran closer to him and grabbed his raggedy shirt,

" You may be telling the truth but I never asked you for that, I asked you when you'll continue the story."

He briskly turned his head, giving a frowning look,

" By midday we will start where we left off. Now let go of my shirt before I smash your face in." he said.

I grinned, but quickly let go of his shirt.

" Until then, Old Man;" I said as I made my way to my shelter.

Later that night, I tossed and turned, wanting to know more information about the child and its mother that the Old Man spoke of. I couldn't stand it, thinking of possibilities of what was yet to come, the feeling of wanting to know was so intense that I couldn't sleep at all . All I could do was wait for the next morning to arrive so I could hear the rest of the story.

The morning came shining brightly over the beach. The sand was covered in washed up branches and rocks from the storm last night. Likooshas, who was secretly afraid of storms and always drank to blot them out, woke up with a terrible hangover. He was even more sore when he found out that we weren't ready to leave to the Atlantis yet.

Almost everyone woke up sore, everyone except the Old Man. He woke up with a large pleasing grin on his face. He seemed to enjoy the morning light more than the evening gleam.

He stretched and yawned and began striding around, kicking everyone to get up and start work.

" Come on you lazy buggers, you want to get a good sixteen hours worth of work done on the boat before nightfall." he shouted as he continued to get everyone up.

He seemed to enjoy telling people what to do, I guess that was why he wanted to be part of this voyage, thinking that he would have complete control over everyone.   Fat chance of that with Likooshas around.

Throughout the day, the Old Man was telling the crew how to attach the large tree trunks onto the ship. This would be for the extra mast that would fold in and out of the ship to hold more sail.

That seemed to be the main project all day.

The later it got, the more anxious I got , wanting to hear more of the story. It was not until nightfall that he got into the mood of finishing up where he started.

"So, about the slave boy who was sold for six pieces of gold. Will you continue from there?" I asked as I started the fire near the shelter.

He sat down, warming himself near the fire and then gave a sigh of relief. " Listen to the sound of the crashing waves, it's breathtaking yet calm. The ocean is a wondrous world, boy, I believe you think the same thing." he said.

As I got comfortable on the sand, I rubbed my blistered hands and waited. " Yes you're right but what does that have to do with the slave boy?" I finally asked.

He laughed. "I'm sorry, I was just making a point which was in the moment. Anyways, back to the story. Yes as I remember it, it went like this: Let's see,"

He looked up with a smile on his face, Let's start with an introduction shall we ?"

I looked at him, wanting to hear the story.

" Alright," I said, waiting.

He laid back and closed his eyes, remembering a part of it. "Eighteen years had passed since the slave boy was sold off. That part won't have anything to do with this part for now. As I said before, the story goes like this:

The North was a world where advancement of oneself was not important. Only the advancement of the Clan. So the acceleration of technology was for the clan, not for profit. A world where outside conquest is irrelevant.

A world where technology is continually worked on, not to make it faster or sinister or elusive, but to make sure the clan could last forever. And to show loyalty as well as reliability was also very important. These people were people you have never heard of. These were the true wise ones. These were the people who lived in North Atlantis. Women mostly. In a world ruled by women . . ."

Drums were being beaten as hundreds of people roared with joy. The streets of the great city in the civilization ruled by women, were filled with liveliness. A parade was going by. Different rows of Clan women marched alongside giant wool-hoofed horses mounted with women warriors. Great mammoths decorated with war paint and ritualistic armor followed.

The women marching along, playing the drums and keeping the rows in unison were all wearing different kinds of armor. All of them were parts of different clans from all over the Northern continent of Atlantis.

Ritual instruments were being performed for the spectators who stood and watched.

This great day was "The Day of the Beginning." of the great Empire which spanned from the Western Ice-Capped mountains to the Eastern shores.

This City-state, Lina, was no ordinary place. Amongst all the other territories, provinces, and towns, this was the capitol of the Great Empire.

As the Parade went past the clay and stone houses, and the thousands of spectators, the Empress Ameraldia watched out of her grand three story balcony on the top of a mountain and gazed at her proud subjects. Her old thin hands rested on the cold stone and her grey hair was tied back to keep it from getting in her view. Her old eyes showed that she wanted to be part of the crowd. She knew that she had the power to arrange an outing but she worried for herself. For a woman of the age of 89, there was no telling what would happen to her.

Sassaska - The Chosen One

Although she wanted to be out in the environment, she knew that she couldn't. Not because of her health but because of the Empire. If she was harmed in some way, the throne would be left to an heir that was uneducated about the ways of governing.

It was a sad sentence that she made herself go through but it was one that she would have to carry out. Not only could she not leave the palace, she also had to accept the fact that another woman from outside of the family would have to rule. It was that way because she was unable to produce any heirs, herself. And it was much too late now.

Though the Empress was old and was expected to die within a few years, she felt that she had boundless energy now and was quite willing to become more of a mentor to the young heir - who had recently been chosen, so that the Empire would continue to be as strong as it had been for thousands of years.

The Old woman knew that her dynasty would end with her, yet she looked at it as more of a freedom than a failure. She had learned a long time ago that change was a part of nature and if something was not changed then it would soon destroy itself from the inside out, changing glorious accomplishments into feeble minded mistakes.

As her inner peace calmed her emotions, she began to hear footsteps coming to her. She turned around, seeing a slender woman standing in the doorway. The young woman's gown suggested that she was a high priestess, and, on closer examination, the way the woman's beads were intricately wrapped around her arm, showed she was one of the highest of the high.

The young priestess knelt down and bowed to the Empress without saying anything. The old Empress smiled dearly at her. "You may stand." she said.

The priestess stood and looked into her eyes, "You called to see me Grand Empress ?" she asked.

" Yes child. I wish to see who was to be the next woman in line to lead this great Empire - do you know yet that you have been chosen ?."

"I was just informed, Empress."

The Empress looked at the young woman's attire; a plain robe with a necklace that had ancient text written on it. The priestess' serene face showed youth and naivete, but there was a strength there, bred into her by a thousand years of Arkaiton Warrior Women.

She would do.

With experience and guidance, she would do just fine.

The grand old woman patted the girl's hair then, looking at her necklace, and she smiled once more.

" Empress Sassaska Batusha Girshy, doesn't that sound rather nice to you child ?"

Sassaska looked away in embarrassment. From the expression of her face the Old Woman could tell that she didn't seem to like the title.

" What's wrong child ?" She asked in curiosity." Don't you want to become the next ruler ?"

Sassaska turned to the old woman. "Grand Empress, I was born and raised a priestess. I don't know anything else. I don't know politics, strategy, or even the provinces that I will be controlling."

The old woman laughed gently, " Child, do you think that I knew what to do when my mother left me the throne? If I had the choice back then, I would have been a priestess myself. But I didn't have that luxury, child and nor do you."

She sighed and looked away to the side where the parade was still streaming by. "My life was a good one. I was a strong leader to this Empire and I only wish that I was able to bear children. To continue the line. My family reigned for two hundred years, bringing forth the Golden age of Atlantis."

She turned around and smiled at Sassaska. "For two hundred years, the rules and traditions have not changed. Slaves are still slaves, Borders are still borders, and order, organization and Government are still exactly what they used to be."

She gently stroked the side of the girl's soft cheek. ". . . But sometimes change is needed . . . to improve, to excel, to heighten. Perhaps we are too stiff and set in our ways.

Sassaska, when you become Empress, after I am gone, I want you to be one that will be remembered as a woman who changed the world - rather than one who simply, like me, kept it in place."

Sassaska tried not to show any negativity to the old woman's words; " I'll try my best Grand Empress. To become the great ruler you want me to become."

The old woman looked into Sassaska's eyes, now having both hands on her shoulders.

" Sassaska. Your family has always been loyal to the dynasty and when I die, your family's loyalties will be rewarded. Their reign will become as great as mine was. Perhaps greater. However there is one thing I want you to do. This will help you when you become Empress, a training course that I wish I had had when I was chosen."

The Empress then turned away, slowly walking towards her study area. Sassaska followed in curiosity. The Empress reached for a key under the cushion of the seat and unlocked the old, wooden cupboard. She reached inside and brought out five scrolls. She smiled as Sassaska inspected the scrolls. The Empress looked at her eager eyes, then unrolled one of the scrolls. The sketches on the unrolled parchment revealed four symbols scratched on with charcoal. Over these symbols, there was an outlining of a map. The map showed the entire continent and the symbols marked clan boundaries in each of the three provinces. The paper itself looked centuries old.

"Here are some facts that not even the High Priestess knows. It is information only the Empress can have access to. This is the one true map of the entire Arkaiton Empire."

"I never knew the Empire was so huge"

" It is not something we wish people to know - otherwise they will realize how difficult it is to govern efficiently and might decide to take a piece of it for themselves"

"Has it always been so big ?"

"Nothing much has changed for over two hundred years. In the west where we are, the main population of women clans are Arkaiton. Noble, brave, and loyal to whomever is on the throne."

"I thought it was an even mix of the clans."

"A thought we promote - but in fact the vast majority here in the west are Arkaiton - ready to protect their Empress at the heart of the Empire."

Sassaska smiled, " Natural born Zealots," she said.

The Empress laughed to hear her saying that. " Yes, that's right. You see - the priestess caste knows some secrets. Now, the symbol here in the middle, going further south than the rest are the territories of the Buushu. Their name - and very few know this - means the "Bull women" because it took over one thousand years to domesticate them, and even now some clans still choose to be defiant at times.

Although they might appear to be rude and arrogant, they are the only true allies that would aid in the protection of our capitol. What affects them, affects us. They are the best at weapon making, no one can beat them when it comes to markswomenship. They are brave fighters, the best. They can be your greatest friends or your worst enemies. Now the last one is. . ."

Sassaska stopped her before she could go on. "I'm sorry to do this to you, but why are you telling me information that is irrelevant ?"

The Empress looked at her with displeasement. "Once I die, there will be no one to guide you at all. You are about to become Empress. When you are, everyone will expect you to know all the answers, even to the questions which have no answers to them. You must know all there is to know - and only then can you use that knowledge as you see fit. It is the foundation of your reign."

Sassaska lowered her head in embarrassment. "Forgive me Empress . . . I am just too young and too naive to -"

The Empress smiled at her with a mother's sereneness. The Empress knew that she just had no idea what was involved in governing an Empire of women The Empress then rolled up the scroll and slowly put it back in the pile.

Sassaska stared at the several scrolls that Ameraldia took out next.

"Now Sassaska. You have no choice, you cannot continue your studies as a priestess and live the enlightened life until you die. Once you were chosen, that all ended for you. Unless you die in the next few months, you will reign. And, reign for decades in the most turbulent period the Empire has ever known. It is the greatest sacrifice anyone in the Empire has ever been forced to make. The life of an Empress is not grand. You will have to be able to hide your emotions, put your own personal loves and family aside and do what is best for the Empire every day of your life.

You'll be expected to approve hundreds of papers and agendas, you will have to order women to be executed and send your friends and family into battles that they cannot possibly survive. You will become cruel and selfish and obsessed with the health and welfare of your greatest lover - your Empire. And even when you pick or are assigned a man for marriage, you will barely see him and no matter how you feel, you will have to put all other citizens before him.

It is not a life for a sensitive woman. And so all of your sensitivity will be beaten out of you before you take the throne. Remember the life you had mapped out for yourself. Peaceful. Serene. Rewarding. It is not to be. You have a new life now and the eyes of history are upon you. Both lives end in the same path. They both end up with you alone, but the difference is responsibility.

In the old life, you are only responsible for yourself and the few children you might have had. Now you are the mother of millions. So I give you the advantage that I never had as a child-empress. If you want to be a mediocre Empress you may leave, never look back to this day, and you will become so.

If you want to take the route to greatness, then ask for these scrolls and listen to what else I want you to do. The choice is yours."

Sassaska looked into her old, warm eyes. The priestess bit her lower lip, knowing that she would regret any path she took. She then looked to the scrolls with despair.

Suddenly she turned around and started for the door. The Empress sighed in disappointment, slowly walking to her cupboard to put the scrolls away.

Sassaska reached the doors. She was about to open them. As she pushed the doors open, she looked to the hallway. Seeing the beauty of the tiles and the stone statues of women warriors, she began to feel chills go down her neck. Her heart pounded with a feeling that she had made a wrong decision. She tried hard not to cry but she didn't understand what was happening. All her life, she had been raised and trained as a priestess. Sassaska felt that she knew what to expect from it. But the path that she had chosen for herself was now gone forever. She gulped, thinking about her decision again, then closed her eyes, unsure of what she wanted now. She had spurned the help of the only person in the world who knew how to do the job that Sassaska would soon have to do. She looked back to see that the old woman was again staring at the parade, silent and upset at Sassaska.

"Grand Empress," Sassaska said as she slowly returned and stood behind Ameraldia.

The Old woman did not turn around, she only sighed.

" Yes Empress ?"

Sassaska started to slowly approach closer with nervousness in what she was about to say, " Grand Empress, I - I want to deny the fact that I am no longer destined to become a Priestess. Even though the Council has chosen me, I can still become unchosen. I can go to the provinces, deny my name and live in some small monastery. The only problem is that my mind tells me that if I made that choice, I would regret it for the rest of my life. I know what to expect if I go down the path of religion - I have thought of nothing else all my life - but I just don't want to take that safe religious path anymore.

The fact that I was chosen - that I did not vie for the throne, yet it was given to me anyway, tells me that there is a destiny involved. Perhaps it is my fate. So I will be Empress."

The Empress turned around with a stern face, covering her true feelings of forgiveness. " So... Your decision is made. Empress.

It is well that you submit to it. Your dream of being a lowly monk in a far flung province would never occur in any case. The Council would find you and bring you back. Once you have been chosen, there is no exit but death. So it is good that you have come to this decision on your own. If you were forced to reign, it would be a disaster and I would kill you myself to protect the Empire. But now that you know that you are destined to take this royal road you should do it to the best of your abilities. Your destiny demands it."

"Let me get the scrolls . . . " Sassaska looked with unsureness in her eyes. "Grand Empress, surely destiny, if it has chosen me so far, will protect me in future. The life that I have lived until now has been a life of solitude. I would prefer to continue in that life, even as Empress." she said, slightly nervous.

The Empress looked into her eyes. "Oh solitude you shall have - even in the midst of crowds.

Believe me, you will never be so alone as when the crown is upon your head. Destiny does have strange twists and turns doesn't it child?" she said with a mild smile of happiness. "But destiny only gives you the potential. The rest is up to you."

Sassaska reached her hand towards the Empress' hand. "May I have the parchment ?" she said mildly, accepting what the Empress wanted to give her.

The Empress went to the cupboard and handed her the scroll. "Sassaska . . . I want you to learn about the lands that you will be governing. I want you to go on an expedition to these provinces - if nothing else, "she said slyly, "you can look into small monasteries. But seriously, I feel that in order to receive a good education in government, you have to experience the governed. Discover their problems and worries. Discover what makes them happy and what they will settle for. To actually understand what you are ruling will make you a better ruler . . . As I said before, you'll need these scrolls to help you."

She took the large scroll which showed the overview of the country and handed it to Sassaska. Then held up another: " This map will help you travel. It shows all the villages, territories and clans, recorded from the West coast to the East coast. I have a travelling bag ready for you." She walked over to her chair, picking up a heavy, leather saddle bag, unbuckling it and throwing the four remaining scrolls into the bag.

"These have more information about every province."

Sassaska unrolled the map scroll, seeing the side key. It listed four symbols for four different clans. Most of the symbols, she was familiar with. The Arkaiton, which she was born into. The translation stood for 'the Zealot Followers'. The Buushu, which the Empress had explained, meant 'bull women, bull warriors'. The Makaiton,' the Night Warriors', a people which lived, hunted, like any other, but were notorious for fighting completely in the dark.

The last Clan symbol was near the bottom of the map over on the south continent. The southern region seemed to sink down and shrink into a small, curling isthmus leading to the southern continent. She looked to the odd squarish symbol with what looked like warning abbreviations, in old grammar, on each side. The symbol read '!The Sud!' The name translated clearly meant 'The South.' There was no special meaning for it. The abbreviations were unclear. Probably a warning or something.

Sassaska remembered the symbol though, to her it seemed rather familiar. Not the abbreviated symbol, but the warning about the South. It was in an ancient tale that was told to her some years ago. She wondered and tried to remember the whole tale, but it was still too distant to recollect here, in front of the Empress.

Ameraldia smiled and stroked Sassaska's hand. Sassaska looked at her. Both of their eyes were gently focused on each other. The old woman slowly passed the leather-heavy saddle bag to Sassaska.

"My expedition of discovery will take me a long time, will it?" Sassaska asked, slowly rolling up the map scroll.

The old woman nodded slightly. "It will probably take my lifetime. I trust in you to be confident in leading this Empire when you return from your journey. If I am still alive, I will turn the Empire over to you at that time. But I am frail. Be prepared to receive the message of my death at any time during your journey. For that will make you Empress immediately and put you in great danger.

The roads selected on that map will provide you easy passage through the land without any trouble. Take as few with you as possible. This is not a royal visit."

Sassaska nodded and picked up the saddle bag. As the male slaves came in with fresh linen, walking to the wardrobes and beginning to clean up, the Empress walked Sassaska out. They both strolled down the grand hallway, looking at the statues, and the Empress noticed that there was something puzzling Sassaska. She could see it in her eyes, in the way that her eyebrows were slightly raised and in the expression of speculation on her face.

"What are you thinking about ?" she asked.

Sassaska turned to her, wanting to unroll the map and show her.

" The sign on the map, the symbol of the Sud. Is that a warning of another clan on the other continent ? I heard tales of boogie men from the south when I was a girl. Is it the same thing ? I see the regions that cover the Empire on the map but they end where the land bridge starts. Why is that if there is a Sud ?"

The Empress started to laugh with amusement at Sassaska's question. " Oh child, that map was copied from a tacky one that was centuries old. The original map had legends written all around it telling the stories of a lost clan called the Mox-Sudutan who rule the southern continent."

" Isn't it true?"

The Empress slowed her stroll and placed her hand on Sassaska's shoulder. "Sassaska, the only thing out there down in the south is rain forest, small patches of desert, and a lot of ice. Ice so tall it crushes the rocks beneath it. Ice that goes so far, you could walk for days and never come to the end of it. Some sort of frozen paradise which, I'm sorry to say is too vast to conquer. It's all fantasy really.

The Ancients probably charted the Buushu Lands and thought they were much further south. Someone else added the tribe called the "Sud" - and a myth was born. Another reason why the story is fantasy is because the name Mox-Sudutan in ancient Marsollan dialect means"

" The Men of the South ?" Sassaska interrupted.

The Empress smiled, " Yes, The southern Men. Buushu are closest to this land and the Buushu women, who are hired as guards here say that a civilization run by men is like a mammoth doing cartwheels - something to laugh about, but nothing you will ever see.

I take the word of a Buushu woman any day. Besides, our little housemen running a grand empire ? Ha ! They might want to clean it up or decorate the ice, but a civilization of men ? It's unnatural. " The old Empress rolled her eyes.

"I heard tales from our Buushu guard when I was a girl", said Sassaska. " She claimed, beyond the ice was a city of three rings. That it was run by men and had wondrous machines powered by ice crystals. That these men had conquered the whole world. She claimed that they could even fly . . . "

"A tale that no one will ever know the answer to." the old Empress interrupted. "Some Buushu say they don't exist. Some Buushu say they do. We Arkaitons believe that Marsolla exists and Makaitons believe there are cities of gold. And I'm sure you've heard the rumors of men with black skins who come and steal boy babies ? Why is the South such a mystical place?"

After strolling down the hallway, Sassaska reached the staircase descending to the lower gates. They were guarded by six women soldiers, all armed with long seven-foot spears. She turned around to Ameraldia and wanted to say something to her, but her thoughts were shy and were not racing to her tongue to say anything.

Ameraldia felt that Sassaska was rather uncomfortable and unusually nervous. The old woman gently placed her hand onto Sassaska's left shoulder once more.

" I hope you have a safe journey, one which you will come back from with a better feeling about the throne."

41

Sassaska lowered her head, trying to avoid showing her the uneasiness on her face for making the decision to go on the trip.

" I shall . . . and when I return," she paused, biting her lower lip to keep herself from once again regretting what she was doing. ". . . and when I return . . . I shall be ready to lead this empire as a good and strong leader, will I ?"

The Empress slowly touched Sassaska's chin and moved her face up so that she was able to see her face. The Empress smiled slightly, " Don't feel that you made the wrong decision. When you return, you'll be thanking yourself for making this journey."

Sassaska smiled then looked away. " Until I return, Grand Empress." She then knelt to her in the customary way that any one bows to the Empress.

"Good-bye child." the Empress said.

The Empress turned around and started to walk back to her room. Sassaska kept in her bowed position, slowly coming up. She sighed with regret for going with her feelings of adventure rather than taking responsibility right away and learning to govern from the Empress right here in the capitol. But the thought of a journey - all over the empire. With no duties. No worries. No expectations.

As she began to walk down the steps and the guards slowly opened the gates, she skipped a little before going outside.

The Old Man stopped the tale and stood up from his sitting position, beginning to stretch. I began to worry that he was going to stop for tonight. I wanted him to at least finish a little further on. I didn't want the story to end that soon.

The Old Man turned to me, his face dim and hard to see in the low light of the flickering fire. I could see enough to notice that he seemed a little tired so I lowered my expectations that he would continue the story.

" Can you imagine a world run by women? Not to mention women who have the strength of ten men yet at the same time remain slender and beautifully presented ? Strong yet retaining their softness and smoothness in the texture of their skin.

Although they were strong, they still kept most of their feminine traits, making them very attractive - even when you knew how dangerous they were. " he said as he stretched.

" You make it sound like you were infatuated by one of them, almost like you fell in love." I said.

The Old Man turned around to me and grinned, not saying a word to my comment.

"Well Old Man . . . Good night." I said, as I struggled to stand up.

" Why are you so anxious to go back to sleep ? I still have quite a lot to tell you tonight. It's not even that late, boy."

I gave a mild smile and nodded, " All right Old Man, I'll listen a little longer."

I sat back down and waited for him to begin once more. He lowered himself back into his sitting position on the sand, leaning on a rock, and getting into the mood once more. He closed his eyes, trying to remember where he left off.

"All right, well she just had walked down the stairs and was going outside right ?"

"Yes. Skipping. So she was really happy about the journey ?" I said.

"Ecstatic."

"I would be too."

"Good, now shut up and let me begin . . .I'm an Old Man and it is a long story. I may not live to finish it. So, as I was saying: the Palace of the Empress was unfinished. . ."

" What ?"

" Oh, I'm sorry, I forgot to tell you that didn't I? Well then. Outside the Palace, the Empress was having a wall constructed. Men and women slaves were both working on it.

They threw giant stones down and placed wood skeletons to mark where each new stone would go. Of course the women, being smarter and stronger, did the heavy work. The men were just assisting. The women slaves worked and labored in putting the precise stones into place. In the background, the men slaves, grunting and angry, mixed the sand and pebbles and mortar together to make concrete. They used their hands as they poured powder in and clumsily threw pots and pans around, making a mess of the area."

Sassaska walked out, looking at the unfinished walls and the women slaves grunting as they carried up blocks of stone and wood. The atmosphere around her was laborous. Everywhere she looked, there were slaves and overseers with long spears, not like the guards or the soldiers' kinds of spears with the elegant, two blade, wavy barbed heads. These were flatter, and used to smack and bluntly hurt the slaves if necessary.

Sassaska walked to the stables, carrying her bags, watching a herd of men slaves, who were working at cleaning and grooming the horses. When she walked over to her own huge horse, the man slave who was grooming it. got scared and started to walk back from the horse.

Sassaska grabbed the horse's braided mane, throwing the saddlebag over to the slave. It hit him in the chest, knocking him over and fell to the floor at his feet.

Sassaska jumped straight up eight or ten feet, effortlessly, and sat on the horse, both feet in the stirrups, looking straight at the slave. The slave froze with a frown on his face.

Suddenly the horse grunted and shot out air from its nose. It startled both the slave and Sassaska. Sassaska shook her head, feeling jumpy from the startlement and looked to the slave once more.

" Fasten the bag onto the horse, man."

The male then lowered his head as he walked over to the bag, He knelt down to pick it up. Fearing that the wooly-hoofed animal would kick him if he got too close, (of course horses wouldn't kick you if you were just bending down but he was new to the stable and jumpy from being knocked over as well.)

He worked rather clumsily in front of Sassaska. As he fastened the buckle around the leather belts of the giant horse, the slave looked up at her, fearfully.

Sassaska raised her dark brow, " Yes, slave ?"

The slave looked down immediately as soon as she addressed him.

"Mistress, are you the High Priestess who was chosen to become Empress?"

"I am she, slave."

"You are a High Priestess of Marsolla ?"

"I am."

"Before being a slave to the Empress, Mistress, I was a slave to the Goddess Tierra and her prophet Julbax."

"She is a mighty woman but follows a false god, man"

"She had a vision of you, Mistress."

"Tell me."

"I tremble to tell you, Mistress."

"I said tell me, slave - I will not ask again."

"You will be the next prophet of Tierra, Mistress. Soon Tierra will talk to you directly."

"You are right to tremble, slave. My life is devoted to Marsolla - Empress or not. And Marsolla speaks to no-one. Nor need he. We know what to do. We need no half mad prophetess to tell us."

"I mean you no offense Mistress - but all in the service of Tierra know of this prophecy and await its fulfillment"

"An Empress of Tierra ? Not in my lifetime, unless I go mad."

The slave only bowed his head as he slowly backed away "That too is part of the prophecy" he muttered to himself.

Sassaska rode out of the stables. She didn't wonder about the peculiar action of this stable slave. Men were emotional creatures and often fell victim to hoaxes and supernatural scams. They were like children most times - and slaves the worst of the lot. After all, the poor creature was a man, a slave man, one born only for one purpose: to serve whomever was his mistress. A code that most were bred to live by. Sometimes male slaves were mutilated at birth so they lived their lives without the ability to talk. Some women believed that this was an advantage for them. That it would push them into their rightful place, as appliances used only for insemination and soft labor. Although there were women slaves, they were usually women defeated in battle and given the choice to serve or die.

None of them were as looked down upon as the highest free man. Women slaves had the opportunity to impress their masters to let them free or to work off their time of servitude. All males, however, were virtually born slaves. Either in law or in fact.

All males belonged to their mothers, who had the full right of life or death over them - and could marry them off, sell them or dispose of them in any way - and no other woman could say a word.

Looked at with slight disgust because of their scruffyness, their masculine actions and their instincts to resolve things by primitive standards, the weakling men were a joke among all women. Although women had similar instincts, they were able to control themselves better and their superior strength and reflexes made sure that they could do better jobs in most of the things that counted, like fighting, governing and building. Men were inferior in hunting, gathering, and even in staying hygienic. Poor things.

Sassaska knew this ever since she was a child. She was taught by her mother to think of men as subhuman. Sassaska was not heartless though. She had never hated men or even wanted them to obey her. She knew that there were women who loved the company of men and that there were some who loved the company of women. There were no true barriers to love. Her mother taught her that it was all right to love another woman, another person to share intimate feelings with, not to mention partnering for sex.

She was raised in a culture that believed in the dominance of Women. That the female body was beautiful and superior to all others. She believed in it too but sometimes she would wonder and question it. She wondered why women were not bothered by having a man one night and a woman the next. She wondered why women kept separate from men until they reached heat and wanted offspring. A woman who was -

" Wait ! Old Man,"

I couldn't take it anymore, I was cracking up, I had to stop him before he went on.

"I never knew that you were the one who could think of such perversion, you old dog you !" I said, trying to hold in my laughter yet failing at it.

" What ?" He said unsure of my humor.

"A world ruled by women, Ha ! That's a good one Old Man ! Women, they can't even cook right, let alone build a working civilization. Stronger than men ? Ha ! That was a real good one ! Women having sex with each other ? Ahhhh ! I'm dying. What would possibly they stick in each other ? What would they do ?" I said, justifying my outburst.

Suddenly he reached over to me. "Well then the fact that the story is about such women will make it a memorable story won't it?"

I nodded as I giggled still.

Suddenly he slapped me.

I was startled and shaken as I fell to the sand. I was more shocked than hurt. I scurried up and sat back on the log, angry and distraught.

"What was that for ?" I asked.

He grinned, getting comfortable again.

"For doubting me, you young bastard. And, since you live only by what you feel - to make you feel something about this story. So it will be a memorable story I am telling, boy." he said.

I looked at him with an unusual curiosity.

He grinned and chuckled at my expression and confused look and leaned over as if to smack me again.

I flinched.

" See, you've learned something already. Now, may I go back to the story ?" he asked.

I nodded, still shaky and frustrated.

He closed his eyes once more and sighed, getting the mood back, to finish where he left off.

"All right. Hmmm. Yes, now I remember.

Sassaska had left without a second thought for the strange stable slave. She rode slowly down the dirt road surrounded by slaves laboring to complete the wall. She was in no hurry. After all, she was heading for one temple to gather her things. And another to gather her companions.

A few minutes later, she got off her horse at the monastery where she lived. She grabbed the reins and tied them to a post outside the walls. It was considered rude to bring horses inside the courtyard. She walked into her rooms and made a small bundle of the clothes and the few things she possessed.

As a high priestess she had given up most material things in preparation for a life of the spirit, so there was not very much to take.

After informing the Less High Priestess that she had a mission from the Empress and would not return. She went back to her horse to find a few women standing around it.

Now that she had the priceless scrolls from the Empress, she had learned her first lesson - suspicion. A possibility occurred to her now that had never occurred to her before - that people might steal things if she left them unattended. Having never before had anything worth stealing, she had never considered security before.

Now it was uppermost in her mind.

She shooed the women away - who, in fact, were only admiring the horse, and rode across town to another Marsollan monastery - one she had not visited for many years, but still knew intimately.

This time, after tying her horse, she made sure to grab her saddle bag.

She started to walk towards the temple, keeping pace with the peasant women, who were carrying woven wicker baskets of wood chips, to be used to stoke the aromatic fires of Marsolla's temple. The peasant women all were strong and tall, covered up in rags from head to toe. They looked like ghosts of some sort, doing penance for sins that were committed long ago.

She watched them with a keen eye. Sassaska saw one of them stare back at her with the same curiosity. She immediately looked away, stroking her long hair and handling her bag closer to her.

The peasant woman walked closer to her and said " Go with Tierra, Chosen One."

Sassaska started and turned to watch the peasant woman walk away with her heavy basket. She shook her head and continued walking to the temple. As she looked to the side shops, all with men hammering away with tools she noticed how their female masters supervised them and piloted them through their work. Nothing out of the ordinary here, she thought. Only that slaves and peasants kept telling her that she would soon worship another God. How ridiculous.

She stopped at a tall building. The wooden gates and walls were beautifully carved with religious symbols and the front of the ancient cracked doors were decorated with the symbol of the Arkaiton spear. One of the two female guards at the door wore a head cloth with the symbol of the Buushu sun. Both warrior women were Buushu and had lengthened braids coming from the top of their short cut hair, acting as a family insignia, for every Buushu braid was done differently for each individual. At the end of each braid, there was a knot tied around smooth stones.

The guards' uniforms were not Buushu but Arkaiton, since Buushu were individualists and refused to have a clan uniform other than their family braids. For money, however, they would wear the uniforms of any other clans.

These two had brown, plated chest armor, with grooves and decor made to mimic that of the human rib cage. They wore leather harnessed fasteners around their stomachs and abdomens to allow maximum   maneuverability.

They wore imperial boots with round plated buckles to the soles, and each had a side blanket tied over the shoulders of their shield arm. Sassaska knew that Buushu were one of the only clans which allowed their warriors to be hired by others. Most of the other Clans needed whatever warriors they had just to defend themselves. Buushu were all warriors, so there was always a surplus. And always a demand.

Most of the warriors of other clans were honorable and skilled but when it came to ultimate honor or raw hand to hand, the Buushu were recognized as the best. It was usually because they were in training from birth and also because of their battle drink which made them berserkers before fighting.

But Sassaska was not going to the monastery to recruit fighters. Although she was going to get company to go with her, it wasn't going to be mercenary women. Sassaska was here to bring along her onetime lover Brelinka, the Governess.

Brelinka was the only person she trusted to protect her. And she was good company besides. Brelinka was the type of woman who enjoyed the outdoors, she knew of all sorts of ways to hunt game animals, such as buffalo, mammoth, sloth and even the great bears that roamed the forests.

In addition, she was a great intellectual to talk with and an excellent lover. Brelinka was the only one who understood her. Sassaska felt more comfortable around her and was able to talk to her about things that she would never talk about with anyone else. But their affair had ended three years ago.

Once she was appointed as Governor of Lina, the capital city, Brelinka ran that great city day-by-day while the Empress concerned herself with the empire.

The two women, High Priestess and Governor had become much too busy to continue their affair and seldom even spoke anymore. But if there was one person in the Empire who would be her choice for a travelling companion, it would be Brelinka. If she could be spared. If she wanted to give up her high position for a long journey. If she hadn't found a new romance. If, if, if.

Sassaska sighed and looked at the gates once more. One of the guards gazed back. Sassaska then walked towards her.

The guard raised her brow, " Yes ? What is your business here at the monastery?" she asked.

Sassaska looked at the walls around it. The beautiful wooden sculptures of women who ruled before Amereldia, all around the slits in the walls. Sassaska then gazed back at the guard.

" I am here to talk with the Governor Kriemik."

The guard lowered her eyes and looked at the beads that were wrapped tightly around her upper arm. The guard immediately knew then that she was an important priestess. The guard turned to the other one and nodded. The other one knocked on the door, a small slant opened up, and in the small opening were two suspicious eyes.

"Open the gates, we've a High Priestess to see the Governor."

The doors opened up and the guards moved out of Sassaska's way as she slowly walked in.

The doors closed behind her. Immediately the environment changed from the outside smell of dung and herbs to the sweet smell of incense. The sounds of the peasants work songs were not to be heard, and there were no cries of horses.

There was total silence all around. The totem shrines within the gates were carved out of the best woods in the area. Underneath them were sticks of burning incense embedded in sand so that the grass would not catch on fire.

Sassaska smiled. The silence and the smells were familiar. She closed her eyes to enjoy the memories of her childhood here in this very spot, when she was a young student. She remembered sitting outside, reading about the battles of long ago, and smelling the burning flavor of crushed flowers. To her the smell was irresistible.

One of the inner guards walked over. The guard didn't want to be rude in disturbing her so she waited for Sassaska to notice her. Sassaska slowly opened her eyes and turned to look at the young woman.

" Yes ?" she said.

"Priestess, I am glad that you have come to our monastery. The Governor is waiting for you now."

Sassaska smiled, "Good, will you show me to her place ?"

The guard nodded and started walking her to separate dwelling place within the large courtyard. As they were walking the guard turned to Sassaska.

" Priestess ? The Governor was very pleased to hear that you were here today. Where do you know each other from ?"

Sassaska looked to the guard. The guard was very young, she was a woman but still had a few girlish pimples and blemishes. She was beautiful with her thin strands of curly red hair and her brownish-red eyes. Sassaska could tell that she was around 17 or 18. Sassaska gazed at her naive face, seeing that she was the curious type, like most young women.

Sassaska then smiled. " How old are you young girl ?"

" I am . . . of age, to be a soldier." she said, as she pushed out her chest a little more. She wanted to give the appearance that she was a battle hardened soldier but she was doing a bad job at it.

Sassaska smiled. "I'm sorry . . . I met the Governess when we were both students here. I was being taught to become a Priestess and she was being taught to become an Arkaiton soldier."

Monasteries acted as academies to train soldiers as well as temples to ordain monks. Both types of students worked and lived amongst each other, and both were trained well to attain certain types of disciplines.

"We became . . . friends." Sassaska said, thinking that she was too young to hear that they were much more.

The guard smiled. "You must be Sassaska. Brelinka talks about you." she said as she nodded her head.

"She does ?" Sassaska said.

"Oh, every now and then. When she's telling all her secrets."

The guard saw a signal from another guard further inside the compound.

" Well, my sister is ready to see you." she continued, " after she's done her morning exercises." she said.

Sassaska smiled once more. " Sister ?"

The young guard nodded. "Yes. Sister." and walked to the door waiting for another signal.

Sassaska followed her, "What is your name young woman ?" She asked.

"Elana... Elana, Seanna Kriemik." she said.

Sassaska smiled and pushed the door open. "Elana . . ." Sassaska said to herself. "Let's interrupt her, even if she's not finished."

Sassaska waited for Elana to go in first, she was being polite to the sister of her lover. Elana walked in and patiently stood there, looking at a woman outside in the garden, who was half naked and practicing Arkaiton martial arts.

Sassaska looked at her too, seeing the line of her back as she went through her moves smoothly with a wide-bladed Lopper. It was a special sword with a tempered iron blade that was almost two feet wide and weighed hundreds of pounds, yet it was sharp as a razor.

Her arm was trembling, trying to keep the balance of the fat blade, which was as wide as her body, through the intricate sequences. (This sort of blade was for training strength with skill, but only the very strongest of women would actually use such a heavy and clumsy weapon in battle - though it was a mark of honor to try and it was devastating when used well.)

Sassaska continued to stare at the woman, watching her quietly to see what she would do next.

he woman slowly moved her leg to the left side, still balanced. She then immediately bent her arm, holding onto the sword and swung around in a circle. She pushed with all her force, stabbing with the huge Lopper, and then her feet left the ground. She flew into the air in a surprise move and turned a cartwheel in the air, and landed facing the opposite direction, with the sword ready to lop again.

She then executed a series of twirling movements which made the wide sword sing through the air - heaven help anything that got in it's way.

Just as suddenly the sword stopped it's mad swishing, and stood rock steady as she landed on her feet, like a graceful cat. She then revolved her neck to loosen it up as she started to walk over to her office carrying the Lopper casually.

Brelinka looked up and her eyes widened as she saw Sassaska and Elana there. She was expecting to see Sassaska but she wasn't expecting them to watch her do her acrobatics.

"Oh . . . Sassaska. It's been too long. I'm sorry, I thought you were still touring the monastery."

Sassaska smiled at her. She was happy to see her again and the feeling was mutual. Elana had picked up a cloak hanging off the edge of the chair and a pair of skin boots which were lying on the floor.

She then walked to Brelinka to hand them over.

Brelinka smiled at Elana, thanking her with the expression of her face. She then put them on and tied the knot on the cloak as she walked into the room. Sassaska moved out of her way and watched her walk over to her table.

Elana, not wanting to eavesdrop, crept out of the room and closed the door behind her. She knew that what they were going to talk about didn't need to concern her.

Brelinka sighed as she sat on her seat at her desk. She looked up at Sassaska, leaning at the side of the bed post.

"Bree - what's that on your head ? You look like a Makaiton. " said Sassaska.

"Remember when I was away for a few years. I was Assistant Governor in Makatia. The Empress decreed that we should adopt the native customs, so I designed it myself. You like ?"

"I love." said Sassaska, smiling.

" Please, sit down. We've got a lot to catch up on." Brelinka said.

Sassaska put down her saddle bag and pulled up a wooden chair and sat down on it. She gave a smile to Brelinka. They sat there, both staring at each other, not knowing what to say. It truly had been a long time since they had thrown glances at each other.

It had been three years since they were lovers and nearly two since they'd seen each other, even though they both now worked and lived only a few minutes from each other.

They had been students at this very monastery and had a long relationship afterwards before each went her separate ways - one in the priesthood, the other in politics and war.

Brelinka had been in battles all over the empire. Sassaska had stayed in solitude for years, seeking guidance from Marsolla.

Now they were back together again at the height of their powers. One a military Governor, the other a High Priestess.

" So, I see you've met my sister Elana." Brelinka said.

Sassaska gave a mild laugh, "Yes, she's rather adorable, from what I've seen. But I never knew that you had a sister. She seems rather young to be related that closely."

Brelinka sighed. " Yes, I know. My mother had many offspring but all were men, poor things.

Brelinka

After all, she had three men house-slaves and used them all for much more than cleaning. Elana was the last child and the only other girl child . . . she was really too old to have another baby but you know us Arkatan girls - we want girls to carry on the line - having Elana killed her. "Brelinka grinned, " The ironic thing about it was that it happened over eighteen years ago.

I knew my mother had died but I didn't know there was a child. I only found out about Elana when I was appointed Governor. Since my mother owed many debts, and all of her other children were men, the collectors accounted all of my family's belongings to pay off the debts.

My brothers were married off to rich women. My mother's Buushu bodyguard took baby Elana and raised her. I was off in the academy."

" That's right" said Sassaska, "I remember when your mother died. We were about 12."

"Right. So I couldn't have raised the kid, even if I knew about her. And the whole family's estates and fortunes were gone.

So Elana got a Buushu upraising, poor kid, but not in Buushu territory - so she's unaware of real Buushu customs.

Yet she's allowed to wear the clan braid of her bodyguard - although she had to earn the right.

She may not have Busshu blood, but the Buushu discipline and the Buushu toughness - she's got that."

"I sensed that, just in a few minutes I had with her."

"Then the bodyguard passed on. Elana was left all alone with a letter to me. So I took her in and had her learn from the teachers here in the monastery. Soon she'll be the most highly educated little Buushu bitch in the Empire."

" That's rather sweet of you Brelinka. what is she being taught as: a military officer, or a priestess ?" Sassaska said.

" Both. I want her to choose for herself. She seems to be leaning to the side of a soldier. She's the type of girl that thrives for adventure."

" You talk of her as if she is more than just your sister."

Brelinka looked at Sassaska with a glitter. "In a way I feel like she's my daughter, yes." Brelinka said as she nodded.

Sassaska looked at Brelinka's curly, hair which she had let down after her exercise, as it waved in the slight breeze.

"So, did you stop by just to say hello or was there more?" Brelinka asked. "I've been hearing strange rumors about you in the last few days - is it true you're the Chosen One to be Empress next."

Sassaska nodded, reaching for her saddle bag. "You probably heard that one before I did. I just learned today. I came out of seclusion only because the Empress had sent for me - and they told me on the way there. What a shock. The Empress has no other heirs and I am the closest in relation to her. I didn't want to do it. I was happy in my little world, adoring Marsolla and helping people. But I was summoned there to talk to The Empress, to understand why I must be the next ruler of the Empire."

"Congratulations. I'm happy for you-"

Sassaska held up her hand to stop her friend, then reached into her bag to grab a scroll. She then took out the map and placed it on the table and unrolled it in front of Brelinka.

"There's more. She wanted me to spend the remaining few years left before she dies, traveling around to these marked provinces. She believes that it will enstrengthen me if I go and actually see what I am ruling. She's given me a lot of scrolls to read up on. To understand the customs of the other clans and show the outlying provinces that someone in the capital cares about them."

Brelinka raised her brow. "So you, want an expedition partner to go with you. To . . . keep you company."

Sassaska smiled. " You can read me even better than before. Of all the women in the Empire, I wanted you to go with me."

Brelinka looked down, feeling the texture of the map.

"Sassaska, I am a Governor.

I just can't leave like that. I have reports to do, cases to check out, organizations to approve. The list goes on and on."

"I felt the same when I talked to the Empress. She persuaded me that my selfish desires didn't count - only the needs of the empire. I intend to make the same argument to you - that is, if you want to go."

"I don't know"

"Where's your sense in adventure, your flame and desire to see the world, your feelings for the outdoors? Don't you want to experience that again ? You and I have spent our whole lives in a domesticated world.

True, we've been out on trips and you've been off fighting with armies - but never the two of us together. Not on a long term journey like this one. It'll be a chance to grasp life right before dying . . . if you are still the Brelinka I remember."

" I am. But that Brelinka is buried under years of bureaucracy. I yearn to go - but I couldn't. The Empress would have me executed." Brelinka looked into her eyes, She could see in Sassaska that she had missed her. She could sense that Sassaska missed her touch, her conversations and her presence all together.

Brelinka was shocked. She didn't know what a large effect she had had on her. Brelinka found herself holding back tears, but her eyes and tension in her lips told the whole story.

"Has it been that long ?" Brelinka asked. "It's like it was only yesterday. I'd like nothing more than to come with you and be free again. But I have sworn an oath to do this job . . . "

Sassaska said nothing and only tried to smile as she nodded.

Brelinka reached her hand over, moving Sassaska's fine black strands and placed them behind her ear. Sassaska felt relieved and slowly moved her head back.

Brelinka sighed, stood up and looked at the garden.

"Brelinka - the Empress gave me many scrolls. I'd like you to look at this one." she said as she pulled a short one with an Imperial Seal out of her bag.

" It's a blank parchment !" said Brelinka. "Yes. It authorized me to take anything or anybody I may need in my special mission from the Empress. So if you want to go - this will get you out of any oath or contract instantly."

"Sassaska, I've served here as governor for three long years and I have many able assistants. If I can get out of my oath, I can easily appoint a long term substitute." Brelinka closed her eyes and leaned her head against the bed post. " I'll go with you, under one condition."

Sassaska's eyes were filled with joy.

" If I go on this so called journey of a life time, I want to spend it with one other person other than you."

Sassaska slowly stood up, "Yes? A new lover?"

"No - no time or inclination for that. May I take Elana with me ?"

Sassaska smiled in relief.

"I'd love you to bring her along with us. I want to get to know her, maybe teach her something worth while during the trip." Sassaska said. "and maybe learn something from her - she's certainly had an interesting life so far."

Brelinka smiled.

Suddenly there was a sound outside and both women went outside to check.

There were two girls fighting and a crowd around them were cheering.

Brelinka shook her head with displeasement. "What has Elana gotten herself into now ?" she said as she stormed into the crowd.

Sassaska followed to see what was going on.

There was a large group of students watching two women fight on the outside patio. One of them was Julyo, the 20-year old Buushu guard from the outer gate, slender, thin-nosed, and confidently-handsome. She was casually fighting with Elana in a skirmish. They had no intention in hurting each other for the blades they used were blunt.

Brelinka turned to one of the older priestess' watching the fight. The Priestess was still too caught up in the action going on to notice Brelinka's staring eyes.

Brelinka tugged her shirt. The priestess pushed her fingers away without looking to see who it was. Brelinka suddenly turned the priestess around, startling her.

" Oh, Governor." she said as she bowed her head in forgiveness.

"Priestess, why is my sister fighting with that guard ?"

" Well, they were talking and making jokes and all. You see, they're good friends Julyo and your sister Elana. Like young people do at times, their conversation went out of control.

They were arguing.

But then that Buushu woman, Julyo over there, tapped Elana's head with a spoon. Elana took it as some sort of insult. The Guard tried to apologize to her and then they broke into fighting."

Brelinka felt worried, she felt that there might be some accident even though the swords issued to students and guards are blunt.

The Priestess looked back at the fighting and began to speak once again. "I am truly sorry to say this, even though I am a priestess, but I'll venture to say that the Buushu can win any time.

She's just toying with your sister. I just believe that Julyo wants a little fun instead of an actual confrontation. I mean it's that girl's last week here before she leaves back to the plains to her family. That's how Buushu work. They do the work, You pay them, they leave. "

"Why do you say that ?" asked Brelinka.

"That's the Buushu way." replied the Priestess.

" What's that supposed to mean ?"

" Well if she wanted to, she'd kill Elana like a cat killing a mouse, but Buushu seldom kill for fun. Only for money - and so far, no one's offered her a penny."

The priestess turned around with a grin on her face, back to cheer on the show.

"Priestess, Brelinka whispered, " I don't think you know my sister very well . . . "

Brelinka stood there watching, straining from intervening, and feeling relieved that it wasn't really a major duel. The slim, slender guard had a thin head band holding back her short brown hair. Her two family braids swung around as she precisely went through the battle movements, holding her sword up high.

Elana gracefully swung her sword towards the guard's face. Their both blades clashed and sparked.

" You're getting better girl." said the guard.

Elana grinned as she pulled back her sword and swung it to her heel, causing the guard to jump and fall to the ground.

" And I'm not even warmed up yet." Elana said as she backed up and got into her acrobatic combat pose.

The Guard flung her legs and flipped up, throwing the sword into the air and trying to kick Elana's hand. Elana, still holding her sword, quickly grabbed Julyo's kicking leg and tried to topple her. As she did, the guard caught her sword from the air and kicked with her other leg onto Elana's chest. Elana was about to fall over but she cart-wheeled and stood quick to face the guard, tapping her in the head as she passed.

"Julyo, this started with a tap of your spoon and now you've been tapped back. Had enough ?"

The guard grinned, "Ha, never enough. And I still say that you're overreacting. It must be all that weight on your head. After all, little girl, your hair is too long for you to become a warrior.

Why don't you let me cut it." Julyo said, feinting one way and slashing her sword close to Elana's head and cutting off a lock of the wildly flying hair.

Then she stopped, beginning to giggle.

Brelinka's eyes were wide. "I thought you said they were blunt blades ?"

The priestess beside her merely shrugged.

"But you - you don't dress well enough to be in civilized company. Let me give your suit a better cut. " She flipped her blade at Julyo's boot-tops and clipped off a small piece of legging material.

The Buushu woman swiftly moved to her side. Elana spun and swung again. Immediately the sparks from the two swords clashing erupted. Elana then spun to the other side, swinging her sword to her left. There Julyo blocked her incoming clash and held it there with leverage.

Elana looked up to Julyo, " Tit for tat ?" Elana said as she panted. Julyo then growled as she raised her eyes with excitement and untangled her sword from Elana's. Both of them slowly backed up to give each other room.

The guard slowly shook her head with a sinister smile on her face. Elana was concerned a little and flattered. Elana knew that the guard was flirting with her.

Elana swung her blade once more and held it above her head, then charged towards the guard, twirling the sword around her fingers and trying to slice to the right. There their blades met once more. Suddenly the guard grabbed Elana's bare shoulder and spun her. Elana felt the force and was about to fall over, but she stuck her sword into the grassy ground and leaned against it. Elana was almost bent over in front of the guard.

The guard seemed rather pleased and then turned her blade to the flat surface and slapped Elana's behind.

"I was never a tit girl" said Julyo. "More of an ass woman, actually."

The crowd roared. Elana, feeling the smack on her behind stood up, feeling humiliated and embarrassed. She stared around at all the women laughing at her. Elana's cheeks started to flush, she lowered her brows and turned around to the guard.

Elana started to swing her sword around wildly over her head and started to try and hit the Guard. The Guard ducked on every attempt of Elana and the two parted for a moment to get their breath. "You're amazing. Julyo, I'm not sure what surprises are to come." Julyo raised her eyebrow. " Enough about me, what about you Elana ? Do you have any surprises left ?" she asked.

Elana noticed that Brelinka was watching and winked at her. When Julyo attacked again, Elana pushed her sword out in front of her, exactly as Brelinka had done in the practice court. Elana used the weight of the sword to cartwheel right over the Buushu woman, landed on her feet and jabbed Julyo in the behind.

The crowd laughed and cheered even more.

Julyo looked angry for a minute, but even she finally broke into a mild giggle.

"That's one hell of a surprise" she said as she put down her sword and reached over to Elana's armor and pulled her towards herself.

She then kissed Elana on the lips.

The crowd went crazy, clapping and cheering. Elana was shocked. She felt weightless as her eyes widened.

She was scared, feeling the firm yet soft hands of the guard run through her hair and caress the back of her head.

Elana immediately dropped her sword in surprise. She began to push away from the lips of the woman. Julyo was stuck in the moment and didn't notice that Elana was trying to pry herself free from her.

Suddenly Elana stepped back and ripped herself from Julyo. Julyo looked at Elana's expression. Elana was shocked; shocked, humiliated, and disturbed. As she panted, she wiped the saliva of Julyo from her mouth.

Julyo felt sorry for what she had done. She went too far with her. Julyo walked up to Elana and held her by the shoulder. She looked to Elana's stunned face, only to see Elana trying to avoid eye contact with her.

" Elana... I'm sorry, I got caught up in the moment. I -"

" That's fine Julyo, just... Don't do that to me again. Please ?" she said quickly.

Julyo stroked Elana's hair and still felt a little upset at herself for what she had done.

"Truly Elana, I didn't want you to feel uncomfortable like that.."

Elana held Julyo's hands from her hair and shoulder and slowly moved them away from her.

"Julyo, it...it's all right. Now don't worry."

Julyo was beginning to feel shattered, yet her honor as a Buushu warrior kept her from showing her emotions out in the open.

"... Is there anything I could do, anything I could-"

Elana stopped her from going on. "Just...we should stay apart, good friend... That's all."

Julyo nodded to her resolution.

"Alright. Elana, No more kissing. from now on . . . only spooning." And with that, she pulled out her spoon and clunked Elana on the head with it -the very same move that had started the fight in the first place.

They both laughed at that and patted each other on the shoulder. But Elana was still uneasy, not wanting to make eye contact still.

Julyo was crushed. She let her emotions jump too quickly. Very usual for a warrior in combat but not in casual entertainment. Julyo slowly bent down and grabbed her sword. She put it in the scabbard strapped to her thigh.

She looked at the crowd which were once roaring and cheering the game but were now feeling sorry for Julyo even though she had tried to make amusement of it, the joke had backfired somehow. Julyo hated it and looked away from the crowd and back at Elana to get some positive sign from her but Elana was too uncomfortable to even look at her.

Julyo lowered her head, seeing that Elana hadn't picked up her sword lying to her side. Julyo slowly bent down and picked up Elana's sword hoping to show her one last strand of compassion.

"You dropped your sword." Julyo said. Elana quickly snatched the sword from Julyo's hand.

"Thank you." she replied quickly. Julyo said nothing, feeling that she had done enough damage and slowly walked away.

Brelinka watched Julyo, feeling slightly sorry for her and angry at the same time. Unwanted sexual advances, even between women, were frowned on at all levels of society.

Sassaska stared in awe, not knowing what to say.

She felt that there was nothing that could fix the atmosphere of shame and heartbreak.

Julyo walked past Sassaska. She was staring at her. Julyo was keeping in her sorrow, trying to make no contact with anyone.

Suddenly Brelinka stopped her. Julyo sighed and looked at Brelinka. She saw the eyes of Julyo grey with tears trying not to fall, thinking that she'd be less of a woman if she started to feel helpless. After all, she was Buushu.

Brelinka admired women like that. Women who were truly passionate but refusing to show it. She believed that it built character. A strong character, fighting honor with feelings. That was the only reason why Brelinka didn't punish her for kissing Elana. And it was a surprise move in a fight full of surprises.

Brelinka gave a slight smile of forgiveness, nodded and patted her on the back. " It's not your fault young Julyo. She's just not ready for a relationship yet. She's still young. Much younger than you."

Julyo sighed once more. stuffing her emotions away, " I know. That's what makes it hurt even more." Julyo then brushed Brelinka's comforting hand out of her way and stormed out of the patio.

Elana stood there, closing her eyes and not knowing what to feel. She liked Julyo as a friend, nothing more. She wanted to be alone. Instead she was surrounded by eyes, watching her and making the situation worse.

Brelinka watched Elana, feeling sorry for her. She wanted to go out there and comfort her but she knew that Elana was not a little girl. She needed to help herself out of it.

Sassaska leaned her chin on Brelinka's arm. "Such a shame to see something like that out in the open. She must be going through all sorts of emotions." she said.

Brelinka turned her eyes to Sassaska. " I think that it would be best if we started that journey tomorrow. Elana needs it."

Sassaska removed her resting head from Brelinka's arm: " Are you sure that's what Elana wants?" she asked.

Brelinka gazed at Elana. She sorrowfully stood there looking stressed and tense. " Yes, I think that it would be best."

He always stopped just when I was getting to feel as if I was right there, inside the story. But I knw beeter now than to shout at him. So I went to bed and dreamed dreams of Atlantis. How could I not ?

The morning came, and the droplets of rain hammered down onto his shelter. It was cold and it was damp. The salt water smelled vibrant as the cool wind blew and crashed savagely.

The later it got, the more anxious I became , wanting to hear more of the story, but it was not until nightfall that he was in the mood of finishing up where he started.

" So, are you ever going to return to the tale of the slave boy, or the threee women or are you going to make another jump to yet another insignificant beginning of a tale ?" I asked as I tried to start the fire in the moist hearth.

" The story I am now going to tell you takes place 27 years later in another place far away from the North. All that I have told you about Six Piece, about Elana, Brelinka, and Sassaska will be suspended for a moment but do not think that they are different stories all together for they shall connect with each other later on."

I was eager to hear it any way, At this point I didn't care anymore about the story, if it all connected up or not.

To me it was all the same. A long legacy of some sort of tale which had happened to this Old Man somewhere in time.

" This story takes place where there are no blizzard snow storms, no ice-rocky paths and no sorts of giant, wooly animals. Where this story takes place is much further south - so far away from the North that it is almost a different world all together.

This story takes place in a world of logic and greed; a world which has forgotten most of its traditions of honor; a world run by men. This world was what everyone knows today as Atlantis. This is the world that Likooshas wants to find. The world of treasures and marvels.

To the world, they were known as Atlantis. To themselves, as the Sudutan Atlanteans. To the clans in the north, they were known as the Sud: a mythical place where men ruled supreme over women. A concept that no one from the north could ever conceive of. Just as no one in the South - or in your colonies for that matter - could imagine a world run by women ten times stronger than men. Thus, by lack of imagination, they were oblivious to the very existence of each other.

The Sudutan civilization had thrived for only two thousand years. It was an enlightened glimpse of human ingenuity at its peak, but alas, it was already dying.

These Sudutan people were a civilized and cultured bunch whose technology went beyond anything you could imagine, young Greko.

But these people were not considered great scholars or philosophers.

These people were conquerors and engineers, bent on finding resources and precious metals for their own benefits, to feed their hungry beast-like machines and to save their dying world.

They built grand half-diamonds or pyramids to manage the diamond mining around the area and for the rest and comfort of the overseers. They were also the diamond-collection points for the region and served as beacons to tell their flying machines where to land to collect the diamonds.

These places were so luxurious that when they were abandoned, after the diamonds ran out, kings of the native people filled them in and used them to be buried in. Strange practice, that.

The Sud also built giant coliseums all over so that they would be able to play, to spectate and to wager on the usual games that they had brought and educated the Natives to learn.

These things they built were considered great monuments to the ones they conquered but to the Sudutan Atlanteans, these things were bad copies of the originals, hastily thrown together to be used briefly in these backward outposts so far from home.

Diamonds were the resource that powered their technology. And if they were to run out, their whole existence would have crumbled into chaos" he finished.

"Now let me remember; there was a young man who wrote."

" A male scribe ? Did they let males read and write ?"

" Yes, they did. But I'm no longer in North Atlantis, boy. Where am I ? Oh, yes . The young journalist." the Old Man started up again, after pausing to get things in order

This man, Kline, was no ordinary man of the South. He was a writer, a scholar, an elite member in the High Council. He was a man who was considered a dangerous one. Not because of his strength or his will but because of his knowledge and tongue. He had a gift of telling the greatest stories and of describing the undescribable. His nickname was 'the man with the warrior's tongue'.

It was a gift that he had had since the day he was found. He grew up near the borders of the rocky and endless mountains along the great Isthmus and his parents were suspected of dying in the cold.

The only remnant of his past was a necklace that he wore. And on it were the writings of a language from long ago. That was why he became a writer: to find out his past. Yet he could never translate it, almost as if it was incomplete. All he could tell was that it meant 'Free.'

He didn't know of his past or where he came from. But in his gut, he knew that he was from somewhere else, perhaps one of the colonies to the east. Perhaps from the uncharted North. That was why he was so obsessed with it. Every chance he got, he studied every tale, every legend and every song written about the North.

So now I start, I begin his tale twenty seven years after Sassaska goes on her journey Now, I start with the chronicles of Kline. . ."

It was night time and the streets, temple-like towers and the local houses all were quiet. After a whole day of using their energy-powered lights and household appliances, it was time to turn them off and light candles. It wasn't a religion or custom to these people to do such things; it was a rule that had to be followed or their entire state would be in danger of burning away every piece of resource they had. It was the price they had to pay for conquering most of the world and using up what their ancestors thought were endless amounts of energy and wealth.

One pyramid tower had lights on inside as people and guards busied up and down the giant staircase.

There, inside the tower, was the Congress of Journalists and Scribes burning the midnight oil; discussing the latest news updates in the constant search for diamonds, mainly. All except one young man, dressed in a long grey cassock with a dark blue cloak over it. He looked up to the wall, studying an ancient map leading to the North continent, standing and staring at the map, oblivious to the people and voices swirling around him.

The chatterings of the others carried on. He raised his thin dark brow as he looked at the ancient old map. The ratty old parchment lay mounted in glass, its torn sides eaten away and the fading ink sketches told its age immediately. It was a map he studied every time he came here, searching for his history - or perhaps his destiny.

Kline

As he reached for his necklace for comfort, he began to see something he had never noticed before: an almost invisible symbol on the border of the North Continent of Ice. The symbol was written in the same writing as his necklace, very faintly - and only visible because some unique trick of the weak flickering night - light.

The man looked and strained over it, trying to decipher what it meant. He was always interested in the north ever since he was a boy of 10. He felt that he never fit in with the world he was brought up in. To him, the language of the Ancients seemed more familiar to him than any other language he grew up with.

As he looked at the map, he closed his eyes and took a deep breath, trying to recapture a distinct scent that had stayed in his system. That too was also sowed into his obsessions in going up north.

Suddenly it came into his head. It meant 'Beware of Women. . .' The young man translated. He thought about it for a minute and found it rather unusual.

At that moment the lights went off and the only glow of luminescence was the moon and the many torches mounted around.

" Damn energy rations. . ." he thought to himself, irritated from his meditation and studying of the map. He sighed and then released his hand from his necklace.

" Kline ? After you're done reviewing that map, why don't you join us in our discussion?" said a voice.

Kline turned around and looked to the voice who called him. He was met with twelve eyes staring back at him, waiting for him to sit down with them. Kline grimly walked over to his seat and was about to sit. Out of the six people there, he was the most important one. He was the Vice-Head of the Journalist's Department in the Outside News. Mostly, it was an organization where the truth benders and the liars for the government worked in harmony. Without them, Atlantis would have fallen years ago.

He was the head of an important sect of the government and he wanted to go for the approval of the Elite. He wanted to become part of the scholars and writers known as the Elders. To be one of these, you had to be more than a good writer. You had to be a journalist who either discovered resources somewhere, or invented something that was beneficial to the continent of South Atlantis.

" Well then, from the reports and written documents of the outer colony to the north East, I see that no progress has been made at all." said a man.

" That can't be true. The Elders reviewed the given maps in that area and had predicted that there would be a hefty resource." defended Kline.

" Well I am sorry but they are wrong;" the man said.

"Alright Councilman . . . Is there any written proof other than charts and death rates?"

A man from the far end of the table slowly picked up a scroll and read it to him.

" This is one of the quotes from Scholar Joan, posted in the continent to the North East:

I believe the time has come to tell the world that Atlantis has twenty more years until it's bled out of all the juice that we've given it. The workers dig day and night at the predicted mountains and the predictions are about as close to correct as purple is to yellow. . ."

Kline thought for a minute.

"There are no diamonds in the North East continent. But the mining still goes on in the other colonies. They are bound to find something."

" So should we release the latest news ? There are people who are wanting to know about their colleagues in the far away colonies."

"No, we mustn't let the news out. Not yet. . . We must keep it under the lid until we find something to lift the spirits of everyone."

" But Vice Head Kline, we've only got twenty years left until -"

"I know, I know . . . That was why we must expand. We few who know must take up the burden. We must send expeditioneers to places which have not been charted or imagined to go." he said.

Suddenly a humming sound lightly rumbled a bit. The glass tubes began to glow a pleasant green. The black out was over, the city's lights were on once more for government buildings and special groups - the common people followed the rules and used their endless candles and oil lamps after sundown, but the elite - for the good of the nation - had power whenever they wanted it.

" The power is always going to go off thirty minutes every day during the afternoon to try to cut down on peak usage.

It already causes trouble in everyday life. And we all know it's gong to get worse unless we have a major diamond find soon. I side with Vice Head Councilman Kline in theory . . . But in practice, where's left to mine ?

We've been sending expeditions to everywhere that is imagined already with no luck and three of the traditional diamond colonies have run out.

Possibly we have mined all the diamonds there are. Maybe we should be looking at some other power source."

Kline sighed, resting his chin on his hands as he glimpsed around at the concerned eyes.

" I can tell you that there is a place that counts as an untapped area. I bet that there's millions of deposits all over . . ."

" Where - the North ? Your favorite daydream. " the man said with a little chuckle.

Kline gave no answer. He slowly stood up and faced the oddly curious council members.

" Please, if you come this way. I want to show you the map . . ." he said.

" Why ? That map's a piece of scratch paper from the ancestors. The translations come to a rhyme, a fairy tale. I don't believe that it's even accurate. . ." said a Councilman slowly getting up.

" Councilman Hux, if, may I remind you that we are the Department of Journalism and Current News. You of all people should know that there has been a separation between meaningful language and written slang.

For example: the great Grova Hip games, heres what the game-reporters write: The winners collect the heads of the losers and then the losers bodies are sacrificed to the gods . . .

Tell me what the journalist truly meant if you knew how to read the language . . . "

Kline waited for an answer.

"You know very well that it really means that they win the gold - head-shaped trophies and when they lose in the temple championship they have to give in their championship body tags to the temple officials - and can only redeem themselves by doing physical labor at the temple." he said.

Kline nodded and said; "Now if you were literal to the point of exact word to word translation, then you'd think that our culture was a bloody cannibalistic society of brutes and goblins."

Kline slowly started to walk down the smooth granite floor back to the map. He looked up at it as he spoke;

"Keep in mind all of you, deceiving the people, bending the truth and fixing up the knowledge of the government is what we're all about now. The news has become secondary. We protect the people and the nation in this way. Otherwise we would have chaos.

But what if we are not the first truth benders. We assume, because we are running into trouble now, that we have invented this idea of "truth well told" - or, in many cases, not told at all. But what if it has really been going on all along - even in the ancient good times when energy was plentiful and there was nothing to worry about. Wouldn't it be ironic if we were deceived by our ancestors, in the same way that we deceive people today ?"

The group was now standing under the ancient map.

"What if they lied to us about this entire area up north," he pointed to the top of the map. "What if it is not totally covered by ice after all ?"

A man with a slight pot belly being imprinted through his dark cassock, spoke up;

"Why would they lie ?"

"The same reason we do - to protect the people"

"From what ? Frostbite ?"

"Maybe something up there frightened them. Frightened them so badly that they never wanted to return - and didn't want anyone who came after them to go up there either. But those were ancient times. Now with our modern technology we can deal with any beast or problem we encounter - we've conquered every country and culture and terrain we've ever entered. Nothing can stand against us anymore."

"Kline, what is it that you're proposing ? That we should send people up to the North ?" said a voice familiar to Kline.

Kline slowly turned around, looking at all the sceptical faces of his council and then focusing at the one who asked the question.

" Dole, my most trusted colleague . . . I've known you ever since our youth. Try to figure out what I mean when I translate this old passage, ready ?" he said.

Dole shook his head with an expression of disinterest.

" Alright Kline, we'll all play your little game. . . Shoot. . ."

Kline took out a little notebook and read out loud:

"Beyond the cold ruler of the Ice lay the world of the old; the world where ice is merely the servant of the women, as are men and all other creatures. Where the world revolves around the green, the grey, the blue, and the yellow; the world considered no man's land. .'

What does that mean ?"

The council sniggered a bit.

" A world run by women. . . quite laughable Kline." Dole said.

"No, no not that part . . . I'm suggesting the part about the Ice. Beyond the Ice lays a world which revolves from green to yellow to grey. . . The seasons. Don't you see ?

The Ancients who originally explored were trying to tell us something. . . they were telling us that the world of ice was disappearing, that a plentiful world was born centuries ago."

Dole sighed a bit.

"Ridiculous"

"But look here on the map " Kline pointed to the faint warning he had noticed earlier; "It says "Beware of the women" - it all ties together."

"Alright, maybe there is a liveable world up there. . . What makes you think that anyone's going to go up there to prove your theory ? There is no evidence that there are diamonds up there. Expeditions cost money and time - and no-one has either anymore. People are no longer daring and adventurous. . . with so little resources left, they can't afford to be."

Kline smiled a bit.

" With so little resources, they can't afford not to be. Not all people are that way you know. . ." he said with a little anxiousness.

"What, alright, the crazy ones are usually up to it, but people with common sense are usually sceptical about these great measures." Dole argued.

Kline slowly but casually backed away from the map a bit.

"I have a little common sense in me, not only that, I have a gut feeling about it."

Dole and his other colleagues began to look at each other.

" Kline, you're surely not suggesting on going up there yourself are you ?" he said with a mild concerned tone.

Kline only nodded.

" With most of your support and permission, friends, I propose that I do go on this mission. I am ready put most of my fortune into this expedition, hells I've even planned to train with the soldiers that I have managed to mandatorily volunteer into it. . ."

He chuckled a little.

". . . Well, I'm sure that this will get me into the ELDERS. . ."

Controversy started up amongst the Council.

Dole looked into his eyes, knowing that ever since childhood, Kline had been a jokester, but this time he saw no-one playing the fool; he only saw an eager man testing his theory with the giant bet of losing everything he had worked for. If his hunch was correct, he would be a rich prospector who would be written down in history. If he was false, then his whole fortune, his rank, and his privileges would cease to exist at all.

Kline's face showed confidence, a confidence so strong that his theories were utterly convincing to the council. Besides which, with Kline out of the way, they would control all outside news and not be subject to Klines' overseeing. To Kline, it was a chance to satisfy his desire to go to the North.

Ever since he was a feeble child of six, he always thought that he was from there, yet he also knew that it was probably a child's story that was told to him that got him thinking in that manner. He still felt that he would be more at home in the North and always thought his birth parents were from the North. He felt that if he returned, he would be where he thought to belong. . . that was if his hunch was true and there was habitable land up there at all. He knew that it was all only fantasy in his mind, but it was still something to desire.

Dole looked into his eager eyes once more, seeing his confidence in more depth.

He then began to feel confident as well, not at the passion that his colleague had about the North. He only saw the possibility in making millions if they found any sort of diamond deposit up in the North. He started to think of the many prospectors that would have to pay taxes if he became an outpost master.

Immediately his eyes widened.

" Kline, I think I speak for us all when I say that we all welcome the chance to get rid of you - possibly forever."

The group laughed. " But if we are going to give you money to support your wild plan, I think we need someone else from here to go along and oversee our investment."

The others nodded.

"I propose that this overseer be me." Dole said.

Kline grinned, knowing that his friend was beginning to like the idea, not for any idealistic reason, but because of the potential money value up there. Nonetheless, he appreciated Dole's vote of confidence and enthusiasm in wanting to join him as he went into training.

An hour went by, and the council, now animated with the idea, talked and began to mold into the possible reasons that the North would be something worth excavating.

Kline sat patiently as he laid out his papers of temporary dismissal from the vice head of the council, and recommended the fat man for the position - a recommendation that was agreed to by the council immediately. It would take effect the very next day when Kline decided he would leave to training.

As the council went on, they started to come to the conclusion that there might be a chance that his theory had some merit.

Kline saw that they were all beginning to go to his side, so to make sure everyone approved of his plan, he began to point at the map once more. " For twenty years, we've mined in the few regions by the land bridge. Most of us knew that they were not possible places to have diamonds but we were desperate and hoping for a miracle. It was the forbidding geography which made everyone negate these areas up here for hundreds of years. Remember the old days and the stories of the prospectors who are now known as the heroes of our text books almost all of them went where everyone said they couldn't go. To Europe. To Africa. To Asia. They ignored everybody saying it wasn't possible and went there and started up mines in those areas.

If you do not trust me now, think about how everyone would react to you if you were proven wrong years later after I am gone. You will be viewed as the villain Councils of the past who tried to arrest the hero prospectors who saved the nation." he added to their conscience.

At that point, the Council reluctantly agreed, and finally, after a few drinks, agreed with caring arms, hugs and the verbal promise of financial help.

They all smiled at the thoughts of the profits and the acknowledgments of being heroes for not only agreeing, but funding it.

Even if the project was a big failure, the Council would still be given praise for funding impossible projects in the hopes of saving civilization. It would show that they cared for the state of the nation. It was something that would boost their profits and prestige at home no matter how the expedition turned out. If it disappeared altogether, the Council won nonetheless.

Kline cleverly knew this and had sold it to them bit by bit as the evening wore on. He felt the glows of their faces and egos as they came to the final vote. He only licked his lips as he awaited their official decision.

" Vice Head, Kline. Not only do we give you the permission to go up to the distant north, we wish to sponsor you as well ." one of them said.

Dole smiled with delight as they said those words.

He knew that most expeditions were expensive and was afraid to use his own fortune as lavishly and as wastefully as Kline did. But since the council members were going to sponsor the expedition, he knew that he could rest assure that he wouldn't have to spend a dime at all.

Kline took a sigh of happiness. His dream of going to the north was about to happen and he knew that he was going to find many new discoveries that were going to be considered valuable findings.

He felt that he was going to be immortalized. He prophesied it when he was in scholar school, and now it was time to fit the last part of the bargain. It was time to go up there to find everything.

I was silent, more in confusion than fascination of the story up to now.

From warrior women to a culture of scribes and magic - lights without candles and great pyramids and flying machines. Diamonds that burned somehow and gossips who seemed to control the news instead of just reporting it..

" Where are you Old Man ?" I asked in frustration.

Following the story was going to be more complicated than I realized. From the beginning to now, the story was heading further and further into dark territory. Chaos was taking its toll on it.

The Old Man leaned in and shifted a little.

" Why I am only telling you what I remember. I am sorry if you are too incompetent to follow along." he said.

" Incompetent to follow along ? You're the one jumping from Buushu to Sudutans, thank you very much !" I defended.

The Old Man nodded.

"Aye, boy you do have a point. Think of it this way, my story is only testing your understanding of the complex diversity which the world of Atlantis held.

Let me continue on and hopefully you will be able to follow on." he explained.

"Will you be explaining about the Atlantean culture of the ants as well ?" I asked sarcastically.

The Old Man smiled and then patted my back,

"All in good time, Greko, all in good time."

It was another day in Sudutan Atlantis.

The Council members took their seats on the balcony facing the game field and eagerly watched as the game began to get interesting. Kline sat near the edge of the balcony, crossing his fingers that the home team would win.

" Dole, I think that you're a traitor. . ." he suddenly said.

Dole laughed.

" Why's that ? Because I bet on the opposing team ? I never knew we passed a law saying that betting on the opposing team was punishable by death." Dole said.

Kline chuckled to his comment.

"Maybe we should institute that into the laws. . . Therefore we'd eliminate gambling," he added.

The early evening was radiant and alive at the game stadium right next to the pyramid where Kline worked. The glowing, green lights brought daylight brightness to the cobbled, indoor field. All around the sides, resting aside from the protective walls, were the journalists dictating to a man broadcasting the game through a complex crystal radio. As the Home team shouted out the command to block the opposing team, the man holding the small ball on his mowhawk then throwing it up into the air to bounce it off his shoulder. Immediately the man was knocked off his feet and the ball was bounced off the side of the standing man.

The crowd started to roar like crazy as the man hit the ball carrier on the shoulder with the side of his head.

Three other men ran to stop the opposing team from kicking him over.

The first man tackled a man dead on. The man carrying the ball jumped over the heap and continued on. The more he came closer to the goal line, the more everyone became excited.

" The Goal line shall be Breached !" shouted the journalist excitedly. As the man, holding the ball to the side of his neck, jumped over the line, confident that he had won the game.

Suddenly as his foot was about to hit the ground, a man came flying through the air, tackling him and knocking him away from the line. The man carrying the ball let go of it, letting it bounce next to his team mate who was right next to him.

This man tried to sweep it with his mowhawk- his high crest of stiff hair - but he lost balance and instinctively grabbed the ball with his hands.

The crowd became silent and started to moan in disappointment.

The priests started to hit a drum three times.

The Home team, frustrated with anger for losing were kicking the walls. The captain of the team gulped as he looked up, regretting being cocky.

" Game over. . . you lose your head !" the Priest said, pointing to the opposing team.

Controversy started amongst the crowd immediately as the Priest briskly strode down to pick the head of his choice.

" The Priest now makes his way with the team to choose one of their heads. . ." explained the frustrated and depressed journalist on the side lines.

The team walked into the changing room and the priest followed. He looked in there for a while then came out, holding a golden trophy in the shape of a screaming head.

The Priest held it up

" Behold, the head of the team. . . Now yours." he said, waiting for the captain of the other team to approach him.

The captain quietly bowed his head and nodded as he slowly grabbed hold of the golden head.

As he did, he started to grunt indefinitely, getting quicker and louder with every huff. His head rose up as his grunts got louder. Then the whole other team started to grunt which became louder with every pulse as well.

It was their victory song, a developed song made for fun.

"The Zimina team has conquered the field. They have won the game. . ." said the journalist, signalling for the man controlling the crystal radiobroadcaster to stop. Everyone was disappointed at the game as they began to pack up, even the council members who watched from their special seats in the balcony of their pyramid building.

There Kline sat, very disappointed by the game and angry for betting on his team.

Dole on the other hand, was as happy as a lama grazing in a field.

He had won the bet amongst his colleagues, he alone had bet on the opposing team.

" Alright then, pay up." he said confidently as he held out his hand and waited for everyone to give up their money. The others grumbled as they stood up from their seats in the balcony and handed their lost money to Dole.

" Thank you, thank you, I am looking forward to the next game in town. There, there - all of your luck might change boys;" he gloated, chuckling away as he counted the amount he made.

Kline still sat down, not moving or making any preparation to leave. Instead, he waited, holding his face in his palms, regretting the bet.

Dole came up to him, knowing that he had to collect his booty from Kline." Well, well, well Kline. I see, this is the first time in a long era that you lost.

Well, I don't mean to be sore or anything, but a bet is a bet. So you're going to have to do it." he said.

Kline, sighed and removed his face from his palms.

". . . I thought that you'd consider a gentlemen's bet ?"Kline said, trying to elude his way out of the deal. "Just for the academic aspect of it - not for real goods or services - or heaven help us, for money ."

Dole grinned.

"Why Kline, this is not like you to try and sneak your way out of a debt. You lost so now you've got to do it. Pay up. " he said.

Kline looked at Dole with a laborous expression.

At that moment, Kline regretted making the bet: that if he lost, he would go with Dole to some local stinkhole and would have to drink twelve glasses of the bitterest beverage it had. Dole made it up because both of them were too cheap to bet any money at all.

Dole started to laugh, picturing what would happen if Kline did it.

" Come on Kline, you know that I'd do the same thing if I had lost like you."

" Yes, I know Dole. But you'd drink anything that was fermented for months. And lick your lips afterward."

"Excuses, excuses, excuses Kline. . . You're a whiner you know that, don't you ?" Dole said jollily.

" No I'm not." Kline said.

" Then quit stalling and lets go to Jok'ork's." Dole said.

" But I don't want to. . ."

" Whiner. . ."

" Stop that. . ." Kline defended.

" Nothing but a little -"

" Alright, I'm going, I'm going. Just let me stand up." Kline said, immediately getting out of his seat and feeling a little light headed from standing up too fast.

" You better stick to the agreement. . ." Dole said, waiting for him.

"I will, I will." Kline said with a mild sigh.

" You better drink too -"

" Whatever you choose; right, ?" Kline finished.

Dole grinned.

" Kline, you'll be thanking me in the morning once I choose the twelve drinks that you're going to have to drink down."

The two left the balcony and began to make their way to the public bar.

It wasn't much of a trip for the two because it was right across the street. As they walked in slowly, they saw the lights glowing green and blue over desks filled with what appeared to be Imperial officers sitting about. Their bright red and black mowhawks were all precisely centered amongst their military knots and their facial tattoos, symbolizing their personal tales of adventure.

"Oh, by the way Dole. I want to make an appointment with a technical engineer before we leave," Kline said.

Dole turned around as they were going to their conveniently reserved seats.

"Why ?" Dole asked.

" I want to jot down a few notes on diamonds and crystals. I need a basic idea of how we extract the energy from them, how we find them in the wild and anything I need to know about mining and transporting them. They are so important to our society."

Dole's face seemed enlightened as he found their table.

"You really, honestly expect to find diamonds up there?"

"We've found them everywhere else - and that's the only place we haven't looked. I want to get an education."

Dole and Kline took their seats and relaxed for a moment.

Dole then leaned a bit forwards, his eyes looking to see any servant girls that had a free hand. Although his eyes were wondering, his ears were still listening to Kline.

". . . I'm sorry, you want to do what ?" he said once more.

" I want to take notes on how one diamond can power our day to day vehicles and appliances we use - just in case we have to slam some technology together up there to impress the natives."

" What do you want to do that for ?" Dole said as he began to wave for a servant girl near by. The servant girl saw him and started to make her way over.

"Don't waste time. Did you know that Bringington down in Zimina has already gotten word about your expedition and is probably getting ready to embark within the week.

You know that Bringington has been at your neck ever since you threw his life down the pipelines with that article you published on the Zimina Council department. . . ." Dole said, but Kline wasn't paying attention.

Kline had glimpsed over to the servant girl and was now totally attracted by her. His eyes were locked on her curves and the many other attractive features that appealed to him. She seemed very different from the women he had grown up around. She had a discolorization in her eyes that made them a very dark greenish color, something that was uncommon for the main population of Sudutan Atlantis.

Her hair was shorter and a little brighter than straight black. Nonetheless, he continued to try and talk about what he had thought was important.

"I...Um... what were we talking about ?"

His imagination started to work overtime. He completely lost touch with reality in his anxiousness to meet this young girl.

Dole gave a chuckle at his stupefied look, snapping him out of it.

"...Oh, right. I was saying that I want to take notes about mineral fuels because I find it really interesting and because we'll likely need it on the expedition."

Dole raised a brow, not fascinated at all about the topic.

"Really, who, in the most powerful continent of the world, knows even a little bit about how we use diamonds and crystals for fuel and energy ? Nobody I've ever met. It's like that waitress you're mooning over - we may use her - but who knows how she works. And, Kline - tell me - who really cares.

Kline strained his head up, trying to catch another glimpse of the waitress as he talked: "To me, personally, crystals are a mind boggling mystery. And if I was able to talk to an engineer, a person who devotes their life to building works of art that are powered by these things, then I would be able to write it down and tell others in Sudutan Atlantis about it."

"How noble. But aren't you at the least worried about Bringington and his crew ?" Dole remarked.

Kline went silent as the servant girl approached them.

Her face was a little darker in skin tone. Although her nose was not long and elegant like most other women, it was smaller and bluntly rounded - a trait that was considered ugly in most men's eyes. And in the land of Sudutan Atlantis, a woman's only job was to look appealing to a man otherwise her life would be tough and lonesome.

She waited for their order in a quiet, yet impatient manner.

" Yes ? what will it be ?" she finally asked.

Dole's eyes widened with a mild surprise. He felt that she had a lot of spunk for a servant girl. Most would just wait, dumbly, until they were spoken to ."Oh, I see that you're a frisky, forked-tongued little sssssserphant, aren't you ?" he said.

The girl sighed and ignored his comment.

Then, when they still didn't order, she spoke again: "Yes I am. It's a long night and I don't expect you to make it a little worse." she said. "If you do, you'll feel the fangs of this little serphant. So be nice guys, Order something. "

"Ah, a complaining one I see. . . what's your name girly ?" Dole asked, thinking that he was charming.

The woman raised an eyebrow. "No, my name is not Girlie. What's yours - boyie - or maybe shit in a suit ?

Then she ignored him and turned to Kline.

"What is it that you and your friend want ?" she asked him.

" Well. . ..um . . . My friend - he was meant to choose the drinks." Kline muttered, stunned by her beauty.

She waited patiently not remarking to his answer even though she was already fed up.

"Twelve cups of your finest but bitterly strongest drinks, my dear piece of ass." Dole said as he grabbed her hand where he placed a few gold plated coins.

Kline gulped in concern as he looked at the girl's silent but insulted face.

" Dole, please. . ." Kline insisted, thinking that his friend was speaking out of line.

Dole maintained eye contact with the girl.

" Now why won't you be a dear and get us those drinks, my friend is getting thirsty right about now." he said as he reached over to kiss her on her hand.

As his lips approached her hand, she spat on him and pulled her hand away.

Dole chuckled.

" Ooooh, I like a girl with spunk, don't you Kline ?"

Kline blushed in embarrassment. She looked at Kline's face and gave a very mild smile. So tiny that it still looked like she was frowning.

". . .Um, pardon my friend but he's-"

Immediately she interrupted Kline as she held out her hand in front of his mouth.

"Don't even . . . try to explain . . ." she said, taking off to get the drinks.

Kline was in awe as he watched her walk away. Dole, on the other hand, was having bundles of fun. All in one night, he had won stacks of money, agreed to an expedition, and had gotten fresh on a woman. This was heaven as far as he was concerned

Kline looked at him and felt a little bad about the girl.

" You know you didn't have to do that. . . I mean, she's just a poor maid girl you know. I think that the last thing she needs is a wisemouth putting her down. . ."

"Oh shut up, Kline. Just because you've got struck by Marsolla's love needle, it doesn't mean that you have to go soft on me like that."

" What are you talking about ?" Kline said to his defense.

Dole watched the girl as she began to load up her tray with twelve cups of drinks.

" Oh, yeah she's cute. . . But her hair and facial features ruin it all." Dole started, then he looked at Kline with concern in his eye.

" Anyways, like I was saying earlier. As your adviser in your expedition, I am telling you to watch your back and. . ."

" From what ? If Bringington wants to tread on my project then let him do it !" Kline interrupted sternly.

" I guarantee you that without any sort of idea and good will, he won't last two seconds out there. Besides, if we go up there and bump into him, there will be no charges held to me for killing him . . ."

" You mean if he doesn't kill you first. . ." Dole said.

"Right." Kline said nervously nodding his head.

The girl came back with the drinks.

All conversation came to a hold once more as her presence was made. She slowly lowered her tray with the drinks.

Her anger was controlled, anticipating the next word to come out of Dole's mouth. She slowly glimpsed at Kline as she was placing the drinks on the table. Kline felt a little shy, not knowing what to say, so he let the first word that came into his mind come out.

"Um, I've never really seen you around here. " he said, waiting for an answer.

He received no answer from her.

"Are all the Savages in the oversees colonies as bad tempered and strange -looking as you ?" he said, only then realizing what he had said was slightly insulting.

She froze for a moment. Not just a little insulted from what he said. She was furious, " I hope that both of you rot and die of something embarrassing." she said.

Dole was ready to say something back, but Kline insisted that he keep his mouth shut.

Kline nervously apologized, hoping to end any tensions between them.

Instead, she spat onto the table and walked off.

Dole watched her walk away, stroking his beard.

" You know, I'm a little surprised that no one has raped and killed her yet. I can guarantee you that anyone who does that would share a beer with whomever her father is." He said.

" Dole," Kline said with a slight dark tone.

" What ? I'm just saying that if some one was to do it to her, no one would accept damage charity from her family. They'd probably be glad to get rid of her." he defended, smiling.

Kline leaned back and sighed.

"Come-on Kline, she's a lama. . . that spits. You could tell that her father is having problems selling her off." Dole finished.

"Dole, just drop the topic." Kline insisted.

Dole sighed and then gave in. He nodded.

" Fine. . ." he said.

" Now, let's talk about the expedition a little bit." Kline said.

Immediately, he took out a small paper, a rolled-up scroll with miniature pictures on it.

" You actually carry identification files along with you ?" Dole said as his brow went up. " Kline, I think that you need a life." he finished.

Kline unwrapped the scroll as he talked,

" Now I wanted to talk to you about the selections that I have made for my expedition team. See if you like my picks," Kline said as he handed the paper over to Dole.

Dole looked at the first person on the list.

The picture showed a young man in his twenties. His beard covered his cheeks, but was shaved clean where it touched his chin and mustache, leaving a small paint brush patch of hair on the point of his mouth. His hair was short, and his eyes were slender.

"Demet're Fillo, nicknamed Dusty Fill because he once dived in a Dragquad at one hundred miles an hour and immediately came to a stop only three feet from the desert floor up at the Sieka Province. His history background: He was once an officer in the Sudutan, Imperial Service. His accuracy and efficiency reports show that he's a bright, creative individual, and he's the best engineer you can find when it comes to aero tech." Kline said, pointing to his profile.

Dole read a little more of his background.

" You forgot to mention his criminal record:

Kicked out for raping his commanding officer's daughter. . . and refusing to pay damage charity to him; he had also been convicted of shooting civilians without giving a reason to them; he has been thrown into a mental correctional facility overseas." Dole said looking up at Kline.

"So. . .er. . . he's been in a little trouble. He's still a great engineer. Alright, if you're not impressed by our engineer scout than check out our long range observer: Luca Berndinand, Nicknamed Luca Beard for his long beard extending to his belly. . .."

Dole looked at his picture. It showed a round face with a darkened tattoo barred across his eyes and nose. His beard was thick and bushy. His hair was short and entangled with feathers coming out of the small knots braided along the top of his head.

"Well, lets see. . ." Dole muttered as he read his background.

" He was a sniper during the Savage Control Wars; He's one hell of a shot; Excellent in mathematics and aero-geometry; and had positive conduct. . ."

Kline smiled.

" See, there's a good one." he said.

". . . Until the age of twenty. He has several convictions and penalty fees that he had to labor for because of his alcoholic addiction.

He's killed three civilians in the past five years; The last man he killed was a year ago because his beard was cut off during a drunken orgy. The man was then picked up, thrown out of the window, then dragged into the street where Luca beat him to the point of unconsciousness."

Dole gave a slight grin as he read on.

" And that's not the end of it:

After the man passed out, he took him to an aero field and threw him into a Be-Quad trying to take off. The man literally painted the town red !" he finished with a sick little chuckle to himself.

". . .Er. . . At least you can see that when he's committed, he's willing to see a job all the way through. . ." Kline nervously said.

Dole wasted no more time going through the list one by one and skimmed through the rest of the selected bunch.

" All of these men: Clubio, Squirrel, Dav'inne, Vittorio. All of them fit the needed requirements yet they all have heavy criminal records. I am surprised that you picked these bunch of lost people." Dole said.

" I can only guess that you hired them because they were. . ." Dole looked up at Kline's embarrassed face.

Kline gave a pathetic cough.

". . .cheap. . ." Dole finished.

Kline cleared his throat, then turned to watch the servant girl serve someone else.

He anticipated her to notice him and when she did, he quickly turned around.

Dole noticed him doing this and kept quiet.

Dole began to show a slight smear on his face.

". . . You picked these men so that you wouldn't have to spent too much of your tight budgeted expedition."

"Just in case I was to find that everyone was right and I was wrong." Kline said, letting his eyes harmlessly wander to look for her.

" Ah, that's a good trait that you've developed. Always anticipating the worst."

" You know that if we find nothing up there you will have every shred of dignity that you have worked to build, stripped, until you are a good for nothing radical." Dole said.

Kline's eyes were still wandering eagerly as he continued to look for the girl.

As he looked around, he noticed one tall, Imperial officer (easily recognized by the knotted, red and black mowhawk and the distinctive hair rows across the sides).

Rolled up, across his wrinkled royal red and brown uniform was a long, fat strap which was a high ranking decoration given to those of Imperial office.

His nose was straight, seeming as if there was no actual point indicating where his nose ended. He was a hard, experienced-looking man.

He walked into the room with another man who appeared quite a bit smaller in body structure.

The smaller man's hair had a few feathers across his scalp, his hair knotted to keep them tightly strung. His uniform was slightly similar except for the symbols on his strap which indicated that he was a lower ranking person than the tall officer.

Kline felt that they were mildly familiar, then he grabbed the scroll out of Dole's hand. He matched up the pictures, positive that both of them were members of his expedition team.

Dole turned around and looked closely at the two men." Oh great.," he said, sarcastically, "Now we see the elite crew in person..."

Kline looked at the pictures again, and then found their names.

The shorter one was Dusty Fill, the Aero Engineer slash scout.

And the taller officer was Clubio, the Imperial supervisor who was to report on all aspects of the expedition back to the governmental branch - just to make sure the truth matched Kline's final report.

Kline then turned around to Dole. Dole, on the other hand, was looking at the drinks on the table, licking his lips in anticipation.

" Clubio and Dusty Top are a lot taller in person than their descriptions suggest, aren't they?" Kline said.

" So ? They're all a crazy bunch of coca smoking, puff heads. Whatever you saw in their records will not get you to the north continent. . . on the other hand, Bringington's team is made up of -"

" You know what, let's stop talking about that bald, illiterate, little heretic for tonight shall we ?" Kline sternly interrupted.

Dole nodded and moved his hands up, expressing that he was backing away from the topic." Alright, alright, I'll stop talking about Bringington for tonight." Dole said.

Kline looked around to find Clubio and Dusty but instead, he found the strange-looking girl cleaning up at a table near the bar.

" You know what ?" he said with his eyes locked onto the girl.

Dole looked at the girl too." What do you plan to do, oh great war general of Atlantis ?" Dole asked, waving his arms around to give Kline a false aura of greatness.

Kline watched the girl closely as she crouched over to reach for a rag. The curves and structure of her body seemed to entice him even more. The more it enticed him, the more he wanted to go and meet her.
" I'm going to go and introduce myself to her." Kline said.
Dole turned around, gazing at her. Then he turned back to Kline."Who, the beast ? You're going to get fresh on the savage beast ?" Dole's eyes rose in interest and then reached for a drink on the table. He gulped it down.
Kline grinned as he nodded.
Dole then reached for one of the twelve cups, but Kline quickly grabbed the very same cup.
" Wish me luck!" said Kline as he gripped the cup that Dole was reaching for and sucked up all of the drink, sparing no drop.
Dole grumbled a little as Kline quickly got up from his seat, and staggered - partly reacting from the kick of the drink and partly from his eagerness to introduce himself to the girl.
Dole sighed and slowly began to sniff the other cups of drinks to find another potent one.
As Kline made his way to approach the girl, he had a quick glimpse of Clubio and Dusty in the side of his eye. He paid little attention to the duo and walked up to the bar.
The girl was still cleaning about, barley noticing Kline standing over her.". . .Um, I wanted to thank you for putting up with my friend, Dole. . ." Kline started, just to get her attention.
"Um, hm. . ." she mumbled as she ignored him, still cleaning the table.
" I'm Kline by the way." he said, receiving no answer at all.". . . well what's your name ?" he finished.
" What's it to you ?" she snapped very harshly as she stormed to another side without turning her head.
Kline slowly followed her to the other side of the bar." Because I am interested in you. . . you see you're unique and I've never seen you here in Prox before. . ." he struggled to say.
Suddenly, he heard the doors open once more.
Kline and the girl quickly turned to see who was coming in.
There were two well built soldiers with bluish black feathers and waxes woven beautifully in between their mowhawks.

Their uniforms were brownish with bright red straps across them. Immediately, Kline recognized their division. They were the elite officers from Zimina, a province along the western shore of Sudutan Atlantis. Their bands meant that they were part of an expedition team.

These were obviously Bringington's men and wherever Bringington's men were, Bringington himself was somewhere close by.

Then, predictably, the rather bald, sinister-looking runt of a man walked in. Bringington looked around the room almost as if he was trying to sniff Kline out. Kline quickly panicked.

He wasn't afraid of Bringington himself, but he was afraid of Bringington's entire team. After all, Bringington had sworn in public to kill Kline. So, out of good sense, Kline quickly looked for somewhere to hide.

The girl gazed over at the newcomers and came to a stop in her cleaning, standing right next to Kline. Immediately Kline grabbed the girl by the ears and pulled her close to him. He then ferociously kissed her. She was shocked. She struggled to break free from his clutches. Her eyes widened in anger, fear and humiliation as they had when Kline mistakingly insulted her over at the table.

Meanwhile, Bringington began to slowly walk to a table, unknowing that the person he was passing, who was kissing a stuggling girl, was Kline.

He was slightly disgusted by them

" People of your kind do not deserve to live here. . . Hideous beasts! That was why rooms were invented. . ." he said as he walked by - but put them out of his mind as he noticed Dole at a far table.

Kline watched with the corner of his eye, seeing Dole in Bringington's line of sight and hoping to Marsolla that Bringington would not sit next to him.

But he did, and where Bringington went, his goons went with him. They took the table next to Dole and began to interrogate him.

Kline slowly released the girl, noticing that she wasn't fighting as much anymore.

She was surprised and afraid by Kline's actions.

Kline didn't know how to explain himself to her, so instead, he gently grabbed her hand.

" Hello, my name is Kline. . ." he said nervously, trying to get out of a long, hard explanation. "Sorry but that man has sworn to kill me." The girl's face backed up a little bit.

"Hello. . .. my name's Ennis. . . and I may kill you first " she said, a little shaken up from the long hard kiss.

Then she slapped him.

He fell hard onto the stone floor.

". . . Never kiss me without my permission again. . ."

Kline felt sore from the slap and felt that he had to do something at that moment. So he stuck out his thumb signalling an OK to show he forgave her.

From the floor, Kline looked quickly at the tables where Bringington and Dole were, then he looked around, until he found Clubio and Dusty.

He immediately stood up, placing both elbows onto the table under which he'd fallen.

He looked into the eyes of Ennis. Kline nodded a lot, showing that he was as surprised by her actions as well as she was.

"You hit well . . ." Kline said.

She giggled a bit but kept her face solid as she looked at him.

"I'd love to continue this great conversation and get to know you even better, but I have to go over there now and try to save my life. Nothing less than this threat of death could draw me away. . ." Kline said, thinking that it was now important to go over to Clubio and Dusty.

If he was going to survive until tomorrow, then it would have to be dependant on them.

Kline blinked and then turned back to Ennis.

"Well, I enjoyed our little chat but as you can see here, I have to get back to wiping up the drool of high council members. . .. Good bye. . .." she said to him sternly as she grabbed her tray and stormed to a far away table.

Kline froze there for a moment, watching her leave. He gasped, an aftereffect from the slap.

" Clubio and Dusty. . ." he muttered to himself as he began to cup his hand to cover his still-stinging face. He slowly tried to manoeuver himself over to the table where Clubio and Dusty sat with a different waitress placed on Dusty's lap.

The girl was uncomfortable and Kline could tell that she wanted to get away. Unfortunately, this girl was of no concern to him.

Kline stopped in front of the table, grabbing a chair.

"Please, could you let me go so that I could go back to my job ?" the girl pleaded nicely.

Dusty nibbled on her neck. She held herself from crying.

" But your job is supposed to be satisfying our 'every need.'" Dusty said.

Clubio laughed as he took a drink and watched them.

Kline was surprised that they had not noticed him.

He stared from the corner of his eye to look at Bringington, to see if they had killed Dole yet. The peculiar thing was, they were actually laughing and patting each other on the backs. Then Bringington turned around and glimpsed Kline. At first he didn't notice that it was him, but he caught on really quickly.

Immediately, the goons and Bringington got up and started to make their way to the table where Kline was.

Kline turned around and cleared his throat loudly so that Dusty and Clubio would notice his presence.

Dusty slowly turned from the girl he was molesting and Clubio gave a silent growl as he sharply stabbed Kline with a stare. Even the girl was silent.

"Yes. . ." Clubio said, focused and locked onto Kline as if he was prey.

"Hello, my name is Kline. . . I'm the Cummundore of the expedition. . ." Kline said.

Both of them looked at each other and then back at Kline. They said no word.

" You know, the expedition to the North continent ?" he said, trying to refresh their alcohol-marinated brains. They were silent for a little while, and then they slowly started to giggle. Then their giggles turned into laughter.

Kline, feeling the goons coming closer and his life as he knew it coming to an end, got perturbed:

" What's so Marsolla-damned funny ?"

"You're the notorious Kline. . . The one with the warriors tongue?" Clubio asked.

"Yes. . ." Kline said, a little ruffled.

"We've always had the impression that you were a wider, broader shouldered, taller and more adventurous looking man." Dusty said.

Kline looked at his shoulders, then back at the two.

" I've got the broad shoulders, I'm five foot. . . What's so damned funny?" he said.

" Your face and your voice. . . So whiney. . . You're too much like a woman. . ." Clubio said.

They continued to laugh at him and even the captive woman was smiling now.

Kline gave a sigh of frustration.

"Nevertheless can . . . can I ask you both for a favor ?" Kline asked.

"Sure. . . later. . .After this drink" they said, trying to get over their humor.

" No . . . no,no." Kline insisted, "you don't understand. I may not be alive until then. . ." Kline said.

" Why what do you mean ?" Clubio said as his tone changed a little.

Kline gave a smile of satisfaction. Finally, someone was going to listen to what he had to say.

As Kline began to speak, he felt a firm hand land on his shoulder.

Kline closed up his mouth and gulped, knowing now that the end was near.

"Kline, long time no see." said a voice.

There was no real suspense or twists to describe. Everyone knew who it was. It was Bringington and his goons coming to kill him, to be rid of their only competitor.

Kline turned around to look at the sinister bald facade of his rival.

" Bringington, glad to see that your still shorter than everyone these days." Kline accidently said out loud.

Clubio, Dusty and the waitress roared with laughter.

Bringington grinned,

" Still never knowing when to shut up I see." he said as he spat in Kline's face.

Kline gulped and wiped his face.

"That does seem to be the popular event this evening, doesn't it " he said, commenting about the spitting.

Bringington quickly ordered one of his blue feathered goons to pick him up.

With one yank, Kline was taken from his chair.

Clubio nodded as he finally understood what was going on. " You still need that help you were asking for?" he said putting his cup down.

Dusty slowly reached for his pistol lodged between his groin and the waitress's ass.

Kline looked at Dusty, then at Clubio. He wanted to say that he would want them shot right there, but he felt that he would have to write tons and tons of articles and paperwork to get him out of the labor camps in the outer colonies.

Kline, although respected by the ELDERS and everyone else in the upper class, was still a lazy slouch that wanted to cut corners. He quickly thought to himself, hours and hours of community service, or a clean and painless death, taking him to Marsolla.

It was finally decided:

" No that's alright Clubio. . . I believe that everything is under control." Kline said, still immobile in the grasp of Bringington's goons

Clubio and Dusty looked to each other, then nodded.

Clubio sighed then said, " All right, suit yourself."

Dusty went back to molesting the waitress and Clubio went back to drinking.

Kline wasn't expecting that sort of an answer. He thought that they would jump out of their seats and start a brawl on their own - without his urging, so he couldn't be held responsible, but , it seemed, there was no chance of that.

Clubio was three drinks away from puking and passing out while Dusty was busy nibbling on the waitress's neck, both knowing that nothing was going to stop them from their goal.

Kline sunk his head, realizing that death had him. All he could do now was take it like a man.

"Take him outside," said Bringington to the goons.

As they began on their last walk-through, Bringington ordered that Dole should be taken out too. So the other goon got him.

They were escorted out into the stone street. The traffic was busy with large, beetle like transportational units stomping around in an organized manner.

They forced Kline and Dole to pretend that there was nothing going on, they continued on their destination towards an alley way.

Then both Dole and Kline were thrown and pinned to the wall.

" You know, ever since you published my article about the colonial underground, my life has been hell ?" Bringington said.

Kline looked down at Bringington's shiny scalp, knowing that that was the only part of him he was able to talk to.

" Bringington. . ." Kline struggled. "You sent it to me. I thought I was doing you a favor. What the hell do you send it to a reporter for if you don't want it published?"

Bringington smiled as he brushed himself up.

Then he punched Kline in the gut.

" You were supposed to fix it up. Use your warrior's tongue on it to make it sing. Instead it was seen as poorly written. Stupid even. It made me a laughingstock - as you fully intended it to, you bastard. Because of you, my sponsors left me. . . It took me months to get new ones to finance my work. . ."

Kline still gasped from the force of the punch from the little man.

Dole then felt that it was a good time to cut into the argument.

"Excuse me, but I am a dear, dear friend of Kline's and there's one thing I can tell you about him: He's the most dishonest, dirtiest, notoriously perverted, scruffy looking-"

Kline then stuck his head up.

"Scruffy looking ?" he interrupted.

Dole then smacked him in the head followed by another punch to the stomach by Bringington.

" Please go on. . ." Bringington said.

"To make a long list short, you knew what you were signing up for when you chose him to be your editor . . . If the history didn't lead you, then the deserting you along the Nilippika River should have made it clear to you . . ."

Dole pointed with his head." Kline is famous for his lazy, self-serving ways. This is not a man to be trusted." he said.

Bringington bit his lower lip as he nodded." That is all true. . . You left me stranded in the middle of nowhere. For months, I fed on what I could find. Bathed in plagued waters. Prayed to Marsolla while being preyed upon by the local predators . . ." he reminisced.

" You know Kline. . . if it was up to myself, I would kill you right here, right now. . ."

"Oh, and in front of so many witnesses ?" Kline said with a slight sarcasm intended.

Bringington chuckled grimly. "Always the jerk in tight situations, aren't you ?" he muttered.

"No. . . I have dreamed of the day that I would see you dead. . . To caress your skull in my hands and then to fly over a cliff to throw it off and watch it break into thousands of pieces.

Unfortunately, that is not the reason why I have sniffed your vile little rear out this night . . . My sponsors say that it would spark interest throughout the Sudutan Empire if your team of measly criminals team up with my thirty professional expeditioneers to head for the North Continent within four days.

No hassle with customs, training or even paperwork, using the finest in Bequad winged transportation All smooth sailing.

Oh, don't think that I won't kill you though,"

"But of course. . ." Kline said as he rolled up his eyes.

" For accidents do happen out in the wilderness. . ." Bringington continued with a grim giggle.

"And my other option ?" Kline asked.

"Well. . . You could spend the four weeks learning to use the explosion-notorious Drag- Quads - with a measly group of convicts that are a fine hair away from killing themselves. . ." he said.

Kline sighed, hearing the humming sounds of a Drag Quad flying by with freakish coincidence.

" You do know that money and sponsorship doesn't matter at this point. . . For the papers have been signed and cut into stone. You know that if we join up together, it wouldn't mean anything at all. No extra sponsors, no extra money, worst of all, no credit for either of us." Kline gasped. "I'm sorry but my answer is no. . ." he said.

Bringington grinned and nodded.

Dole, fearing for his life immediately jumped in, "Keep in mind that whatever the result he gets for what he just said, I have nothing to do with him at all."

"I'm sorry, but you've turned down a great offer." Bringington said.

He then looked to his blue frilled mowhawked goons.
" Drop them. . ." he said.
Dole and Kline fell to the floor, still shaky and anticipating their end." Let's go. I see that our presence here isn't going to be respected at all." Bringington said as they began to walk out of the alley way.
Kline slowly stood up, surprised from the whole outcome.
" Wait a minute !" he said.
Bringington turned around."What do you want now ?"
" Why didn't you kill us off like you swore to do? Why the dramatic walk away ?" Kline asked.
Bringington raised a brow." Why would I kill you here? I would incriminate myself - as you so rightly said. I have sworn to kill you. If you wind up dead, they'll look to me first." he said. He took a step then he stopped and turned around once more.
" Unless you want me to kill you . . ."
"No, no. That's quite alright now. Just. . . curious." Kline said nervously.
"Huh. . ." Bringington said as he turned around to walk out.
"Wait !"
Bringington stopped again.
"I'll return the favor then. Here's some warriors tongue for your Sponsors. Tell them that you would never ask an enemy like me to accompany you. But that there will be much more interest and money generated throughout the empire by following a race between two deadly enemies who will do anything to win over one another. A race to save our very way of life."
"I like it. So will they. You've destroyed me, now you've saved me. Maybe I'll let you live to go on your expedition after all." Bringington said, then left.
For a few minutes, Dole sat there relieved that no one pulled out a projectile.Kline paced, still a little shook up from the encounter.
" Well that was rather exciting, don't you agree ?" Kline said.
Dole looked up and spat at his direction. He was frustrated and tired, not wanting to hear another word for the night.
Kline stopped in front of the spit and then walked over it, not caring."Why is it that everyone enjoys spitting at me tonight ?" he muttered to himself.

The storm came and went. The Old Man had spent days ordering the crew around, yelling at this one and yelling at that one. Likooshas spent the time in his cabin, drinking and cursing, not used to waiting for anything.

Finally I caught the Old Man sitting down on the beach one night, a few nights after my last installment of the story.

"I'm ready for more." I said, sitting down beside him.

"What do you remember so far?"

"Warrior women and the boy sold for Six Pieces of gold. Elana, Sassaska and Brelinka. Kline and Dole and Bringington and the big expedition. It's a big story."

"Who do you want to know about the most ?"

"Kline." I said without hesitation.

"Well then, I'll tell you about somebody else." he said, getting comfortable.

I hid my frustration and let him go on. He could tell me about going to the vomitorium and it would be exciting - he just had a way of telling a story.

" So they left the next morning heading west to their first monastery on their long journey." the Old Man said.

I was unsure where we were at this point. The Old Man was first talking about a child being sold, then he had jumped to three women, two of which were in love with each other and the youngest one which was a little unsure of herself, but fought like a demon.

As far as I knew, the Old Man was going all over the place in his story. Nothing seemed to make sense at all.

" Why was it that most of the women characters in this story have long names ?" I asked to get a few points straight.

" Well, it was because they were proud. Most women would carry their mother's last name for honor but they made up a middle name which was to be their own last names once they bore children." he said, thinking that I would understand.

" Huh?" I said confused as ever.

" Well, I'll use an example. . . Um, Well let's use Elana Seanna Kriemik. Her mother's name stays with her forever, but once Elana had children, their last names would be Seanna."

The Old Man began to look concerned as if he had just thought of something disturbing. "Yes. A child named Seanna . . . Kline Seanna. A boy-child named. . ." He began to seem distraught. He then went silent, trying to calm himself from tearing up a little.

" Are you all right Old Man?" I asked

The Old Man gasped a little but appeared to be back to normal. "Yes boy. . . I'm alright now. . . So, anymore questions?"

I felt that I was getting a hold on this saga.

" About the story?"

" Yes boy ?"

" So what did the trip by the women have to do with this mysterious child ?" I asked.

The Old Man grinned. " I was just setting it up to make it a better story. That's all."

" Huh ?"

" You see boy, if I only told the story of the slave child, it would be one long, boring story without delivering any grasp on what kind of culture he was being raised up in. What I have told you sets up the culture and the story nicely. Like building a strong foundation for a house. I did it so that you'd stay interested." the Old Man explained. "And so I'd stay interested too."

" So are you going back to the sold boy like it really was or are you going to make up more changes in the story to have it be a little more interesting ?"

The Old Man laughed. " Just listen. Now, I go back to the women.

the child will appear in due course" he said. He then sighed. " Now, we left off with the boy being sold off right ?"

" Yes Old Man."

" All right ... hmm, After he was traded for six pieces of silver he was then traded again to a woman priest. The priest owned many slaves who worked in the great monastery further north. There he learned how he became a slave. The priests told him the story of his merchant mother who traded him into slavery. They felt that it was necessary for him to know he was unwanted by all but them. That was his roots, his roots as a slave. But they also taught him to read, write, and sense other people's thinking which would make his life as a slave very much easier. But, in addition they taught him all along to know that his life was worthless. Of course, he was taught these things to do this menial work for them. He was a labor saving device - a recording device whenever they needed it. Every time he poured hot water into the baths, he listened to the priests talking and chanting. I must hand it to him, he was a clever boy - much like you. There he grew up and knew the great monastery as his home. His name was Nurix, or that was his Mother-or derivative - after the merchant who sold him to the priest when he was six, but the monks found it more comforting changing it to his price - Six Piece, thinking that it had a certain meaning to him, and would keep him in his place as a slave.

Although it sounds as if he has had a tumultuous life so far, it was not until he was eighteen years of age that his real story began. I remember it as clear as glass, and just as fragilely . . ."

Elana

It was morning and the priests were outside in the patio. They all sat in silence. Six Piece was out with them, observing them keenly as he scraped the snow off the stairs.

They all were sitting in deep meditation while the high priestess was standing up. Then she began to speak: " For all the ones who have died and suffered, we remember them and for the ones who will be born and prosper, we give them our respect. That is why we give no praise to any god nor give thanks to any saint. We pray to all who need praying for, and give thanks to the living. Nothing more and nothing less."

For another half an hour they stayed in meditation, calming their thoughts and thinking of nothing, it was even hard to hear them breathe. Six Piece sat down, thinking of what the High Priestess said. He began to wonder why she gave no thanks to any god.

He sat there, rubbing his hands and shivering because of the cold temperature and came up with no satisfactory answer. As he wrapped his scarf tighter around his neck and got ready to leave, he began to hear a cry of a horse.

He stood up and looked outwards to the snow covered dirt road, seeing in the far distance a large flock of horses trying to make its way through the snow with only five people mounted among them. Most likely they were going to be raiders.

Six Piece quickly ran for the security inside the walls. He went right past the meditating priests, without stopping for a minute. He'd interrupted them before and had the scars to prove it. But, at the last minute he stopped. They were the only family he'd ever known and he couldn't leave them in danger.

"If I intrude on them now, I'll lose time and get myself killed by the raiders," : he thought. "But if I don't intrude, I might die anyways - and what a way to die, with such guilt on my soul."

He then ran across the patio where they were all sitting and ran up to the High Priestess, tapping her shoulder. She grabbed him by the arm and squeezed it tightly with one hand, while, with the other, she smashed him across the face with a mighty blow that almost knocked him out.

" What are you doing Six Piece? Why do you intrude during the morning prayers?" she scolded.

Six Piece looked up at her, gasping for air and breathing deeply, " Mistress, Mistress listen. Raiders are coming . Raiders! If you don't wake up from prayers, they'll kill us all!" he shouted.

The other priests stood up in fury because of the intrusion of the slave.

" Is what you say true, slave?" asked the High Priestess,

Six Piece began to get fearful of her. That she wouldn't listen.

" Yes Mistress. What reason would I have to not tell the truth? I saw them from the high steps up there. They are nearly upon us." he said fearfully.

The High Priestess was still angry but then, as she rose her hand to slap his face, the sound of ten horses trotting and coming to a stop cooled her temper with the slave, but she still held on to him in case she changed her mind and wanted to hit somebody.

Suddenly a giant bell rang out from the entrance as the raiders announced themselves by tugging on the rope outside the massive gates. The high priestess let go of the slave and slowly walked to the entrance gate. She looked over the top of the wall carefully, fearing an arrow or worse.

She saw five women, two slaves and three warriors, the three all wearing dark brown cloaks over their thick, wooly warmers.

Their armored shoulder pads were decorated with saber fangs and their swords were strung on their backs for easy access. The High Priestess leaned further over the wall and fearfully made herself visible.

"Yes, what do you want?" she said briskly. One of them, the one with long, wild, curly brown hair that had red streaks - dark red streaks made from root skin sap - running through it, looked up and rode closer to the gates.

"I am Elana Seanna Kriemik. I am an appointed Adviser, traveling under the request of the great Empress Asmeraldia."

Immediately, both the High Priestess and Elana muttered, " May Marsolla bless her spirit." Sassaska and Brelinka echoed the prayer.

" These two are my sister Brelinka Shuwe Kriemik Warrior-Governor of Lina and the other is her Royal Highness Sassaska Batusha Girsy, Highest of the High, Priestess-Queen of the Marsolla Temple at Lina and Next-Chosen of the Council and of the Empress herself." she finished with a flourish.

A gasp came from those watching over the wall at the announcement of such exalted company. The priestess held her hands on the gate, and tried to show that she was not impressed. " What is your business here?" she asked bluntly.

" We are on the Empress' business" Elana replied importantly. "We've come on her instructions to chart and re-link all the other city states which exist up here in the far north -and to promote peace among the Provinces."

The priestess looked them over one last time, thinking they were a cunning trio of Bandit-girls. Her eyes seemed to glare an interest in Sassaska, looking eagerly at her long straight black hair, thin aristocratic face and her slender body.

She began to grin and slightly lick her lips, suddenly feeling the stirrings of lust. "Can you prove what you say Arkaitan?"

"We carry the Royal Seal of the Empress and a letter of safe passage in the Empress's own hand."

"Does the Empress send any personal regards" asked the High Priestess, sarcastically, almost positive now that the three were an advance party of raiders, trying to ruse the gates open so the rest of the hidden horde could charge in.

Elana was momentarily stumped.

Sassaska, for the first time, looked up at the old Priestess and spoke softly, so all had to strain to hear her.

"Yes Priestess. The Empress does have a personal word for you."

"And what is that word, oh young Exalted One ?" the priestess laughed, still not believing. She signalled archers to take positions on the wall - and pointed to the back wall, in case this foolishness at the gates was but a distraction.

Sassaska finally locked eyes with the High Priestess and the older woman felt the full power of her personality for the first time."That word is 'Mo'Lalla !" she said loudly, in the old language.

"What the hell is that " whispered Brelinka, "A magic spell ?"

"It's the old language" whispered Sassaska back. "At a certain level, all High Priestesses must know it. It is our secret means of communication."

The High Priestess was shocked. She signalled the archers to stand down.

"Oh, yes" she said, flustered. " Forgive me, Mistress. Come in. Make yourselves at home here."

She waved to the gatewomen. "Open the gates"

She turned back to the travellers. "Eat your fill. Rest a while. My monastery is at your command. I give all I have willingly to the great Empress and all who travel in her name."

She hurried down the stairs to greet these guests personally, as the gates opened.

"Old language or not, what did you say to her ?"

"It is the traditional conclusion to a request from the Empress." Sassaska replied, as they dismounted, waiting for the gates to open.

"OK, but what does it mean ?" persisted Brelinka

"It means 'Tremble and Obey'"

Brelinka tried to smother her laughter as the gates opened and the High Priestess stood in the opening to welcome them in.

Her eyes were fixed on Sassaska as the gates opened wide enough to admit the party, which was now on foot, leading their horses.

Elana smiled, and stepped boldly onto the bottom step which was directly in front of her.

The priestess took a deep breath and began to look insulted.

" Arkaitan ! Has it been so long since you have been in a place of Holiness, that you've forgotten the Rule of the First Step." she said angrily.

Elana stepped back quickly, looking rather sorry for insulting her. The priestess crossed her arms. and looked at her

" What rule?" whispered Brelinka.

" Its considered a great insult here in the North, if you step on the first step of a monastery." Sassaska replied softly. "Don't they teach you soldiers anything ?"

The priestess began to beat her foot on the ground, " Well, I hope that this is not how you're going to create peace up here, Arkaitan. If you never learned our customs or if you have forgotten, let me remind you of that important rule. 'Never take the first step for the first step to everything is filled with what you least expect. " she stated.

The priestess nodded her head and grinned once more, having re-established her superiority in at least one thing after looking foolish in front of the visitors.

" You and your companions may come in." she said with a sly grin as her eyes fixed once more onto Sassaska.

As Sassaska stepped over the stone step, Sassaska smiled back at her. "Thank you for your hospitality, Priestess." she said, diplomatically.

Brelinka noticed the lusty stare directed at Sassaska and looked at the priestess with jealousy in her eyes. The priestess turned around to see her in. Her seductive glances quickly changed to a stern face in front of Brelinka.

Brelinka, angered over the humiliation of her sister and still with the rage of her jealousy, stomped her boot onto the step, twisting it as if she was putting out a small fire.

She looked at the priestess becoming insulted and gave a sly grin of her own,

" I was never the religious woman my young Empress is. I am Governor of Lina and warlord general of the Arkaitan kay. And my first rule is this 'Crush whatever is under your foot and thus you will never encounter anything unexpected.'

I hope you can respect my first rule. If not, I am ready to give you satisfaction in a personal duel."

She then gave a playful gesture, moving her thin brown eye - brows up and down quickly.

The priestess gulped as she faced the seasoned Warrior Woman. She began to feel rage building inside herself, but was not foolish enough to give in to it.

"That will hardly be necessary, Governor-War Lady" she managed to say.

Brelinka began to walk and caught up with Sassaska and Elana. The priestess, still filled with fury from the encounter with Brelinka saw the slave boy already at work cleaning up the patio and dusting the seating cushions.

She stormed towards him. She briskly pushed him to the floor. He was startled and accidently hit the priestess with his cushion beater as he fell.

Using this as an excuse, although she didn't need one, she released her anger on him, beginning to hit him, kick him, and continuing to knock him back onto the ground.

" Stupid Little Man, be more careful when you do that! You struck me, you ingrateful twit! You deserve to be frozen in the winter for all the foul-ups you do, Boy!" she shouted.

Brelinka, Sassaska, and Elana quickly turned around and Brelinka sighed, " Oh, look at that sad old Priestess, taking her anger out on a weak man like that. Then again, why should we care. it's just a man." she said.

Elana looked at Brelinka with despair, "How could you say that, sister? It's our duty to protect men. They are helpless. We must help him, Empress."

Sassaska looked at her. "I would if it were another woman she was hitting, but like she said, its just a man and she is entitled to treat her property in any manner she chooses. I am not here to make enemies, girl."

She then turned around and began to walk away with Brelinka. Elana gasped and began to walk over to the priestess, who was telling the slave boy to plea for forgiveness.

" Excuse me," said Elana.

The priestess turned around, " Yes, Can't you see I'm trying to teach obedience to my stupid slave here?"

Elana looked at the slave huddled up in a ball.

" Well that's what I wanted to talk about. Perhaps he has learned his lesson already. I believe that you are being a little abusive to him."

" Listen, Arkaitan, when you buy a slave of your own then you get to do whatever you want with it. Until then, stay out of other people's affairs!"

Elana then gulped once more. She saw the Priestess get ready to kick him again. As she pulled her foot back Elana couldn't take it any more. She couldn't watch a young, handsome man be treated in such a bad way.

"How much do you want for him?" she asked briefly.

The priestess looked at her once more, pulling her foot back.

"What?"

"How much for the slave?" Elana asked again.

The priestess began to grin.

"Well, Why would a bodyguard like you want to buy this snivelling slave? To help in your journey ? I've got more efficient ones, bred for such tasks, out in the back. This one's useless, mindless and stupid. If there's one thing he can do right, I guess that it's . . ." the old priestess raised her brow naughtily. "Is it for sensual pleasure you want him ? I guarantee you that you don't have to buy a slave for that. It could be considered part of my hospitality to the Empress if you need him for an hour or two - if you know what I mean," she said.

Elana was disgusted with her question, feeling uncomfortable as she did around any question of sexuality from man or woman. Also, she felt that the old Priestess was getting personal and that the old bag was a pervert as well, thinking, as she obviously did, that everyone else's needs were as perverse as her own.

Nonetheless Elana reached into her money pouch and prepared to play the game, pretending that the Priestess's suspicions were true.

" Sorry, your Excellence, but an hour or two is simply not good enough for a rough soldier that's been on the road too long. No. I need a particularly stupid, disobedient and ugly man-slave like this for my own evil ends - which he will not likely survive. And I'd hate to take someone else's property and love him to death - so let me buy him."

The priestess stroked her chin and thought about it. "For a fine young slave like this, I would want seventeen pieces, big pieces of gold."

"Too much for such a wreck of a man - especially since I'm just going to break him up and throw him away by tomorrow. I'll give five and you can have the body afterwards to feed the pigs."

"Ten and you dispose of the body yourself." said the Priestess.

"Seven and I will actually pay you, instead of just taking my pleasure, killing him and asking the Empress to make it part of the Hospitality Package."

"Done for seven" nodded the Priestess.

"Done" Elana said, looking for seven pieces.

"And you dispose of the body" added the Priestess.

"Agreed." said Elana.

She found them, then threw them onto the ground and swept them to the priestess with her fine tailored boot. This was not an insult but part of the tradition of buying an adult slave.

The Priestess motioned for the slave to pick the coins up and hand them to her. "Man-slave - this is your price which has been given to you and which you have given to me. Go with your new Mistress." she said the legal words of slave transfer out loud, for all to hear.

The slave quickly stood up, still keeping his head low amongst their presence. He tried to not cry, moan or show in any way that he was badly hurt. Instead, he tried to cover all the bruises on his ribs with his hands.

Elana looked at the slave.

The priestess turned to the slave. " Well, You are no longer my slave, you heard the words. Leave me! Go with your new mistress - for the rest of your life. No matter how short that may be."

She laughed cruelly and walked away. The slave, looked up at her as she left. He felt grief and abandonment from the only person he knew as mistress. He didn't know what to do.

Elana slowly walked over to him, softly gripping his shoulder. The slave lowered his head once more. He slowly turned around to see his new mistress. He only saw her cloak, thinking that he was not allowed to look up at her face. As he waited for his next task to be given to him.

Elana tried to see his face but his head was bowed. "Please, your face, may I see it?" she asked.

He slowly began to look up at her face.

From the shape of her body, he could tell that she was a young and fair woman. As his eyes climbed further on up, he stopped in fear, He then turned away.

" What's wrong?" Asked Elana.

" Please Mistress, give me a task to do or a chore, something, don't kill me for your pleasure."

"Please, I want you to stay calm and steady. Don't worry about what I said to the Old Bag. I don't have much money and I needed her to think I only wanted a Pleasure Boy so I could get a better price. Loving and killing slaves is something she thinks happens all the time in bigger cities. So she believed I would have done it with or without payment. Now may I see your face."

The slave finally gave in , still trying to hide all his fear, his anger, his frustration and his pain, He looked up at her face. At that instant, he began to feel a nervousness coming from the inside out. Looking at her fair skin, her brown, curly hair with its partly dropped dark red streaks, her thinly pointed nose, and bright brown eyes topped with perfectly aligned brows, he was struck speechless.

She was so slender and dark, yet with such pale skin and fine features that she didn't seem like any warrior or merchant he had ever seen before. She seemed much more beautiful to him than anyone he had ever seen and suddenly, she not only owned his body, but his heart, too.

He relaxed a bit and that caused him to begin to feel the effects of his beating. He couldn't endure it much longer. The throbs from the aches from his stomach and his ribs became intolerable. Elana could tell that he was in a lot of pain now that his fear of her was gone. She reached for him as he began to crouch.

" Oh my," she said, grabbing on to him to keep him upright. "You need medical attention, let me carry you into the Great Room. They must have a medical woman here. "

The slave began to look away from her. He tried to hide the pain once more, " No. Please. Give me a task to do. I'll not mind the pain. I'm used to it. If it bothers you, I'll try not to show it."

"That's nonsense, I'll take you now." The slave suddenly fell out of her grip and onto the floor, coughing out blood and starting to moan once more. He soon passed out from the agony.

Elana picked him up easily, even though he was bigger than she was, and ran with him into the monastery building. Once inside, she then threw him on an eating table. "Somebody get me a cleric of healing!" she shouted,

The priestesses started to rush out to her calls and finally the cleric appeared. She was an older woman with a sour face. She carried a well worn bag of supplies and seemed weary.

"Did someone call for healing," asked the Cleric.

Elana quickly ran to her. "Please, I need you to treat him," she pointed to the slave on the table.

The cleric looked at the slave and did not seem anxious to save him. " You want me to save this Slave boy?" she asked" He is property of the High Priestess. I will not touch him without her permission."

" Please do, no one deserves to die so young. Slave or free."

The Cleric sighed, " It is the law. If he is in this state it is because his mistress wished him to be in this state. And, if history is any indication, she put him in this state herself and usually lets him suffer for a few days to learn his lesson before she allows any treatment to begin. She does it every few weeks."

"He belongs to the High Priestess no longer. I have just bought him. Many of your sisters here were witness to that fact. He is mine and I permit you to fix him."

"Is that so ?" asked the Cleric.

"I saw it done" said one of the crowd.

"Well, in that case, I guess I could save him but keep in mind, you must trade something for it." Elana watched desperately as the slave breathed shallowly, seeming to be sinking deeper and deeper into death.

"Tell me your terms, Medicine Woman"

The Cleric woman took out her thin spectacles and a piece of parchment paper. It was titled 'Things to trade for saving lives. . .'

Elana couldn't believe her eyes. At this moment, instead of saving the young slave, she was discussing things to trade with Elana. It irritated her.

" Skins, a scroll of poems, something useful." the old woman rambled.

Suddenly Elana slapped her parchment paper out of her hands.

The Cleric got a little frightened.

Elana grabbed the tunic of the Cleric and lifted her easily off the ground. "Here are my terms, witch: save him now and you will live to see tomorrow. Otherwise you die when he does - but more painfully." The Medicine Woman only used to dealing with peaceful priestesses, nodded, terrified, and Elana let her down.

" I will pay you fairly if you save him but now is not the time to be concerned about personal finances, old woman." she said sternly,

The old woman looked on the table, seeing the slave trickling blood from his nose and mouth. She sighed, then reached into her medicine bag.

She looked at the other priestesses watching her, " Well, what are you all doing? I need assistance here." she said.

Three came up, whispering to her on what to do. She started to grind up roots and berries, taking out white flowers and pressing them for the juices, then passed the bowl to one of her assistants. As the other woman mixed them up, the Cleric tore the shirt off the slave, revealing his bruised stomach and ribs.

"The blood is from the stomach" she explained to Elana. "I've seen it before with this boy after he's been beaten. It may be a nervous stomach - I'd be nervous too if I got a beating every two or three weeks."

They made him drink one potion and started to pour the thick ointment which was just mixed onto his stomach. He relaxed almost immediately after drinking the potion.

The other female monks started to rub the ointment on him. Others started sticking wooden slivers into his body at precise locations.

"It is not serious, then ? " asked Elana.

"It is. Without treatment he very well might die. "

"What treatment will I need if it happens when I leave here."

"A potion to calm and stop the bleeding inside his stomach. A powder to stop the pain and balm to coat his stomach and help it heal.

There is an open wound inside that heals and then is re-opened by his worries and finally by his beatings. If you can coat the stomach wall and keep his worries of beatings down for a month or so, he will heal forever. If not, keep a balm handy. I use the milk from the Purpleweed, mixed with a bit of blue clay and a few drops of mashed up sweetseeds." the Healing Cleric then held up the head of the slave, taking out a potion from her pouch.

117

Before she poured it into his mouth she turned around to Elana. "Or you could use the one that you soldiers call Stomach-Mortar"

"I know it well" said Elana.

"The ointment and the picks are for the bruises and the external pain and, for the ribs, we'll wrap him tightly with tunic-cloth.

The Medicine woman paused before pouring the potion in the slave's mouth.

"You know that if we treat him with this, he will go, well, in rut?"

"Really, that never happens to soldiers who take it. "

"These men, even though they are much weaker than us, have their own strange ways. A good dose of the stomach tonic gets their blood racing and they become almost insatiable. That's why the High Priestess loved to have him treated with this potion. She had a smile on her face for days afterwards."

"I thank you for the warning, but he is my slave to worry about."

The Cleric sighed as she poured in the potion, then stroked the slave's neck to help him swallow without choking while he was unconscious.

She then laid him down and quickly pulled out the needles in his stomach. The other monks lifted him and began wrapping him tightly with a long cloth. The cleric walked up to Elana, frowning and nodding her bald, old head.

"Well it is done, and I warn you, the tale of the mistress who saved her slave ended when the slave killed the mistress in a crazed sexual state. Even though they are the weaker sex, their sexual organs drain what little blood they have in their brains and make them even stupider than they normally are."

Elana looked at her gleamingly, "I will be taking that chance Healer."

The healer rolled her eyes. "Oh, I'll never understand warrior women like yourselves, who leave things out of your control. But enough of that. Let's talk a fair price now. "

"A sixteenth gold" Elana said. "But if he dies before I leave, I'll have it back."

"That's more than fair." the Cleric said. "This one has a hefty organ. Look, the potion is beginning to work already. If you want to ride it while he's still unconscious, my sisters will help."

She laughed as she walked away.

Elana shook her head and paid no more attention to her.

"Marsolla!" she thought. "These dry old monk women don't think about their god all day. They only think about sex."

Her worrying eyes were focused on the slave's face, although her glance did stray lower for a moment. He lay there quietly, sound asleep. More relaxed and better looking than when he was awake.

She slowly approached him, seeing a warm cloth soaking in water next to him. She sat on a nearby chair, took the cloth out of the bowl, and began to pat his forehead with it, wiping his face and squeezing the water out into his eyes.

Suddenly, his cold hand grabbed her wrist lightly.

It startled Elana.

The slave looked up at her. "Why did you do this?" he whispered.

Elana continued wiping his brow and gently took hold of his wrist, using her superior strength to put his arm back down at his side.

" I saved you because it wasn't your time to go. Besides it would be really sad if the first slave I ever bought managed to die before I ever got to use him."

He chuckled a little. " Well then, I thank you Mistress -" he paused, waiting for her name.

She sighed, "You shall address me as Elana."

He quickly bowed his head, " Thank you Mistress Elana." he said.

She smiled.

"Anyways, I must gather my things. I shall also get your bed ready for tonight." he said as he started to get up.

She pushed him back down on the bed gently. " Relax a moment until the medicine begins to work. "

They both looked down at his obvious erection.

"It seems to be working well already, Mistress."

She laughed. Do you have a name as well as a huge reaction to medicines, slave?" she asked quickly.

The slave stopped struggling to get up. " My-my name is Six Piece, given to me because I was bought for that amount by a merchant when I was an infant."

"So I got a bargain - I only paid a little over your child-price."

"I am ashamed to cost so little."

"I am only a poor bodyguard. It was every expensive to me. Maybe I should call you Fortune - since your cost has pretty well depleted my fortune."

"You are my new mistress and you can change it to anything, if you like to." he said shyly.

"Do you like your old name?" she asked.

He began to look deep into her eyes, almost getting lost. To him such a question about how he felt was never asked. Because of his history of abuse, he had never been able to express what he wanted.

" Any name will do. I'm yours to keep."

She smiled amusingly to his logic, raising one brow. She then took a seat. " All right, Six Piece, I'll give you a name. But it will take me time to find one that fits you well. In the meantime, you will still be Six Piece."

The slave lay still, waiting to be dismissed.

" Oh, right. Well, if you feel you can get up now, you go do whatever you were going to do."

The slave nodded, gulping nervously. He rose up slowly and got off the bed. His first couple of steps were shaky, but he soon recovered and he went out of the room to gather his things and fix a bed for her.

As he grabbed blankets from the cabinets and straightened them out on the bed, in the guest room, his mind was still on Elana. He had never felt this way about any mistress. It was partly because of her attractive body but mostly it was because of the way she treated him.

" A mistress that treated you like a normal person? Did such a thing really exist?" he thought to himself.

He folded the sheets carefully around the mattress, which was full of feathers and straw, tending to the cushions and fluffing them up on the bed . Suddenly, there was a loud ring from a bell. It was dinner time for everyone. He sighed and walked back to the dining hall where most of the priests started to feed.

The priests and the new guests all sat on the main table, all having soft cushions to sit on and clean wooden forks and spoons to use. They all waited for their dinner to be served.

The slave immediately put on a serving mitten and started to rush into the kitchen. There, the pots all boiled with hot dew bubbling out on each side.

The other male slaves were rushing around like wild animals, picking up steamed meats and rushing out to serve the mistresses.

"Out of my way!" shouted one servant, as he stormed and pushed his way through Six-Piece. He became nervous, walking and beginning to carry the boiling pot. As he stumbled to the door, the other servants got out of his way, ignoring him and rushing out to the tables with jugs of water and freshly baked bread.

He walked over to the table, trying to place the pot of soup on the table. The monks were talking and paid no attention to him. His arms were trembling to the weight of the pot and he needed help in placing it down. He looked to the side seeing another slave coming by,

"Will you help me place it?" he asked.

The other slave ignored him like everyone else.

Suddenly his arms over the handles of the pot began to strain. He fell onto the table, slamming the pot down and splashing a few drops of hot water on a couple of the monks.

He stumbled backwards and almost lost balance to himself, leaning against the wall.

Suddenly a monk stood up and grabbed the arm of the boy and was about to slap him across the face. As she swung her arm for the blow, it was blocked by another hand. The monk looked up, seeing the firm face of the slender Sassaska.

"What are you doing? Can't you see that I'm trying to discipline this slave?" The monk shouted.

Sassaska raised a brow. "You are a monk who believe in the studies of the great ones. Verse 54 of the books are not to take out anger on weaker individuals. Besides, he's not your property anymore." she said.

The monk let go of the boy, "How is it that you know so much about the Ancient texts, traveller?"

Sassaska only grinned and then said something to her, "Mishu d'oake Sall ave 'o."

The monk became shocked and dropped her mouth. She then looked down and acted as if she was a slave herself.

"Grand Solla of the Priestess Congress, I'm sorry, I didn't know, I thought -"

Sassaska changed her tone, "Would you have acted the same if I didn't tell you who I was?

As a first rule, all priests are taught to respect smaller forms of life and especially to restrain from beating them. The code of every monk is the same as every warrior in the empire. We are all trained to only fight when necessary. What rank in year are you, Monk?"

" First year, Grand Solla" she said with discomfort in her tone.

Sassaska only sighed and nodded, "Such a shame for such a young student to forget the first teachings of verse 54."

" I'm sorry Grand Solla." she said fearfully.

Sassaska only sighed once more and then put her arm around the monk. "We only learn by making mistakes. Perhaps you have learned something valuable here today"

She then looked at the slave, " Come, sit with us. You are part of the family now and I feel that you'll find it more safe there."

She guided him to his seat near Elana, Brelinka, and the other two slaves they had.

As she sat, she waited for the slave to sit down.

He stood, thinking that they were waiting for something,

" Won't you sit?" asked Sassaska.

The slave looked at them then slowly sat down, anxious and un-sure of what they were wanting. He saw the others begin to eat. The slave began to fondle his fingers and twiddle his thumbs as he watched the others. His lips became moistened by the touch of his tongue glid-ing between the two.

He gazed as the other two women slaves ate thoroughly like the their mistresses. Elana, chewing her grains, looked at the slave. She moved a piece of chicken to him.

He gulped and nodded his head politely.

Elana then swallowed her mouthful.

" Are you hungry?" she asked politely.

He gulped again, not knowing how to answer, " Well, mistress, I was taught at a young age that slaves were supposed to eat after ev-eryone was done. In case anyone wanted any other food, they didn't have to poke slaves to stop eating and go cook," he stated.

Elana gazed at him, not really understanding his answer.

" So, you're not supposed to eat in front of the masters. But you still didn't answer my question. Are you hungry?"

The slave then started to feel uncomfortable,

" Well, I am. Pretty well all the time. "

Elana smiled, " All right, then."

Elana passed a piece of flat bread to him along with a few vegetables. The slave began to take small portions of both and started to chew the bread timidly. As he started to eat, Elana gazed at him. " Since we talked before, I've been wondering what to name you. A name's important. It helps create who you are. And you have to be comfortable with it too. You see, I could give you any old name and you'd be stuck with it until the day I die or the day you are sold off." she said.

The slave suddenly stopped eating. The words   " sold off," seemed to bother him. He tried to hide it through his face but in his eyes and his clenched fist on the table, Elana knew that what she had said seemed to terrify him.

"Is it all right if I ask you a question," she said gently.

The slave looked into her eyes, wondering what she wanted, he then looked down to his food and gave out a sigh, " I'm a slave. You can do anything."

" Yes. You are a slave - and a man. But you're still a person. And you deserve a bit of dignity. What was your name before you were sold off to this monastery?"

The slave paused, showing a undisguised expression of despair.

"The merchant who sold me to the monastery told the story of how I'd been bought for six pieces of coin - they thought it was funny and called me Six Piece. But I learned to read a little here. I found my original bill of sale. It said my name was Nurix. The reason why I had that name was because the original Makaitan merchant who sold me gave it to me with the last syllable of her last name and the ending of my first, for identificational purposes.

I don't know if she was my mother or just another merchant. That is all I know, I am sorry if that was not the answer you wanted but it is the best one I could give you."

She raised her thin brow, " Do you prefer the name Nurix or Six Piece?" she asked.

The slave lowered his head and started to move a potato around. He looked up at her at that moment, his mouth lay slightly open about to say a word.

Elana waited for him to answer, She looked to his eyes wanting to know.

" The name Nurix, it's a real name. Not a description. It makes me feel like a real person."

She grinned with a mild expression of relief. " Then Nurix it is. I believe that name to be a good one, better than the one that these monks have given you."

Nurix chuckled, not giving out a sound through his mouth. His eyes were still locked onto Elana's face. She slowly reached and put her hand over his face. She stroked his hair, then felt his ear.

" I believe that Nurix suits you. Nurix, Meanna-Kriemik. It seems to tell a story of a strong character." she said.

She then moved her hand away from his face. She looked at her plate, clearing her throat and wiping her mouth with a rag.

" Well then, we should get our rest. We've got a big day tomorrow. More miles, miles of snow and trees for as far as the eye can see."

Nurix nodded his head. He then stood and waited to be dismissed by Elana. She looked at him as he stood up slowly and couldn't understand why he stood there then it came to her.

" Oh, right. Um, you may go." she said.

Suddenly a giant wave crashed onto the beach and destroyed the concentration of the Old Man. I looked at him with anxiousness.

" Well go on, tell me what happens when they wake up. Do they travel further? Does he die? Will you please tell me more?"

The Old Man started to laugh powerfully as if he was drunk.

" Listen boy, do you see the boat that we're working on?" he pointed to the boat.

I looked to it, barely seeing it through the thickness of the dark.

" Yes, but what does that have to do with Nurix, or Elana, or Brelinka or . . ."

" That's enough boy, I think that you've heard enough for one night. Look at the evening sky, I believe that it's almost midnight. You get your sleep if you want to be able to hear more of the story tomorrow, after we work."

I was irritated, fed up and curious. I wanted to know more about them. I felt that he was trying to keep the story going by breaking it up into small chunks to make it take a long time to tell. Then again, I feel that there might be more to this story than what he was telling me. That's the problem with a good story - you want to find out what happens, but you don't want it to end. Whatever the case, I had to wait until the next day.

The next day was hot, humid and the sting of sweat was in everyone's eye. It was late in the afternoon. Even this late, the only part of the day that was not hot was the ocean water slapping down onto the sandy beach. The water seemed to taunt everyone.

The men had worked on the boat and had broken a hole in the hull as they were walking down the exterior of the ship with melted bees wax.

Likooshas was angry and was even more furious once the Old Man told him that we might not be able to set sail for a long time because of it. The men all stood around a rock, seeing Likooshas slamming his good arm onto the wood of the hull,

"Why must there be always something wrong with this boat?" he shouted as he tried to keep in his furiosity.

The Old Man, ignoring him, was squinting and trying to see where to cut the wood of the hull. He held out his thumb to estimate the length of the hole. " Well, I believe that we're going to need to build something else for the boat since a part of the original hull is broken off." he said.

Suddenly Likooshas turned to the Old Man, having the urge to hit something, " How much time have we spent on this boat? Why would one hole in this great boat be such a problem?" he barked loathesomely.

The Old Man sighed and threw a look of sorrow to Likooshas.

" Can you swim? If you can that's good because with this little hole, you should expect to be swimming within a week" he said.

Likooshas grumbled a little in front of him. " You said that we should be building something?" he said unwillingly agreeing to the Old Man's authority

" Yes, you must start with a fire heating a lot of water, You must be able to dampen and steam the wood enough to make it flexible so we can bend it to match the hull here. It's the only way a patch will work - unless you want to build a whole new boat."

Likooshas looked at three of his men, " You three, start digging a ditch, we're going to start it right away!" he shouted impatiently.

The others started to listen to the design specs of the Old Man. He told them to start building a small hut long enough to hold a ten foot length of plank and wide to let it be bent through an arc of about three feet over it's length. It needed to have fasteners inside to hold the plank in a curve and it needed to be mobile, so the men could lift it and place it over the pots of boiling water - so the plank could be steamed - to hold it's curve.

The Old Man told them that the steaming hut would take a week if they hurried. The men started work, digging in the sand and creating what the Old Man told them to create.

The labor began to exhaust everyone. By the end of the day, they were all dreaming off into nausea-zation and dizzyness. The Old Man sat staring at the fire that he had started and looked to the setting sun off at the far horizon. And there I watched him, waiting for him to start the story once more.

As the dark blue of the sky started to become livid and as night began to catch up, the Old Man turned to me. He sighed looking tired and bothered.

" Is it possible that I tell you two days worth of stories tomorrow instead of telling you one today?"

I shook my head. "You can't. You left me wondering of what was to happen next. I'm your audience. We have a deal. You talk - I listen. In a way ,Old Man, you owe it to me to tell me what happens next. So far all I can remember is the slave getting his name. To me that isn't really interesting, in fact it's rather boring. Besides from what you tell me, this seems too far fetched to be a true story - so just make something else up." I said impatiently.

The Old Man raised a brow. " I tell you the true history of people who changed an entire civilization forever and you tell me it's boring and far-fetched ? Why is this story too far-fetched to be real? Please explain, boy." he said stingingly.

I gulped, thinking of what to say next. " Well, um" I tried to say something, " Well, why is it that women are the masters of men and why do they seem to be stronger and much more built for combat?" I said, thinking that that would prove my point.

The Old Man grinned; " You talk like a truly arrogant person. You believe it to be a false story because all you know is that men are superior to women. All you see is that and all you believe is that. If you haven't seen it in your sad little world, then it must not exist ? Well I'll tell you the reason why it's true. The world of North Atlantis was great because women ruled it as the superior sex. Their culture was based on women and it was a far richer culture than any ruled by men - no matter what you were taught. Boy, you must realize that North Atlantis was not a world that anyone was used to.

It was almost a whole other species. Their customs and their beliefs may have sounded far-fetched but to them it was part of their everyday life.

If I was your mistress, I would smack you for asking such a naive question, but since I'm not I'll let you believe what you want. If you want to think of this story as just another fantasy than think nothing when you listen to it. But if you believe it to be true, then listen with both ears wide open and focused for there is much of value to learn from it and I will not tell it ever again. Not to you and not to anyone else." he said.

I sighed, thinking of the possibility of it being true. My logical mind told me that it couldn't of been but inside my gut as I looked into the Old Man's eyes, I felt that it was all true to the very last detail.

I gulped again, " I'm sorry for saying something like that. I still believe it to be false but I will remember it all - for that is my gift - and, I guess, that in time I will convert my thinking and evaluate it a little more."

The Old Man smiled and then rubbed the top of my head. "Alright boy, well said and probably the most I can hope for. Just for that I'll tell you one of the most exciting parts of the story:"

As the night became long, Elana, Brelinka and Sassaska got themselves up the stairs to go to bed. The slaves, on the other hand, went outside to the stables, sleeping next to the horses in bunches of hay and wheat.

There Nurix, the new slave started to see what kind of people the others really were.

It was dark, pitch black as Nurix lay on the irritating hay. Suddenly he heard a person walking and searching through a saddle bag. He heard foot steps walking closer to him, then he sensed someone kneeling down.

He began to hear two stones clash with each other, causing a spark of light. Suddenly a small fire was starting up and becoming a great force of light pounding and throwing heat all over the stable. The horses began to get slightly startled by it, but they immediately calmed down when they saw it was not going to burn the stable down.

Nurix squinted to the light as it tortured his eyes with brightness. He then saw that it was the woman slave. She began to walk over to open the stable door a little. Nurix slowly sat up and crossed his legs as he stared at her.

Suddenly the other woman slave got up and crawled over to the fire and lay there, waiting for the first one to come back. The first woman slowly walked back and then sat down laying her back against the hay. Both of them were silent as they saw him staring back at them.

All three of them at that moment resembled well-behaved dogs waiting for a command. The woman who had lit the fire began to talk. " So you're the new slave they bought. Yet you're not a woman like us. You're a man slave." she said.

Nurix nodded and gulped, not knowing what to say to such an obvious statement; " Yes, I was bought by Mistress Elana."

They both seemed to be amused at what he said.

" Well then, I guess that she's given you a name?"

He twitched his nose at them, not giving her an answer.

"What's your name Boy?" she said superiorly.

"Well she never gave me a name. she made me choose my own name." he responded quietly.

Her amused expression to his naiveness began to contract. Nurix twitched once again.

"You never answered my question Boy, What's your name ?" she asked once more.

Nurix then began to blink as he focused into the fire," My name. It is Nurix. Anything else you want to know about me?"

She started to laugh as she shook her head, the other one gave a glimpse to her then at Nurix. Nurix began to feel comfortable around their laughter.

" Well then, will you tell me what are your names?"

The one then turned to him. " You're talking out of order Boy !" she barked.

There was the silence from the two. Nurix was beginning to get furious yet he was afraid of what he wanted to say. But he said it anyway: "You are more pathetic than I am. Your thoughts of being superior are just to cover your own wounds of grief and sadness. After all, I was sold as a babe in arms - nothing I could have done about it. You two, on the other hand, would have had to have been defeated or shamed or sold yourself in order to be slaves."

She nodded and smiled, then spoke , "My name is Taboo. Her name is Rhyme. I believe that that is all that you should know for now."

Nurix nodded then continued to focus in on the fire. He looked up at Taboo.

"The mistresses talk about re-opening up all the routes to cities all over the north, what's going to happen?" he asked.

Taboo stared at him, her smile fading. " Why is it that you ask me a question such as that boy ?"

" Will you tell me ?" Nurix asked.

" We never question the mistresses, we only do what they tell us to do. It would not be honorable to do otherwise. We lost a battle and agreed to become slaves for a term, rather than die. Our word binds us more strongly than any shackles. We will not dishonor our pact even in so small a matter as questioning the mistresses. That is the way of our lives. I thought that you, being a slave yourself, would know that." she said. "Don't be such a weakling. Don't be such a man."

"I asked about what's going on. Not whether the mistresses, themselves, were right or wrong. Besides, I made no agreement to be a slave. And never forget; I'm a man and can have no honor in any case. Now will you please tell me the answer if you know it, oh great but temporarily humbled warrior?" he said passively, with a smile.

Suddenly Taboo stood up. "You're rather cocky when you're not around the mistresses, especially for a sad little man." she scolded, even though the young man was taller than she. Then she grinned a little and lowered herself back into her hay. " But I don't blame you a bit. This is your whole life. For us it is a punishment. I had a free life before, and after my term, I will have one again. I just have to pay for my crime - the crime of losing in battle. And make no mistake, losing is the worst crime you can commit. Or rather, that I can commit.

You, on the other hand; you were born to lose. You're weaker, clumsier, more emotional and less intuitive than any woman. And with all that against you - you are a free-market slave rather than a protected male relative or a houseband. I can see where you'd be interested in what's going to happen next. Because next is all you have to look forward to.

There is no life in your future. Nor in your past, likely. The mistress you had treated you badly- we saw that coming in. Probably beat you even worse than we saw, certainly thought less of you than a pet, maybe even forced you to do sexual jobs. I understand the despair of being a slave. Probably even better than you do. After all, I used to be a warrior. I had slaves of my own. Now I'm also a slave. So I know the feeling of being property. The feeling of being lower than everyone else We chose it. The alternative was death.

Yet many of our close friends chose that alternative, and willingly. We chose the humiliation and vowed to be humiliated and not fight back. To live in humiliation..."

Nurix stared at her." Well then, you should know that you get used to that kind of thing."

Suddenly Taboo furiously stood up and began to shout. "Never! Never!" She brought herself under control as Rhyme looked on, then began speaking: " Never say that! Although we're slaves, we also feel emotions. But we are trained as warriors to do our duty. This, now, is our duty. It is a hard mission and for a long time, but we will complete it with honor and pride. If we were to get used to these unthinkable chores then they've won!

And more importantly, we've lost.

Again. Some day I will be free and I live for that day. Slavery is a terrible thing to be brought into. But it is the cornerstone of the Empire. Without it the entire culture would collapse.

But I can say that easily - for someday I will be a slave no longer. There is no such hope for you to cling to - you will always be a slave Yet you seem so passive in it. Is this just your natural manliness to be so accepting. What is your view of it ?"

Nurix looked over at her, breathing heavily through his nose yet not showing any provocation. Even Taboo sat down to see what he would say

"As far back as I could remember, all I can see are chains. I have always been in slavery ever since my mother sold me for six pieces of gold, when I was only a few weeks old. I guess you're right about me being passive. I know no better. To tell you the truth, I don't really care either. Mistresses always replace you or trade you off when something better comes along. Mistresses are mistresses. They are all the same. If there's one thing I learned, it is that you can't change the world around you, you can only adapt to it. And as a man I have to.

There is nothing in life for any man but slavery of one kind or another. I can never own property nor even have any money. I have no voice in any council nor can I bear weapons to defend myself. Life itself, for any man, is a harsh mistress."

Taboo nodded to Nurix. "Well said, young Nurix, and true. I pity you. You cannot even have a dream.

My dream is all that sustains me. It is my Freedom Dream. I will serve my term. I will be free again. And I will come back to face those who owned me as a free and equal warrior and any who mistreated me, even a little bit, I will kill . . ."

Suddenly the door opened up. All three of them turned around from their small fire. To their surprise, Brelinka was standing there. She looked rather surprised herself to see them all talking together, but she still slowly walked in.

The slaves all looked at her. She cleared her throat as she pushed her curly strands of hair coming down on her face to the side of her ear.

" Well, um. I just came in to tell you that you should prepare for travelling in heavy snow. Feed the horses and pack the gear accordingly. The Priestesses tell us that there's a blizzard storm coming in, but Sassaska insists on leaving at first light."

Suddenly Taboo turned to Nurix, giving him a mild frown, then turned back to Brelinka.

" Yes mistress, I'll get it ready for you. Depend on me."

Brelinka looked around at the three, " All right then, sleep well you three."

The three slaves stared at her as she slowly walked out. They feared that she had heard them all talking, not sure on how to put an explanation to her sereneness.

As she slowly closed the barn door, the slaves were silent for a few minutes, staring at each other, feeling rather terrified about what had happened.

Nurix sighed and eased up. " Well, I don't know about you both but I am going to go to bed, we've got a long day ahead of us."

" Do you think she heard us ?" whispered Rhyme. " If she did, I wouldn't care."

Taboo said "If she did, we'd likely be dead already. You know her reputation as a War lady. Although maybe she has a more fearsome punishment in mind."

Nurix paid no attention and turned around, trying to get warm. As they threw sand on the fire, there was silence from both of the women. Still, after three minutes, they started up again, talking and worrying if Brelinka had heard them or not.

Nurix chuckled to it, the thought of these two tough slave women talking big yet acting like timid children once in the presence of their mistress. Or in the thought that she had heard them giving out their innermost feelings. The thought of their worries brought a funny picture in Nurix's mind. After all, knowing no other, Nurix didn't mind his life as a slave.

"Then what happened Old Man?" I asked eagerly.

The Old Man stroked his scratchy beard with his fingers.

" That's the end of the slaves on that night, The story I mean."

" What ? You mean that's it for tonight? What happened to the slaves ? Did Brelinka hear them and order them killed ? Did they talk their way out of it ? What did they do ?"

The Old Man smiled as he gave a chuckly yawn. "They went to sleep."

"Oh, come on."

"You have to realize boy, that in stories, and in life, there are long chapters and short chapters."

"Which is this?" I pleaded, thinking it was over no matter what I did.

" I said that it was the end of the story of the slaves tonight, not the whole story of that night.

You'll never guess what happened next . . ."

Earlier as Brelinka had walked out of the monastery, she had slowly made her way to the barn, thinking of the hard trip tomorrow and hearing the chatterings of the slaves.

Brelinka started to slow down her walk as she heard the passion and excitement in what the three slaves were talking about although she couldn't yet make out the words.

She stopped at the door, still trying to make out what they were saying, wondering what could bring so much passion to a slave.

She then opened the barn door. She stood there looking at Taboo talking angrily: "And I will come back to face those who owned me as a free and equal warrior And any who mistreated me, even a little bit, I will kill . . ."

That much Brelinka heard.

All three of them turned around guiltily. The slaves all looked at her with a slight expression of fear and surprise, certainly not expecting her to walk in on their conversation.

She raised one brow and slowly walked a little more forward. She cleared her throat and told them about the blizzard noticing that Taboo turned to Nurix, before turning back to speak.

She looked at them and wished them a good sleep, raising a brow suspiciously at them, still unsure of what they were talking about. She then turned around and slowly walked over to the barn door.

She turned around one last time, looking at them, to see they were still staring at her, like a pack of dogs who had done wrong. She then closed the door and shook her head. " Why did we have to buy such strange slaves?" she said to herself. She gave a small giggle to it. She was a War Lady long before she was a Governor and she knew barracks talk when she heard it. She had no more fear of the women slaves turning rogue than she had of the sky falling - and she knew that humbled warriors had to make their empty threats and bluster in order to keep their morale up.

As she walked back to the monastery, she stopped at the lit lamp outside. She began to rub her hands together to keep the chill of the air away. As she sighed , a gust of warm air came out of the lamp and washed over her like smoke in the afternoon sky. Like a dragon of some sort.

She then stepped to the entrance of the inner monastery chamber and looked down at the giant first step blocking her way.

" Bad luck, huh." she thought.

As she went to step on it, just to be contrary, she kicked the step by accident and fell into the inner chamber, hitting the floor hard.

Lying there she heard a chuckle echoing through the walls of the giant monastery. She slowly stood up, looking through the dim lamp light. She saw a dark figure sitting on a cushion staring right at her.

Brelinka started to walk forward to the figure. From the way the stranger's body was draped in darkness, Brelinka felt slightly attracted to the figure. From the chuckle, she could tell that it was a woman. As she began to get closer, the figure suddenly stood up and walked into a darker patch of shadow.

Brelinka stopped. She heard nothing but gigglings and footsteps echoing from wall to wall. then a full, heavy silence. Suddenly she felt someone tap her shoulder. She suddenly turned to her left, seeing the dark shadowy figure run into a patch of darkness again.

Brelinka grinned, amused at this playful game. There was silence once again. Nothing moved, not even Brelinka.

Brelinka smiled, sensing something giving off a warmth behind her, feeling a sort of object blocking the drafty air blowing on her. She slowly turned around. To her surprise, the figure wrapped her arms around her waist and kissed her cold lips.

Brelinka stepped back, startled but in pleasure. She then wrapped her arms around the figure, feeling her warmth all over her, even in her mouth as her lips were locked on to those of the mystery figure. Brelinka was not startled anymore. She knew who it was now. She knew from the shape of her beautiful body , the giggle, and last, the way her tender tongue embraced her own tongue.

The figure was the slender Sassaska.

Brelinka stopped kissing her and placed her temple affectionately to Sassaska's. Feeling her neck warming up.

Still embraced with each other, they stood there, not saying anything but rubbing their heads against each other like affectionate cats rubbing their heads and purring to the fingers of their masters.

"Have you reviewed the northern scrolls?" Brelinka asked.

Sassaska gave her a serene look. "I did but there's one problem."

" Whats that?"

"It would take close to four months if we were to take the normal routes."

Brelinka kissed her cheek, " Whats wrong with that ?"

" Brelinka, I never told you this, but I hate the winter. I hate the cold and the snow and the short days. That's why I've always stayed in the capitol where it's warm all year.

Four months in the snow and blizzards is just something I don't want to look forward to. It's too depressing."

" Yes, I know, but your mission is called a tour of the NORTH-ERN territories. The south has already been charted. And it is the beginning of winter."

Sassaska let go of her waist and laughed. "I guess when you put it that way . . . it's even more depressing. It means I chose this. Hmmmm ? "

"And what does that say about you, Sasssaska ?"

"Thanks, Bree. You've brought me out of my blues. Ever since you brought your kid sister with you to travel with us, I've grown attached to you both. Almost as if we were a family. It's so nice to have people close to you who can cheer you up. I haven't had that for a long time."

"We're just trying to suck up to you - after all, how often do you get to know someone who will soon be Empress ?"

"Brelinka, I don't even know if I'll be able to handle everything in this tour, let alone the whole Empire."

Brelinka smiled at her. " Shhh, you'll get yourself caught up into a wedge of thoughts. You should be proud. Not too many High priestesses get chosen for the position of Empress every day."

" Only when an Empress can't produce an heir to the throne."

" Well, good luck for you that she didn't." said Brelinka; "What's the problem."

"What's the problem ?" Sassaska started to turn her back on her friend, walking to the light and stopping. " I know it's rather normal in the Empire, but we're still both women. Every other animal has female-male relationships."

" But Sassaska, that's what makes us better than the animals. How far we've come from that state, where we had to depend on the opposite sex to live a happy life. We've learned to be happy with the same sex, using men only as fertilizers at least we don't eat them afterwards like some beasts do. It's wonderful, don't you think?"

Sassaska looked at Brelinka with a worried face. " I am 35 years old, and this mission may last years. I'm running out of time. I'll be another of those dried up old Empresses with no heirs."

"You're determined to be depressed tonight. First it's the snow, then it's the responsibility. Now it's your fertility. What's next ? Do you think the sky is falling ?'

"Brelinka, you're my first love. And probably my last. I've never been with a man. Is that natural ? I'm beginning to feel that maybe it's our love which is unnatural. It bothers me slightly, doesn't it bring some sort of discomfort to you?"

Brelinka glanced at her with a hurt look. "I have been with men, and let me tell you, it's not all as beautiful as most would think. It's messy. It's smelly and, more often than not, you're left unsatisfied. And, even though they are weak and we treat them as pets, there have been some cases where they can have a strange effect on a woman and cause all reason to flee.

It's sometimes quite frightening. I'm sure you've heard the stories of great houses being run from the slave quarters, when some man seems to take possession of an otherwise intelligent woman.

You're best staying away from all that.

Especially now, when you will soon rule the greatest empire the world has ever seen."

Sassaska turned around with a mild smile on her. She reached over and gave a hug again. " Oh, Brelinka I'm sorry, I'm just. . ."

" Don't worry, I'm not angry at you. We're in love, we've proven it before to each other. I know it's difficult to go on sometimes but together, we'll manage to get through. You'll learn to trust us and to trust me. "

They kissed once more. Their foreheads met and touched each other softly. They stared into each other's eyes. They then both started to laugh.

Suddenly a priestess walked in. She was startled to find them this way.

" Oh, I'm sorry." She stood there staring at them both.

The two women only turned their heads at her. Waiting for her to say something.

" Well, Um, high priestess, I had found some of the ancient scrolls for you - the ones you asked for earlier - but- I guess that you're -." She was nervous, she cleared her throat. " I'll be going now, I'll um, I guess, Um, I'll put the scrolls in your room."

She backed away slowly and disappeared into the darkness.

They could hear her running footfalls. The two women stared at each other again.

"Maybe it's not so common after all ?"asked Brelinka jokingly.

Sassaska broke into laughter. They kissed once more and walked to Sassaska's room.

I gulped with an uneasiness.

I looked at the Old Man to see if he was showing any form of fibbing. For some reason, the story started to feel rather far over the head to me.

" I told you that Atlantis was an odd place. And we've only gotten into a small part of the whole story." he said,

" The women had sexual relations with, well, with each other ? How could that be ?" I said.

The Old Man raised a brow. " In the Empirial times, most of the males were slaves. Even when they were free and raised to be married, they were kept as sort of housepets. Mostly they were used for cleaning, cooking, and pleasuring and fertilizing their mistresses.

Keep in mind they were much weaker physically - and in human groups, the weaker members are always thought to be contemptible.

There were female slaves to do the hard manual labor like harvesting foods and transporting goods for their mistresses, and taking care of the horses."

I was rather confused about something. " Wait, You said that some men were married off. Then how could there be these same sex relationships if there are men getting married to women ?"

" That's a good question, boy. Most times, the men would only get married to act as a personal servant.

Most times a woman would have a lover and a husband at the same time. That was considered normal. It was their culture."

" Then what was the difference with a slave and a husband ?"

" Nothing really" The Old Man chuckled a bit. "The difference was that if you were a husband, you had more chance of living a longer life.

Male slaves were usually every much at risk since they were weaker than women. Husbands usually had a life inside the bedroom while a male slave had a life outside of the bedroom, seldom allowed to go in - although most slaves live in the house and do the chores there - even when there is a husband."

He looked at me." Any other questions boy ?"

" Yes, well - I wanted to know about Brelinka and Sassaska."

" How they enjoy themselves ?"

" Yes. How is it that they- well you know what I mean."

" Like all other animals do it."

" Well, yes, I guess but, they've not got the -"

The Old Man raised one brow as he wondered what I wanted to know.

" What else is there to know boy ? They mate. That's all."

" Yes but - what about the actual act - I mean, they lack. . ." I looked at the Old Man, who was not understanding my ramblings. I guess that I had to take the Old Man's words on it. They mated like any other kind of animal regardless that they were both female.

The Old Man started to laugh gently as he reached over and patted my shoulder. " Well, boy, growing up, I learned not to ask too many confusing questions, because when you ask them you're not going to get the answers you want."

The Old Man gave a little chuckle, then looked out to the evening sky. " See those stars ?" he said. I looked up, seeing the millions of stars scattered around. Some of them were clustered together, while others were alone, glowing frail and dim.

" Yes? What about them ?" I asked to broaden my knowledge.

"That is how we're going to travel to Atlantis, boy."

" Isn't it only past the point of the peaks ?" I asked.

The Old Man turned to me. " No, those are only the first borders. They are the warning point of no return.

Once you go beyond those peaks, you'll have to sail the sea for months. Once you're out there, there's no end to ocean. And all you have is the wind and the stars and a slender hope.

That is why people believe that Atlantis sank. Because of the vastness of the ocean.

Atlantis no longer comes here because they have mined all the diamonds that exist here and have no further use for you. And you people are too undeveloped to ever sail to them. So you believe Atlantis just disappeared. But it did not. It stands there today, larger and more civilized than all your sad little villages put together.

Most think the same thing as you. That it is only past the points that the world ends. But trust me, it only begins there."

" When do you think we'll be able to set sail, Old Man ?"

He looked at me with concern in his eyes. " To tell you the truth, I often feel that our toy boat will never get us there, no matter when we set sail. I keep putting it off thinking that we can add a bit more here and a bit more there. But it won't make any difference. If we catch the winds and don't catch the storms . . . "he shook his head, then continued,

"Old men are too cautious. That boat, as strong as it is, was made to sail the Mediterranean Sea. Once we're out there in the ocean, it will face the Wrath of all forms of Gods. Waves the size of mountains, fish big enough to swallow you whole, and the thought of hopelessness eating at you. It is truly no man's land out there."

"But Likooshas still believes that we can get there."

The Old Man began to sneer. " Yes, that fool pirate, he thinks he can get there on will power alone. I admire him. His urge and instinct is strong and his greed stronger. Even I will come to depend on his force when we get too far into this foolish quest to turn back."

" He will succeed." I said.

" Yes. . . I depend upon that - but we'll see. . ."

It was early evening. And the morning sores had finally caught up with me. I was tired from working all day then staying up and listening to the story.

No one seemed to notice that both I and the Old Man were dozing off. They were still building the steam house. The Old Man roused himself and wandered over to talk to Likooshas.

Likooshas was a pot always on the boil but he was even more furious when the Old Man told him that upon reflection, they really didn't need the steam house after all. And that the hole could be fixed with some fine carving and a bucket of tar to hold it all in place.

It seemed that the Old Man only ordered people around for his own amusement. Or he had decided to forget doing every job perfectly and was ready to settle for just 'good enough'. Or maybe he just changed his mind often. I didn't know. Nor did I care. So long as he continued to tell me the story. I was hooked now.

The hours went by, and the hole in the boat was finally fixed. Likooshas had demanded that we be done on the end of the week, going by the Old Man's count of 14 days as one week.

The boat itself seemed to be in shape for sailing but the Old Man still refused. He told me details that should be on a boat which I had never even heard about. All I knew about boats were that you needed oars, a tub of wood and a sail connected to a mast. The Old Man made it so complicated to keep up, it was a wonder how we got anything done.

As usual, dark came later than anyone expected. A couple of the men went and hunted a boar, and liberated a goat from a farm near by.

They also traded some of their working tools for two barrels of wheat whiskey. We had feasted that night and most of them were dead drunk. That was everyone except me and the Old Man.

The Old Man sat at his usual spot and stared at me, getting comfortable once more.

" Ready for tonight's tale ?" he asked.

I smiled as I sat up. " All right Old Man, hit me with your tale of women warriors and worriers. Give me your version of Atlantis." I chuckled a little.

The Old Man raised an eye brow, to my outburst. " Yes. . . My version of Atlantis. . . All right, Hmmm, Yes. How about this, then:

The next morning, Sassaska and Brelinka had woken up refreshed and somewhat glowing . . ."

" Yes, I wonder why." I interrupted as I laughed a little.

The Old Man sighed and strained to continue. " Now, Elana had gotten a few supplies from the Monastery. A few blankets, a few woolly capes, dried meats and vegetables, and some Mammoth spears.

These spears they received were Buushu made. The best of quality, and rather hard to come across, if you weren't Buushu, I mean. Since the Monastery was only filled with priestess' they had no need for such weapons of raw power as these."

" What was the big deal with these spears ?" I asked.

" They were six feet tall, the spear heads were wavy blades meeting at a point, and they were spring operated. Once in impact, they split apart to lock onto the animal." The Old Man said.

" Was that it ? What else does the spear do ?" I asked thinking that these spears were a minor thing.

" The spear then split in half and it had the capability to explode."

" Explode ?"

" Yes. Have you ever seen a piece of wood in a fire when there's a knot ? It blows apart. Imagine the same thing a hundred times more powerful. That was what kind of spear I am talking about."

I gulped.

He grinned. " Now boy, will you let me continue with the story or not ?"

I nodded, knowing that he was getting irritated with me asking too many questions.

The Old Man laid back now, getting into the trance that he always gets into. He sighed once more and I moved a little closer to listen.

" It was morning, all of them, the slaves, the mistresses and the priestess were up. Sassaska was getting the scrolls offered to her by the high priestess. Brelinka was packing up her things and supervising Rhyme and Taboo as they fastened all the bags and one last time, checked over everything. And then there was Elana.

She was packing her things and fastening their weapons onto the saddle of the horse. She was working with Nurix by her side. It was early and still dark, although the mountain tops glowed with the radiance of the rising sun. Elana was fastening her supplies down while Nurix was struggling to carry her weapons.

Elana watched as Nurix's hands shook from the weight of the bag flung over his shoulder - a saddle bag she had carried downstairs easily, with one hand. He walked over to the horse and then grunted as he threw it over the creature's back. The horse cried in shock from the weight but did nothing else.

Nurix, exhausted from working all morning, leaned on the horse for a while as he tried to catch his breath. He then noticed that Elana was gazing at him, holding her new spear that she had bought from the priestess. Nurix immediately bowed his head and walked over, still panting but trying to silence it.

" That was the fourth bag loaded and buckled around your horses mistress Kriemik."

Elana reached to hold his chin, slowly moving it up, so that Nurix looked up at her.

" You don't have to look down when you talk to me, Nurix."

Nurix then looked at her eyes. He wasn't going to put up a fight about it anymore. He felt that what he had been taught no longer mattered. He was with a new mistress now. And when there was a new mistress, there were new rules to follow. That was a key point that Nurix had forgotten over the years, since he had been so long with the high priestess.

" All right Mistress Kriemik, I won't look down in your presence. Not unless you tell me to."

Elana smiled, Nurix nodded his head, too polite to ask what should he do next.

Sassaska came up to Elana, who was startled by her sudden appearance. Nurix stared at them both. Sassaska looked to Nurix, curious to why he wasn't staring down. But she didn't take it as a problem. Elana turned to Sassaska.

" Yes ? Are the paths on the route still clear ? What does the old woman say ?" Elana asked.

Sassaska unrolled a parchment paper which was a map. She leaned the map onto the side of the horse.

" Yes, she says we probably have most of the morning, so we should get going. Everyone is loaded up now, and we're going to start down this way," she pointed at a line on the map. "Hopefully that route will only take us around three weeks to get out of the mountain regions and onto the plains." she said softly to Elana.

Nurix stared, hearing little bits but not sure what was going on. Elana seemed to be agreeing to what Sassaska was saying; then Sassaska whispered some sort of question to Elana.

Elana smiled and glimpsed at Nurix.

She then seemed to be explaining something to Sassaska. Sassaska paused and then turned to him. Nurix felt uncomfortable with the eyes of Sassaska looking at him. He quickly turned around to look like he was grooming the horse to his left.

Sassaska rolled up her map, patted Elana on her shoulder and walked to Nurix. Nurix, pretending to work, heard her footsteps coming closer to him. He began to feel nervous but kept himself cool. He didn't know why he was beginning to get nervous, it was an instinct reaction that he was going through.

Sassaska stopped walking, Nurix was afraid to turn around and continued to buckle and unbuckle the saddle bags. Sassaska then cleared her throat to get his attention. Nurix slowly turned around, bowing his head and trying not to make eye contact Sassaska looked at him pathetically.

" Have you loaded up all the horses, boy?"

Nurix nodded his head. " Yes, Mistress Sassaska."

Sassaska then nodded her head expressionless. Nurix could feel that Sassaska was a kind of person who looked down on slaves, especially men, yet she was hiding it from Elana for some reason.

Nurix was surprised.

He knew Sassaska was this way because he had a gift in reading people, especially in reading his mistresses - a gift which had kept him alive many a time in the past. But why the soon-to-be Empress would hide her feelings from a low level companion like Elana was a mystery to him.

" All right. Slave. Well then," She sighed. " Get ready to leave."

Nurix nodded and gave an unconvincing smile to Sassaska.

Sassaska took no notice of it. A horse cried in the distance and Sassaska then walked away.

Nurix watched as Sassaska went over to Brelinka, he saw them caress each other then give a mild kiss. They then called their slaves over. Each slave was to go up on horseback with their mistress. The mistresses sprang up on the giant draft horses and helped their heavily laden slaves up behind them.

Nurix didn't know what to make of it.

Elana watched him stare at them. She smiled, grabbing the reins of the two horses and bringing them to him.

Nurix felt their presence as soon as the horses nose was towering over him. He turned around, staring right at the horse. Suddenly, the horse snorted at him and turned it's head. Elana patted the shoulder of Nurix.

Nurix glimpsed at her, still uncomfortable at the idea of looking up at his mistress. He stared at her, seeing her serene face. It wasn't like the others. Her face was kind, pleasing and enchanting. It had the kind of look that you'd find in a friend, someone who cared for you. It wasn't the look of a mistress, there was no look of arrogance or disgust and low tolerance. Out of all the others, he liked Elana's look the most.

"Yes, Mistress Elana ?" he said.

" Hold the horses for a minute. I need the horse to be stable as I get up." She said.

Nurix nodded. Elana then handed him the reins of her horse, leaving the other by itself. Elana, as graceful as a cat, quickly got up there in three steps. One foot on the stirrup, other leg immediately over the saddle, and finally sitting down. She stroked the neck of the horse for being calm while all this was going on.

Nurix looked up at Elana and handed her the reins.

" Thank you Nurix." she replied.

Nurix nodded as he made his way to get the other horse. He brought the other one, which was packed with supplies to her, thinking that she was about to ask for that next

"You get on that one" she said.

Nurix looked at her, terrified.

Elana smiled nonetheless, bowing her head to show a sign of encouragement. But Nurix wasn't encouraged. He was trying to figure out how to get on it.

The horse didn't make it easy for Nurix. It twirled and grunted every time he tried to get on it. Finally he got his foot in the stirrup and attempted to swing his other leg over the bags and weapons. Suddenly, the horse jumped. It startled Nurix severely and caused him to fall to the ground. Elana was slightly amused but not for long. The horse was still jumpy, frantically swaying and changing from kicks to side steps.

Elana immediately moved her horse to the other one, trying to calm it and at the same time, make a wall around Nurix.

He then struggled to move away, trying to stand up but ending up crawling on the ground.

Elana patted and stroked the mane of the frantic horse. The spooked horse snorted at Elana's. Elana paid no attention to it and turned around, seeing Nurix panting, his eyes wide, and his body shaky.

He slowly stood up, then just stood there, staring at Elana, then at the horse.

" Was it something I said Mistress Elana ?"

Elana giggled.

Nurix grinned pathetically back, but then remembered that it was improper for slaves to joke, so he immediately stopped his expression and approached her.

Elana reached her hand over to him.

" Here, I think you'll be safer if you ride with me." she said.

Nurix slowly walked over and smiled at her offer. " I guess you're right Mistress." he said as he grabbed her hand and was pulled up behind her as if he weighed nothing.

" Come on Elana, let's go before the daylight's gone !" shouted Brelinka, moving down the dirt road.

Elana glimpsed to her back, seeing Nurix trying to get a hold, but too polite to grab onto her waist.

Elana giggled once more, thinking that Nurix was too unbelievably naive for a slave. She then grabbed his hands and placed them around her waist. Nurix was unsure of what to say.

" Just so we won't lose you on our first journey. Here, you hold the lead of that other horse" she said as she handed him the rope attached to the pack horse, then turned her horse around and got going in the early morning half-light. Nurix nodded and felt childish but he was still amused at her comment.

"Then they made their way down the mountain from the monastery. For hours they traveled. Nurix and Elana said nothing. Elana wanting to say something to reassure her new slave, but not sure what would comfort him and what would make him even more nervous and Nurix, too scared out of his mind to say anything. They both waited until they made a stop to talk.

Although they had covered a lot of ground on the dirt road out of the mountainous territory, the road was twisted and treacherous and they were still only a few miles from the monastery. And on a collision course with the biggest blizzard they had ever experienced.

And as for the rest I will only tell it after I get a drink of water."

" All right I'll wait." I said, thinking that he was going to get up and get himself some water. All he did was stare at me. I stared back at him. I waited for five minutes not knowing why he wasn't budging. I raised my brow and was puzzled.

" Well, What's wrong ? Why aren't you getting your water Old Man ?" I asked.

" What, you thought that I was actually going to get up and get it myself boy ?"

" Then how are you going to get it Old Man?"

" Well Greko, You see. . . if you want to hear the story, you have to participate as well. In other words, You have to get it for me."

" What ?" I asked. "

" You heard me right boy, get me some water." he said smiling to his answer.

I grumbled as I stood up. I walked to the boat, trying not to stumble over the sleeping bodies of the crew. I then grabbed a wooden cup and dipped it in one of the barrels of water. Then I thought a moment: what if I gave him some salt water. After all, he didn't specify what kind of water he wanted."

I grinned to the thought and grabbed another cup, walking towards the tide and then filled the cup with sea water. I walked back to find the Old Man was laughing at me, thinking that he was so smart. I then handed him the cup with salt water.

" Oh, thank you, boy. I need this from all the laughing I was doing, looking at you."

As he grabbed the cup, he sipped it then noticed that it was salt water. He was about to spit it out but noticed that I, the ragged-assed boy was grinning at him.

The Old Man then proceeded to finish the cup. I watched him guzzle it down and I was shocked. Either I gave him the wrong cup or he was a tough Old Man. I didn't know what to think.

" Ah, that water was good boy. Oh, may I have another, I'm rather thirsty." I took a guess that he took the wrong one, so I handed him mine, in fear that I might be holding the sea water. I then watched him drink it down too. He grinned and looked up at me.

" Well boy, do you want to hear any more ?" he said.

I gazed at him in awe. Then I sat down once more on the sand, near the fire. I had underestimated the Old Man, or he out smarted me. Or both. So now I owed it to him to be quiet and attentive.

" All right, now that I had my refreshing drinks of water," he leaned and looked at me with a mild chuckle, " Now I can continue with the story." he finished.

I nodded.

He sighed and leaned back into a comfortable position.

" . . . Hmmm. They reached the part of the mountain where trees grew and they traveled for a few more hours in these woods and set up camp at a grassy location. Brelinka had set off to hunt their supper and the slaves started to set up the tents, tie down the horses and unroll the warm, Mammoth wool blankets.

When everything was set up, they all waited for Brelinka to come back.

Hours went by and everyone, even the slaves, were doing things to pass the time. Even so, it was a long few hours, waiting for Brelinka's return.

Sassaska waited in her tent, fondling the beads on her bracelet as she studied one of the new scrolls she had picked up at the monastery.

Elana was lying on her sleeping bag, staring at the sky and admiring her sword at the same time.

The slaves were grooming the horses with wooden brushes. Scraping the sides of the horse, and Taboo was grumbling along with Rhyme giggling to whatever she said.

Nurix was silent, thinking that Taboo was talking to him. He thought that because he suspected that Rhyme might have been mentally ill. Whenever Nurix had encountered them before, Rhyme seldom talked and when she did, it was to introduce a point that Taboo was going to make or to repeat one that the other slave had just finished making.

Suddenly a hand slapped Nurix's back and he stopped thinking to himself. " Have you been listening to a word I said ?" Taboo said in a loud tone of whisper.

Nurix immediately turned around and nodded his head, not wanting to say anything to provoke her.

"If I had a weapon and was free from my vow of honor, you and Rhyme both know that I would run in there, slice the throat of that mistress then go over to the younger one and slice her from the bottom to the top." she said.

Rhyme giggled hysterically at her comment.

" Right, I know you would." Nurix said as he turned around to groom the horse's tail.

" You know I'll do it, it's only a matter of time you know." Suddenly she stopped preaching.

" Yes, Mistress Elana ?" she said.

Nurix could hear from the shuffles that Taboo was bowing in front of her.

"That's alright, you don't have to bow in my presence. Oh, by the way, can you hold this for me ?" said a voice.

It was Elana.

Nurix turned around once more. Elana stood there and right beside her was Taboo. Nurix glimpsed in shock, seeing Taboo holding Elana's sword.

Taboo just looked at it. probably thinking that it was her golden opportunity, yet she just stood there.

Elana smiled pleasantly at Nurix.

Nurix, remembering what she said about looking down, stared right at her eyes and smiled mildly back to her. " Yes Mistress Elana, is there anything I can do for you ?"

She gave a small chuckle and started to look away, almost as if she was embarrassed.

" Well, I was bored and I wanted someone to help me with assembling my spear."

She began to look at the horse and pat it as she talked. "Is this one all right ?" she finished.

Nurix noticed that she wasn't making eye contact like she usually did, almost like she was shy about something,

" Is there anything wrong ?" Nurix asked.

Elana immediately took her hand off the horse and looked back at Nurix. " What ? Oh, no.. I was just, you're very good with horses." She nodded her head as she stroked the horses neck quickly. " Yes very nice job . . ."

" Thank you Mistress." Nurix replied.

She sighed; "Well then, will you follow me to my horse ? I haven't unpacked it yet."

Nurix nodded and stared to Taboo.

" By the way Taboo, do what you always do so well, you know. Sharpen it for me."

" Oh, yes mistress. I'll have it back for you at the end of the day." Taboo said as she ran off to sit down and sharpen it.

Taboo, seemed to change her whole character. Instead of the tough grudge-holding slave-warrior, she was now a quivering scared little servant, doing whatever her mistress wanted.

Nurix found it quite amusing.

" Well, come on." Elana said, tapping Nurix on the shoulder. Nurix nodded as he followed her to her horse.

She flipped open one flap and there, fastened comfortably sticking out horizontally from the right side of the horse were her spears. Long and elegant, they were beautifully decorated in Buushu artistry. Its outer wavy blades encased the inner mess of spring- operated spikes adding to its fascinating charm.

" Forgive me, Mistress for saying this but it looks rather complete and assembled to me." Nurix said.

She unfastened it and held it up. To her it seamed weightless, elegant.

She then turned and handed it to him.

Nurix grabbed a hold of it. Elana let it go and immediately Nurix felt it's true weight of 20 pounds. It wasn't that it was heavy, it was just heavier than he expected it to be - something of such elegance and balance. He then realized that it was a woman's weapon, never meant for the weak grasp and use of a man.

Nurix held the spear upright. He had never seen anything so unusual to him before. He noticed a handle which seemed to twist around the pole of the spear. Nurix, curious as he was, grabbed it thinking that it was how you were supposed to hold it. But he began to twist it too far. Suddenly the blades split in two, releasing the hooks and spikes upwards like a stretched porcupine hide.

The spring action was so strong that the whole spear bounced up, out of his hands.

Elana immediately grabbed the spear. She twisted it to the right and the spear closed up once more.

Nurix's eyes widened, startled by it.

" Next time, don't twist that part." She said.

Nurix nodded immediately.

"Um, so. What was the part you wanted to add on to it ?"

She took out three large metallic capsules in the shape of acorns. "I need to place these capsules in the dipped hooks inside the spear."

She handed the capsules to Nurix.

Suddenly there was a large growl echoing from the trees. It was so loud that birds flew and snow lying on the tops of the pines fell to the ground.

Sassaska ran out of her woolly skin tent, drawing her sword. She had thought that a monster had come into their camp.

Taboo had stopped sharpening, and Elana dropped her spear. Everyone was silent. The noise sounded like nothing they had ever heard before, but that was it. One roaring-moan-like sound. The horses were jumpy at the sound, panicking and trotting around, trying to break loose from their tied down reigns and run away. Sassaska dropped her sword and went to calm them down but was having some trouble. There were four horses and one of her. Elana looked to Nurix as she picked up her dropped spear. "I'm going to help out Sassaska." She then threw the spear to Nurix and ran over to help calm the horses. They continued to cry but the real excitement was over. The other two slaves felt this logic too and went back to their jobs in starting a fire and sharpening the weapons.

Elana came back to the tent and they went inside, but Elana kept fidgeting.

"I'm worried about her." she finally said. "Stay here - I'm going to take a horse and have a look. "

She put on a heavy cloak - then went out into the snow.

Nurix waited inside, not sure what was happening. To make good use of the time, he took the spear and tried to attach the capsules.

In an hour she was back, covered in snow and anxious. "I found her trail - and before the snow covered it up, I saw something else - going the same way. Tracks of a Giant Bear "

The Old Man stopped at that point. I thought he was remembering it all and trying to keep it all in order, so I just kept quiet.

Then he started snoring.

That was it for the night.

I chased him around for another couple of days but never got him in the mood to tell tall tales. He had directed the crew to take nearly the entire boat apart by now and in result, it was all lying around in piles and stacks.

I thought it would be really funny if one night, he just slipped away into the forest and left us there with all this stuff - none of us knew what the hell he was designing and we had cut up most of the original ship so it wasn't likely we could ever put it together again.

But I never said anything to him about this joke, for fear of giving him ideas.

I worked hard all day and was hiding after dinner in the hopes that no one would see me and think of a chore for me to do. The Old Man sniffed me out and sat down across from me.

"You look like a boy who needs a good dose of Sudutan Pride," he said, and launched into the story right away:

The sound of humming was rich this morning.

Kline and Dole had gotten home late that night, after their run-in with Bringington and now, with hangovers in place, were going through their first day of training.

The six chosen men were there alongside Dole and Kline. Unfortunately, they didn't seem to give the same expected respect to the trainer as Dole or Kline was giving. They all had their diamond-powered Drag Quad wings on, to gain the feel of the sheer power of these compact wonders of the sky.

Clubio let his mind wander somewhere else, Dusty refused to put on his armwear, Squirrel hadn't even turned on his wings yet, and the rest of them argued and laughed at the Instructor's commands.

This morning's training was in the use of Drag Quads. For three hours, they were taught to put on the leg and arm braces, head gear and anything else to assure their safety. After all, these machines were not only notorious for exploding, but also for dropping their wearers out of their harnesses as well as slicing off limbs.

The man in front of them, an old Imperial Officer with his thinning out frill and over belt belly, was harnessed into his own Drag Quad. He charged up the crystal radio on his left side. He rung up the generator and turned a knob right next to the handle.

" This is your standard communications apparatus. All expeditioneers are expected to wear this," the Instructor yelled easily over the sound of their wings beating 100 times per second.

Sudutan with Six-Pick Drag Quad

Kline looked at the others with the corner of his eye, seeing all eight other men uninterested in the lecture.

" There is a cable connected to your communications apparatus."

" What's it for ?" Dole yelled out.

" So that you wouldn't have to worry about catching it."

" What's so bad about reaching to catch it ?" Kline curiously asked.

"If you bend your arms and forget to set yourself in hover mode, then you can kiss your arm good bye !" The Instructor said with a grim laugh. "Your wings, in forward mode, will slice it off."

"Is that why the air corps are called the one-armed bandits," yelled one of the men.

" Yes. We have many, many Imperial officers that have lost limbs flying these things. That is why we train you to be able to understand the dangers of these machines."

The Instructor looked at all of them.

" Alright you can turn them off now !"

All at once they yanked the kill-cord, depressurizing their powerhouse engines. The humming came to a stop.

Kline was almost knocked over by the powerful stop that he endured.

He even heard the air intakes suck in a giant breath to cool themselves down.

" I see that you are now all acquainted with your wings. Love them, care for them, and last of all, buy them." The Instructor said.

"Tomorrow, after you've paid for them, you will learn a little more about the safety policies that have to be followed carefully." he said as he began to unfasten his brightly painted wings.

Kline quickly tried to release all of his equipment all at once. It was over forty pounds bearing upon his body and it was rather uncomfortable when the wings weren't beating one hundred times per second.

All the knowledge and information that he was experiencing, he wanted to record it all down, to publish later on in a book of his journey when he had returned from the trip.

As he saw the Instructor make his way to the officer's lounge, he shook off most of the braces, unfastening the alloy buckles and calling him at the same time.

"Mr. Instructor, sir ?" he yelled as he raced over to get him.

The old officer turned around and stood there waiting for Kline.

"Yes, Cummundore ?" he replied, instantly knowing Kline's rank by the color of the feathers fastened to his leather helmet.

Kline stopped and caught his breath for a moment.

" Can I help you with anything ?" the Instructor asked.

" Yes . . ." Kline said getting out his notebook and a pencil to get down his notes. " I wanted to ask you a few questions . . ."

" Questions ?" the Instructor replied, a little unsure about what kind.

" Yes... about the flying apparatus... The -er . . ."

"Drag Quads ?" the Instructor completed.

" Yes. Thank you."

The Instructor stood there, nodding his head and feeling confident to answer any sort of question about the flying apparatus.

" But before I begin, could we go back to the air strip to look at an example ? My questions might go into inexorable detail." Kline warned.

The Instructor looked at him, trying to imagine the types of questions that he might ask. Nonetheless, he agreed.

Kline's expeditioneers had left their Drag Quads on the air strip and were lounging around under a shade tree quite a distance away.

Kline and the Instructor came across the closest Drag Quad pack which had its two pairs of wings painted bright yellow, so that it would be visible from long distance.

They both crouched down.

" Now, let me start with the most obvious of questions: Why is it called a six pick Drag Quad ?" he asked.

" Well, because there are four wings which resemble that of a dragonfly's - that gives you the Drag and the Quad for four.

The term six pick comes from the way the engine is designed." he said stern but brief.

It was obvious that he was in a hurry.

" Can you go into detail on what the six pick stands for then ?"

The Instructor nodded and opened the back hood of the wings. There lay an intricate, precise powerhouse engine. There was a lot of gold wiring and on each wing joint and hinge was gooped in lubricants to keep it from building severe friction.

There in the middle, were six gold and silver bars jabbing themselves into a fingertip-sized diamond which was placed in the center of the whole engine.

" See those bars - they taper down to become thin picks - they're right there, pressing and creating the pressure to keep that little diamond in ?" the Instructor asked.

Kline nodded.

" That is why it is called a six pick." he said.

" Obviously." Kline muttered under his breath as he made a rough sketch of the design.

" What ?" asked the Instructor feeling a little insulted from his comment.

Kline looked up, " Oh, nothing... Go on..."

" Anyway. This design beats any other kind of Drag Quad... Because of the Six pick.

The six bars keep a very sound and smooth hum instead of a rumble and clank that you get with a four pick or a single, and the heat is equally distributed among the six so that there is less of a chance of overheating to cause an accident ."

" An accident ? You mean exploding ?"

" Yes."

" I thought all of these wing packs had a chance of exploding if you pushed them ?" Kline said.

The Instructor gasped." Um, technically, yes. I mean that if you used any other kind, there would be a seventy thirty chance of nothing happening, but the thirty percent possibility is a result of explosion. The six-picks take that percentage down to under 5%"

" What's the maximum punishment that a six pick can take ?"

" Punishment ?"

" How fast can you go for what amount of time before you can explode ?"

" This one in particular ? Around one hundred fifty miles for six hours before the engines overheat and burn away the lubrication of the rotation joints of the wings. One hundred is already considered the red-line for all kinds of Drag Quads." he answered. "After that you should strip them down and overhaul everything - and in between overhauls you have to keep lubricating - do it every time you land."

Kline took a breath through his nostrils.

"So the lubrication is still unreliable ?"

"Yes."

" How long does the diamond last ?"

"Excuse me ?"

" The power source." he said as he tapped the diamond. " How long does it last before you've got to replace it ?" he asked.

The Instructor scratched the side of his scalp and took a guess. He was no real diamond expert at all but he knew that average rate for check ups." I believe the change rate is once every five years for a diamond like that."

" You believe ?" Kline said. " Such a juvenile thing to say even at your age." Kline said under his breath.

" What ?" said the angering Instructor.

" Nothing. How does the breakdown of the diamond work ?"

" The breakdown ?"

" Yes. The whole technology behind it. How do we extract energy from it in order to power the wings. And why does a diamond have to be replaced. Does it shed layers ? Does it melt ? What is inside of the diamond that makes it such a valued resource for us in these wings and everywhere else, other than its pretty appearance ?"

The old Instructor feeling a little overwhelmed by the way the question was addressed closed his eyes and gave a sigh.

" It's too complicated to explain to you in one sitting. The main source is the carbon within these diamonds. The diamond arranges the carbon atoms in precise rows within the crystals. The power comes from splitting these atoms, one by one - breaking the carbon-carbon bond and then breaking each atom up in turn. Since they are all carbon and all lined up, the atom breaker device doesn't have to change focus or change power. All the carbon atoms are right there, in a row."

" You can't be serious Tubbo?"

"What ?"

" Damn it - atoms and bonds, rows and focus. There must be more to it than that. How does the atom get broken. Are you sure you cannot tell me anything about that - it's all so mysterious?" Kline asked, looking up from his notebook.

"Kline," the old Instructor started.

" Learning half of these things took me twenty years. I don't be-lieve that you'll be able to learn the breakdown of carbon from a dia-mond in twenty minutes."

Kline looked at the engine and pointed at certain parts.

"Are you sure you cannot tell me anything more about it ?"

" No." he said.

The Instructor began to get up.

Kline quickly pointed to another part,

" What about this ?" he said.

The Instructor then closed the hood of the back blades.

" I've got to go."

" But -"

" Listen to me Kline, I am this close of reporting you to your Spon-sors for your attitude and disrespect towards your seniors."

" Disrespect ?" Kline said with slightly over exaggerated expres-sions.

" Yes. Now I have to get going and you've kept me.

" Only for a few minutes more . . ."

" Good-bye Kline." he said as he began to walk off.

" Damn !" Kline thought to himself as he closed up his notebook.

He looked back at the Drag Quad.

" I guess that your secrets are safe with him, eh ?" he said as he put his book away.

Later that night, Kline returned to the bar where he first laid eyes on Ennis. He was drawn to her because of her physical appearance. She seemed to remind him of a lifetime long ago, something that was serene and warm to him whenever he thought about it. The way her brown hair curled like no other woman he knew in Prox.

Also her eyes, the stare of a cat. It seemed to keep him on his feet.

There he sat, opening his journal and reviewing previous sketches and pages to pass the time by as he awaited the bar to open up.

This was no ordinary notebook. It was a veteran which had ac-companied him through the harsh and dangerous times of his career.

The roughs of five articles discussing the abuse of natives and savages overseas which outraged the distant diamond colonists in Egypt, Europe, and the Islands. The crackdown on crime lords, risk-ing the lives of many others.

He had sold his soul to writing and he held it in that journal.

As the bottom lights began to shine and glow, Kline looked up to see what was going on. He noticed various people sitting around, talking to themselves.

Kline felt uncomfortable and slightly disgusted.

Although he was in a high class Imperial bar, he still felt that he was with the lowest of scum. To him, they were all the same. Rich or poor, they were all a little vile in their own way. He cringed as his hair stood up.

He then went back to reading his notebook.

Ennis appeared from the door, carrying a box of goods. She walked past Kline without noticing, or noticed but didn't care. She walked into the kitchen and dropped it off. Then she immediately walked over to set up the chairs and tables, getting ready for the evening's pay.

Kline slowly closed his little notebook, slipping it under his reddish black dress band, the long strip of cloth colored to tell the class to whom the individual belonged.

He gave a little smile and barely made a noise as he stepped off his chair.

Ennis looked through the corner of her eye at him.

" Oh, it's you again. What is it that you want ?" she asked firmly.

" Oh, nothing." he said.

She grabbed the chair and placed it on the floor next to the wooden table.

"...I..."

She briskly walked off as he tried to speak to her, moving to another table.

Kline followed her.

" ... I wanted to apologize. . . " he said.

She turned around with an impatient look on her face.

" Apologize ? You already have apologized for your fresh talking friend." she said as she walked away.

Kline felt a little bewildered. He continued to pursue her nonetheless.

"... Oh, no ... " he began.

" I meant for the moment that I kissed you. I truly didn't mean to startle you that way, I just. . ."

She immediately stopped and turned around.

" As I said before, why is it that you are apologizing for kissing me?" she asked as she slowly leaned towards a table.

" I just thought that I put you in an uncomfortable position. That's all."

She looked him up and down.

" You're sick . . . " she said plainly as she walked over to place more chairs under the tables.

" What are you getting at ? How am I sick ?" he asked.

" Men don't think to care about women's feelings. Why is it that you, out of your own gender stereotype, choose to be different ? Why come back to this bar just to apologize ?" she asked

" Because I . . ."

" Oh no," she interrupted. " I'm not done. Why is it that you come back here, the place where your alleged rival stalks, waiting for this very moment. Why, come apologize to me ?" she said.

Kline thought for a moment, realizing how truly peculiar it really was.

" Therefore I conclude that you're sick . . ." she concluded pausing and storming to the bar.

Kline continued to think. He noticed that she was an intellectual woman, something that was considered a nightmarish thing for Atlantean men.

He figured out that she was expecting a very intelligent answer. After all, she seemed to be a stubborn, confident, hard headed, violent, spontaneous woman who loved watching men squirm with blank stares. She was looking for a fight, and he was willing to give it to her once he prepared a valid argument.

In other words, Kline fell in love.He smiled as he looked at her once more.She ignored him as she cleaned up a messy area of the bar.

He stormed up towards her and placed both hands onto the table. He cleared his throat. Ennis turned around.

" Your observations are actually wrong, you know," he said.

" Oh really, why is that ?" she confidently asked.

"The reason why I came here wasn't because I had intentions in apologizing to you. I am attracted to you and I find you rather refreshing to be around."

She raised a brow, unsure of his answer.

" You mean to tell me that you came here because you felt that my body was pleasurable to your eyes ?" she asked.

" Precisely." he said.

She was silent, a little scared knowing the fact that Kline had eager thoughts about her. Flattered though, by his honesty and confession.

"All right, now that you've spilled your emotions onto the table, what do you expect me to do? Clean them up ? Fall down immediately to satisfy your every need ?" she asked.

" No. I just want to talk, to chat, nothing more after that." Kline stated.

She smiled," Obviously that's a lie." she said.

Kline stared at her surprisingly,

" Why do you say that ?" he asked.

She sighed as she crossed her hands, "Because you're a man. You've always got something in mind for a woman that goes far beyond chatting, most likely something unpleasant. For me anyways."

Kline smiled." May I come back tonight for you ? May I take you somewhere ?" he asked.

She raised a brow." I can't trust you."

" That's not answering my question." he started.

" Will you go with me somewhere tonight ?"

She paused for a little while, hearing the owner of the bar calling her name in the back room.

" We'll have to see tonight." she said as she quickly turned around and made her way to the back room.

Kline rejoiced internally, opening his notebook and writing a reminder for himself.

Later that afternoon, as the sun began to go, the city generators were still worked up, so that the evening lights would be on. Kline made his way back to the base he had set up with a grand enlightenment in his eyes.

He was so happy that he felt rather social that evening, he wanted to talk with his expedition volunteers, not just to study them as he first intended, but actually getting to know them was something he was wanting to do now.

As he walked into the pyramidic bunker, he saw one man lying about on a bunk bed, reading papers and stories published by Kline's official bureau, another was leaning on a chair with his feet up.

But the main group sat at a table, playing games with empty bottles and clay beads.

Kline smiled and pulled up a chair.

The group was jolly but took notice of Kline, a stranger and an outsider in the group which they considered themselves the leaders of. They stopped their game.

"Yes ?" Dusty asked sternly.

Obviously the men felt uncomfortable with Kline's presence.

Kline smiled and tried to seem friendly.

" Oh, nothing." he started. " I just wanted to get to know you all... If we're going to be traveling for six months to conquer the north, I believe that it would be helpful to be good acquaintances with each other." he finished.

The men were silent with his answer.

Squirrel blinked with a slight confusion.

Dusty smiled and chuckled to himself. He stroked his prickly beard.

Luca raised a brow.

Kline looked at them all holding cards with their hands about to release their small carvings of wood, symbolizing many thousands of soldiers.

" What ?" Kline asked, with a feeling of uneasiness.

The feeling of angry eyes focused and locked onto him.

" So the little rich boy wants to be our friend now, but I bet he's writing a scandalous article that would really sucker punch us in the gut, eh ?" Dusty said.

The rest later followed with his laugh.

Kline smiled, not knowing whether he was insulted or not. For he was really going to write that article.

"Of course. That's where the real money is. But you, Dusty-boy - you. I'm going to write up as a swishy homosexual, just for that nasty comment."

That got a good belly laugh - even from Dusty. Everyone eased up a little more and began to ask him questions about the expedition.

Kline anticipated this and expected for the worst.

"Sir, I feel that the trip would result in our deaths." Clubio said with a little enchantedness.

" Ya," said another.

" A suicide mission if you ask me . . . " he finished.

Kline smiled. He was getting to an equal level of understanding with the men - since they looked to him for answers they would also eventually look to him for leadership.

" If you believe that the expedition will be a great massacre, why did you sign up ?"

"The money !" shouted one other man.

The whole room was filled with agreeable laughter.

" The money ?" Kline asked.

Dusty then stood up and looked at everyone, holding his whiskey mug up.

" Face it sir," he started. "We're going across a cold sea, we're going across the endless ice, we're training in the most rugged and crude form of aero-tech available, and you; our gracious expedition leader have a name like Kline." he said, raising his cup.

All of the men did the same.

"I mean you no respect sir, but I'm pretty sure that Kline means 'small' in some dialect over in the plains next to the inland cities."

" We all did it for the money." Dusty cheered and then turned to the jolly men.

"For the money !" he said. Everyone toasted for his comment and someone started to sing songs of fortune.

Kline gave a plastic smile, irritated by their comments and excused himself from the table.

He then walked over to the stairway and watched them go back to their games. He felt that the men weren't ready to talk to him, nor was he to them. So he respected it and let them go back to their mindless fun. But he stayed in the shadows and watched to see how each of his ruffians matched up with their files.

First there was Dav'inne; a short haired man with no real need to show his class to anyone or anything. A man nor also, with no real need to gain a woman for marriage. A man who lived only for himself, but was haunted by grief.

His smile on the table hid his true feelings towards everyone. His fear in showing his true class and education revealed a sad tale of a Medic losing his pride after the loss of a patient whom he arrogantly promised would be fine.

Because of his grief, he began to do the unthinkable - to make mistakes. Although he was not caught out in hundreds of careless mistakes, when the infant son of an upper class merchant died because of a negligent overdose of pernicious drugs, he was thrown out of the profession and all his fortune seized.

Next to him was a man named Squirrel: A man with a short frill to show his power and upper class status. But he wasn't upper class. When he was a third year engineer, although he had won honors, not he nor his poor family was able to pay for any further education and in fact his current loans were due and there was no money. So he wasn't able to gain more formal knowledge to broaden his horizon of skill. He had to begin working in the lower ranks of engineers and had been there ever since - unable to rise. He was a gifted man yet hardened by the years of submission to the richer and more powerful people who wanted to become engineers for the sheer title of it - yet did not have one half of his knowledge and skill.

" Ha, I've conquered your army again ! Now pay up before I have to kill and eat your women and children." said the proud looking Clubio as he broke into laughter after someone made a crack at him.

Clubio was an Imperial Officer who was accused of beating a savage girl once to death. This was a petty excuse for women were usually beaten all the time and quite often died form it, but as long as the woman price was paid to the family, nothing usually came of it. But, in reality Clubio was thrown out of the Sudutan army because of his refusal to share her with the Imperial Governor of his province. His large Imperial tied frill, sloppily knotted, moved as he turned his head to talk to Dusty and Luca Beard.

All of the men in the room had an interesting story, which made them a unique team. All of them were unconscious of each other's past nightmares and sadness. Kline only knew them because he had read all of their reports when he chose them for his team. And he planned to keep them secret and confidential , thinking this knowledge, like all knowledge, might be of advantage to him some time in the future.

He was amazed at them all, all having a different story yet all stories ending in the same way: them being thrown into the discriminatory class where everyone looked down upon them even though their skills and knowledge were quite marketable.

It was ironic, for the Sudutan society called for them to rebuild themselves and even if they did, it was only to find that the Sudutans would never hire them again. Society only wanted to be rid of them from their great cities. Which forced them to the colonies or into a life of crime.

This was what Kline feared most, that his time was coming up soon too. He had risen high on merit alone, but had no powerful family or friends to catch him if he fell. And worse, he had no real sad story to keep, to establish his character - no one to blame his mishaps on but himself.

He was lucky so far, but he knew that it would run out someday, when he least expected it.

Then again, luck was the least of his problems.

He went deeper into the barracks thinking gloomy thoughts, but managing to cheer himself up by the time he reached the bed he had assigned himself.

Kline smiled as he went to sit down on his bed. Then Dole came up behind him, seeming to bear bad news.

He hurried himself as he came towards Kline. Dole was in such a panic that the knot in his hair was riffled and disorganized.

He panted as he leaned his arms on Kline's shoulders.

Kline laughed and patted him on the back.

" Why Dole," he started. " What in the world happened to you ?" he finished.

The men stopped their game and looked over at them in the gloom.

" Looks to me like he had some fun with a girl back at the bar !" Luca Beard said jollily. Immediately, the eight men spewed out laughter from his comment.

Dole paused, ignoring the men and faced Kline.

" There's something that you should know . . ."

" What is it ?" Kline asked, thinking nothing for Dole's feelings.

" I've got important news to tell you . . ." Dole panted. "There's good news and bad news." he finished.

Kline thought for a moment. Obviously he wanted to hear the good news first.

" The Emperor, Zex . . . He wants to Sponsor us . . . " Dole started. " Therefore, we'll be getting more of the supplies we need . . ." he finished.

Kline smiled with delight. "Where did you hear this ?" Kline asked. He felt that this was a blessing from the God Marsolla himself. He was almost happy enough to run through the streets naked.

Then his sceptical, cynical, and grim logic kicked into play. His smiling came to a stop. The information was too good to be true.

"What's the downfall to this ?" he asked with a little paranoia in his tone.

Dole gasped a little; " Well, we'll be doubling up on what we have now . . . More iron tipped pellets for our guns, spare transportable wings in case we have accidents, an extra diamond for each man."

" In other words, more useless junk which isn't essential to us." Kline said. "Is there anything else ?" Kline asked.

Dole gasped once more as the sweat rolled down his greasy forehead.

"Well out with it . . ." Kline said sternly.

"It's Bringington . . ."Dole said.

Kline's eyes widened. His interest was reinstated.

"What about Bringington ?" Kline asked, grabbing Dole by both arms.

As Dole tried to speak, the room started to rumble. The pieces on the board game which the men played, slowly fell lopsided as it moved from the lightly vibrating table. The lights slowly swung back and fourth.

Kline looked around as the room went silent. Everyone stood up.

He then looked at Dole,

"What about Bringington ?"

"Emperor Zex wants to Sponsor both expeditions . . ."

" We're both working together ?"

"No," Dole said.

" On the contrary . . . the Emperor feels that it would be most interesting to watch both of you start from the same place. More to watch then, as the competition heats up."

171

"So it's to be a race. Just like I proposed to Bringington out in the alley the other night ? That treacherous little baldie bastard - he stole my idea and proposed it to Zex."

Suddenly the vibrations became more violent. The sounds of large beating wings chopping the air took over everything. The only sound in the world was suddenly a thunderous mix of explosive humming and groaning and the air was actually compressed in bursts. The wind moved violently, causing the open shutters in the barracks to slam open and closed.

Clubio ran to his bed to look out of the bunker window.

" Six Be-Quads ! " he shouted; "There's a couple more coming !"

The others ran to the windows, watching the giant, beetle-like cargo carriers flying to the landing pad. Their clunky, oval shapes were unmistakable. It was as if the world was being invaded by a horde of huge, voluptuously-shaped insects.

The men stared in awe as the sheer power of the wings from the mechanical beetles shook the building. And it continued, like a symphony from hell as the Be-Quad pilots looked for a place to land.

" The deal is that he's coming to the training base . . ." Dole finished, shouting over the noise and a little frightened by the beetles.

Kline then let go of Dole.

" That's not the worst . . ." Dole said.

"An Emissary from the Emperor himself has come to introduce you both."

Kline was surprised.

" Introduce us both ?" Kline said.

" Yes" Dole answered.

" Your team and his have to be out there to greet the diplomats."

"When ?"

"That's the funny part . . ."

A thought ran into Kline's head, causing immediate discomfort. His eyes widened.

" You honestly don't mean . . ."

Dole nodded frantically as he wiped the sweat from his brow.

"We've got to meet them in thirty minutes..."

The waves crashing on the beach became a little more violent and water began to sneak right up to where we were sitting. Immediately, the Old Man closed his eyes and pressed his grubby hands against his face.

Both of us stood up and got out of the way of the slushing sea water.

The Old Man stretched his neck a little,

" Mechanical beetles ? Drag- Quads ? These sound like the work of gods to me, Old Man."

I said to him, speculating that he was exaggerating.

He grinned and smelled the ocean air, and took a piece of burned charcoal from the tip of a burning branch.

"Give me a rag, Greko ?" the Old Man asked.

I gazed to my side, ripping some of the cloth from my blanket cloak wrapped around me. I handed it to him and waited for him to continue with the story.

He drew well, sketching a gloriously rounded looking beetle. It was graphed completely out of metal. The bolted sides beautifully lined around the outer metal shell where the wings would be. Its legs were a unique collection of tubes, pulleys, and metal spheres. All of which acted as substitutes for muscles and joints. My mind was trapped in the mechanics of the Beetle-like machine. He then turned to the other side to draw me another picture.

"All will be explained as we go on..." he asked.

I sighed,

"These still sound like the works of Gods !" I stubbornly stated.

"They were. " he said quietly.

It was a cold night. Dark and windy as the last transports landed, digging the tips of their monstrous legs into the ground, fastening themselves tightly.

The rowdy eight stood in unison, wearing the uniforms which Kline had provided then with earlier for their practice on the Drag Quads.

So all dressed sloppily in brownish aero wear. Unlaced boots, uncleaned outer jackets showing red with the stains of dirt and mud thrown at them by the winds. And last of all, unshaven faces, all of which looked as if they never believed in the tradition of combing out the knots of hair which they possessed.

Their leather helmets, which were issued to them by the Drag quad Instructor, were ripped on the tops. They were previously put against the wings by the men for some odd reason, giving them all the appearance of barbaric savages who had reluctantly been introduced to the idea of wearing clothing.

All of this was the result of a panic fit thrown by Kline at everyone, not thinking that he could have pre-warned the incoming visitors of a respected and needed intermission for his boys. Nonetheless, there he was, the savages including himself, having a helmet lop- sided, so the ear covers fit perfectly over his left ear but uncomfortably sagged to his jaw on the right. His body band was wrinkled, and so were everyone else's.

Kline stood still, as he placed himself in front of his angry six. Dole ran and stood next to him. Kline cringed as he looked out at the Beetle-like, mechanical aero transport units flapping away weakly as they sat fatly on the ground, dropping their exit hatches.

" What do you think they'll feel of us ?" Dole asked.

Kline, squinting his eyes as the dust and wind from the transport units chopped its currents at them, gave a grim look at him. Then he looked at the six savage-looking men behind him.

" Oh, I believe they'll think highly of us." he said sarcastically. "Being that we're the cleanest, most sophisticated bunch of gentlemen and all," Kline finished.

Everyone turned and looked at him with soreness.

Kline only raised a brow at them.

Suddenly the many engines amongst the many transports cut simultaneously. The last ship, ready to unload as it's open shell awaited the rapid beating, wings revolving and flapping, to come to a stop.

As all of the Aero-ships slowly shut down, the wind spun frantically trying to stay alive but only a the remnant of the tornado that had been blowing only a moment ago.

Their outer shells slowly slid over the wings which had come to a stop.

Both Kline and Dole sucked in air, puffing up their chests, feeling their nervousness work overtime as the thirty soldiers of Bringington, the ten Imperial guards escorting King Zex, and the seven other representative Sponsors formed up far away.

Kline's eyes widened in fear as he made immediate fix ups upon himself.He straightened up his helmet, feeling uncomfortable as the hairs on the top of his head felt they were about to rip. They were caught in the thick slit designed for soldiers who bore military sharp Mohawks. Unfortunately, Kline never believed in the popular trend, thus he accepted what he would have to endure from the poetic justice of fashion. His helmet would have to stay uncomfortable until the end of the day.

Dole's hands shook nervously as he tried to straighten up his wrinkly shoulder band.

"Oh boy," Dole muttered to Kline through the side of his mouth." Here they come . . ." Dole finished as he quickly grabbed his hands in front of his belly.

In the distance, the blurred faces of Bringington's men became visible. With a plain of blue, perfectly arched frills coming towards the measly eight, who were colored in an embarrassing shade of brown.

The Blue army, all of whom were organized-looking, disciplined, and identical in appearance. All of them had long and full blue and black spotted Mowhawks around five inches from their scalps and all had faces which showed the coldest of expressions.

They were Zimina's best, fittest, fastest, and brightest ready to go and conquer the new northern world right from under Kline's nose.

Right in front of the blue-haired army of thirty were the ten Imperials, dressed rather nicely. All of them had matching clothes with bright shades of orange and red zigzagging through their hair. They seemed to be the only ones whose hair was cut short to give a prickly appearance and, right in front of them, leading both small armies were Bringington and the King.

Bringington: The shoe-shining scholar, wearing a thin, brown wig, trying to make it as believable as possible to everyone.

His buckles were engraved with patterns resembling those of tribes far away. His black gloves made him appear even more diabolical than he really was.

It all made him look taller as well.

Next to Bringington was King Zex himself. It was surprising to the others, for he wasn't wearing a crown or lavish clothing like everyone expected. Instead, the young king, only in his thirties, wore the clothing of a commoner only differentiating from the others by the golden plate with the imperial symbol fastened over his cloak. Of course, when you looked closer you could see the brown wear, telling his family name and the many, many rings on his fingers with crystals and gems embedded into them. But his hair was shortened and tightened, painted to dark and heavy red from root to tip.

Kline then looked back at the six men he had. His misfit crew. He looked at Clubio with a little fear in his eyes. He feared what the Emperor King would think of him. Clubio's knotted and multi-separated frill, brightly lit with red and black spots, stood out like a burning bush. His whiskey-stained uniform shirt, wasn't concealed by the many cheap necklaces around his neck. And his eyes still bore the visions of the late night and many drinks. This was the man who was supposed to be his Imperial supervisor and this man couldn't even dress like a cadet.

Kline looked him up and down quickly as he heard the synchronized steps of the soldiers marching towards him.

Clubio, who was facing the colorful army, noticed Kline staring at him. Being the paranoid type, he hated people looking at him. It made him feel violated in some way that he couldn't explain.

He focused a frown at Kline.

" Look alive now..." Kline mumbled sternly at him.

Kline then turned back around.

King Zex noticed them as he addressed them with a wave.

He seemed excited to meet Kline. As he formed a smile, Bringington formed a frown.

" Kline," he shouted with enthusiasm.

Kline's hairs rose. Bits of them prickled out of the slit of his leather helmet.

Then King Zex stopped and Bringington took a step too far, stopped and hopped back behind the king. The red heads came to a stop, then the Blue-haired army halted, all in perfect synchronization - hair waving from the sudden stop.

Kline shrugged as the King approached him. Bringington stayed behind the Emperor king, not in the mood to be placed next to the man who had destroyed his scribehood ambitions.

Kline bowed respectfully to Zex.

" It is an honor to meet you King Zex." Kline lied. It was quite the contrary for him.

Kline felt irritated by King Zex, a spoiled little boy who gained the title after his father died of unexplanatory reasons. Kline was more in favor of Zex's father; the one who had spread the idea of conquest to the people for over sixty years.

The King now, Zex, did nothing that would have matched up to his father's legacy.

All he did was spend the treasury on lavish things. Building luxury houses over at the colonies, wasting the power and fuel to build diamond burning factories to produce clothing for the rich and famous, guaranteeing his friends places in the government, and ignoring work all together.

Zex laughed jollily.

" You may rise now," he said.

Kline smiled and nodded.

There was a silence for a moment.

NEIL LEE THOMPSETT   NO MAN'S LAND

Zex looked at Kline's riff raff band of people.

One long range observer, one medical personnel, one aero engineer, one Imperial supervisor, one Sponsor and two scouts.

Zex was about to laugh.

Kline, the most famous scholar in all of Sudutan Atlantis had a skeleton crew.

Dole cleared his throat.

"I see that you are impressed by our fine crew of men." Dole said.

Zex cringed for a moment, politely keeping his mouth shut, but then couldn't resist. "I have truly never seen their like, Tongue Warrior:" he said.

Bringington laughed.

Kline felt embarrassed.

"Is there something you'd like to say Bringington ?" Kline said sternly.

Bringington stopped laughing,

" Why no Kline," he started. "Nothing at all my good man. You've got a bunch of men, the like of which we have never seen before. A bunch of drunken savages who look as if they had escaped from the animal observatory."

Bringington laughed a little more.

Kline looked at his men. They gritted their teeth a little.

" It takes a small man to grasp at every opportunity to increase his stature." Kline said with a smile.

The men started tittering and even Zex was surprised into a guffaw.

Bringington turned red, trying to keep on ignoring his comment.

" What - no come back ? Or is it too difficult to try to talk and keep your hair on at the same time ?" Kline said, reaching out; "Here, let me hold it for you while you compose your reply." he said as he laughed.

Bringington jumped back out of the way.

Even the Reds and Blues were grinning now.

Bringington tried a shaky grin himself, holding it for a moment before it collapsed in anger.

"That's really funny Kline," he started.

"It is, actually;" said Zex, grinning himself now.

"Your reputation of having a Warriors Tongue is quite well earned."

Kline laughed out loud at his comment.

" But you know what's really funny Kline ?" Bringington tried to regain momentum. " remember that time when I almost killed you in the alleyway ?" Bringington laughed a little too hard. "The look on your face when you thought that I was going to kill you ?" Bringington continued.

Kline nodded his head, waiting for his turn to strike a blow. Then it arose.

He simply ignored Bringington and spoke to Zex.

"My king, " he said; " Ever since I became a journalist, I have supported and hailed your policy of helping the severely mentally retarded people of our great kingdom, to work and live in the community."

The king nodded at this, proud of this policy himself.

Kline pointed at Bringington. "But, Sire, making one of them a Cummundore of an expedition might be taking that policy too far."

The king and the King's men broke into outright laughter, as did Kline's mismatched seven.

Bringington was shaking in anger now. He was reaching to find any kind of wit at all to keep from being laughed off the parade ground.

"Oh yeah ?" he said. " You think that's funny - well you want to know what's really funny ? It's when I was doing Kline's sister and she was screaming like a comfort girl and yelling Kline's name !" he shouted.

There was dead silence.

Kline shook his head, as if disappointed by the actions of a small child.

He spoke again to the King, ignoring Bringington's quivering anger.

"My King, when, in the fullness of time, you order Bringington to be shot with a ball of his own shit - there will certainly be no shortage of ammunition."

Everyone laughed.

"Especially if that last weak attempt at wit was any indication." he added another punch-line.

Even Bringington's own men were laughing now.

But even then Kline had no mercy.

"As everyone knows;" Kline continued. "I have no sister. Only that bastard daughter. Mr. Bringington's young sister Bella."

There was dead silence for a second as everyone considered the implications of this.

Then the laughter was thunderous from everyone on the parade ground, no matter what their allegiances.

Bringington, after hearing the comment about his sister - and finally understanding the insult, called for his men to stand at attention - then to present arms. Immediately the men drew their guns and pointed them menacingly at the measly eight making no noise, even though many of them were still grinning at the skill of the Warriors Tongue.

Zex, who was rather bored at the moment felt excited and stepped out of the way. His men quickly marched to the side of the ground and opened their ranks to let him get inside. They immediately drew their own weapons.

Kline shook his head again, disappointed, then frowned and turned around.

He called for his six to stand up to them in a bored voice, then turned to face Bringington again.

"Still small in stature, and in spirit, I see" he said.

"Apologize, Kline," yelled Bringington; "Or I'll have my men shoot you and your ragtag crew."

"Hah!" said Kline, unwavering; "Each of my expert marksmen will only have to kill 4 or 5 of your men to make things even. Pick your targets, men !" he shouted.

The king and his guard were laughing aloud.

Kline turned to the side to bow and noticed that his men were no longer close behind him. They were backing away, step by step - slinking like abused dogs, intimidated by the thirty thick frilled bunch.

It was Bringington's turn to laugh now. " Your men have deserted you Kline. Apologize or I will shoot them all."

"Hah ! They are only getting in better shooting positions" Kline said, turning back around ad puling his pistol. He aimed it right at Bringington's head.

"Besides, " Kline said, "You've already proven that you can't even shoot the shit, so how do you expect to shoot my Courageous Contingent?"

Kline began to sweat.

Bringington grinned.

Kline looked back behind him and saw the men fearfully backing even further away.

Kline turned quickly to Bringington.

He smeared a nervous smile,

"Excuse me Bringington but will you be so kind as to grant me a moment. I must discuss strategy with my men before we begin this blood bath ?"

Bringington smiled. "Not a chance in hell . . . " he began.

"A gentleman's right" the king interrupted. "Granted !"

" Thank you, Bringington." Kline said, sarcastically.

Bringington nodded his head irritatedly.

" You're welcome Kline." he said.

Kline turned to his cowardly men.

"What are you doing ?"

Dusty looked at him.

" We're not paid enough to die for you, Kline !" he yelled.

Dole nodded and pointed at him with agreement.

"I'm going to have to go with Dusty on that one."

"This is not the time or place to be negotiating." Kline said.

The men backed away a little more.

" Fine!" Kline snapped, "I'll double your pay !"

The men kept walking.

"You mercenary bastards. OK. I'll triple your pay." Kline said.

The men stopped and looked at each other. They looked at Kline.

Suddenly they drew their guns. Clubio drew his rifle, Luca drew his long sniper rifle with the enlargened barrel, Dusty took out his fine triggered rifle, and the others took out pistols, knives and a comical assortment of weapons.

Zex applauded enthusiastically and his guard laughed aloud.

"In disciplined order then - advance" yelled Kline.

Screaming like mad men they ran up in front of the robotic, blue haired men and stopped a few feet in front of them.

The six men screamed and yelled, making hideous faces like demons, laughing and gibbering, jumping around like burning monkeys - yet their weapons remained steady, each locked on a man.

Kline felt a little relieved as well as a little embarrassed, but didn't let it show.

Bringington rose his brow, looking at Kline's men raging on as they screamed with their tongues out, waving their heads all around. They acted as they looked, like a bunch of savage animals.

" Are they mentally ill?" Bringington asked sternly.

Kline gasped, as the sweat rolled down the sides of his head. He felt unsure how to answer Bringington's question. For he partly agreed with him on that.

"A strategy we've been working on to deal with savages in the North" Kline said, finally.

Bringington shook his head.

The emotionless soldiers were unsure what to make of them either. They turned to one another with confusion. Kline's men kept screaming and yelling getting louder as they noticed the Emotionless soldiers' bewildered look. They had found a weakness in the Blue haired army but didn't know how exactly to take advantage of it. They didn't know what else to do but continue. And did so.

Bringington felt a headache forming from the screaming idiots.

Kline began to feel foolish, regretting that he pleaded to his men for help. And regretting even more that he had promised them triple pay.

Bringington closed his eyes trying to block out the babbles from Kline's men.

" Kline, may I shoot them now ?" Bringington asked.

Kline turned his head, seeing Vittorio, Dusty, Luca, Clubio, Dav'inne, and Squirrel all red-faced and about to pop veins. Kline was almost about to say "God - please do. And the sooner the better." But didn't.

Kline sighed.

" Let nothing hold you back except common sense." he said. "And keep in mind that you will die first as I am a master pistolero." Kline raised his eyebrows and tried to twirl his heavy pistol around his fingers, but dropped it.

"I can see that." Bringington grinned. " Shoot them men. On my mark." he finished.

Suddenly, the emotionless soldiers, bewildered though they were, snapped to their training. Almost as one, they pumped the air into the compressors and cocked a bullet into their chambers.

The compressed chambers now awaited for the pull of the trigger.

As they were about to fire, Kline closed his eyes and lowered his head in shame. He tried a last gamble.

"Increased Monkey Mode, lads," he shouted and his men, if anything, heightened their mad gibbering and jumping.

Bringington was enjoying every minute of Kline's suffering. He stretched it out as long as he could, but then looked as if he was about to give the order.

Then, the most peculiar thing arose.

Zex came in between the two lines laughing his head off. He was completely amused by the deadly duel. To Zex, this was all a great comedy performed in front of his eyes. He thought it to have all been made up completely for his amusement.

After all, he was known to be very conceited.

Bringington gritted his teeth. He wanted to tell his men to fire through Zex but he knew that it would cause controversy, not to mention provoking the King's Guard, who already had their weapons drawn and looked much more capable of causing damage than Kline's baboon squadron .

"Please, Please," Zex started to speak as he wiped a tear from his eye." No more. I can't stand any more laughter. You both can stop the act now." Zex said.

Immediately everyone turned and looked at Zex, even Zex's Imperial guard looked at him in a state of bewilderness.

"Stand down" said Bringington.

The Emotionless blue-haired army twitched as they released their air pressure and slung their short-barreled rifles across their shoulders. They gave each other a confused look, not sure if it was all an act.

Kline, ever the opportunist, yelled. "Unmonkey !"

His men stopped their wild behavior, as if it were a command they were used to and stood still suddenly, panting and sweating.

Zex heard a silence as they all looked at him.

He felt their eyes and felt as though he was surrounded by a troupe of actors, awaiting applause.

" That was brilliant. How long did you have to rehearse ?"

All of them gave one answer to him:

" What ?" they all said.

They all knew - as did pretty well everyone in Sudutan Atlantis - that Kline and Bringington were deadly enemies, at each other's throat and likely, eventually, to kill one another. And yet Zex seemed to have no clue. Kline thought that there were two possibilities here: Either Zex was incredibly smart for diffusing the tense situation in this novel way. Or he was incredibly stupid and had no idea about the two's angry past with each other.

Yet, whatever the case, the situation had been resolved without bloodshed.

"And Kline - I thought that you dropping that pistol after announcing that you were a Master Pistolero - I nearly pissed myself. That was nearly as good as Bringington' pretending to be angry - I've never seen such remarkable acting.

What a race this is going to be - if you guys can keep it up, we'll have the whole country in suspense over this expedition."

Bringington and Kline put their pistols away as they looked at Zex. Kline then turned to Bringington, taking off his leather helmet and holding it under his arm. He tapped him on the shoulder as if congratulating him.." Bringington, he's right. Your anger act was so good I was getting scared myself." Kline said.

Bringington rose a brow as he frowned at Kline." And having your men run away then be tempted back by triple pay - inspired. When did you come up with that ?" Bringington snapped back.

Zex nodded.

Bringington moved closer, as if they were great friends.

Zex turned to talk with his guards.

" Smile now but never forget that I mean to finish what we have started !" Bringington sail softly around his forced smile.

Kline motioned with his hands to keep his gun where it was.

" I wouldn't agree more with you, but our feud shouldn't get in front of our greed." Kline said as he straightened up his shirt and stroked his beard.

"After all, we are Sudutan gentlemen and reasoning is a natural born necessity with us."

Bringington nodded his head and leaned closer. His face was stern as he spoke into Kline's ear:" From one gentleman to another, my dear Kline," he started. " I hope this isn't any of your sinister schemes to shoot me in the back as you've always done."

"Why no," Kline struggled to say, past Bringington's powerful breath. "I'm too interested in getting rich to waste my time scheming about you - but now it seems we have to work together to get rich - just pretend to hate each other for the public." Kline said as he turned his face away to get a breath of fresh air. "Shouldn't be difficult."

As much as Bringington wanted to start shooting then and there, Kline did have a point. And Bringington also wanted to get rich. He moved away from Kline and patted his arm.

"Very well," Bringington sighed.

Both of them straightened up, and turned to the Emperor king who was now coming towards them.

Zex saw their seemingly friendly behavior and was very amused by it. If he knew it was an act, he gave no indication of it. The idea of a great race to save the nation was something that would benefit him greatly - whether the rivals actually liked or hated each other. He didn't care, as long as they played his game before they left for the North.

Zex frowned as he looked at all the soldiers staring each other off.

"Why is it that both of you are acting this way ?" Zex said, facing them. "Now you're looking too friendly."

Bringington and Kline looked at each other then back at Zex.

Both of them tried to speak and explain themselves. To explain to the King that they were really both arch rivals whose only goal was to see each others fall in death or into poverty.

The King fused his two fingers into the side of his head as a headache arose inside him.

"For Marsolla's sake; " he yelled, "Don't you get it. You begin as friends -end up as enemies. "

"What ?" said Kline.

Suddenly the King's legendary temper rose.

"Sponsor advisors !" he shouted.

Dole nervously jumped, so did four others in Bringington's group.

If he was going to make this production work, Zex realized, he was going to have to make it work at all levels. The Sponsor advisors would be able to explain it better with a softer tone of grovel, which the king liked.

"Here, now !" Zex yelled as he waled a few yards away and pointed to the ground.

Immediately all of the Sponsor advisors ran towards the King. They all began to huddle up and discuss, with arch looks;the issue of: "What the hell's going on !"

Kline looked at Bringington.

"What do you think they're talking about ?" Kline asked as he watched all of the Sponsors, including Dole, grovel at Zex's feet.

" They're talking about how stupid he is." Bringington said.

Kline nodded in agreement. "Surely a topic which could last for hours."

There was a long talk among the advisors from both parties with the King. Then the King came up with an explanation which would cover the events of the day.

He told the advisors his plan.

They bowed in thankfulness as they dispersed back to the expedition leaders: Bringington and Kline.

The four men wearing blue cloaks and stiffened prickly points on the tops of their heads went to discuss what was going on with Bringington.

Dole came close towards Kline.

Kline looked back at Bringington as he huddled with his Advisors.

Kline then looked at Dole, feeling ashamed that he didn't fish around for more Sponsors. Nonetheless he distanced himself from Bringington.

He grabbed Doles arm and whispered.

" What in Marsolla's name is going on, my friend?"

Dole looked back at Zex who was tapping his foot in frustration.

" Well there was a misunderstanding when Bringington's advisors and I sent the request for him to take charge - in most of the funding. So the Journalist Council is out now."

Kline squeezed his arm a little tighter.

" Funding from the Emperor ?" Kline said in surprise. " Does he even know how to do that ? I thought he'd just get money from his rich friends."

Dole sighed and insisted that Kline release his arm.

" You see, I sent the message that you and Bringington were the best of friends. If you weren't we would have no extra funding at all." Kline rose a brow in suspicion.

" Wait a minute, you said that the king was doing this out of his own free will?"

" Well I could expl..."

"- Not only that, but you told me that the King knew Bringington and I despised each other."

" As I said, I could explain."

Kline crossed his arms.

" Then explain yourself, good friend." Kline stated.

"Simple, I lied." Dole said proudly.

Kline nodded. " Good answer."

Dole chuckled a little. " Anyways, the deal is that we told him you both were having a slight difficulty with Sponsorship and funding, but that you had the great idea to appear to be enemies to drum up interest in the great race to the North - and that both of you were still friends.

"Still friends ?" Kline was appalled.

He turned around to look at Bringington. Bringington did the same as he heard the news interpreted by his advisors.

They looked deeply and then frowned at each other turning back into their huddles.

Dole patted Kline on the shoulder.

" If you can keep up the scam until you leave then everything is good."

" My dear God Marsolla, what in his name are you thinking about now ?" asked Kline worriedly.

" Think of this," stated Dole. " If the King funds money for both of us then commercials will be made for both sides. Official truth benders will take sides and tout their own hero. You'll both become icons. Not only that, but more people will want to join up later if there's habitable land up there - you can head start your own colony."

Dole rubbed his hands.

" Do you know what that means ?"

" Fewer stupid people in Sudutan Atlantis?" Kline asked.

Dole shook his head. "Kline, could you please be serious for a moment ?" Dole asked irritatedly.

Kline sighed. " Fine, tell me what it means."

Dole grinned a little.

" That means more money for the Empire, that means more developments of fuel and power substitutes, that means another golden age for Sudutan Atlantis."

Kline yawned.

Dole signed once more. He knew that the only interest Kline had was how things would effect him and his own vanity, so Dole started telling him what he wanted to hear.

" That means a lot more money for you,"

Suddenly, Kline's interest grew.

Dole continued to speak. "That means popular fame, not to mention Historical fame."

Kline smiled. He then turned to Bringington. He grinned." You know, Bringington and I were once the very best of friends. Not to mention Gentlemen." Kline said.

Dole laughed." I know you both were."

Bringington in his group received the same news as Kline. Bringington looked at Kline's grin." What's that monkey up to now ?"

"The same thing you're going to have to do." said one of his advisors.

Bringington turned around."What ?"

" If you agree to be the best of friends with him. It shall mean a guaranteed place in history. Kline's advisor had told him that."

" You mean that I've to act out a friendship with that glob of lama spit ?" Bringington said sneered.

" Only in front of the Emperor. Look on the bright side sir, we're receiving millions."

" We've got enough !" Bringington stated stubbornly.

" Which we'll pocket, and we're getting the finest and purest diamonds from the Imperial reserve, and the best of all, you can kill Kline as soon as we cross the border of the Atlantean Isthmus."

Hearing the part about getting rid of Kline sparked his interest.

" We get to kill him ?"

All three advisors nodded their heads. " Not only that, but if Kline's dead, all credits go to you."

Bringington smiled diabolically as a shocking thought came to him. "Kline's a crafty fellow, what if he survives ?" he asked.

" If and when he survives, you'll have already received all of the credit as well as his own seat in the ELDERS, throwing his career further into debt and poverty."

Bringington nodded in agreement." Damned if he lives, damned if he dies." he said as he pinched his chin.

Bringington then looked at Kline.

" Well, we were always the best of friends weren't we ?" he said.

Both of them smiled as they looked at each other, both containing plastic smiles as well as a slippery personality change.

Kline walked over and threw his hand over Bringington's shoulder.

" Friend." Kline said with his overzealous smile.

Bringington hugged him and patted him on the back.

" My friend." Bringington said.

The King smiled with relief as he walked over. He was liking what he was seeing." Well, I'm glad to see that you both have worked to show your true colors." the King said.

" Unfortunately we're color blind and see no prejudice." Bringington said fakely.

Zex didn't notice.

Kline nodded as well as gave a false laugh.

Zex laughed along with them. Then he threw his hand over both Kline's and Bringington's shoulders.

He looked at them both; "Now that we're all acquainted with each others game, let's get a drink over at the Officer's lounge, shall we ?" he said jollily.

Music played in the warm soft house. There, the hearth burned brightly, reaching the edges of the steel railings protecting people from falling in.The dim color of red gleamed from the walls it was painted on, the polish-finished wood floor's reflecting surface revealed itself in white shapes, hardly able to be made out.

The air was warm, but the draft of coolness from the outside seemed to make the overall environment refreshing.

Small chitchat arose as servant girls and comfort girls flirted around, showing themselves to the gentlemen who cooed in their ears with aroused excitement, wanting their "petal lips of beauty" as a great Sudutan poet would say.

There, doing the most cooing, being the most excited, not to mention the most drunk, was the young King Zex. He lay on a felt couch with two comfort girls doing their jobs which were drilled and told to them over and over: to please a man of stature one way or another.

Although Zex was a man of high stature, and therefore a gentlemen, it seemed that he wanted to be pleased in the manner of the commonest. Which explained how occupied Zex was at the moment.

Over on the left of the hearth were the two arch foes, falsely turned friends for both their own benefits. It was a pose they needed for personal gain.

They sat at a table with a board game between them.

Bringington sat on one side of the small table as a sweet smelling, seductive looking comfort girl acted as if she was in love, although she bore no interest to him at all.

Bringington stroked her back as she sat on his lap. Both her arms swung around the short, but strong man's neck. Bringington smiled as the dark haired girl pressed her lips against the surface of his cheek.

Kline, on the other hand seemed impatient as he stared at the game board between them.

The game was called Victor, a strategic game of conquest. One was given twelve banner figures, which resembled regiments and one moved them from province to province all over the known world.

He sighed as he moved his piece to the Isthmus of Sudutan Atlantis.

He looked at the game board, seeing the North continent portrayed as a fat chunk of ice. This made Kline feel like moving his toys of regiments to conquer it.

His hand struggled to move his piece further on, but then he gave in to his addiction to the game and its rules. He moved it across the seas to the lush jungle representation of the Mhazi state in Africa, one of the large territories.

Bringington, who wasn't paying much attention towards the gentlemen's game, gave a brief look at where Kline's piece was. He smiled with serene delight.

"Oh Kline, why is it that you insist on playing this game ?" Bringington said, moving one of his pieces towards an overlooked province where Kline's piece lay vulnerable.

Kline looked at it with shock, he had forgotten about this piece, only now realizing the consequences.

Bringington took Kline's regiment piece and replaced it with his own." A lonely province in the middle of nowhere, not looked at for three turns." Bringington tisked.

The girl giggled with projected delight.

" Hum, such a careless mistake there. You've left fifty men in the middle of nowhere, no food, no shelter, no dreams and no future . . . much as you once left me - as I recall - old friend."Bringington held Kline's regiment banner in his hand, studying it in front of Kline.

Kline frowned.

"They're starving, they're mad, and their officer abandoned them. Then I come in, give them food, give them shelter, make them as my loyal subjects..."

Bringington rolled his eyes away from the piece and looked upon Kline. He smeared a smile.

" This game does resemble true life doesn't it ?" Bringington said with revelation.

" That one's because of luck." Kline pointed out. "And it's just a game..."

" A game, yes." Bringington said.

"This summoned prophecy of supposed turnouts and acceptable losses: proving probabilities, possibilities, and random abilities. Testing, experimenting, accumulating and formulating theories. All in the sentences: 'I'll try', 'I win' or, 'I lose'." Bringington forced the Regiment piece aside from the table. "It's not a game at all to these pieces."

The comfort girl nibbled at his ear.

" In a lot of ways Kline, this board game is a foretelling of the future yet to come."

Kline, who was stung by his definition as to what a game really was, sighed in shallowness.

" Oh really ?"

" Yes. You see, in this game you and I are competing for power and fame.

Like the game, I have more pieces than you. Like the game, I look for every chance of admittance to a victory I can receive. Like the game, I will beat you and make you miserable, vengeant, and disease ridden. Like the game, I will kill you and laugh at your lifeless cadaver with the relief that another ruthless man is no longer present, but instead is where nothing can be salvaged, when nothing can be saved.

Like the game, I will have the delight of saying 'game over'..." Bringington said as he moved one of his random units towards Kline's capital.

" We all have fantasies, Bringington." Kline said as he rested his back a little. " We all have wet dreams of defaming each other, beating each other, killing each other. It's civilized. It's human nature to bare these tendencies."

Kline looked at Zex, very pleased with the women around him as he took another sip from his cup.

" But like all dreams, we must put them away in the face of reality." Bringington replied.

Kline turned back to Bringington.

"After all, we are gentlemen serving the crown."

Bringington bowed his head in agreement, having a firm grip on the girl.

" Indeed we are, my friend." Bringington muttered.

"And we both need the money which Zex will be handing us."

" But of course..." Bringington muttered once more.

"We shouldn't think of such evil things, so raw, unplanned so soon. Keep all your ideas to the day we reach the other side of the Border, my friend. There will our true day of judgement be confronted."

Kline then looked at the board. His capital was surrounded, sieged, and unhelpable.

Bringington had won the game without even stressing over the movements he made.

"Reality" he said, "Makes itself known in it's own way."

Kline tried to console himself After all, Bringington was an experienced officer who went to school in military academies.

He looked at this game as child's play, a joke.
Bringington snickered to himself, kissing his one night stand on the mouth.
Kline's eyes widened with brief surprise.
Bringington lay back in his chair and squeezed his comfort girl's body a little tighter to get the feel of her.
Kline took a drink and sipped a bit as he nodded.
He then looked up at Bringington. He gritted his teeth in frustration, then tried calming himself by saying it was just a game.
"Speaking of reality and the urges of Human nature, why aren't you enjoying some of these lovely little girls?" Bringington said stroking the cheek of the one that was sitting on his lap.
"Ripe young age, I must say, you're a sweet one aren't you?" Bringington cooed in her ear with a little grin.
Kline began putting away his pieces on the table.
" My mind is occupied with other things at the moment." Kline said as he scurried all the pieces into a pouch. He tied a knot and then put it in his pocket and tidied himself up.
He smiled at one of the comfort girls." I truly think that you are one of the most beautiful girls I have ever seen and I would give up my right arm to spend time with you - but, sadly, I am on a mission where much more than my arm is at stake and I must go." he said politely.
The comfort girl blushed and smiled at his comment. Kline felt honored and a little enchanted.
Bringington looked at Kline suspecting his strange behavior.
" You must enjoy the gifts of life for I'll kill you soon enough," Bringington said as the comfort girl on his lap turned herself around and ran her fingers through Bringington's false hair.
Kline sighed and nodded as he helped himself stand up."Yes, Yes, I know the age old argument: I die, you live, reality stays, life prevails. Hurrah !" Kline mumbled.
Bringington stared at Kline, then focused himself on the comfort girl, fondling her like a fragile little doll. " I know, I know."
" It's just that you're usually the dog in heat. Usually the Alpha male if you know what I mean." he finished.
Kline turned his head in immediate disgust. "Much like you to compare me to an animal of such class.

If I were to reply in kind, I'd say that you're a little pervert, but, of course, being a gentleman I'd never do such a thing. Besides, like I said; there's something on my mind right now."

Kline took out a wooden tube from his front pouch.

It was a powder drug called Cuca. An excerpt from the Cocoa plant which acted as a stimulant. Very popular as well as very addictive amongst the aristocracy of the Sudutan Atlanteans.

Kline was an addict of Cuca.

He took a sniff from a few drops he made on his palm, afterwards offering a bit to Bringington.

" Would you care for some ?" Kline asked politely.

Bringington shook his head politely.

" No thanks." he mentioned.

Kline shrugged and stood there thinking. Something was on his mind - he just didn't know what. And the cuca didn't make it any clearer. Kline was worried that the night was ticking away.

Then, suddenly, he remembered:

He had promised his new found love interest that he would be there to take her on an outing. If there was one thing Kline hated, it was the idea of leaving someone abandoned. Ironically, cheating, lying, stealing, and abandoning Bringington many years ago, were another matter.

The idea of abandonment, however, was his greatest fear of all for he was an orphan and suffered the trauma of nightmares and flashes.

Bringington studied Kline's frown, his discomfort and change in opinion of comfort girls almost gave it away. And as he found out, he spoke: " You've found a woman haven't you !" and saw Kline blush with annoyance.

Kline kept quiet.

" Ah, I knew you were a dog after all. Probably going after the curly disordered-eye sort of women like usual ?"

Kline furiously pushed in his chair.

" It is nothing of the sort !" said Kline,

" You stick to your own business with that Lily on your lap." Kline scalded, jousting his finger at Bringington.

Suddenly the comfort girl turned her head,

" The name's Betsky."

Kline bowed his head in apology,
" My fault Miss Betsky." he apologized.
Then his focus was on Bringington once more.
" Now, if you'll excuse me, I've an appointment to keep." Kline said. Without haste he made his way towards the door, slanted to work with the structure of the building.
Bringington smiled with cynicism,
" Yes, and Zex has an empire to run !" he gesticulated.
Then his attention turned to the nubile Miss Betsky.
As Kline had promised, he headed back to the downtown bar, awaiting a carriage to stroll towards him on the road. When one came along, he stepped in and sat in the four legged, mechanical car. A marvelous adaption which was able to move itself instead of being pulled by lamas just by imitating the simplest of creatures : insects.
"Marsolla never shrugged on the Sudutan Empire." Kline thought to himself as he felt around in the carriage.
The driver immediately turned around, noticing him getting touchy with the cab.
It was as if Kline had never seen a cab before in his whole life. Obviously, for a man of his stature, not to mention a writer serving for the people, this was hardly the case. Kline was fascinated by the advances made in the past thirty years.
Kline then turned his head and told the driver where he wanted to go.
The bar even that late in the evening, was alive with action. The blocks which ran down the corners of the building had the evening lights lighting downwards on the posts. The design was so ingenious that the appearance of a segmented caterpillar was formed. Music flowed from the open doors and the smell of scented people hit Kline like a wall of lead.
The bar was packed with young people as well as Imperial officers taking time off from guard duty. Security was tightened for the Emperor Zex.
Kline glimpsed around and caught the eyes of the busy Ennis, who served drinks at demon speeds. He smiled as he walked over to her, pushing his way through the clustered men, who were all clinching their comfort women tight as well as carelessly spilling beer.

Kline rested his arms on the counter, awaiting Ennis to stop what she was doing.

Obviously Kline thought highly of himself. No working woman would stop for anyone, especially for men who weren't arranged for them. Nonetheless, he waited patiently for her to come to him. He smiled and bobbed his head.

She sighed and rolled her eyes. She quickly walked over to him, quickly sliding a cup to a neighboring customer.

" So are you ready ?" Kline asked out loud.

Ennis turned around and grabbed a giant bottle, large enough to hold a tiny cat.

She managed to heave it under her arm and pour a cup for another demanding customer.

As she handled it, she stared blankly at him.

" You're late."

" Oh I know," Kline stated as he placed his hands down on the counter.

" The night shift has all ready started. Because of you, I'm stuck with it." she said, throwing a whole jug at an intoxicated officer reaching for her.

Kline rubbed the back of his neck, thinking of a reason for her to escape.

"I'll pay your employer to let you go." Kline said.

Ennis rose her brow.

" You're kidding me ?" she stated.

Never before had she ever seen a man so obsessed for her. She was flattered even more than the last time.

Kline nodded his head, undrawing his money bag.

" How about fifty ?" Kline asked.

Ennis' mouth dropped a little.

" I'm not worth that little," she said.

" Sixty ?" Kline pleaded.

Ennis turned away and crossed her arms.

Obviously, she felt that she was worth a little more than double digit numbers. She was playing hard to get with the strange scruffy man named Kline.

Kline sighed,

" How much do you think would cover for you ?" he asked.

Ennis rolled her eyes back and forth from him to his money pouch.

"One hundred-sixty . . ." she muttered with a smile as her employer, actually her father, staggered through the crowds towards her. His belly was large, a sign of a rich man, wealthy enough to keep himself at such a round, over healthy size. He too carried the pigmentless eyes and curly hair.

His uneasy frown pressed onto his face.

" Ennis," he ordered in an alpha male kind of manner, " You're behind in orders ! Five tables are threatening to never come back. Now get back to work before I tear another hole in your head !" he said.

Ennis smiled.

"Kline, this is my father."

Ennis yawned and leaned herself next to the nervous Kline.

Ennis's father was a large, terrifying-looking man. The sort that would eat children in the night time. The kind that was able to take on three men and have enough energy for three comfort girls all in the same day. His curls were vertically rowed and elongated at the tips, creating the illusion of fins. His thick beard and mustache was tied together, forming long tentacle- like whiskers sagging over his double chin.

He intimidated Kline, but Kline was obsessed for his daughter and had to do the honorable thing, he had to pay him for her.

" Good evening sir," Kline said.

The giant was silent.

Ennis patted her father on the belly.

" He wants to give you an offer for my dismissal for the evening"

The father's eyes widened.

" Under no circumstances are you to leave, especially at this hour of the evening. Things change during this time and many people may become dangerous."

Kline smiled." I'm honored that you care for your daughter, sir." Kline said respectfully.

The frown returned into the fathers face as he turned his eyes at him." I was talking about the people inside the bar without my daughter, the bar could be demolished and vandalized by drunks . . ." the father stated strictly.

197

Kline erased any idea of her father being honorable at all and continued on.

" Oh, well I've got a solution for that." Kline said as he drew out his money.

The father's eyes peeked down the endless hole of Kline's pouch. "I've negotiated with your daughter here and she says that she's worth around one hundred- sixty."

" Make it four hundred, plus any damages done to my bar by drunks." the father quickly interrupted.

Kline's mouth fell open while the father's smeared a grin.

Kline gasped, rethinking if Ennis was worth all of that trouble. The father held out his hand.

" Four hundred, what for ?"Kline said sorely.

The father crossed his arms.

" A security deposit. Just in case you rape her too hard and kill her, I need insurance money to pay for all the years of raising my woman for you." he nodded,"I do believe that it's the law,"

Kline frowned,

" I don't believe that your daughter's worth that much."

" No payment for my woman, no deal for you !" the father scalded.

" Now look here, I never intended to hurt your daughter like that, but if you insist, I shall pay you . . . to show you and Ennis here how much of a gentleman I am." Kline said, regretfully throwing his money bag at the father.

The father's grin was seedy and made Kline's conscience turn. He patted Ennis on the back as he jollily laughed staring at his new earned money.

"Well then, you kids have fun now." he said, taking a keg of fermented wheat and setting it up for serving. And so they did, leaving the ever crowding bar, and taking a crawler cab to the air strip. The region in which Kline insisted on going.

There, they lay on the grass hill, watching the Beetle-like cargo transports get touched up by the bald mechanics. Soon they were drawn to each other and had a frantic bout of intercourse. When they finished, Kline knotted up his shirt, noticing that his notebook was out of place. He straightened his over cloak and chest band where he hid it stored.

Ennis sighed, brushing her curls with her hands as well as tidying up.

Both of them were silent during that time. Kline refused to look her in the face.

Ennis lowered her head, wrapping her arms around her knees. She turned,

" Well then," she started. "Now, you've marked me. What now?" she asked.

Kline pulled her closer to him.

" I'm not sure now." he whispered. " I hope to see you more. I hope to come around, come to talk." he finished.

She threw his arm away from her.

" Nighttime promises disappear with the moon. They're only good for the moment, the time, the instant after."

" Yes, that's true. But I mean it." Kline said gently resting himself against her. " It's interesting that you mentioned time, how one man's experience for that moment, that second, that occurrence in time could either be an eternity or a flash within."

" Yes, the moment that I slap you if you're just being nice for my sake." she said.

Kline snickered, patting her leg as he emptied the wooden tube of his Cuca powder, pouring a stream across his other hand and inhaling it through his nostrils.

He took a heightened breath then gasped from the intense feeling he was getting from the drug.

"The moment that I am spending with you, I hope will last an eternity within the few minutes that we've spent together. I hope you feel that way too." he said.

She was flattered, and at that moment, she was his.

"Besides, I did pay your father for the damages. I feel that it was too much . . ."

Ennis slapped Kline.

Kline cringed and gave a frightened smile,

". . .But it was money worth spent."

" Hey Old Man ! Keep your clucking quiet. We're trying to get some sleep here !" shouted one of the men in the far distance.

The Old Man took that as an offense against him and stood up.

" Why don't you just drink some more so you'll be knocked out pirate!" he shouted.

I heard some grumbling and cursing in the far distance, then silence.

The Old Man breathed deeply then slowly helped himself back down.

"Old Man, please. Continue with your story. Any part. Did Kline keep Ennis with him. Did he take her back home ? Did they see each other again ? Or the other one - you know the slaves went back to work after that terrible roar and Sassaska and Elana were calming the horses. Elana found the bear tracks. Then what ?"

The old man yawned and began the story again.

" OK - OK let's move to that one.

Well. A few more hours went by and everything was back to normal.Even though she was worried about Brelinka, Elana went back to Nurix. There was nothing she could do. If she went looking in the snow, there would be two sisters lost. Best to wait and trust in Brelinka, she thought.

By the time she got back to him, he'd been working on the spear and had already finished placing the capsules into the hooks, and waited to hand the spear over to her.

Elana didn't know what to do then. There was nothing left to do. She was bored and anxious so she wanted to make conversation with Nurix.

It took a while for him to open up and it didn't happen until Elana gave him the permission to ask questions and socialize whenever he wanted.

Elana was getting used to the idea of owning a personal slave, and Nurix was getting used to the idea of having a good Mistress."

The Old Man chuckled a bit.

" All I could say; " the Old Man said; "was that their relationship with each other was beginning to blossom."

Elana smiled and nodded, looking at Nurix and expecting him to say something. They both were sitting down and Elana was trying everything she could to make conversation.

Nurix stared at her, thinking that he was doing something terribly wrong but rather afraid to say anything. All he did was nod and answer briskly.

" Are you enjoying the journey so far ?"

Nurix nodded.

This kind of reaction had been going on for a while.

" So um . . . how old are you."

" I'm a slave, how old do you want me to be ?"

Elana didn't expect that answer but in her mind agreed that it was a valid point. She nodded once more.

He grinned. " Mistress, I'm sorry if that wasn't too clear but that was a joke. I'm 18 years of age, Mistress Elana." Nurix said.

Elana laughed, feeling quite foolish at her reaction.

"Isn't that strange" she said. "So am I."

She then sighed. " Why is it that you're so silent ?"

" I have no say in anything. All I have to do is serve. That's my purpose." he answered.

Elana was speechless. She realized that she was talking to a slave but she thought that slaves were able to talk, at least enough to make conversation.

"So why are you three on this journey ? Where are we going ?" Nurix asked shyly.

" Sassaska is going to become the new Empress and the old Empress wants her to travel all over the expansion of the territories. She wants her to understand what she is ruling.

Sassaska came to my sister to ask for her company. Well to make a long story short, here we are. In the middle of nowhere." Elana answered, finally glad that Nurix was opening up to her.

" Sassaska and Brelinka seem to be very close."

Elana chuckled serenely thinking about it. " Yes, they're close companions. Real close companions."

" The reason why I ask is that I thought that only Priestess' were allowed to love other women. " he said; " How about you, Mistress Elana? Do you have any close companions of your own ?"

Elana looked at Nurix with a mild flushed look in her cheeks. She then sighed. " Not at the moment. I mean, I feel that I'm too young to start one and all..."

" Oh..."

Elana and Nurix were both silent now, not knowing what to say. They both stared at each other and nodded their heads.

Elana then found a question to ask him, thinking that it wasn't too offensive. " Well do you enjoy it as a slave?"

Nurix didn't give an answer ,

Elana than realized that it was a question that wasn't meant to be asked.

" Oh, I'm sorry. I just -"

" It's alright... I was born into it, and I don't know of any other kind of life. I don't enjoy it, but I don't regret it."

" You don't ?" She asked.

"Ever since I was a child, I was told the tale on how I became a slave.

I became a slave when my mother, a poor merchant woman with two girls back at home needed money. So she sold me. At first I was sad that my own flesh and blood sold me but I realized that they loved me enough to keep me alive for so long. And they didn't cook me when they wanted food. I know that for a fact.

I grew up with other slaves who were kidnapped as infants, found on the streets and thrown into it, or even brought into it to pay off debts. I was the lucky one, I was born into it." he said shamelessly but still instinctively shy about saying it.

Elana reached her hand over to him. Stroked his cheek and ran her fingers down his neck. "I'm sorry you had to grow up living that kind of horror." she said apologetically.

Nurix nodded.

"Thank you, Mistress Elana."

" You don't have to address me as Mistress. You have my permission to call me by my name."

Nurix smiled but then looked away.

Suddenly, the sound of forceful trotting filled the air, followed by a sound of something big dragging on the ground.

Elana and Nurix stood up.

Brelinka had come back from her hunting. Her horse, had its eyes covered with a black scarf from Brelinka's cape. Both the horse and Brelinka looked tired.

Sassaska came out, stunned at what Brelinka had dragged back. The two women slaves stood up and walked towards her in awe.

She finally came to a halt and everyone stared at the eleven foot bear, dead. It's body was covered in slashed cuts, and scrape burns from dragging it.

On it's back lay her spear wedged in deeply. Around the jab of the spear there were burn marks and an open circle of wound.

Brelinka, not feeling brave, but exhausted, got off her horse and walked over to the bear to pull out the spear. She twisted the greasy part, slowly pulling the spear back together.

Still, the spear was lodged inside.

Brelinka pulled with all her might and ripped it out, taking a chunk of the bear with her. She then walked over to the two slaves, who were looking stunned at the monstrous animal.

She panted a little, then leaned on Taboo. Taboo could smell the sweat of her. The smell of blood and perspiration together with every pant she gave.

" Taboo, Rhyme, skin this bear and cut it up. We've got dinner tonight . . . and possibly for the rest of the week." she said.

Sassaska then ran to her, asking her if she was alright.

Brelinka only smiled relieved, wanting to go to the tent and rest up a little.Taboo and Rhyme stared at each other, then at the bear.

Rhyme then broke into laughter. She broke into hysterical laughter with no apparent reason - but Taboo didn't question her. Taboo always had only giggled and laughed and probably didn't know any other way to communicate in strange situations.

Taboo sighed amongst the constant noise of laughter from Rhyme.

" Let's get to it then." Taboo said, getting a dagger and slicing at the ridge of the neck.

Elana stared at the heap-sized bear right in front of her, still in awe, finding it utterly impossible to think that Brelinka, her sister, took a beast such as a Great bear down and beat it to death.

Nurix looked at it and only saw a dead bear - and, in fact, coming from that part of the country, had seen many.

He was not as amazed as Elana.

" Elana, shall I begin a fire so that we could start to smoke the meat ?"

" Huh?" She said, still amazed, imagining the battle of Brelinka and the beast.

She then turned around to Nurix,

"Oh, right. Yes. Treat the flesh and um . . . do what you usually do with it;" she said.

Nurix was about to get the poles to set up a fire when Elana grabbed him softly.

Nurix looked to her. All she did was gaze at him, wanting to say something.

Nurix, looking at her lips, her pointed chin, her nose and finally to her eyes, said; " Yes Elana ?"

She smiled at him. Nurix could tell that she was beginning to get fond of him. Nurix didn't mind, he actually was beginning to enjoy her company more and more.

" Nurix . . . You're . . . I want you to think for yourself. I want you to ask questions, listen and . . ." She sighed. She didn't know what to say.

Nurix understood what she wanted though. She felt sorry for him, she wanted him to feel free yet she knew herself that he was a slave.

Nurix smiled and nodded his head.

" Alright Elana . . . I will."

Elana smiled once more, stroking his hair and then touching his cheek.

Nurix, thinking that she was touching him too much over the past day didn't stop her. He had masters before which never thought of touching him or stroking his hair. That was why he let her. He felt that he was finally worth more than a slave to someone.

" Well . . ." Elana said; "Get that fire started and we'll hear the story of the hunt later tonight."

A giant bear being defeated by a woman. Alright, by now I knew that they were stronger than men but still - an eleven foot bear in the woods ?

" An eleven foot bear ? There's no such thing, Old Man." I said. The Old Man laughed joyfully.

" Yes. An eleven-foot bear. They were pretty common to find - bears of that size - back in those days. In fact, every animal over there was more ferocious, gigantic, and stronger than the animals that exist over here. It's like they never grew in this continent - perhaps never had

Falcons with wingspans of ten feet, Giant woolly elephants which were two times the size of elephants over here, packs of monstrous timber wolves, horses which were - well, the fact is horses over there are quite tiny in nature - but they had been bred into huge draft horses. And to this very day, they are still that way in Atlantis."

The Old Man grinned as he raised a brow.

" Women who   were beautiful and ten times stronger than the strongest of men . . ."

" Why was it that everything was larger ?"I asked.

" There was once a time, and not too long ago either, in North Atlantis when Giant Glaciers - miles of ice, hundreds of feet thick - covered most of the north. The cold came and challenged anyone, anything to try and survive it's wrath.

Only the ones which proved to be worthwhile, adapted to the cold. They needed to be big and fat and hairy.

The smaller, weaker animals either left or died off while the strong ones stayed.

Over time those animals became stronger to better their chance of survival out in the cold. Ancient Elephants grew wool; lions grew saber teeth to pierce through the wool; bears grew bigger to hunt bigger game, and women grew stronger also - to survive the cold, to protect their children, and to fend off larger animals which would try to provoke them. But also because in the North, the women had always been the hunters. The predators. Possibly they had to grow stronger as their prey grew stronger. I don't know. In the North it is simply accepted that women are stronger. Everything in North Atlantis had to change, in order to survive and keep on living.

Most of the rest of the world went through the same thing, but not as harshly and not for as long. So everywhere else, it was the men who became stronger to hunt and to protect their families.

" Strange. Women grew strong at Atlantis while men grew strong everywhere else ? That makes no sense." I said.

" Nature has many ways of helping the ones in need, maybe men were in the need of women to help them." he said with a nod and an enlightened look on his face.

I knew that he was holding back from grinning.

I was unsure what he meant by his answer or his actions. But I didn't bother to ask anymore, after all. I wanted to hear the rest of the story.

" Alright Old Man, I'll take your word for it that everything was larger. Now, may we continue on with the story ?"

The Old Man laughed jollily once more.

" Ha ! I like your style, boy. Curious, wanting to know a definition for everything you hear but at the same time wanting the story to go along with it.

Either you're a brilliant man who wants to know more or...you're just a dumb boy with no attention span whatsoever."

" May we continue with the story, Old Man ?" I said, wanting him to get to the story.

The Old Man's smile turned into a faceless expression.

He raised his brow

" Well, now I know which you are, Boy . . . and it's not the former."

He sighed and threw another piece of wood into the fire.

" Alright . . . I'll continue with the story. Let's see :

So Nurix finished starting the fire. By then, there was a giant heap of every type of insect imaginable trying to feed on the bear carcass. So the slaves cut some of the meat off and hung it near the fire. They thought that the fire would keep the night animals from coming near it.

Brelinka had cut off the head of the bear. She wanted it for currency. Bear paws, fur and head were worth something once they made it to the plains.

That was a saying when you had no money: "When in financial trouble - hunt."

Anyways, later that night, Brelinka, Sassaska, Elana, and Nurix sat around the fire and listened to her story:

" I was in the forest, looking around to see what to hunt. Originally, I was going to try to get a wild boar but then, near a stream I saw it. I saw the bear sniffing around and stretching in the sun.

By the smell, I could tell that it had killed and feasted on something.

So I quickly ran back to my horse. I blindfolded the poor girl so that if the bear came near, she wouldn't get spooked. I then grabbed my spear, to test it out.

I ran back down to the stream and waited for it to get up. It gave me enough time to put the three capsules into place."

" You mean the metallic ones ?" asked Nurix.

Suddenly Brelinka stopped telling the story.

Everyone went silent and turned to Nurix. Brelinka didn't know what to do. She wanted to stand up and punish him for talking out of place and interrupting, but she knew that Elana had something to do with it.

Brelinka was not quite fond of slaves, especially Male slaves.

Nurix began to feel embarrassed with everyone looking at him. He felt like he did something wrong and had provoked Brelinka in some way.

She then turned to Elana. Elana's expression showed that she wanted Brelinka to answer him like he was one of them. Brelinka thought that Elana was being soft to a slave but she answered Nurix's question.

" . . . Yes . . . That's . . . Correct." She said.

Nurix nodded.

Brelinka then went back to normal,

" Well , where was I ? Oh, right. Anyways. I loaded my spear. I then looked out to see if the bear was there. It wasand it was getting up to leave. Then it spotted me. It growled a warning but I stayed. I was scared because of it's huge size but I wanted to see if I was as well-trained as I thought I was.

She gave one to a few little grunts, then took matters into her own hands.

She started to charge towards me in the bushes.

I quickly jumped and flipped around, ready to stab it. But to my surprise it was so fast, it was right in front of me, standing on it's hind legs. It roared at me a bit.

So I roared back at it.

It then swung a paw at me and I leaped over to it's left. It tried to turn around and get me but it was too late. I had flung the spear into it's back. It wasn't dead yet, only struggling from the pain, so I went over to put it out of it's misery.

I made the spear explode.

Flames shot out and meat splattered all over the forest ground. The bear actually caught on fire, charring the open wound around it.

The bear gave the loudest cry I'd ever heard in my life. Birds for miles around all left from the sound . . . even the trees were shaking.

"Yes - we heard it here " said Elana. "It scared the horses."

" Wow - that far away ? Well, anyways; that's how I killed the bear." Brelinka said.

" You warriors are all alike. You all kill, then you gloat about your glory." Sassaska said, wanting to scold because she was worried; "What do you think the bears' cubs think about you gloating like that."

Brelinka chuckled a little. " First of all - it's a male bear. There were no cubs. And even if there were, why this would be like a motivational speech. Those cubs would grow up to become even stronger bears and hunt me - or any other human they find - down for vengeance." she said jokingly.

" And if one came into town looking for you and telling everyone that she was looking for a fight." asked Elana, joining in the fun.

Brelinka grinned. "I'd approach the bear, fight it honorably, and see where chance takes us. If the bear wins, I die in peace. If I win, I hope that she won't have any bigger sisters. After all - if I had to fight a bear every day, I don't know if I could , well, bear it"

Sassaska and Elana giggled at her answer.

For a few seconds there was laughter from everyone, then there was the silence.

Then they stared at each other, waiting for someone to say something.

Then someone did.

Sassaska stood up and stretched. "We should call it a night. Tomorrow, we've got to make it through the mountain region." she pointed to the ice-capped mountains in the distance,

Elana stood up, squinting her eyes to see it. " It looks pretty far away. We'll be riding all day and we wouldn't get there." she said.

" That's why, we've got to leave early, so that by the time we make it, there would be a little daylight to set up camp." Sassaska finished.

Brelinka yawned then stood up.

"Good night," she said as she started to walk to her tent.

Sassaska, looked to Elana and ran her fingers through Elana's hair. She then kissed her on the cheek.

" Good night Elana." she said.

Elana smiled and kissed her back.

Sassaska then turned to make her departure to her own tent.

There now, left by the fire, were Nurix, the other two slaves and Elana.

Nurix went up to Elana, staring at the stars.

She turned at the presence of Nurix. Nurix nodded his head and smiled at Elana. "If there's anything you need Elana, I'll be outside with the other slaves." Nurix said.

Elana Smiled back, then slowly wrapped her hands around Nurix's neck.

Nurix stared into her eyes, and she slowly moved herself closer to him. Nurix began to feel nervous. He felt his heart beat faster and his palms begin to sweat.

She then gave a soft kiss on his lips.

Nurix was shocked, he didn't expect it but he didn't mind it.

After all, he was a typical man.

She then pulled away and backed up a little.

" I am grateful for the offer. If there's anything I need, I'll wake you. Good night Nurix." she said with a mild grin on her face. She never took her eyes off of Nurix as she walked slowly to her own tent. She kept eye contact on him until she stood right in front of the flap of her tent. She gave a smile once more.

Nurix returned the gesture as she went in.

Nurix sighed and turned around to head to his wooly mammoth skin blanket in the slave tent. He took amusement in kicking a rock as he walked with his worn down boots wrapped up in dirty cloths to keep the sole and the whole shoe from falling apart. His nervousness was still there and was going to keep him up all night.

Not only that but he noticed that Taboo was staring at him with a gleam, and so was Rhyme, trying to muffle her laughs. Both of them had their eyes locked onto him and he stared right back at Taboo. Through the dim lighting of their dying fire, it was amazing that all of them could tell who was who.

All three went into the slave tent and settled down.

As Nurix came close to his bag, they stared at him as he unwrapped the rags over his decaying boots. He then pulled off his mud-packed boots and placed them in a pair facing away from him. He could smell the mud.

Still Taboo and Rhyme stared at him. He ignored their eyes as he got inside the bag and got comfortable.

Suddenly Rhyme started to break out in a laugh. Nurix still tried to ignore it as he tossed and turned. This process went on for a minute or so until Nurix couldn't stand it anymore. He was frustrated by Rhyme's constant laugh and immediately sat up.

He breathed strongly as he pointed a them.." What? What are you two looking at . . . I mean why are you acting this way ?" he said, trying to soften his shout, but making it into a scold.

Taboo grinned and chuckled a little. " Oh, nothing Slave boy. We were just curious about something." she said.

" Oh? What was that ?"

" Well, Little Mistress Elana seams to be getting a little wet around you. We were just thinking if you knew that. Well do you ?" she asked, beginning to laugh.

Nurix began to flush around his cheeks, partly caused by his anger and partly by the cold.

" Elana's just lonely. Since most of you around here are either silent, old or not even in tune with the world. I'm taking a guess that since she's roughly the same age as me, she can relate with me, to a certain extent." he said frustratedly.

Taboo then nodded quickly, pretending that she understood every word and that it had an effect on her. Rhyme continued to laugh even harder. She wasn't joining in the conversation. She was stuck in her own world far-far away from Taboo and Nurix.

" Oh . . . well it looks like that you're growing very fond of her. Well, I mean she's letting you look up at her face, letting you call her 'Elana'. She's even letting you converse with the other Mistresses. She's a little too friendly if you ask me, boy." she said.

" She is my Mistress and I am her slave. Nothing less, nothing more. Now, good night." he said as he immediately lay back down and looked up to the tent roof, trying to get to sleep and ignore the laughs from Rhyme and Taboo.

Taboo then jumped up and crawled closer to Nurix, now coming right over him like she was trapping him. Nurix opened his eyes feeling scared, knowing what a strong woman could do to a man.

"Who knows, maybe she'll be more than just your mistress." she said, raising her brow and giving him winks, teasing him some more.

" I am her Slave, she is my Mistress. Nothing More! Now Good Night Taboo." He grunted as he gritted his teeth.

Taboo laughed some more and then rolled off of him continually laughing along side of Rhyme.

Nurix turned to his side, wanting to ignore them completely.

What Taboo had said got him thinking though. He began to think of the possibility of Elana growing a bit too fond of him. The thought bothered him but didn't frighten him. All his life he was taught that a slave was not allowed to talk, smile, or even grow close to their mistresses. It was a rule which was part of tradition, especially for male slaves. He knew it like the back of his hand yet when he thought about it now, it didn't trouble him at all. He actually liked the idea of Elana growing to love him. Then the thought of reality hit him.

His fantasy was crushed.

What reason would Elana have to love him. He was worthless, literally.

Elana wanted him to be her friend. At least that much he was sure of.

" Nurix was tossing and turning all night but he finally went to sleep.

Rhyme and Taboo finally quieted down from their teasing.

And that's all I can tell you tonight."

" Well, at least you've left it at a good spot for me to be without any cliff hangers tonight when I sleep, Old Man."

The Old Man smiled.   " Here's one thing to think about then - when you camp -never leave a big pile of raw meat out in the open. It draws danger like shit draws flies."

"Did danger come that night ?"

"We'll see boy, We'll see . . ."

The morning came grey and foggy. It was a little cold but not cold enough to call off working on the boat. Yet most of the men laid around and said that they had worked enough on it.

The Old Man told them that they would only need a few more days of working if they would be a little more efficient. Likooshas, then jumped up and shouted for everyone to go back to work once he heard that.

" Alright. We've fixed the hull, fastened the water barrels into the sides of the boat diagonally to make the weight less of a burden. We've smoothened down the extra mast.

Once we fasten it on, then we'll be able to set sail."

"We'll need to fasten it on somehow. We can't possibly nail it down ?" said a man.

The Old Man laughed and then looked at the boat. "No, we won't nail them on but we'll tie them on. If we connect them both diagonally to the main mast and tie ropes to the starboard bow and the back, all running up through the edges, then we'll have ourselves two more stable masts."

" But how will it be done to make it stay that way ?"

The Old Man then explained every detail to him. I honestly couldn't say what he said, only a boat engineer could understand his gibberish. Anyways. They all started work on trying to fasten the masts and twigging a few other things.

All that day, the main concern was to get the masts fastened and the sails to fit on them. To me, it was a busy day of bringing the water, carrying extra ropes, hauling all sorts of scrap wood and so on.

Although the boat was everyone's concern, my concern was to hear the story. I was intrigued by it, even though it had nothing to do with the coordinates, or the greatness of the civilization. It was just a normal story, well if you took out the super women, the flying machines, the huge animals and all the other weird stuff.

Still, I enjoyed it more than anything I had ever heard before.

The night came and the fog was still rather thick and cold. Nonetheless, it didn't bother me and the Old Man. To the Old Man it set the mood for the next part he was about to tell me.

" Ah, this weather is perfect. Funny that it had to be foggy."

" Why's that Old Man?" I asked.

" Where the story takes place, fog is a big part of the scenery."

" Well Old Man, let's hear it." I said, having a brief smile of anticipation smeared on my face.

The Old Man grunted a little.

" But this wasn't as cold as what they had to go through."

" Huh ?" I said, surprised that the Old Man had said that.

" Well, you asked if it was as cold as now. So I answered."

" I didn't ask you that - though I thought it," I said.

" Oh . . . Well . Same thing, really. Now let's get on with the story." he said, wanting to change the subject.

"Yes, let's."

"They had traveled for six hours straight. They were heading towards the middle of two grand mountains. Sassaska felt that it was going to be much safer than taking the rigid, twisting route through the other mountain regions."

" There were a lot of mountains there ?" I asked.

" Yes. Merchants and travelers knew it as the Western Wall because of the mountains. It led from the far north all the way to the southern regions. There was another mountain range like that called the Eastern Wall but when we get there, we'll talk about it. Anyways, back to the story.

The mountain was steep so they all got off the horses. The Mistresses led the way while the slaves pulled the horses behind. The higher they went, the colder it got and the harder they had to trek. Still they went further. They wanted to avoid camping out in the middle of the mountains as much as possible ."

The snow under every step they took was a foot deep and if they continued , it would probably get deeper. Nurix felt chills, even though he was wearing the thickest woolly blanket he had. The other slaves were red around the nose and cheeks. Same as the Mistress'.

Elana stayed close to Nurix and her horse. She was rubbing her hands together to keep them warm. It seemed like everyone was too cold. No combination of clothing worked. Every breath anyone took came out as smoke and their ears were painful from the cold. Only the horses seemed to be enjoying themselves. Stomping the snow with their wooly huffs, and their long manes covering most of their necks. For them, it was just fine.

For hours they traveled up the steep valley, hoping that they'd make it to the other side, but even the valley was rather high up. As the sky got dimmer, night began to get richer and fuller. By that time, they were at the top of the valley, more the cleavage between the mountains.

A particularly strong gust of wind blew by as Sassaska, wrapped in her wooly cloak dipped in red dye, looked further on. She had noticed that there were a lot of trees, growing thickly together up ahead where it was flat as opposite to the few scraggy ones that grew where the party now stood.

The thick trees made it troublesome to set up camp. They couldn't light a fire because the snow packed on the trees would fall, and they couldn't set camp away from the trees because it was all sloped downhill. Sassaska sighed as she looked to the nearby trees.

" We should put up the tents here near these trees!" she shouted, hoping they would provide at least a partial wind break without giving her the problems that the thicker trees would present.

Immediately the slaves, including Nurix stomped over to the two supply horses, unraveling the tents and beginning to set them up. It was hard because their fingers felt pricked with thousands of needles with everything that touched their hands.

Also, by now, there was only the moonlight to work with. And that wasn't bright enough to work on anything.

As the slaves worked, Elana and Brelinka, shivering and wrapped in their cloaks, walked over to Sassaska who was standing up straight, thinking and overseeing the work.

" Sassaska, why are we setting up camp here ? We're in the middle of the valley." asked Brelinka quietly, so the slaves wouldn't hear, giving a stern look unable to be seen in the dim light.

Sassaska nodded.

" I know. It's not the wisest of choices to make but it's for our own good. We can't hang the tree hammocks because it's too cold. If we continue further in this light, we might miss a step and fall.

If we try to camp outside of the trees, the wind will blow the tents over. This seems the only place that we're safe. "

" What about mountain lions ?" Said Elana.

Both of them went silent.

"They'll be as cold as we are and probably won't venture out. But speaking of cold, I don't think we'll be able to find enough firewood here to keep a big fire burning all night, so we're going to have to bundle. Let each slave sleep with their Mistress. Brelinka, you've got Taboo. I've got Rhyme, and Elana You've got Nurix."

"What about the horses ?" Asked Brelinka.

They all turned and looked at the horses. All five of them were standing together in the deep snow and seeming quite comfortable.

" I think that they'll be alright." Sassaska answered.

" It's only going to be this bad tonight.

Hopefully, tomorrow we will reach the plains." she said, then beckoned the slaves. "You three - come over here a minute."

The three slaves stomped over to Sassaska and all except Nurix bowed their teeth-chattering heads.

" The tent's are ready for you Mistress'" Taboo said, "we just have to put up the slave tent now."

"Don't bother - we're bundling tonight." said Sassaska.

Taboo nodded as she made her way to get her blanket. Rhyme did the same thing enthusiastically.

Nurix looked to Elana. He was about to join them in getting his own blanket, not sure what was going on.

Elana stopped him by touching his shoulder gently.

" Nurix . . . You'll be joining me in my tent tonight." Nurix stopped and turned around.

" What ?" he said mildly. Curious to why she had said that.

He could barely make out Elana's face but he knew that she was there.

Suddenly, Sassaska walked through them, pushing Nurix back briskly to get him out of her way.

" Taboo, you're sleeping with Mistress Brelinka tonight. Rhyme, you're with me."

" Yes, Mistress Sassaska." Shouted Taboo in the distance, followed by Rhyme starting up a giggle.

Sassaska then looked to Elana. " Well, don't stay up too late or make too much noise. You might be right about mountain lions." she said as she started out to her tent.

Elana raised her brow. She felt that Sassaska was treating her like a small child. She felt a little intimidated by what she had said.

"I think that I could handle a feeble mountain lion, Sassaska." she said snottily.

Sassaska stopped walking, barely showing an expression of concern in the dark.

" One mountain lion can be stopped easily in daylight but at night, the world is their ground of play." She slowly walked up to Elana and then hugged her and laid her head on Elana's shoulder,

" Just take my advice Elana; if you go out, don't stay out too long." she whispered. Her warm breath tickled Elana's ear, warming it.

"Alright, I won't." Elana said.

Sassaska smiled and then kissed her on the cheek.

" Good night Elana, I'll see you in the morning." she said as she unraveled her hands over Elana.

Elana smiled." Good night Sassaska."

Sassaska smiled as she walked to her own tent.

Rhyme was giggling slightly and waiting patiently outside of Sassaska's tent. Then they both went in.

Elana looked up at the moon, seeing the bright oval shape and the many stars all around. Nurix slowly approached her, chattering his teeth and rubbing his crossed arms to keep warm. He waited there, watching her. She was still staring up, looking for a star. Nurix could see her curly red and brownish hair luminescing in the moonlight, her dark red cloak loosely resting over her shoulders and the finely-made golden cloak buckle lying on her left collar bone.

Nurix thought that the moonlight made her even more glowing in angelic light than ever before. It made her beauty come more alive than just a plain girl's face. It outlined her eyes, her gaunt brows and her thin, long nose.

Her blackish red lips, began to seem lighter and softer in the light. Her features were pleasant to Nurix's eyes. The more he watched her, the more he began to feel lifted.

She still searched for one of the stars, walking around inside the light of the moon.

She then stopped and smiled. Nurix watched her dimples form and her teeth shine gently in the light.

" Nurix?" She called out.

Nurix slowly approached her, still caught in the awe of her beauty in the light. Nurix smiled mildly as usual, not knowing what to say and still too shy to say what he wanted to.

Elana's eyes were lit up with an excitement of accomplishment. She then pointed.

" See dim blue star over there?" she asked.

Nurix nodded as he looked up.

" Yes. I see it."

" When I was a little girl, I was taught about the great exodus from that star. It is a world like ours. It is Marsolla.

They say that Great warriors traveled through the vast ocean of the stars from the power of their minds. One of the first legends from the Ancient texts in every monastery. Are you familiar with it ?"

Nurix nodded again, looking at the other stars.

" Yes . . . I do know the Exodus . . ." Nurix replied.

Elana slowly stroked the back of his neck.

" I remember that the ocean of stars was far greater than the ocean of water. And though both were completely different in length and density, that both oceans were truly the same. That sailors of these great oceans navigated by their thoughts and the stars around them." Nurix said.

Elana, still stroking the locks of his hair running down his neck, sighed.

" All distances can be long or short. All matter can be thick or thin. All you think and all you deal-"

"Are all toys your mind can twist and feel . . . " finished Nurix.

Elana lowered her eyes to Nurix and slowly nodded her head with her grinning smile pressed on her lips.

Nurix just stared into her   brown eyes and literally got lost in them.

" That is correct . . . " she said softly.

Nurix smiled, having his eyes locked and focused onto hers.

They stood there for minutes not saying a word. They were enjoying the moment.

They were both still outside, in the light of the moon.

Elana liked the way he was and the way he looked in that soft light. He was quiet and nervous yet relaxed with her. His rough moustache and beard barely filled in because of his youth. And his heavy eyes locked to hers.

She found all that intriguing about him at that moment and didn't know what to do or what to say.

That night both of them were waiting for someone to say something and then some one did. But it was neither one of them.

Suddenly, in a burst of loudness, giant laughter exploded from one of the other tents.

Both Elana and Nurix jumped at the bursting of the sound.

They turned to the tents and had only one word to say:

" Rhyme . . . " They both said, starting to giggle themselves.

Elana then sighed

" Well follow me. I bet that we've got a long day ahead of us tomorrow." she said.

" Right." Nurix said, a little edgy from the burst of Rhyme's laughter.

They both walked slowly to the tent. Not saying anything at all.

They then reached it. Nurix stood there, waiting for her to go in first.

Elana opened the flap.

" Well you go in first." She said. Nurix, thinking that she was supposed to go in first nodded and ducked his head under the flap but he quickly turned around and looked at Elana for a moment.

" Thank you . . . " he said.

She smiled briefly as she got in. Elana then immediately grabbed her spear and bits of her laces from her shirt and tied the spear to the pole so that the point of the barb was touching the flap and rammed the other end into position against the main tent-pole..

Nurix watched her work on it in the dim light and was curious.

" Why are you tying a spear to the pole ?" he asked.

Elana, finishing the final knot turned around and laid down, facing Nurix.

" Just in case a mountain lios decides to join us tonight."

Nurix looked at the flap tied down and swaying to the spear.

" Oh . . . " he said.

Elana then got comfortable in her sleeping side and turned to her side so her back was facing Nurix. " Well good night." Elana said.

Nurix started to get comfortable himself.

" Yes . . . Good night . . . " he said as he slowly turned to his side as well.

Nurix tried to focus on sleeping but the cold was getting him. His blankets over his trench cloak over his sleeping bag didn't seem to help. But he thought he had no choice. He sighed, used his arm as a pillow and closed his eyes.

Then he heard Elana's voice in the dark. "What are you waiting for - bundling means we bundle together. Get near me."

He slithered in and the warmth soon overcame his thoughts.

He slept like a baby.

The next morning came. The sun was barely up but Nurix was up with it.

He first tried to go back to sleep, wedged in behind Elana, but he couldn't. First came the sounds of the morning birds chirping to themselves, then came the cold air passing through his stuffed nose, and finally his eyes slowly revealed the blurred vision of the inside of Elana's tent.

Nurix sighed, knowing that he couldn't surrender to his dormant passion for sleep so he gave into the morning. Not moving but lying there with it for a moment.

He felt something heavy under his arm and another something bending across his chest and a large soft and long and warm something almost fastened along his back and legs.

At first he thought that it was Elana's cloaks and blankets being pushed to him from her getting up, but when he felt the body of mass expand and deflate, pressing on his back, he began to know that Elana was right next to him, cuddled up and wrapped around him. Probably because she was cold and needed the heat from Nurix to keep her warm. But Nurix didn't care the reason at all.

He smiled serenely, feeling her arm on his chest, he slowly held her hand and pulled it closer to him. Her soft texture of skin contrasting to the tight, dense muscles under it made her body pleasant to the touch. Her laceless shirt covered her breasts pressing with every breath she took, her legs entangled with the back of his. She was unbelievably warm and her soft breathing on his neck gave him slight goose-bumps right on the scalp of his head. And familiar tingling in other areas.

Nurix then closed his eyes, holding onto Elana's hand. He wanted that moment to last forever.

He heard the tent flap gently sway from the mild breeze of the outside.

Suddenly the spear split and shot out with a metallic clang.

" Oh my Marsolla !" said a scared voice.

Nurix immediately sat up and looked. Elana slowly yawned and sat up as well.

Nurix was scared, he thought that someone got hurt and slowly began to crawl out to see who they had hit.

Elana rubbed her eyes, not seeming worried at all.

Suddenly Brelinka's frowning face popped into the flap.

" Elana, what the hell were you thinking ? Why did you rig the spear to the flap ?" she asked firmly.

Elana, slowly waking and gracefully sitting up, looked to Brelinka. "I thought that there might be a hungry mountain lion. I put it exceptionally low so that women wouldn't get hurt."

Brelinka looked to where the spear was tied and un-arguably nodded.

"Well . . . Next time, I hope you tell everyone around that you're setting up a trap."

Elana nodded, resting her hand onto her face, struggling to stay awake.

" Brelinka . . . I'll be out in a moment." said Elana.

Brelinka, still looking in then nodded once more.

" Alright . . . When you get out, we should start to head down the mountain. Oh, by the way. Sassaska and I found paw prints leading to the camp. " she said.

Elana's eyes widened.

" Were the horses killed ?" she asked.

" No, it was sniffing around the bear meat, but the funniest thing is that it looked like it jumped and then was spooked away. The only thing we could think of is that it was Rhyme's obnoxious laugh that spooked the lion."

" Well at least we know that she was worth the money Sassaska bought her for."

Brelinka chuckled and nodded her head.

Elana nodded as well.

Brelinka could tell that she was waiting patiently for her to leave.

" . . . Um, I'll let you dress up then."

Elana nodded; " Yes . . . please go.." Brelinka then smiled mildly and then went out of the tent.

Elana sighed and slowly looked to Nurix.

" Did you have a good night's rest." she asked.

Nurix nodded, not knowing what to say from his experience waking up and finding her wrapped onto him.

" Oh . . . I guess that you could say that . . . " he said.

Elana nodded her head a little and looked to her shirt. She then noticed that her cleavage was exposed but didn't seem to care that much.

" Nurix. Could you untie the lace from the spear ? I think I need it back on my shirt."

Nurix looked at her cleavage and raised a brow,

"Nurix, the lace please."

He then looked up feeling foolish.

" Oh, right the lace . . . " he pointed nervously to the pole.

" . . . Yes, now for . . . the lace."

Elana chuckled at his reaction and tightened her buckles on her pants. She then flapped her red cloak to get it free from dust and wrinkles and loosely tied it on.

Nurix, untied the knot. The split spear dropped to the floor. Nurix slowly handed it over.

" Thank you . . . " she said. As she began to thread it from bottom to top.

Nurix watched her hand push the lace through and work her way up.

She then noticed that Nurix was staring and stopped. She looked at him with a slight grin on her face.

" Nurix . . . Please, can you turn around ?"

Nurix laughed, feeling embarrassed and shy once more and turned around.

She finished her lacing, tied it up and then tightened it. She stood up struggling to put on her high brown boots with the hook-like buckles.

Then slowly crawled out of the tent.

Nurix then quickly put on his own boots, not caring to buckle their worn and tattered up straps but he took extra time in wrapping and tightening the rag bandages around his legs to his shoes. They fastened the boots a lot better than the buckle even though they looked clumsy, dirty, and unattractive. (Typical for a man to continue wearing something so bulky,)

He followed, quickly grabbing his trench cloak and carrying it on his back as he stepped out into the morning snow.

Immediately, he felt the environmental change from cool to frosty.

It sent chills down his spine and shivers through his arms and fingers.

The light was incredibly bright as it was reflected off the snow. It caused soreness in his eyes, so much so that Nurix had to squint to see anything.

All he could see were the horses standing and waiting to be packed. The other slaves seemed dreary eyed and sickly. They both had a bad sleep that night, probably because of Rhyme's bursts in laughter.

Well she wasn't laughing now. She was sad and tired. Both of them looked dead. It was amazing that they had enough life in them to gather some wood to pack on for needed supplies of emergency.

Nurix then turned around to take the tent apart and load it back onto the horse to get it ready, but he was curious on how much further they had to travel.

He looked to the other horses with Sassaska and Brelinka on them already, pointing at the direction of North East. Nurix knew this was the correct direction because he had often studied maps of the region when he was at the monastery. This was the only road. And he had also heard the many stories of travellers lost in the North East cleavage when the snows came early. Most were never found until spring thaw.

Nurix then sighed, realizing a couple of things he could never have known from looking at a map - that it was another slope uphill and that it was going to be a lot longer than a few hours across.

" And he was right. It was three more days of traveling through the mountains.

It took longer that anyone had expected. So long in fact, that Nurix was getting used to sleeping with Elana cuddling next to him.

Nurix prayed for colder weather to continue this state of affairs and his prayers were answered.

The more they seemed to travel on, the colder and faster the wind got. Soon an even bigger blizzard storm had occurred.

Because the storm was quite heavy, Taboo and Rhyme had to get off and ride the other two horses since they kept getting spooked as the winds got stronger . . .

It was the third day and the storm seemed to be getting worse. They had found a cave to stay in the last day and left early in the morning where they thought that the storm was over.

Little did they know that the storm was only resting up for the afternoon. They were three miles away from the cave, then the storm hit with tremendous force.

The blizzard was so strong that they couldn't see where they were going and so couldn't travel any further. Sassaska thought it best if they head back to the cave.

Everyone had dismounted from their horses and pulled them by their reins. The storm was too strong to ride in, and it was easier to control the horses that way.

" Come on ! Only a few more steps. The cave should be coming up soon!" shouted Sassaska on the top of her lungs. She couldn't see anyone but trusted that they heard her. She had tied a rope to all the horses so that she wouldn't get separated.

" Sassaska, can you see the cave yet ?" shouted a voice in the distance.

Sassaska stopped walking, shivering in the cold and trying to push her hair back from the wind as she squinted her eyes, trying to see it.

But she couldn't.

She couldn't see the road. She couldn't see their tracks. She couldn't see more than a few feet in front of her face.

She felt her cloak, feeling around to see if her scroll was still secure, buckled down in her holster for her sword. She was relieved to find it resting there as if the leather holster was meant for it.

Sassaska was getting worried. She started thinking about them freezing to death in the middle of the mountains. It was her nature to think about death, after all she was a priestess which believed in judgement before going to the heaven of true believers.

She was also the leader and she would carry the burden for anything that went wrong. The more she thought about these things, the more it punished her concentration of looking and the more it made her jumpy with nervousness. And the more she was jumpy, the more stressed she got.

Nonetheless, she had to know that if she got them lost. At least it was looking for shelter instead of blindly going on or something else. She then got scared that she had dropped her scrolled map and stopped to check it again. She was ready to panic, feeling around and hoping to run her wondering finger over the scroll, she felt nothing.

She couldn't believe what was happening. She briskly grabbed her holster and felt it all the way to the bottom, finding the map with a sigh of relief.

She shook her head to stay focused and then looked around for any signs of the cave.

She started to walk again. She slowly moved, in fear that she might slip down some of the steep slopes. She still continued to walk, fighting against the wind.

The horse stopped and grunted.

She glimpsed at the horse, "Come-on girl, we're only a few steps away.

She then tugged on the reins. Still the horse wouldn't budge. The horse was getting spooked by the harsh winds and the blinding white of the snow.

" What's going on ?" shouted Brelinka in the distance.

Sassaska struggled to get the horse moving again.

" The horse won't move. She's scared of something. I just can't get her to move." she shouted back.

Sassaska then tugged harder by the mouth, feeling that the horse was dripping it's warm saliva over her hand as she tugged more.

The horse, still shook its head and moved back. It sounded terrified about something. Then suddenly it jumped up, standing on its hind legs and swinging his front. It's wooly huffs stomping onto the ground severely. It's power was causing the ground to get softer.

Sassaska fell over. She was scared of the horse crushing her with one stomp to the ground. She immediately stood up, reaching for the horses reins, to gain control once more but it wouldn't let her. Brelinka's horse slowly came up to it. Brelinka had blindfolded it though and it seemed fine although it's ears were twitching to the sounds of the other horse.

Brelinka stopped and dismounted, slowly approaching the horse, on foot, afraid that it would kick her.

More it stomped on the ground as Sassaska persisted in grabbing for its reins. She finally did catch them, then the unimaginable happened.

The horse broke the chunk of the ice off and slid down the slope pulling Sassaska along with it.

Brelinka was thrown back and quickly struggled to get to her horse.

Suddenly the rope tied to all the horses went tense.

The weight of Sassaska's horse was slowly pulling in Brelinka's.

Brelinka grabbed the taut rope, pulling herself to look down the slope.

" Sassaska ?" she shouted in despair. She was worried and panicky as she waited for an answer. Nothing was heard except the terrified horse.

Suddenly the rope pulled Brelinka's horse closer to the edge.

Brelinka called one more time, now scared if Sassaska was dead or hurt.

Suddenly a faint cry of the horse was heard, still no Sassaska.

" What's going on up ahead ?" shouted Elana.

Brelinka immediately looked back.

" Stay where you are ! Start to pull back ! Sassaska's fallen down the slope."

Nothing happened.

" Brelinka ! Is she alright ?" shouted Elana once more.

Brelinka pressed her teeth into her lower lip and was afraid that she might have died.

Still she wasn't going to let grief blind her from the possibility of life.

She breathed deeply and began to think.

Suddenly more snow started to fall. Brelinka and her horse suddenly moved back from the sinking ice.

" Sassaska!" She shouted one more time.

She heard nothing. "Sassaska ? Sassaska ! Sassaska!!" She shouted louder and louder every time, still there was no sound.

Brelinka fell to the soft snow, thinking that Sassaska was dead. She couldn't believe that it was true. She thought to herself that maybe she could be still alive, barely holding onto a rope, the saddle, or something.

She put her face into her hands and shook her head, trying to find the power to realize and overcome her lover's death.

Then there was a soft touch to her arm. " Elana sent me up to see what was going on.

She couldn't make out what you were saying, only that Sassaska had..."

Brelinka turned looking expressionless, seeing that it was Nurix trying to understand what was wrong and that he saw the rope leading down the narrow steep of the slope, barely seeing the lying horse in the distance - held there by the rope which the other four horses were tensed against.

He looked into her eyes.

She gasped and tried to keep her tears to herself.

" Sassaska can still be alive . . . " he said.

Nurix looked down, seeing the rope taut and leading down to the horse hanging there and paralyzed with fear.

He grabbed the rope, then looked to Brelinka. " I'm pretty sure that she's still alive."

Brelinka looked away, thinking that he was trying to make her feel better.

" Mistress Brelinka, I don't know how to tell the horses to move back. If we do that then we'll find out."

" She's dead, slave. I called out to her so many times. She hasn't answered back. She's gone, slave, let's leave it at that. We have to save the rest of the party."

Brelinka then stood up, and took out her sword. She walked over to the taut rope connecting to the horse hanging and limp on the steep slope.

" No, please, Mistress Brelinka. I am telling you that I think she's still alive down there. If you'd . . ."

Brelinka only shook her head as she placed the sword on the rope.

"Don't say anything. You hear me slave? Don't try to fix me, man. It's all over . . . " she said as she backed her sword up to swing it to make a clean cut on the rope.

She breathed in deeply and closed her eyes to swing. She then swung it,,

Nurix watched her swing and shook his head, thinking that she's still alive, that she's alright, just hanging on.

" Somebody up there ? Brelinka ? Help me, please . . . " came a weak, moaning pathetic voice.

Nurix's eyes blinked. He was right but it was almost too late.

Brelinka's eyes widened she gasped in suspense, realizing that she was wrong and that she was going to kill her beloved Sassaska. As her blade came close to the rope, she immediately rolled the handle with her two hands and stabbed the sword into the ground and fell to her knees. She couldn't believe it. She was going to take her life and didn't even know.

She closed her eyes and sighed.

Nurix sighed in relief, glad that Sassaska was alright.

" I can't believe it. I chose the thought that she was dead without doing anything. I am foolish to think such a thing." She said.

Nurix only looked to her. " It wasn't your fault. Any woman would have done the same." he said, trying to comfort her. "The heart always rules the head - even in a warrior like yourself."

There was a creak.

She then stared to the rope straining .

" Oh, god. I hope that she hasn't fallen now."

Brelinka immediately grabbed onto the rope, happy and thankful for her lover to be alive. She was muttering and joyful as unending streams of tears fell down her cheeks.

She then turned around and immediately started walking over to grab the reigns of the horse. She then turned to Nurix, grabbing his arm firmly.

" Nurix, go and tell Elana to move all the horses back. We're going to pull her and her clumsy horse up. Understand me ? Now Go !" She said.

Nurix nodded and started running as fast as he could. Calling out for Elana, calling out to move the horses back.

Brelinka, then looked down the slope and called out to Sassaska. " Listen, just hold on tight there. We're going to pull you out. Just stay there. Don't move. Please, for me, don't die . . . " she shouted.

She immediately started to move her horse backwards.

The horse grunted stubbornly but moved nonetheless.

Slowly the rope began to move up.

The horses struggled as they moved back, feeling the weight of Sassaska and the horse dangling on the edge .

The horses grunted even more and pulled harder. Brelinka went to see Sassaska. The horse was slowly ascending up the slope.

Sassaska, weak, bruised and scraped al little was holding onto the horses brown mane with one hand and struggling to keep her grip on the reins with the other.

She looked sad, scared and hopeless as Brelinka began to see her more clearly. The horses felt that the burden of the weight lessen and moved back faster. Brelinka immediately grabbed onto the reins and stopped the horses.

" Stop ! Sassaska's off the slope !" she shouted.

She looked to Sassaska who looked depressed and negative about something. She shook her bruised head slowly, like she had lost something precious to a fool.

The horse, seemed to be fine. It was shaky and slowly pulled itself up. As it did. Sassaska let go of the horse and fell to the floor. She lay there looking at the snow in shame.

She then looked up to Brelinka who bent down to help Sassaska up.

Sassaska gasped as she hugged Brelinka. As they both stood up. Sassaska buried her face in Brelinka's shoulder, Brelinka crying in joy that she was alright.

She then kissed Sassaska emotionally, holding her head with one hand, then hugging her again. She was glad that Sassaska was alive and she didn't want to lose her again. So they held onto each other there on that spot not moving at all.

Sassaska rubbed her bruised cheek against Brelinka's crying as well.

Elana slowly walked up to them, seeing that Sassaska was fine. She gasped in relief.

" Oh, thank Marsolla that you're alright." she said.

"I'm fine - just feeling stupid," Sassaska said, then slowly whispered to Brelinka. "Let's find that cave now."

Brelinka smiled to her.

" We will. Don't worry," she said softly, kissing her on the lips once more.

Sassaska felt weak and a little dizzy but she held onto Brelinka tightly, and she felt secure and protected now that she was hugging her. Brelinka had saved her life, and she loved her even more for that, but she still felt that she had failed as a leader.

She felt that way, for it was her that almost pulled them all to their deaths, It was her that lead them into the storm, and last it was her that lost their only way back to their home, Lina.

And, she cursed herself after checking, it was her that had lost the map . . .

The Old Man paused and nodded his head as he closed his eyes.

I was stunned. He had brought me into another cliff hanger and I was left to wonder if they ever found a way out of the mountains.

The Old Man looked out to the sea and sighed.

" I shouldn't tell you this, but I feel that you'd be able to keep a secret.

Our boat is ready to set sail tomorrow but I don't think that we should. That's why I am going to tell them to keep working on it." he said.

I was excited. We were ready to leave for Atlantis, I didn't care that he didn't want us to go. After all, who was he ? Our father ?

" Why is it that you don't want us to leave for Atlantis ?" I asked.

" I don't think that anyone is ready to handle what is out there.

I don't want the crew, panicking when they sail for three months without any sight of land. I've seen the people here, and all of them including you are superstitious. Not a minute goes by that you don't think of praying to some damned God or other. If you all are like this. I don't know what would happen out there on the sea."

" You know, that tomorrow or after a few more weeks, we are going to leave anyways. It makes no difference. We'll all be the same. The difference is you. That's why you've got to lead us there. You've got to teach us how to make it, Old Man, or we certainly will perish out there."

The Old Man turned to me. " You seem to want to go there, even after I've told you this much about Atlantis. I thought after telling you about a world ruled by women, it would make you think that I was crazy."

I grinned and shook my head. " No, you see Old Man. I am fascinated with Atlantis even more now that you tell me the truth about it. That one part was ruled by Women. Ten times stronger then men. That another part of it was ruled by men. Who could fly. This is so much better than the lies and re-written rubbish that the other old story tellers talk about."

The Old Man giggled a bit. "And to think, with all that, I haven't even told the half of it yet."

I was now excited. I was amazed that there was other parts to the story and that it was actually the same story. All I had to do was ask him to tell me the rest of the story.

Then, hopefully, he would.

The more I heard the story, the more it made me wonder. I began to have a feeling, a feeling that it wasn't a story at all that he told, but a piece of history that he had known, that he had lived. I began to think that he was that slave Nurix. Or maybe the journalist Kline. That was what kept me hooked on his story.

The Old Man raised his brow.

" Well then, I've decided to give the crew a few more days. Then I will lead you all to Atlantis. " he said.

"Thank you . . . " I said.

He laughed and slapped his knee.

" Now, let's go back to the story before there is no more evening to tell it with."

" Please, tell away."

He sat and stared into the fire as he reached over to grab another piece of wood.

Sassaska's tired legs couldn't go any further. She was falling deeper into hopelessness and shame. As she slowed her walk and was about to surrender to the cold, Brelinka grabbed her and held her up, forbidding her to surrender. Sassaska gasped and couldn't say that she had lost the scroll because of her selfishness to live.

The storm was at it's peak and Brelinka helped her walk, flapping her cloak over Sassaska's wet, snow- covered one.

Brelinka led the way slowly.

" Just a little further Sask, please don't surrender to the cold. Not today, not any day. Not if you're still with me. Please."

Sassaska said nothing but nodded her drowsy head.

They walked for another hour, fighting against the cold, needle-like winds.

As they went on, Sassaska slowed down. She seemed to be getting weaker as they went on. Brelinka, afraid for her health, began to slow her pace to almost a sluggish motion. She immediately turned around and called for someone to help.

" Elana, come up to the lead horse !" she shouted, desperately trying to keep everyone moving in the storm. Elana ran and staggered clumsily as she came up to Brelinka holding the icy reins of the lead horse, which was now getting tired as well.

Elana gazed at Sassaska, her hair wet and locked with frosty snow chunks and her ever-so-pale face getting even paler.

"Brelinka, she's getting worse." she said concertedly.

" I know Elana, but we can't stop now. It's too dangerous. We've got to keep moving." Brelinka said, now blowing onto Sassaska's hands and frictioning her arms.

Elana, feeling worried as well grabbed onto the reins and started the horses walking again. She knew that it if they were out here for another hour or so, Sassaska would be gone, and that the cold would begin to point its fingers at them for death to do his job on them as well.

Just then, Sassaska couldn't keep going any more. Her eyes were getting heavier and her hands were beginning to numb a little more.

She stopped walking, Brelinka walked a few steps and pulled her.

Sassaska shook her head slowly, she was surrendering and Brelinka knew it.

Brelinka suddenly felt Sassaska drop to the ground.

She quickly knelt in the cold snow, holding Sassaska tightly in her arms.

Sassaska smiled, she didn't want Brelinka to suffer. She looked into Brelinka's eyes and tried to reach her arms around Brelinka.

" Brelinka . . . I've failed you, your sister, and now because of me, you'll perish . . . "

" You haven't failed us. You fell. It was unexpected. Your horse trampled on a loose piece of the ground and caused a mild avalanche. It wasn't your fault, you had no way of knowing." Brelinka bit down on her cold, sore lip, her feelings were coming out, banishing her ability to command and think clearly. Her pain and grief were showing not only through her expressions but through her eyes.

" The cave . . . Once we've reached the cave . . . The slaves will start a fire and you'll be fine . . . " she said as her tears began to fall. Brelinka shook her head as she held Sassaska tighter to her breast.

Sassaska closed her eyes, drowsy, weak and losing all feeling in her tips of her fingers ." No, no you don't understand. When I fell, I had dropped the scroll. It was in my reach, I could have gotten it, but then more snow came and piled on top of me.

I held onto the mane of the horse and could of reached for it. But then I got scared. I looked down, seeing that I was near the edge and that if I grabbed the scroll with one hand, I might of fell. So I grabbed onto the reins as the snow piled up even more.

I held on, thinking for my own benefit instead of everyone else . . . " She began to sniffle a bit. A single warm tear raced down her frozen cheek as she started to pout.

Brelinka only stared to her, controlling her tears and reaching over to her to wrap her arms around her.

" You're alive now. It wasn't your fault. Please don't die. You can't die. I need you, if that doesn't matter to you, then think of this . . . You are to be the next Empress. The lives of the Empire depend on you. They chose you to be the next heir for a reason."

Sassaska smiled looking like she was about to sleep, she slowly reached her hand over to Brelinka's face. She stroked her hair and wiped her tears from her face.

" Oh Brelinka, you've been so good to me. I'm sorry that I've failed you and your sister. Please, leave me. You and your sister may still have a chance . . . "

Brelinka shook her head.

" I, my sister and you, Sassaska. Don't die . . . Don't die ! Not here, not in the snow, I promise you, if I have to die with you right here, we are all going to make it.

Now . . . If you love me, please get up . . . At least walk with me some more . . . So that I could tell everyone that you died . . . Saving all of us . . . ."

Sassaska then wrapped her hand around her neck.

" For you my love, I'll keep walking . . . . For you . . . " she whispered.

Brelinka immediately helped her up Sassaska struggled to keep her legs from falling. She then dragged her sleeping feet one by one with Brelinka holding her stable as she kept on walking.

" That's it . . . I've got you, don't worry Sassaska. Just, let's keep going." Brelinka said, holding her emotions in and moving with her.

They walked and walked, holding each other in their arms. But Brelinka knew that Sassaska couldn't keep walking forever. It was only so long until she fell once again.

The winds were beginning to die down, and the wind resistance was getting weaker. Brelinka held her hands as she walked, trying to keep Sassaska alive, she sighed with relief,

" Look Sassaska, the winds are dying down . . . " she whispered.

Sassaska gave a wan smile "We might have a chance . . . " she said, her pale, icy face and her blue lips stayed with a smile.

But then the worst came.

Sassaska rolled her eyes up and then fell to the snow once more, totally unconscious.

Brelinka tried to help her up. Sassaska opened her eyes staring further along the distance. She strained to keep herself awake but she was already light-headed and too weak to stand up.

She saw the horses being led further on into the winds, then she heard Elana's voice with words she couldn't believe.

" I found the cave ! " she cried but it was as if Brelinka couldn't hear her

Sassaska, tried to say something to alert Brelinka but she felt too weak, then as she kept looking on, she saw the white fog disappear and the dim dark of the caves mouth showing only meters away.

Brelinka looked up as she helped her up.

She was joyful that Elana had found the cave and that the storm had finally died.

As the winds grew weaker, so did Sassaska. Brelinka immediately picked her up and began to carry her. She quickly struggled to hold Sassaska's frozen body and make it to the cave. She saw as she got closer that the slaves were at work starting a fire, but they had not known that Sassaska was so close to dying.

Elana's eyes widened as she saw Sassaska, she quickly ran over to see her and help to carry her in.

Immediately the slaves worked faster to start the fire, but all of them feared that they were too late to save her.

Brelinka and Elana quickly placed her down and started to undress her.

They had to get her into dry clothing first before they could do anything else.Elana raced, pulling out some of the unused cloaks, blankets, and skins. Brelinka tried to keep Sassaska's attention, so that she wouldn't black out.

She then saw that Elana had brought all the blankets and dry clothing she could find. Brelinka carried Sassaska and placed her on a pile of blankets She then started to unclothe herself too.

" Sassaska, we've made it to the cave. I've finished my part of the deal. Now I want you to keep your end of the bargain, I want you to keep looking at me, keep listening to me. I don't want to lose you, you hear me." she said as she stripped down.

Sassaska blinked slowly and kept staring, numbly on her toes now as they took her boots and stockings off her. Elana then grabbed Sassaska's hand and kept talking to her, as Brelinka, now naked, laid right next to her, to warm her up with her body heat.

" Sassaska, we've gotten this far. You've got to pull us through to survive, You led us to the cave. You saved us. We need you . . . " Elana said, getting worried.

Brelinka immediately went on top of her, moved her to her side, and held her tightly as Elana wrapped the blankets around both of them. As Elana continued piling more blankets around them, Brelinka held Sassaska, not letting go.

For now, time would be the only indication if she was to live or not. There was nothing else anyone could do.

Sassaska felt numb all over from the cold. Brelinka, holding her frozen body close, began to feel the heat she was giving off. She then started to rest her face on Sassaska's shoulder.

Sassaska felt tired but struggled to keep awake, she began to feel the heat from Brelinka's body all around her. She felt Brelinka's head lying on her and she smiled.

Sassaska slowly moved her head to Brelinka and kissed her on the cheek.

Brelinka slowly turned to look at her, glad that she was getting better,

" . . . I guess that I should keep up my end of the bargain . . . ." she whispered softly as her sleepy eyes started to get heavy once more.

Brelinka smiled with joy and continued to hold her.

" . . . I love you . . . . I won't let death take you so soon, not without a fight." she whispered.

Sassaska smiled gave a mild, slow, pathetic giggle

" Brelinka . . . Always the Warrior . . . Always the Romantic . . . ."

Brelinka smiled as she looked into her eyes with a glowing look on her face,

" . . . Sassaska . . . Always the mellow dramatic . . . ." she said, trying to make Sassaska laugh. Sassaska smiled as she closed her eyes.

Brelinka gasped with relief and said nothing, she just was silent as she kissed her on her lips and placed her face resting on the side of Sassaska's forehead.

Elana sighed with relief and slowly let go of her hand.

Sassaska, slowly moved her freed hand and weakly pulled the blanket further up to cover them both and keep them closely embraced as they were.

Brelinka chose to sleep there, holding onto Sassaska. When the fire warmed the cave, they were already sound asleep. Brelinka felt happy, she was happy that Sassaska didn't give up on her. To her it showed her that Sassaska loved her as much as she loved Sassaska. Sassaska felt that the fates had given her another chance, that they had forgiven her for failing to be the good leader she wanted to be.

Now she was filled with hope that they were going to get through with her mission, but only time could tell if she was going to be able to show it.

" Did she survive the night ?" I asked, feeling oddly concerned for his fictional character. (I was caught up in the suspense.)
The Old Man smiled.
" That's what we'll find out next time. "
"Oh come on. Just a little more."
"Well, alright then. How about this:"

The sounds of roaring wooden pellets, weighed down with iron noses filled the air.

" Hold !" shouted the Instructor.

Kline panted as he lowered his weapon. Today was shooting practice.

Kline had arranged to be able to have the use of projectile piercing contraptions called guns.

"I said Hold, damn you !" shouted the Instructor, cursing at Luca who insisted in knowing the use of the gun which he carried.

All heard the sound of suction coming out of the air pump connected to the barrel of the projectiles.

These were projectile weapons powered by the force of compressed air. It was compressed by a manual air pump built into the gun and then the pellet, or "mini dart" as the traditionalists named it, was forced out of the barrel with a powerful puff of air. A design which was adapted from the ancient blow darts that the founding fathers used for three hundred years in the early days of the Empire.

The Instructor looked tensely at the others then shouted:

"Reload the chamber !"

Kline immediately pushed up the magazine of the gun until it clicked and aimed at his target: a man made of straw and tied together with ropes.

Kline knew that if the trigger was held down, the magazine wouldn't have to be pushed up to reload the bullet. The power of the vacuum of the loss of air would pull the next bullet in, immediately after firing the previous one.

Unfortunately the "mini dart" pulled rapidly into the chamber in this manner would have half the amount of pressure to accelerate on, so rapid fire was to be avoided.

The gun was called a point five pick, long range, ten shot. It's nick name was the "long observer."

It was a standard weapon taught to all sorts of gun users as the best personal weapon that Sudutan Atlantis could ever provide. Unfortunately everyone had to treat it as a single action weapon.

The Empire was unable to develope anything that would suit the needs for a multi action weapon.

It was all in the preciseness of the air intake. The single action was a step up from blowing darts already and no one felt the need for a major change.

" Remember what happens if you are in a tight situation with savages: Breath . . . Let your gun breath or else your following pellets will not be able to project as well as the first time." the Instructor reminded them.

Kline looked to the side, noticing the Instructor pace past him, and go into vacant stare as he recalled something from the good old days.

The others groaned and cursed him off, knowing what was coming - as the Instructor had done and said the same thing before. But, as he walked by, they continued to shoot.

The Instructor grinned and brushed his frilly top as he began to speak; "My friends and brothers learned a lesson forty years ago. Unfortunately they learned it a little too late. So we came up with a saying so that you will remember not to get in that same situation.

It goes like this:

Shoot too soon - you're a goon

Shot too slow - you'll take a blow "

Dole, who was crouched right next to Kline, sighed in agony,

" Oh no, here it comes, the dreaded war story" he said under his breath. Kline chuckled a little.

The Instructor continued to speak, "When we were under the command of Elder-Cummundore Dav'idine Karakkus, we were posted to hold a position over in Egypt from the savages.

May I remind you that it was forty years ago . . . .

When the Mhazis attacked, me and my friends panicked and held down the trigger, refusing to let go.

We paid for our fears. The first pellet took out one savage. Maybe even the second or third, but after that, the air was so depleted, that they just bounced off. We faced death, right in the eye that day and fully half the company fell.

But it wasn't an honorable death they fell to. It was a savage with a spear made of bronze.

A savage! Can you ever believe that Sudutan soldiers of the greatest civilization the world has ever seen, fell to the spears of

Mhazi-like savages like wheat falls before the cutter?" he emphasized then smiled.

"Well, they did. But you don't have to. Have a little patience when you shoot and every shot will be a killing shot. Load the air pump manually every time. And you'll kill every time.

But you are all lucky to be born in this day and age. The savages are all tamed. You'll never have to go through anything of that sort at all." he said with a mild laughter. "Unless it's an enraged husband."

The next task before the day was over was to fly and stop in mid air, fire the gun at a low target on the ground and come back. A tough task indeed.

It took two hours to strip on the splints, the safety fasteners, the pressure valve to measure the speed of the air in contrast to your own acceleration.

Walking to an open area to take off was like walking on stilts for the men.The equipment was heavy as well as inefficient as Squirrel continued to emphasize and complain about throughout the simulation. He believed that safety was a nuisance if one was to accomplish true sufficiency.

Squirrel was the only one who chose not to wear a few of the essential parts. He convinced Dusty to go on his side. They were the only ones who showed up with the pressure valve cut off, the exhaust holes expanded as well as missing essential pipes.

The Instructor was not as pleased with them as he was with the others. Squirrel especially shunned on the idea of wearing splints over the legs and arms. "An insufficient need for more money to be spent." was his usual line.

Kline began to see why he was kicked out of the Mechanical Engineering Academies: he was an obnoxious know -it-all - who did know it all.

"This is what we call, the leap of faith." the Instructor shouted over the loud beats from all of the wings.

" You shoot a moving target on the ground and then you decline to the target you shoot. This is a tactic taught for shooting large grazing animals from above.

The pellet builds speed, therefore is able to kill anything cleanly." The Instructor said, looking at the rough bunch who were admiring their new rifles.

" What if we were to kill a person with the bullets, would anyone be able to spot us ?" asked Luca Beard, eager to know.

The Instructor nodded in appreciation.

" My motto was always 'Fly hard, die hard' That is the chance all soldiers serving under the Sudutan crown usually take." The Instructor went on with a snaggle.

Luca grinned, strapping down his rugged pig skin helmet with the retractable Monoscope fastened comfortably over his left eye.

" Fly Hard, Die Hard ?" Luca repeated, and nodded his head.

" I like that saying, old timer." he finished.

The Instructor smiled and pointed to Kline.

" You first !" he shouted.

Kline's brow went up under his pig skin helmet.

" Me ?" he answered.

" Ya, you !"

Kline looked around at everyone, flapping their mechanical wings, holding tightly to their long observers, pointing to the floor.

" Oh, I'm not ready for this. I barely know how to take off yet," Kline nervously pleaded to the Instructor.

"Get up and fly, Kline ! I thought that you were the man with the warrior's tongue,"

Kline gulped in fear.

" That's the thing, I try to emphasize the tongue more frequently than just the warrior." Kline said in his defense.

The Instructor then walked over to him, ignoring whatever he was saying, and pulled the accelerating lever next to the pressure valve of his Drag Quad.

Kline looked at the Instructor with terror in his eyes. The sound of the wings beating at maximum pulse and the lift against fall as well as thrust against pull, forced Kline to take off into the sky, fearing for his life.

His helmet wasn't strapped tightly. His Monoscope rattled, bruising the outer eye socket which it rested upon.

Kline glimpsed as much as possible with his free eye on the pressure valve, noticing the speed of the air going slower as he accelerated at fifty to eighty miles an hour, a speed that he was not accustomed to.

He quickly forced his shoulders left to right, knowing that it was the only way to control the direction he went.He now regained control of the direction, but reducing the speed was another obstacle.

If he continued at this speed, the Drag Quad would have a greater risk of losing its wings or causing friction where the grease was, therefore causing an explosion.

If he slowed down too much without pulling the string starter to sustain him in a stable position, he could risk stalling in mid air, falling to his death without ever gaining his lift in time.

Kline trembled in fear as he tried to safely let go of the gun with one hand without dropping it. As soon as this was possible, he reached his free hand towards the lever.

As soon as he pulled it, he found that the wings had come to a suddenly silent stop.

Kline free fell.

He felt his heart leap to his throat, his legs tingle as well as his stiffened arms. Immediately, the wings regained a beating pulse, now slowing his fall and bringing him to a hovering position. Still his body swayed as the air current pushed at him, but his position kept him from falling. He slowly regained his stability and discontinued shivering in fear.

He stared down upon the air strip, seeing patterns of rocks which formed into large signals.

A waving man, telling that it was a safe position to land. A sign that looked like a crow on the bottom, was being held up, meaning to beware of birds flying into the wings.

By this time, the others had already come up, hovered, fired and came down.

This humiliated Kline by far as the worst humiliation he had ever endured.

Nonetheless, he persisted in doing the shot.

Since no one was able to contact him, or he them, he loosened up the Monoscope and elongated it.

He raised his rifle, noticing the hot air balloon being risen. What he had to do now was punch a few holes into it, to let the air free so that it would decline to the ground.

He breathed deeply and pulled down the monoscope strap over his helmet to clip onto the rifle. It aligned and the pieces slipped into each other like assembling a pole, or a wooden chair.

He closed his free eye, aimed, fired, and conquered.

He was still considered the laughing stalk, missing the balloon five or six times before finally hitting it.

But it was a ten shot rifle - and any kill is a good kill.

Kline became troubled as he changed into his casual dress. The way that the training process was being done made it almost impossible to leave during the two weeks time period.

He was anxious to start, ignorant to do anything else. In his mind, the mission was the most important task that needed to be finished. But the sudden changes which occurred almost every moment, made him more frustrated.

First it was the presence of Bringington. Although they compromised the tables so that they would barely see each other, the bald glare from his adversary struck hateful nerves, making his focus unclear.

Even with the presence of King Zex, the procrastinating fool thrown into an important job, pressured his resentment even more.

Kline never disliked Zex, only felt annoyed by him. It was also jealousy that struck Kline's ego. Nonetheless, Kline was bothered and wanted to talk with Zex about the situation so he took a crawler to the Imperial suite near by.

Tall Imperial soldiers stood on guard by the door gripping their Bankra blades: a sword in which the blade was swayed and bent to form a rounded, hook-like appearance.

They stood firm and proud, wearing the full gear of an Imperial trooper. They had the brownish red undergarment with a family heritage band falling down the right shoulder. They had the chain linked, vital straps: a thick metal-linked band which came across the left side of the body to act as an impermeable shield to the vital organs. And their Mowhawks were full and perfectly rounded, culturally showing high class and pride for the Sudutan lands.

Obviously, these men were proud to be in the expensive clothing issued to them. But Kline almost laughed at the thought that these soldiers did anything else except stand around. Kline nodded at them as a kindly gesture as he tried to make his way to King Zex's room.

Suddenly, one of the Imperials turned around and held him by the shoulder.

Kline was amazed that the Imperial actually moved to stop him.

The soldier focused on him with piercing eyes.

Kline looked at this man. The Imperial was a thin-nosed, pale faced, heavy-eyebrowed, native dolt of some colony that Kline didn't care to know the name of. In addition, the Imperial had no facial hair which was considered to reveal a man's womanly features. A weak trait.

Kline eyed the hand which gripped his right shoulder.

" I don't think that you should go inside." the man muttered.

Kline sighed " The King's Official Whoremaster, reporting for duty."

The soldier frowned, " What ?" he asked.

Kline grinned and looked at the man,

" Nothing. I have come to speak to the King about some urgent news." he stated.

The soldier speculated whether Kline was a trouble maker or not.

"Where are your qualifications, sir ?" the man asked.

Kline snorted, not being able to believe what was happening to him.

He was being interrogated by a man whose people had been defeated and undignified by the Sudutan conquerors.

The thought was beyond Kline to even imagine this sorry state of affairs. Kline had no time for people who gave him no dignity.

" Where are my qualifications ?" Kline repeated. " I am the reason that King Zex is here at all. You are too ignorant to ever read the informational journals at all. So I doubt that you have ever heard of the Great Race which wills tart right from here." Kline complained.

The soldier, insulted passively laughed at Kline's remark and then patted him on the back.

" Nevertheless, Sir, I decide who goes past to see the King and, at the moment, my lack of intelligence is contemplating throwing you down the stairs.

So please, Oh Mighty One, I ask kindly of you, leave this area at once," the soldier said calmly.

It was obvious that the soldier was used to ethnic slurs, adapting a thick skin to block out most of what anyone would say.

Kline shook his head.

" I see that you are a persistent man, and one who follows orders well - I'll give you credit for that, but I must see the king at once."

The soldier shook his head.

Kline stood there, planning his next move. He thought that diplomacy might be called for.

"Let's be reasonable here" he said. "There are two of you here. One great warrior is more than enough to keep me in control. Have your comrade go in and tell the King that Kline is here on a matter of some urgency. Let the King decide."

Kline paused for moment to let that sink in, then added another line of attack; "If the king does not get my news in a timely manner, or if you do indeed hurt me and it turns out I am known to the king, his wrath will be much more dangerous than mine. And, on the other hand, if I am telling the truth and give a glowing report of you to the King, your life could be much improved. Don't take a chance. Send in your comrade. Let the King decide."

The soldier gulped quickly. He was overwhelmed with the threats that Kline made, not knowing where his duty lay. It bothered the guard and it bothered the other one who seemed to find comfort in silence. The soldier turned to the other one who was darker in skin.

"Go in. Ask the King if he will see a Kline."

The silent guard nodded and quickly went inside. Then came out quickly.

"Kline ! Get in here !" came the King's voice.

The soldiers looked at each other nervously. Then they both moved out of Kline's way.

Kline smiled and stepped into the hall,

" Good, now apologize for treating me so low and then carry on doing whatever you savages were doing." Kline said proudly, enjoying his given power.

"We are sorry to have caused you so much inconvenience, Sir." one of them apologized. But very predictably, Kline ignored them and made his way to the royal suite.

As he stood in front of the inner door of the thickly built room, Kline knocked, hoping that King Zex would be in the mood to hear his complaints. But no one showed up to answer his knocks, not even Zex's many women servants which he took pleasure in fondling at all times.

Kline waited for a few minutes more for someone to answer the door and then frustratedly knocked once more.

" - Oh, by the God Marsolla, I told them not to let anyone inside !" came a faint grumble through the door.

"Quit bitching. I told them to let him in," came the King's voice.

Kline took a sigh as he anticipated the door opening. Immediately, the King opened the door quickly and the young shaven Zex stuck out his head and sneered at Kline and gave him a suspicious glimpse.

" What the hell do you want ? " he said appalled in his presence.

Kline rolled his eyes,

" Yes, yes it's me, you sack of ignorance . . . " he said under his breath.

Zex frowned,

"Excuse me ?" he requested.

Kline shook his head, keeping from a smile.

"Nothing of real importance. I just said 'It's me who lacks forbearance'

Anyways, I have to come inside - I have to talk with you, Highness;" Kline said insistingly forcing himself through the door while Zex resisted.

" Um, Kline; just tell me from there - I've got a big mess in here. Is anything wrong ?" he struggled, pushing from the other side of the door.

"No. Let me in. I don't want to be overheard out here."

"Is it possible then, that you can come back another time ?" Zex pleaded quickly, but it was too late for Kline had forced the door open and strolled into the King's room, knocking Zex sprawling onto the floor.Zex laid back on the floor and revealed that he was wearing only a pair of undergarments stained with a little blood on them. Zex must have had to have paid compensation to the family of the woman he was fondling the night before, thought Kline. Apparently she had not survived his attention.

A servant - the Ancient Mumbler Kline had heard through the door - ran over to help the King up.

Immediately Zex stood up in fury, and brushed the oldster away.

"Get out of here. I'm tired of you. Come back later and clean this mess up. Not now."

The old servant quickly disappeared through another door.

" How dare you knock over Royalty, Kline !" he joked rubbing his head, "That's a capital offense."

Then he came to the realization that the oldster had told his security guards not to let anyone in, especially rank.

"How, did you get the guards to come in and disturb me, Kline ?" he asked.

Kline rose an eyebrow.

" I am Kline. I have the Warrior's Tongue. I told them that if you were displeased, you would request the colonial armies to execute their families but if they did go in and ask, I would praise them to you and improve their lives." Kline said. "And, keeping my word I sing their praises. Please improve their lives, Sire."

Zex gritted his teeth,

" They left me half defenseless for that ? Stupid bastards. Leave colonial soldiers to do a Sudutans job . . . Well then, I will heed you and improve their lives as well as discipline them for their lax attitudes. I'll just kill their families as you have threatened, after all, whose life wouldn't be improved by eliminating their entire greedy grasping hordes ?

So that's done. What is your business here ?" he said beginning to walk to another section of the room.

Kline walked with him.

" Well, I wanted to request a transfer to another air base to train."

Zex sat in a woven chair across from his bed. Kline stopped and was about to pull up a chair until he noticed the woman from the Officer's Lounge lying on the bed, dead and staring open-eyed, with her wrists slit.

Kline widened his eyes "My god Marsolla, isn't that a little drastic?" he asked as he walked closer and peered at the dead woman.

Zex started to laugh.

"One of the beauties of being Royalty, my friend." he said. "Besides, I believe that they're better when they're fading away slowly . . . just before they get cold and stiff . . . ." he admitted gleefully.

Kline turned away. He was never really into the killing of women even though it was a common practice with the poorer folk to sell their daughters to perverted rich men such as Zex.

" So why is it that you want to change stations when you've only got two more weeks before you leave ?" Zex asked as he crossed his arms.

Kline took a sigh of relief. "Your Highness, to tell you the truth, I wasn't expecting to have you as well as Bringington pushing me towards my goal. I feel pressured and overwhelmed with what is going on . . ."

Zex stood up and strolled to his desk. " Kline, do you have any idea how much this expedition is costing the empire ?"

Kline was lost after Zex went off topic.

Zex turned his head.

" I see that you have no idea. Well, I'll give you a hint. The Royal treasury is spending four million, three hundred thousand. That money goes to supplies, equipment, training and weaponry if there is ever to be any confrontation.

My father had sent many people to the north hoping to find something. All have come back with no eagerness to report what they find. The reason why I am straining all the money I can is because of three things:

The first reason is to spread a good reputation of my name.

So that I could possibly bring the golden age to the Sudutans once again.

The second reason is so that Sponsors here and away will donate money into the treasury thinking it will all go to the Great Expedition and give them shares in the profits. And shares they'll get, if any are there to share. But I expect to break even or even make a great deal more than the cost - even if you find nothing at all.

But the third reason is the most important and the same as my father's and his father's before him. Our diamond mines are depleting over at the colonies. The specialists have estimated that there will be no more diamonds within forty or fifty years. Our proud civilization would fall and the end of the known world would come." Zex stated.

Kline leaned a little in his chair,

"Oh, that's only a rich boy's myth. The colonies are plentiful of diamond mines -"

" I disagree ! All of the conquest, all of the seizing was, in the end, useless. The great promise of earlier generations has all been spent. Mines there are - but near to empty, all of them. Our Geologists don't even know where to begin to find new ones !" Zex shouted. "Every likely possibility in the known world has been explored and found with nothing."

Kline gasped, and sat on the edge of the bed, facing Zex rethinking his argument. "- think of the publicity, the Sponsorships then: First men to go to the North Continent. The unexplored world. The first chance in this generation for a huge diamond discovery. That should be good enough to sustain the treasury. As you say, everyone will want to invest in that."

Zex chuckled," Kline, have you been listening to any word I've said ? You are not the first to go to the North Continent ! Many people have traveled to the north. Of those who returned, and they have not been many - the majority of those poor wretches are not mentally competent anymore to publish anything and the very few who are . . . and they are very few indeed . . . will not, for fear they will be mocked and vilified. There is something terrible up there.

You think that you are special from anyone else ? That you had this glorious idea which no-one else has ever had ? You are just a rich man who wants to have a little fun, but this is deadly serious . . . "

There was a pause, Zex sighed and calmed down a little.

"I don't care if there is land up at the north, all I care about is if there are diamonds up there. No matter how much investment I get because of the publicity, it will do me nor anyone else any good, if I cannot buy diamonds and keep the power running. When the lights go out for good, our civilization will crumble like a house of dust. No matter how good our publicity is. No matter how famous you get - or I get. That is why I have funded so much money . . . " he said, taking a breath for a moment.

" So when you come to me and cry because of your lack of comfortability, I don't see any inconvenience as you do. I see a large disappointment of what I expect of you." King Zex strained. "I expect the hardness of diamonds."

Kline gasped nervously and then shifted on the edge of the bed.

Now he was in trouble. He was stuck in a tight situation where the Empire counted on him. This was no time for him to whine. Now he had to deal with the loathsomeness of Bringington and the jealousy that he had for Zex.

Yawning and nervous, Kline stood up from the bed. The dead girl bounced up and down.

Kline's mouth was pressed tightly together in embarrassment.

" Well I thank you for your explanation and your truthfulness. Now, that you've scared the shit out of me, if you will excuse me, I've got to leave."

Zex put his chin in his palm.

"Remember Kline, the Empire is counting on you and Bringington . . ." he said. "Only you can save her.."

Kline nodded. Then he stepped out.

Later that night, Kline returned to the bar and took a seat. It was chilled in the room of tables, and the business appeared to be slow. Only few soldiers of the Royal Guard, three of Bringington's expeditioneers, and a man who had laid his Bankra blade across the table.

Because of the quietness, Kline took out his journal and placed it on the table. Then he took out his wooden cuca box, feeling that it was an equal opportunity to indulge his eyes in reading as well as indulging his mind in cuca.

He dipped his finger into the soft powder and arched his finger. Watching the zestiness of the drug rest on his finger made his appetite grow. He brought it to his mouth and then rubbed his gums with it. He closed his eyes to lessen his heartbeat as he turned to his journal. Then he began to read a little bit:

" The articles of the Merchant Laws have been broken seven hundred and thirty two times by the Sudutan smugglers taking slaves from the colonies back to Prox . . . " he read.

He smiled, being reminded of the days when he was younger, working with Bringington to bring crime to light and criminals to justice.

" . . . But alas, where there is victory, there is always casualty . . . Bringington will have to fall if the criminals get the punishment they deserve . . ." he stopped and slowly closed his journal, dreading the truth about Bringington, a good man turned corrupt by the greed that Kline had uncovered. A man too worried about his self-image to make the desperate arguments and create the bald-faced lies that could have let him get away.

When Kline had published Bringington's manuscript, it had been more than simply an embarrassment. Bringington, without realizing it, had confessed in his own words, to misdeeds and corruption.

Kline breathed deeply to clear his thoughts. It was then that he heard Ennis approach him. He gazed up at her and smiled.

" Hello Ennis," Kline said humbly, being affected by the drug.

She raised a brow and then took a seat.

" You've come back. I thought that you had your fun." she said gaily.

Kline began to shake his leg." I'm not going to do that."

" You do care for me ?"

" No, of course not. But there would be suspicion if I did not come back to you . . . Bringington's men, you know . . . they saw us kissing that first night. Why they might think I had been trying to trick them and seek a terrible revenge." Kline muttered with a grin.

Ennis was charmed a little bit by his cynicism and quick wit.

" Oh yes, the suspicion about you."

She then turned and intentionally pointed at a soldier sitting at the bar.

" Oh look, an officer from Zimina, do you want to kiss me again
?" she said jokingly. "Only to keep up appearances ?"
Kline paused, a little embarrassed by her actions. Then he offered
her some cuca.
"I would kiss you, but it wouldn't be for escaping purposes like
last time." he said in retaliation.
She nodded,
"Ah, your intentions are to pay for my rape." she assumed.
He nodded.
Both chuckled a little. She then moved a little closer.
" You know, I find you to be interesting." she said, changing the
subject so that the interests would be appealing.
" Really ? Why's that ?"
" You are the first person who has not gloated to me about your
job . . . Why is that ?"
Kline gasped, suddenly feeling the effects of the drugs coming
into full play at the moment. He lowered his head into his hands as the
intensities crashed into his head.
" I haven't told you because I feel that it is unnecessary right now.
If I get associated with you, I'll never see the end of you . . . if not - I'll
never see you again."
She felt mildly insulted yet cherished his honesty.
He looked up with his lowering eyes. " But I hope to never see the
end of you at the moment." he inhaled a large portion of air, then be-
gan to speak once more. " I am a journalist who is being Sponsored by
the Prox division of journalism as well as the Council of Journalists
and the Emperor himself, to explore the North . . . " he said, liking
what he said.
She was not very interested in his job.
His smile began to drop.
" You're not impressed ?" he asked.
She sighed and leaned back in her chair.
" In other words, you've become another Imperial Conqueror for
the Crown ?" she asked.
Kline rolled his eyes up.
" I may be, I may be not. Depending if we find savages up there.
But it is diamonds I am Sponsored to conquer."

She placed her hand on the table slowly. "I find that to be a dreamer's statement. An unofficial position. Many say it, many die because of it . . . "

There was a long pause between them.

Kline studied her face and analyzed what she had said.

She continued to talk. "Haven't the Sudutans conquered enough land for themselves ? I mean, the lists for Sudutan citizenship of the world must be as long as the great oceans. That is one thing I will never understand about men, Sudutan men; they never feel that what they have is enough . . . " she went on.

Then Kline began to speak once more as soon as a valid question came up in his mind. " How is it that a woman of your stature knows so much of everything ?" he asked her.

She left her mouth open in mid-sentence, not understanding the question.

"What ?"

Kline rested both elbows on the table and closened his face to hers.

"You know how to make beautiful sayings. You anticipate every move that any man makes, and you comply with no fear to anyone who opposes you.

Take no offense when I say this; but you are one of the rudest, most aggressive, violent and yet you are possibly the easiest woman I have ever met."

She raised an eyebrow,

" Oh thank you, lover of great words . . . " she remarked sarcastically.

" . . . and I am aroused by it. Tell me how you received those characteristics."

She shook her head. "I was born and raised in the presence of men. No mother, no lady friends, only men."

Another moment of silence interrupted them as they sat on the table. It was then that Kline threw his hand over hers and then looked into her eyes.

" Will you come with me ?" he asked. The drugs were making him act this way. His feelings had no barriers at this moment.

"Where ?" Ennis asked.

" Come with me, to the north.

I can sign you up as a comfort girl, you can be with me throughout the trip . . . Please . . . " he pleaded to her.

She shook her head and smiled, unable to rationalize reality from his highness.

"I- I don't believe that you should be talking like this, especially when you have rubbed cuca on your gums . . . "

Kline shook his head violently.

" I guarantee you that the drugs have nothing to do with what I am saying. I am as sharp as you can make me. Will you go to the north with me ?"

Ennis gave a timid smile. Such a smile attracted a blush, something that has never been seen by any man at all.

She was taken by him and then nodded.

" Yes . . . Yes, I will go with you, Kline."

Kline smiled and then stood up, and began to make his way to the door.

She was bewildered,

"Wait, where are you going ?" she asked.

"Why, to fill out your papers of course."

Then he stepped out with a laugh.

Ennis grumbled a little and then stood up, knowing that, although her life had just changed forever, she still had to go back to work.

The next night had arrived and Kline sat at the table inside the barracks with his expeditioneers. His papers had been turned in with the request for specifically chosen comfort girls. He had not informed Dole about it yet, and was about to tell him.

Dusty and Squirrel had been working on their Drag Quads. Pieces of wiring, blobs of grease, and fasteners lay about the room. They were so scattered that Dav'inne tripped and aggressively picked up one of the pieces to throw at Squirrel.

Clubio and Luca laughed as they sat on the table, polishing their chain- linked, vital straps.

Dole took a sip from his Sponsor-provided drinks recently given to him with compliments of the Emperor King.

Kline sighed with a mild smile on his mouth and Dole continued to go on about the treasury. "So King Zex is spending over four million to fund this expedition ? How daft can a boy be ?" he muttered.

Kline nodded,"He's trying to gain a reputation of resembling his father, unfortunately everyone still hates him . . . "

Dole chuckled.

Kline turned his head to the others, " Do we salute the king ?" Kline asked them.

Clubio raised a brow, " May Marsolla strike him down in the day of Judgement !" he toasted, with the Emperor's own wine.

The others hollered in his favor.

Kline then turned to Dole, "Oh, by the way, speaking of Judgement Day, I've filled out the forms so that we can take comfort girls along."

Immediately, everyone's attention was focused on Kline.

Dole began to whisper, "Does this have anything to do with that savage girl in the bar you're after ?"

Kline looked ruffled.

" I believe that I paid for her fair and square." he replied.

Dole's mouth dropped.

"Your taste for women is repelling, I've lost all respect for you, Kline." Dole said, slightly shocked by the mental picture.

Young Vittorio, knotting his hairs, turned his head. " If you're taking a savage girl, then I'm taking one !" he demanded.

Kline turned with a frown suffering from annoyance. " Good, that makes two women."

Dav'inne then stood up from his bed post. "If Vittorio can take his slut than I can take my wife !"

Immediately a whole quarrel of voices came out. It had appeared that everyone had their own personal girl that they wanted to take along.

" . . . I've got a fifteen year old who's cheep to buy . . . I'm going to get her !" Dusty roared. The interest of the men raised as Kline buried his face in his palms.

Order had to be established so he jumped onto the table and kicked away all of the contraptions left on it. "PLEASE, CALM DOWN!" Kline shouted.

Everyone groaned and lowered their volumes.

Kline looked around."I am the leader of this Expedition, therefore I can bring my woman . . . "

He pointed to Clubio, " You are the Imperial officer . . . . That makes you the second most important so you can take your woman."
Clubio grinned.
Kline then pointed at Davi'nne, the medical person.
" You . . . " he panted. "You can pick the healthiest of the other women to take up . . . But for Gods sake man, if there's going to be partner sharing, leave your committed wife be . . . "
Dav'inne slowly nodded.
Kline looked at all of them and shook his head.
" Everyone Hold On To Your Sluts ! The maximum is three women . . . I've picked mine and the next two. Case closed . . . " he stated.
Kline gazed around reassuringly at the men slowing their arguments.
There was a quick silence and, as Kline departured from the table, Clubio went back to polishing his Vital once again.
Dole stood up and straightened out his cloak. Kline trotted a little on upon his last step to the ground as he motioned to Dole. "I believe that the situation is over with now." he said in a positive ponder.
Dole shook his head, as he made his way outside for a quick breath of fresh air.
Kline took a sigh of relief as he sat back at the table where Clubio and Luca casually sat.
Clubio had finished polishing, pleasingly throwing the Vital on diagonally across his chest.
"You think, this'd stop a slice from a Bankra ?" Clubio asked.
Luca raised a brow.
" No doubt you'd survive a slash across the chest but anywhere else, you'd be vulnerable." Luca said as he tightened the links with a pair of clamps.
Clubio gave a confident laugh.
"I beg to differ Luca. I was an Imperial Cummundore serving the crown ! I can handle my Bankra better than any man." Clubio said, slamming his well rounded Bankra blade onto the table. The main blade curved inwards, almost forming a perfect circle. "The Vital is only for looks. A clever swordsman can easily kill a man wearing one."
Luca was mildly impressed.

His eyes fell dark within the blue tattoo barred across his eyes. " You may have been a spoiled little Sudutan Cummundore, but I was a Long Range Observer during the Rage Wars. I was a one-man army, responsible for my assigned kills. I can use any pistol, any blade. Any time, any place. What I know, I know from experience, not theory. And I tell you that, no matter what your skills, you cannot penetrate the Vital with an ordinary Bankra. It can only be done with a specially altered blade - like the Rebels used. In fact, I can show you. I have the Bankra blade used by the rebel Sudutan, Jeffak," Luca said, walking over to his personal carry bags, and undrawing his holstered Bankra.

He undrew it, revealing a thinner blade only curving half way. It was not as well rounded but the advantage was with the extra blade on the other side of the handle.

" Bankra on top, knife on bottom," Luca said, as he walked over and placed it next to Clubio's blade.

"You can only beat the Vital on the back stroke."

Clubio gasped a little in impressment.

" Stories mean nothing unless you can prove them-" Clubio continued.

Kline paid no attention to the gloatings of Luca and Clubio. His focus was on the new box of cuca he received from his personal merchant.

As he opened up the box and slowly picked out the wooden straw, Bringington, dressed in black, wearing tightened brown leather padding over his belly and shoulders as well as the darkly, well grooved Vital strap across his chest, grabbed Kline by the frill of his garment and quickly threw him to the ground. All happening before Kline could react.

" What in the Hell are you doing ?" Kline asked torturedly.

Bringington gave a fearsome frown.

" You tricky bastard of a man !" was the only answer given.

Everyone in the barracks stood up as they watched Bringington quickly drag Kline out into the open.

The others followed Bringington to see what was going on.

Bringington then picked Kline up by the collar and violently threw him onto the hardened stone floor again. The impact caused a few of his teeth to wabble.

Bringington circled around him as he shook his head.

"You went to King Zex, questioned his plans, and risked the loss of his Sponsorship because of your petty little quarrels with me ?

I thought that we were to be feigned friends, Kline ... " Bringington said.

Kline made it to his feet and brushed the dirt off his cassock.

"There was no risk of losing the mission you little bald idiot !" Kline scald.

Bringington growled, undrew the Bankra Blade from his back holster and slowly approached Kline.

Kline began to circle, weaponless, hoping to grab one of the weapons that lay around the room. Instead, Bringington kicked the back of Kline's leg, causing him to fall over once more.

"Oh, yes there was. The King told me that he is beginning to feel sceptical about the whole expedition because of you." Bringington then began to back up, rolling his blade around in his hand.

Kline grunted from the pain of the kick, then struggled to stand up. "I believe that you're too paranoid for your own good ! You mad, twisted little mess !" Kline shouted furiously, losing his Warrior's Tongue in his fury.

Bringington stormed over to Clubio and pulled his blade away from him. Clubio didn't say a word, knowing that it wouldn't be wise for the moment.

Bringington threw the blade to Kline.

" Pick up the Bankra !" he snapped stepping backwards to make room.

Kline slowly grasped the handle and brought it to knees length.

"Bringington, this is ridiculous. The King will continue with the expedition. Trust me, I know what he said -" Kline gestured calmingly, as if taking to a dog or a mental patient.

His calming gesture was unfortunately misjudged. This only made Bringington more furious. His eyes grew large and his jaw tightened

" Trust you ? I was betrayed by you and thrown into colonial prison camps. Do you know what they do to you there ? They burn the top scalp of your head so that you will never grow a thick mane of hair ever again. They make you eat, sleep, and excrete in a room small enough for a man's coffin to be placed.

They take away your dignity, your class, and your identity over there. So if you believe that Sponsorship from the King means nothing, or what the King feels means nothing, or even what I tell you means nothing, I suggest you take a history lesson from me, Kline.

What happened to me will most definitely happen to you. I'll make sure of it !"

Bringington then raised his Bankra and stormed towards Kline with martial spins and rolls from his weapon. Kline brought up his Bankra and used it to block Bringingtons' grind-like slice.

Both blades rode off each other's curves.

This was a traditional challenge for a duel. Kline brought his face closer to Bringington and gritted his teeth.

" Bringington, you greasy little toad. I will not accept."

Bringington grinned, "But you have to. Or else you aren't considered a Sudutan Gentleman.

If you turn down, I win. That'll only prove that I'm more of a man than you are. Think about it, you have a lot more to show off than a simple duel. Your team seems to believe that you're all tongue and no teeth. A weak old lama, gone in the teeth. Just look at the way they view you."

Kline snorted, trying to resist bringing himself into a Bankra duel for he believed that it didn't resolve anything and also because he was never any good at using the clumsy blade.

Kline lowered his blade. " I'm sorry, but I would rather not fight you."

Bringington nodded slowly. " So you agree that I am the better man than you are ?"

"The better man in insecurity . . . " Kline said under his breath.

"What ?" Bringington asked.

Kline looked up and frowned. He was rethinking the duel, knowing that his pride was on the line.

"Nothing." he said as he quickly as he tightened his grip over his blade and bashed the side into Bringington's Vital strap. This was an acceptance to the duel.

" What would this world come to if there were no more Sudutan Gentlemen like you and me ? " Kline asked taut-lipped as he backed up for room.

Bringington growled as he took three steps towards Kline, swinging his blade powerfully at him. Kline ducked out of the way and ran past him, keeping his own blade in front of him.

Bringington turned around and rested his Bankra across his shoulder, holding out his other arm.

"If there were no Sudutan Gentlemen, and there would only be savages. I'd be king instead of an expedition leader !

You'd be someone's slave or concubine, you little woman." Bringington replied.

Kline sneered as he frantically swung outwards trying to catch Bringington by surprise, but Bringington, only swayed a little to avoid the wild swings.

Bringington gave a smile.

" What are you doing ?" he asked as Kline roared away, chopping down with the blade.

" .... Trying to lop off your limbs ... " Kline shouted, stepping to the side and swinging to his shoulder.

Bringington ducked and then rotated his round blade outwards to clang it loudly on Kline's Vital.

"See what I said" Luca pointed out.

Clubio nodded.

Kline staggered back from the blow, unhurt, but threw his arms up.

Bringington made a quick move and his Bankra flipped Kline's loosely-held blade away.

Kline jerked backwards and Bringington lowered his weapon to lean on it as he crouched down.

"The Bankra is a weapon of delicacy. Used for quick slices and elongated incisions. You're a born Sudutan and you can't even hold a Bankra right. And you call yourself the Warrior !" he said.

The men standing around broke into a mild laughter.

Kline raised a brow as he picked up his Bankra and held the blade to his chest.

" It's the Warrior's Tongue ! Learn to read you illiterate, toothless whore !" Kline yelled, now charging towards Bringington, swinging his whole body into motion.

Bringington yawned, "Well then, Lick this, Tongue boy,"

Bringington stepped to the side and neatly knocked the sword out of Kline's hands again.

"This is pathetic . . . " he said as he threw up his own blade into the air, grabbed a hold of Kline's leg, pulled him to the ground, grabbed the spindling blade with one hand, and grabbed Kline's hair with the other.

As Bringington lowered the hook of the blade to his neck. Kline was fearfully impressed by his quick reflex.

Kline moved his eyes around to see the reactions of the others.

They were startled as well.

Kline gasped, feeling the pressing hook's cold pain slowly cutting into his skin.

" Well then, are you going to kill me or not ?" asked Kline, sounding brave, but closing his eyes in terror.

Bringington panted as he tugged on Kline's hair.

"As much as I am tempted to, I can't kill you now. If you tell me that King Zex is continuing with the plan, you and I are friends. And as long as Zex funds us, we will remain friends.

I fought you just to prove a point; I can kill you at anytime and anyplace. Don't frighten me like that ever again, friend . . . " he said as he pulled the Bankra blade away from Kline's neck. He then put it back in his fat, rounded holster.

Kline dropped to his palms and choked, feeling to see how deep of an incision was made. There was no cut.

"I hope this has been very insightful for you Kline." Bringington said.

"See you in the North," he finished with an amused laugh.

Kline grunted and hit the floor with his fist. He then stood up and looked at his crew. His adrenaline pumped through his veins. He wanted to get him back, but knew that he'd die trying it.

Clubio lowered his eyes from Kline as he picked up his blade. Kline was too humiliated to say anything. Even if he wanted to speak, the men wouldn't listen.

They then went back to sitting around the barracks, as if nothing ever happened. Kline swore and grumbled to himself. He didn't want to say anything, so he left to the only place he had any shred of dignity at all; to Ennis' bar .

Kline casually strolled into the semi-packed bar. The dim blue lights glowed over his brownish red cassock. In the warm humid air, it made him feel more uncomfortable as sweat beads seeped into existence over his forehead. He looked around in the hopes of seeing the eyes of his beloved Ennis but she was nowhere to be found. Only her largely packed father lay present at the ordering cage. The Bar was very much alive with laughter and joke telling, for the advisors of King Zex were putting their pay to good use. Kline wondered if Zex himself was there, fearing that another conference with him would push Bringington off the wall once again.

As he strolled down the entrance way, he noticed Dole sitting at the same table he sat at the day Kline first saw Ennis. It was a vivid moment for him so it symbolized a sign for him as well. His grim smile grew as he came closer to pull up a chair.

Dole gazed up at him with the look of a drunkard. Kline shook his head in disgust.

" Dole, do you always have to drink out the evening ?" he asked.

Dole turned up his chin, unconsciously swaying from side to side.

" Of course I have to drink. I'm a Sudutan traditionalist ! Without the traditions of Marsolla, we'd all be lost." he boasted as he grabbed a cup filled to the top with rice whiskey. He sipped the top of it. His glowing red cheeks gave a soothing aura.

Kline leaned into his chair with a look of concern in his eyes.

"Tradition ? More like addiction I believe." Kline mentioned.

Dole gave a sarcastic smile to him.

" You talk," he muttered, " Don't let me start with your lust for the cuca, my good friend. No one goes through the amount of boxes you go through in a month. Going back to your comment, I believe that it is a tradition for a young Sudutan conqueror to take his share of wine from the grail of Marsolla. Besides if it's my addiction, then it's also my one night stand before the great venture to the North. No more civilization, no more hygiene, no more drink, no more cuca . . . " Dole explained as he took a guzzle. "If both of us are gone for any length of time, the entire economy may collapse."

Kline nodded and slowly took out a miniature cuca box he carried in his strap pocket.

He opened up the rounded top and placed it next to his nostril. He sniffed up and then quickly closed the box.

" Stalemate to your reply, my good friend. Stalemate . . . " Kline said in a tortured voice.

He waited for a few seconds for the drug to circulate through his body. As he shook his head to get rid of the acute pain aches from the drug, he noticed the Sponsors gathering to a longer table near the back of the bar.

There, Ennis was tending to the bottles of expensive alcohol. Kline then felt his whole body sit up as his heart lightened. But Ennis did not notice him.

"Ah, there she is . . . My own woman." Kline proudly stated.

Dole gazed back and forth from Kline to Ennis. Dole nodded a little and took another drink from his elongated cup.

" Speaking of addictions . . . Well, you better get a hold of her before Zex does. He's here you know ?" Dole mentioned.

Kline's face then fell into fear. He knew that Zex was bloodthirsty for women, the same way jaguars were blood thirsty for new borns. If Zex made arrangements with the father already, then Ennis was as good as dead. He gasped in fear as he thought of the consequences being made. His arm pressed onto the table.

" Has Zex talked with her father yet ?" Kline frantically asked.

Dole yawned. " The father ?"

" The large man over there !" Kline pointed.

Dole took a keen look at the overweight man.

His lip pressed inward tightly as he turned, " I do believe that Zex and the large man talked for a while." Dole replied.

Kline's heart then sank. It was almost too late for him to save her now. His dream of the perfect woman ruined by Royalty. His hands trembled as he rested them on the top of the table.

Kline lowered his head in doom.

Dole watched his hands vibrate the table.

" I'm surprised that you're having such a fit over a rude woman. Like I said before, she should have been dead long ago . . . " Dole said, trying to comfort him.

Kline shook his head. "No . . . Not like this, not her. She's the one . . . She's the perfecone . . . " Kline stated.

Dole's eyes widened in bewilderment, not able to believe what he was hearing.

"Kline, you've only known her a few days at the most, how can you say such things ?" Dole asked.

Kline gazed his strengthening eyes towards him.

" That was all the time I needed . . . " he said, slowly standing up.

Dole began to worry,

"Kline, what are you thinking about ?" Dole concertedly asked.

"There might still be time to save her !" Kline gallantly said as he slowly began to walk.

Dole's mouth dropped.

In Kline's mind, his goal was love and he was trying to accomplish it. But in Dole's mind, logic and greed were the main goals and they trying to assert themselves.

"Kline. I think that you're not right in the head at this time . . . It's the cuca that's doing this, isn't it ?" Dole squirmed.

Kline shook his head as he puffed up his chest, staring at Ennis.

"The drug doesn't take much effect for another within fifteen seconds or so." Kline said, as though he knew what he was talking about.

Dole then stood up and went in front of him.

"Kline ! If you go through with this, Zex might scrap the whole expedition. Try to be reasonable about this. No more Elders, No more dream. All that you and I have worked for will have been for nothing." Dole said keeping him from moving any further.

Kline closed his eyes and paused.

Then he gracefully pushed Dole into an empty chair and continued on, not even thinking about what he was going to do as he began to come closer to the Royal table.

Dole grew fearful and jerked himself up to stop him. He was not going to throw away his chance for a leap of prosperity all because of Kline's lust. To him, it was crucial for feelings to remain perfect and under brow as well as confidential.

Zex was happily installed in a lavishly built chair, brought over from his Royal suite.There he sat, near the center of the table, his thin, dark-lined face glowed with charm, his shortened hair, dyed in Royal orange colors reflected glee, and with his strong hands, crossed across his chest, he resembled the perfect picture of a confident soul.

His aura was strong in the presence of most of the men and his rich texture of topics made it easy for all the feigned friends to stay in a constant state of interest. But his eyes followed the motions of Ennis. He winked at her as she poured him a drink at the table, then held her arm as she prepared to leave for another bottle.

"Wait for a moment," Zex asked her.

She smiled obediently, knowing not to disobey a King.

Ennis faked a smile to hide her discomfort. She had been informed by her father that Zex requested to pay for her body during the evening.

She felt complimented by being chosen by a King, but otherwise, for her, it was just another job in what seemed like an endless series.

Ennis slowly came closer to Zex and sat herself gently on his lap. He then wrapped one of his arms around her waist and firmly fastened her within his grasp.

His aggressiveness showed as he clamped her neck and forcefully placed the bottom of his jaw over her shoulder.

" Oh, my. Your highness, I feel . . . gratified that you have chosen me for the evening." she said, already intimidated by his molestations.

Zex sniffed her hair and moved his hands to grip her side.

" Your skin. Your hair, and your features are all exotic to me . . . I felt that I had to have you . . . " he said seductively with a stare that showed fascination more than lustfulness.

Zex stopped talking and began to further his fondling. Ennis trembled, feeling more abstract every time she sensed the solid clutch of his hands around her. But she was used to such things and knew how to put up with it.

The Sponsor advisors, who sat in a crowd around him, paid no attention and now that Zex had dropped out of the conversation, continued to maintain a debate on a field of their interest; which was property assets growing over in the colonies.

The moment only became awkward when Kline appeared and pounded his knuckles to the table.

Immediately, all conversation came to a halt.

Dole was too late in restraining Kline and slowly tried to tap him on the shoulder, but as soon as Kline pounded on the table Dole froze as well, thinking that Kline would be punished more severely than he would.

Zex gritted his teeth, irritated by the pounding that had so rudely interrupted his Royal erotic feelings.

Ennis' eyes widened as Kline approached. She still felt too abstract to say anything but her natural gestures revealed a breath of relief.

"Kline . . . " Zex worded irritatedly.

Kline gave a stinging glance at the Emperor King. His heart pounded and leaped as his jealousy and bias against Zex flowed directly from his unconscious.

" King Zex, I must talk to you at once . . . " he stated briefly.

Zex rolled his eyes, showing annoyance to Kline. Zex believed that he was going to complain once again about Bringington or the Instructor, or the actual town itself.

" What is this about now ? Bringington ? How dare you interrupt my humble feast for such petty issues which resolve nothing. I've told you to live with it !" he ordered without patience.

Kline turned his attention to Ennis.

"This is pertaining to another matter. May we talk somewhere more confidential ?" Kline asked.

Zex shook his head and growled with a pause after every sentence:

" You bypassed my guards to interrupt me earlier today. You interrupt me again during my supper. You suggest privacy for yourself. Do you have any consideration at all, or were you born a rude, vulgar man ?" he asked out loud.

Kline turned to his side and leaned to the table. His other hand rested on his hip.

" I, respect you by all means, Zex. I just feel that the topic I want to discuss has more to do with the girl. Nothing about the policies about the expeditions or the Sponsorships." he explained.

Zex gave a nervous chuckle to his comment. He was feeling more and more harassed by Kline for his appearances at embarrassing times seemed chronic and never ending.

"This is about this girl ? This slut which I am attached to ?" Zex shook the girl on his lap.

Ennis was slightly insulted and immediately tapped Zex's head, catching him by surprise.

"Mind what you're saying your Highness !" Ennis said out loud, "I am a queen in my own country." she joked. But then she fell into an apology, realizing that her temper had gotten out of hand and the King was not laughing.

Zex hissed and tightened his grip around her neck. Ennis' eyes widened as her face flushed.

Kline watched with a gasp.

It was then that Zex noticed the care in their eyes as they looked at one another.

He immediately knew what was going on and released her.

She fell to the floor, choking for the air.

Zex slowly stood. " Kline, have you really come to me to discuss this girl, nothing more, nothing else ?" he asked bargainingly.

Kline watched as Ennis came to her senses and stood, rubbing the sides of her swelling neck.

Kline turned back to Zex and nodded.

" Nothing else will come up for argument, I swear by the words of Marsolla." Kline pleaded.

Zex sighed,

" You and me . . . . in the private room !" he snapped, pulling Kline by the shoulder as they walked into a back storage room.

Zex dropped the flaps to the door and came close to Kline. The brightness of his orange hair began to darken for the lights in the room were slim to keep the goods in storage cool and dry.

Kline was impressed by the absence of sound created by the flaps of the door and paced backwards as Zex came close.

There was a long pause of abstract thinking going on with the both of them. Zex wondered about Ennis, the girl who had smacked him, how it angered him as well as fed his interest for her.

Kline wondered whether Zex would be calm and considerate or ghastly and violent as Kline has seen lately of him.

Then Zex spoke.

" So you wanted to talk about the girl . . . Talk now," he said calmly.

Kline pressed his hands together and then gave a stiffened nod.

" This girl, Ennis . . . I feel very misfortunate that you have found her charming."

Zex breathed in deeply. He was a little overwhelmed by Kline, now finding out that his one night stand happened to turn out to be the love interest of the young journalist.

He gave a nervous, overwhelming smile and wiped the cold sweat breaking across his royal crown. " Not only do you irritate me, but it turns out that my lust for the evening is yours as well. Will I ever be free from you, Kline ?" he sneered at him, immediately pacing backwards.

Kline leaned against one of the slanted shelves of the room.

" I promise you, King Zex. If you let Ennis go, I'll never file another complaint to you again . . . I'll find you another comfort girl for the evening." Kline pleaded, "An even more exotic one."

Zex looked at his nails with a loathsome expression imprinted on his face."Ever since I arrived here in Prox, you've given me nothing but moans and complaints. You remind me of a hounding dog waiting to die." Zex said to him."If you hound me like this, then I shall treat you like a dying dog . . . I do have sympathy for those in need, this is my job as a Loyal King and I see that you are in desperate need of saving.

Therefore, I'm going to enjoy breaking her in as I make incisions into her wrists . . . since I will be doing it for you as well as for myself. You see, I'll be curing you of her.

Permanently.

A healing performed by myself for you, my dear Kline." he finished coldly, turning his attention to his hair as he got ready to step out of the doors.

"The courtship between a man and a woman should be strictly for business contracts as well as political gain. It should never be for the sickness of love, for love can be fatal." Zex added as he reached for the dampening flaps of the door.

Kline paused, speechless to the coldness of Zex. At that moment, all of his anger, jealousy and irritance for the young Sudutan King came out. The final trigger to release all of his tensions toward him was the constantly growing love-sickness which was plaguing him.

Kline slammed his arm and blocked Zex from stepping outwards.

"You are a tyrant of a man !" Kline shouted grabbing Zex by his royal band and throwing him against the wall.

Zex ground his teeth as he straightened himself up. " Kline, what in Marsolla's name are you thinking about ?" he asked, immediately grabbing hold of Kline's body band and slapping him hard across the face.

Kline shook the tingles of the smack and grunted at him. " I have never liked you ... Ever since the beginning when you were crowned, you spoiled little boy !" Kline shouted as he worked his way to grab the King.

Zex immediately gripped Kline by the shoulders, slamming him into a shelf continuously until he was calm again. Zex fastened him by the neck, keeping him on the spot he leaned against.

" After I even stated that I was going to cure you, you still act this way ?"

"You were going to save me through your own hunger for lust. That is not the signs of a martyr, but of a glutton." Kline interrupted.

Zex leaned closer to his face, concerned with the new snapping he was enduring. " Can't you see that this sickness has gone right to your head ? Now you're obsessed about that girl. I thought that there was no way for a man of your stature to fall so low as this, to risk everything over a woman of savage immigrant descent."

Kline grabbed onto Zex's hand, which was then fastened over his neck, and stressed to loosen it up.

" You call me a fool for indulging myself in a savage woman, yet see no problem in a boy like you indulging yourself. Such hypocrisy. Ruining lives on a whim. Your father wouldn't stand for any of it ... " he snapped in gasps.

Zex's lips tensed as his brow lowered. He hated it when people contradicted him or tested his insecurity about his dead father's approval. Thus in retaliation, he attacked Kline, the man with the Warrior's Tongue with the only ruthless strategy he could think of in the situation; extortion.

" You are willing to give up everything you hold so dear for this young woman, just for the lust ?" Zex asked as he paused.

Kline then nodded without a second thought.

Zex then continued. " I can see that you believe that you are a man who can take advantage of any situation just because you can fall back on the prestige of this expedition to the North.

Don't believe it a minute longer.

I can tell you that you are the least of anything. You are expendable, for there will always be sneering little scribes like you who will dream about adventure and will endure anything for a chance at fame and riches... My father had many of them and so shall I.

Your only part in this is to fail. We will stir up publicity about the Great Race and you both will go off to the North - but you will fail. You know nothing of expeditioneering. You cannot lead your men. You have no plan and no idea of what to do with diamonds should you find any.

You are a small actor in this play.

When you shall fail, all the credits will only be appointed to Bringington. Where you fall vulnerable, he shall be there as an untouchable. It is not a conspiracy. It is destiny. He is a high born Sudutan, schooled in leadership and conquest. You are a low-born foundling, raised by peasants. I really couldn't care less whether you make it or he does. The credit will circulate back to me. But breeding will excerpt itself. Your blood is too low to succeed in this.

But I now give you a choice as a good and fair king:

You can have your savage girl tonight. Right now. But there is a price. A small price to pay for everlasting love, but a price nonetheless.

The price is that you will be cut from the Sponsorship program as well as from the expedition, severed from all governmental ties and counsels all over the Empire. Your payment cash will be discontinued immediately and the record files of your identification burned into ashes, destroying any chance of work or travel for the rest of your life.

Not only that but you would have to pay back the treasury for your expedition expenses in full, so far.

A small price to pay for the woman you choose to love . . .

The other choice is simple; let me continue my lust for the girl, never bother me ever again and continue to show a happy face to all.

If you do this, your life will continue on. Your Expedition will be documented, your credit with the government will be honored, your traveling expenses will be paid, and your application to the ELDERS will be accepted.

Your name would be published in every history journal throughout the colonies as well as in all the Sudutan lands.

275

Choose the girl and you will be a failure of the people.

Choose to permit me to have the girl, and you will be a successful hero of the Sudutan Empire . . .

What will it be ?" Zex then paused, leaving him with the options to consider.

His face backed slowly, as did his grip over Kline's neck.

Kline thought many things in his mind. He loved her dearly and was willing to be with her until the end of time, but he loved his career as a highly recognized man of Sudutan Atlantis even more. He knew that Zex would win either way out of these choices. This made the situation even more desperate.

He knew that Zex was like any other rich young aristocrat; charming, exciting, and thirsting for young women to kill.

Within Kline's mind there was no true way out.

Kline loved Ennis, but not enough to stand in the way of his career. The fact of the matter was that Kline lived for this expedition and to leave it all behind him because of a woman was insane. It was painful to tell his conclusion to the man who was going to kill the only woman Kline ever loved. Nonetheless, it had to be said before Zex would take control of the situation.

Kline tensed his face as he forced his grey, water-filling eyes to the level of Zex.

His lips trembled as his head rocked in nervousness.

" You can assure me a seat with the Elders ?" he grimly asked, his decision already made.

Zex grinned as he patted him on the back.

" I am King . . . " he stated convincingly to him.

Both Kline and Zex came out of the storage room silently.

Zex, with a smile on his face rejoiced and ordered another bottle of rice whiskey for his advisers.

Kline looked up at him with weary eyes, wondering how could such a man have no morals, but it was then that he realized that it was he himself who had no morals at all.

Zex, a man who was under the influence of the culture was not the executioner but the victim. The practice of paying peasantry for raping and killing their daughters had been a tradition continued for over five hundred years. It was a normal practice.

And Zex was a normal person while Kline was merely the sceptical one who questioned it.

And who was he to argue with the tradition.

Kline came out and passed Ennis. He hesitated at her glance. She smiled and placed her hand on his face. She came closer to him to give him a kiss. She did.

" Thank you for what you have done for me. Speaking up like that. I thought that the Emperor King might buy me forever - but as long as it's just for tonight, I can stand it." she whispered in relief.

Kline held her hand and slowly lowered it. Hearing those words of naiveness made his heart leap with guilt. He feigned a smile and gasped;

"Yes . . . Nothing can stand in the way of you and I. You will be forever in my mind and I will climb to the top of society for you . . ." he said.

Kline dropped her hand and began to storm towards the door, holding in his mournful grief.

Ennis then followed a few steps.

" Will you pick me up tomorrow ? To get ready for the trip ?" she asked him happily.

Kline stopped midway from the door. He felt the eyes of Zex stalking him, to see if he was keeping to his word. Because of this he refused to turn around and face her in fear of telling her the truth, that he had sacrificed her for his own personal gain.

So in the simplest words he could mutter he nodded and then said,

" . . . Yes . . . " and made his way towards the door, never able to have the satisfaction of her pleasant look ever again.

All he could remember her for was her naive thanks to him and her happy face, expecting to be with him soon - her hero. The man who had stood up for her against a King.

Her face showed that, in the very moment when he had betrayed her, she had loved him more than she had ever loved anyone.

It was something he would never forget.

At some level, however, Kline really thought that he had done the right thing. His expedition was still in production and Bringington seemed to be pleased. His ascension to the Elders was guaranteed.

His life was on an upward track.

All that Kline had done was for the benefit of himself, yet he did not feel the benefit. His temporary madness for Ennis threw him further on into self analysis.

He left the bar and moped.

Later through the night, he neglected to return to the air base to rest up and instead, wandered the thinning streets of Prox in deep thought about Ennis in relation to himself.

" Why would such a woman arouse me for such an elongated period of time, and why would it make my own confidence plummet so low as to bring tears from my disciplined eyes ?" he wondered, replaying all the conversations with Ennis he ever had - which were very few.

He had only known her for such an instant, that it should have never taken such effect. Kline came close to the square-ish stadium where he had watched the wins and losses of many golden heads. He sat himself on the steps facing Ennis' bar right across the street, still in deep thought.

Then he began to try and fit in the element of Zex, the man who pushed him in the direction he had went, so willingly.

"Zex told me that love is a sickness which can infect anyone at the slightest touch. Could it be true, that all of the suffering I go through is because of the sickness. Did I have no control of what I was feeling at all and was only led by the germs which came through my own nostrils into my head ?" Kline asked himself.

As he faced the bar, he began to hear the sounds of Ennis' laughter. He felt her presence standing in front of him, loving him still. His heart pounded as tears began to fall from his eyes. He shook his head, feeling his emotions coming over his own strong will.

His head lost to his heart. Again.

Kline finally got a hold of himself and stood from the stairs. He wiped the tears from his eyes, feeling the sting of his dissipating masculinity to the evening breeze. As soon as he controlled his obnoxious trauma he started across the deserted street for the bar, hoping to seek comfort from his own deconstruction.

He knocked on the door and hoped for someone to open it even though it was long after the hours of business.

Still, Kline continued to knock, this time louder and more prominent with every other pound.

His confusion and anger made his persistence go on, until he felt his knuckles beginning to bleed. Rather than stopping him, this whipped him toa new urgency. He started to bang on the door with both hands, beating upon it as if it were a person.

Suddenly the door swung open and Ennis' father who was in his night gown, furiously grabbed Kline's arms.

"What in Marsolla's name are you trying to do man?" he asked him.

Kline struggled to loosen the grips of the large man.

" Calm yourself down before I call the Imperial Guard on you!" he threatened.

Kline frowned and pulled his hands away from the man's grasp.

"Oh yes, then let them come so that I can toast them a drink. Marsolla knows that I am in desperate need of one." Kline said, lowering his head.

The large man wondered about Kline. He barely even recognized him at all.

"What is your business here, young man?" he asked.

Kline merely slumped over to a table and pulled out a chair. "May I sit down before the Imperial Guards come?" Kline asked him. The man sighed and gestured his hand for him to sit down.

The large man then made his way to the table where Kline was making himself a little more comfortable.

"Explain yourself young man," he requested as he eased himself into a chair. Obviously, the man had not thought of him as important when he paid for his daughter a few days before.

Kline leaned a little forwards,

"Sir, I was the one who payed for your daughter a few days before. My name is Kline, Sir." Kline mentioned with concern.

The man stroked his beard with a weary glimpse.

" Oh, yes. I remember who you are . . . It's the assumption to why you're here that bothers me . . . Ennis isn't here, so should you be here?" he asked sternly.

Kline nervously rubbed his hands together, feeling chills go down his back.

"I felt that I had to come here, almost like a commitment that I owed: To mourn for her." Kline said softly.

The man merely rose a brow.

" To mourn for her ? Is she dead ? She is in the Emperor's care now. She was a burden for me as well as this bar, always arguing with the customers, refusing to go with some of the men. Why should you mourn such a woman ?" he asked.

Kline sat up straight, feeling the lack of respect for Ennis from her own father. Kline was surprised. Out of all of the criticism made on her by Dole and other men, why would her own father also take on their side instead of his own daughter ?

" That was very disrespectful on your part, sir." Kline acknowledged to him.

The man frowned,

" Bah, you're such a woman. You knew that she was a strong girl, too strong for anyone to tame. This was bound to happen anyways. I was surprised that it didn't occur sooner. She was a woman who had dreams and we as men should know that a woman with a dream is as dangerous as the most vicious of beasts." he stated.

Kline's mouth dropped when he heard the man's statement aloud, although it was certainly a thought that many a man had silently.

"She was your daughter. How could you say such things about her ?" Kline asked in a snippy manner.

" I can say such things because I was her father ! And when you are father to a daughter, this is the fate that you know awaits her. She will be sold to a gentleman or taken on the streets by a band of ruffians. I lived with that knowledge every day. I was the one who raised her to be obedient, I was the one who carried her to Prox when I opened shop, I was the one who fed her and gave her sleeping quarters, and I was the one who finally sold her to the highest Bidder: Emperor Zex - imagine my daughter - a Royal concubine."

Kline slowly stood from his seat, feeling the conversation becoming a little more heated for his comfort.

"Then may I ask you if you've been paid by the Emperor King ?" he asked loudly.

The man stood up as well.

" I will be expecting five thousand tomorrow." he said.

Kline leaned on the back of the chair,
" Five thousand. Such a cheap price for a daughter like yours !" Kline said with a sting of anger.

The man took a breath to calm himself down. He knew what Kline was trying to do; make him feel guilt for selling his daughter. He was not going to be talked down by a spoiled man who wanted the perfect fruits of life.

" What has been done has been done. There's nothing you or I could do now. Let us leave it at that." he said, trying to bring an end to the conversation.

But Kline resisted. " But you could have refused to sell Ennis for a few extra credits on your part."

"And you could have convinced him for other persuasions. I saw you come to the table and demand him to stop what he was doing. But, like me, you threw her life away for the benefit of your own career." he interrupted.

Kline was silent. The man went on.

" So you come here to accuse me of your own faults so that you could clear yourself of all sins. You believe that I have no morals yet you do the same and expect to be praised. I may be filled with greed but at least I can say that I am. You are no better than I. For both of us sold Ennis for money and success."

There was a long pause between the two.

Kline kept his eye on the man and fell into deep thought.

The man was right about the situation. Kline was no better than the stingy bar owner standing before him. Between them both, neither had the conception of a good moral to believe in. Kline realized this and concluded that nothing more was able to be said.

Kline then drew his money pouch and threw it onto the table . The man looked at the pouch, estimating about seven thousand in it.

Kline gasped, "Condolence payment for the mourning of your daughter. " he uttered as he made his way for the door.

The man picked up the pouch and stuffed it into his pocket,
" I thank you for the payment Kline, and I accept it - not to pay for Ennis, but to pay for your guilt. But the Emperor is obligated to do the payment." the man said with concern, "So you see - she wasn't so cheaply after all."

"Think of it as insurance for her soul. Just in case he doesn't pay for her. Good evening." Kline mentioned as he stepped out and made his way back to the air base.

"More insurance for your own, young man." the big man sighed as he locked up after Kline, put the bag of money in a safe place, and then went back to bed to sleep soundly.

I was crying. I couldn't stop myself.

"Oh that's so sad. " I said. "That bastard ! How could he just give her up like that?"

The Old Man was silent for a moment.

"I've never understood it myself. " he said, sounding a bit teary himself.

"But maybe she didn't die." I tried to talk my way out of it. "You never said she was really dead. Maybe the Emperor didn't kill her. Maybe she survived . . . "

"God, I've always hoped so." he said.

I was becoming dreary eyed from the emotions.

The Old Man paused to rest his eyes a little.

I slowly stood up and yawned as he rubbed his eyes.

The Old Man then looked at me. " I think that was going to be the last part I tell tonight, was that right ?" he asked.

I nodded, feeling too tired to bother to speak to him.

The Old Man turned and pointed to the boat in the dim moon- light. "Tomorrow boy, we make our final adjustments to it, then we sail out past the Peaks of Stone."

" What ? I thought that the boat was already to sail to Atlantis." I asked, breaking my vow of tiredness not to speak.

The Old Man laughed at my question. " We can't expect to sail a long journey without starting somewhere, boy, now can't we. It's not just a day's journey, you know. It's only once we get past the Peaks that this journey really begins." he said.

"Oh," I replied, re-establishing my vow once more.

The Old Man slowly sat back down.

" Well boy, I think that I overdid it tonight." he said.

I stared at him rather puzzledly. " You're tired, and I don't blame you, tonight's telling was quite long. Even for me."

" That's alright Old Man, the more detail and dialogue you give me, the more I can imagine the story in my mind and remember it." I said as I yawned. "But I wish it didn't end so sad." I wiped my eyes again. " Well good night Old Man." I finished.

" Until tomorrow night, then. And I'll see if I can change the sadness into something interesting, boy." he said enthusiastically.

" Right Old Man.." I said, too tired to care.

The sounds of extreme hammering and shouts filled the afternoon air. We were leaving on our Grand Adventure.

"We need more ropes over here !" shouted one man working on tying down and fastening the main sail.

" Place the barrel below deck !" shouted another, sticking his head through the trap door of the deck.

Everyone was making their last minute adjustments to the boat.

The Old Man, who was ordering them around, walked onto the deck as they all got the supplies ready. All day, most of the crew were taking barrels of water and fastening them tightly into the hold areas that the Old Man had told them to make.

I, on the other hand, was working with most of the other crew members, pulling the ropes tied to the bow of the ship and helping to pull it off the beach.

The boat was tremendous in length and although the back end was in about two feet of water, the front and most of the length was still on the sand. It was proving almost impossible to drag it to the water.

" Pull, damn you !" came a large yell from Likooshas who was also pulling.

Slowly, the boat began to move, but only inch by inch and for every inch it moved toward the water, it seemed to sink down a few inches in the sand.

The Old Man was amused as he saw most of the crew, standing in the water, hooked to ropes, like beasts of burden, all trying to pull the ropes to get the boat out to where it would float.

He stood there, watching us. We all saw him, keeping himself from breaking into laughter.

"Pull harder!" Likooshas shouted once more, trying to motivate the men, expecting us all to have super strength.

The sounds of the men struggling as they pulled and strained were loud. Likooshas continued to call out and the men continued to groan.

The Old Man then grinned happily, unable to contain himself any longer. "What is it that you're trying to do?" he shouted.

Likooshas ignored his rantings and continued to call out "Pull!"

"You're not going to get anywhere pulling something that weighs this much."

Likooshas looked up to the Old Man. "Watch us!" he shouted furiously. He then looked at all of us.

"PULL AS IF YOUR LIFE DEPENDED ON IT!" he shouted as his eyes widened. We all pulled our hardest, straining, groaning, and utterly tiring ourselves. The boat finally gave in, moving three more inches closer to the water.

The Old Man, feeling the whole boat moving, or more exactly - not moving - continued to laugh at us all.

Likooshas was out of breath. He let go of the rope and then huffed and puffed to catch his breath. We all stood there, resting, feeling ourselves being moved by the waves of the ocean.

The Old Man still laughed at our ignorance as we waited there.

Likooshas then looked up at the Old Man. "Alright Old Man, what do you suggest we do?"

The Old Man stopped laughing, regressing it into a mild smile. "Well Pirate, I think that you should get a couple people from the crew up here to get off, and push it from the front of the boat, therefore there is less weight to pull, more men to work and you'll be getting more of a leverage." he said, making his way from the deck to the water, and splashing as he jumped in.

"Instead of four ropes of men pulling from all angles, run all four ropes straight out - and pull together - concentrate your force. And don't just pull - we'll all heave together, rest, and heave again until it starts to move. And it won't start to move until it quits sinking into the sand - so take a few of those log ends we chopped off the new masts, and put them sideways, under the front of the boat - we'll need at least twenty pieces - and as they come out the back of the boat, we need a few men to pick them up and run around the front and put them down again. That should work."

He then looked up at the deck.

" Come on men, we've got work to do !" he shouted, walking up the beach to the front of the boat.

The crewmen on the deck stopped what they were doing, they stopped, shuffling the wood scraps, stopped packing the dried foods, stopped tying down the barrels. They all walked to the side and peeked at the Old Man.

" What, Old Man ?" one of them asked.

"You heard the Old Man, get down there and help us push this boat out to sea !" shouted Likooshas, beginning to lose his patience.

The crew did as he said. They regretfully stopped what they were doing - all easy jobs and dry - and then plopped off the deck to join the rest of us.

Likooshas sent some to the front of the boat to push, some to gather the logs and others to join us on the ropes, which were all pointed straight out to sea now.

The deck crew made their way to their posts and waited for someone to tell them what to do. Others carried out short lengths of logs and wedged them under the back of the boat, which was in about two feet of water.

Likooshas looked at all of us, resting up and now catching our last breaths." Alright all of you ! The ones in the front Push! The rest of us. Pull and rest. Now pull. And rest. Pull. And rest. Pull !" he shouted.

We all grabbed onto the ropes and began to pull our hardest. And rest. And pull. The grunts from the others side all came at once now, all of us were struggling together and focused. And what a difference that made. The boat was moving a little more at every heave and soon began moving smoothly.

" THAT'S IT, KEEP IT UP ! WE'RE ALMOST DONE !" he yelled, satisfied with the results he was receiving.

More and more, it became easier.

" We're almost done !" shouted someone.

I looked around seeing the others beginning to lose their touch with the sand bed as the water got deeper.

The others in the front continued to push.

Finally the boat became free from the beach and floated, as eager as we and headed out to sea.

There was no one left on board.

" Quickly ! Get to the rope ladder !" shouted Likooshas.

Everyone let go of the ropes and placed their hands on the boat's hull, stepping on the soft wet sand under them and slowly moving closer to the rope ladder.

Immediately, three men got up, quickly running over to drop the stone anchor before the boat drifted away.

I was thinking that it would have been really funny if, after all that, the boat just sailed out to sea, on it's own, leaving us all behind.

The Old Man was the last one up, and when he got to the deck, he needed a hand getting off the ladder.

He brushed his hands and looked around.

Likooshas walked around the deck, breathing in the salt air. The others were happy that the boat was finally fit for sailing. The Old Man walked around the deck looking at the sails and opening the trap doors.

Everyone paused from their cheers of victory and accomplishment, knowing that whatever the Old Man thought was important. If he said that the boat was not fit for sailing, then they'd have to start all over again.

"Well, is it sea-worthy ?"Likooshas asked sternly.

The Old Man said nothing as he continued to look around. He picked at the sails, pulled on the ropes, and stomped on the deck. He then shook his head and sighed.

He looked to the crew.

"Well ?" I asked, anticipating what he was going to say.

"Well, it floats doesn't it ?" he said as his stern face changed into a smile.

Once again the crew laughed and celebrated in joy.

Likooshas then shushed everyone down.

He looked at us, "Well. The boat's sea-worthy, let's get sailing before the tide changes and leaves us high and dry again. We've got no time to waste!" he said.

Everyone stared at him.

" But Likooshas, we just finished the boat, can't we take a break now ?" said one of the crew men.

Suddenly all of us agreed.

Likooshas came close to smacking him across the face, but he then noticed that everyone was watching him and would probably throw him overboard if he did.

He held himself from hitting the crewman. He sighed frustratedly, grumbling to himself.

"Okay. One night ! Then tomorrow we sail. But that is it ! No more slack for anyone." he stared evilly at everyone.

" You got that ?" he finished.

All of us nodded.

"Draw up that anchor and take us out a little deeper to avoid the tides. Then take your rest."

He then nodded, looking to the Old Man who was staring at him like he had done something wrong.

The Old Man then turned around and sighed.

" Alright then, lets celebrate." Likooshas shouted as his face lit up. He walked over to the one of the beer barrels which had been loaded and lashed to the deck on top of other boxes.

He screwed a big tap into the bung hole of the barrel.

" A drink to Atlantis !" he shouted happily as he held his mouth under the tap and opened it, sending beer into his mouth, over his had and across the deck.

Everyone cheered and started to draw their wooden cups.

I was puzzled where they got all that beer but I guess that it didn't matter. Maybe they were making it while I was listening to stories.

That whole day, everyone told jokes, drank, lay around and listened to the Old Man tell old tales, not connected to Atlantis. Then night-time came. Everyone was quiet now, and had finished two from the five barrels of their beer reserves.

Likooshas, who had gone below deck for a few hours, came out, finding that most of the crew were lazily enjoying themselves.

He grumbled a bit more as he shut the trap door and sealed it up.

The Old Man lay on the deck of the boat, staring up at the sky.

" Well Old Man , I guess that it's time to continue with the story." I said, sitting patiently on the empty barrel.

The other crewmen looked to me.

" What story ?" one asked.

The Old Man turned around to answer but then one of the other crewmen, who was about to drift into a slumber interrupted him.

" It's the story of Atlantis. This Old Man's been telling it for weeks." he said.

The Old Man was surprised. The curious crewmen looked to the Old Man, then at the crewman who was going to sleep.

" Is that right Sisko ?" one of them said to the sleepy crewman.

" ...Yup ... I've heard it for a few long nights of restless sleep. It's all about these three women who are ten times stronger then men and were sent to travel around the northern continent of Atlantis. Two of them are in love with each other, while the man slave of the other one is about to fall in love ..." he said. "Then, in South Atlantis, there's this guy who wants to explore the north and he's just sold off his girlfriend so he can do it."

The Old Man was amazed at his accuracy.

I was amazed that he had summed up weeks of stories in two sentences.

"If you ask me, nothing interesting has happened yet . . . " he finished as he lay down as if to go to sleep.

Immediately almost all of the crew hustled up around the Old Man and me.

"What's all this ? Women in Atlantis ?" said the one

" Women ?-" said another

"Tell us about it Old Man." said one more.

The Old Man grinned and looked at all their eager faces.

" Alright, I'll tell you all the story, but you can't ask questions until the end ." he said.

He then turned around to look at the drowsy crewman.

"Or you can ask Sisko over there." he finished.

They all nodded, only wanting to hear the story because they heard that there were women in it.

The Old Man sighed, not nervous at all in front of a larger audience. "Alright . . . Um . . . where was I ?"

Suddenly Sisko sat up from his slumber, not able to sleep and then he told it.

" You left off where that bastard Kline traded his woman for his career." he said.

All of the crew turned to look at him.

The Old Man paused once more in amazement again.

" Um . . . Thank you, Sisko."

He grinned lazy eyed, " Don't mention it." he said as he sat back down and seemed to go to sleep.

All of the crew then turned around to focus on the Old Man once more.

The Old Man sighed again and closed his eyes.

"Alright . . . . . well, I'm sick of men and their problems. Let's talk about the women for a while."

The crew nodded, eagerly.

"Where were we with the women ?"

"We didn't know if Sassaska would live through the night." I said.

"No we didn't. But I'll tell you now, she did. But they still weren't out of danger. Not by a long shot.

Brelinka was wrapped up with Sassaska, trying to keep her warm. Elana was with the horses, sitting, stunned, against the rock wall of the cave.

The other two slaves were tired after getting everything inside and unpacked. They felt that their work was done and went on further down the cave to start up their own hearth. They didn't even ask permission from Elana if they could do so.

It was usually expected of them to ask, although it was also expected in all slaves to leave into their own section once all work was done, so it wasn't that big an offense, given the circumstances.

Nurix, on the other hand, felt that there was something else to do. He felt that he was going to be needed if Sassaska or Brelinka called for something.

So he sat there beginning to observe them and waited for something, an order, a demand, or possibly a conversation. But nothing happened. He only got to watch them both drift off into sleep.

He got down, after the fire was going and sat there, content. He gazed as a spectator, as an observer, being silent and courteous not wanting to interrupt.

He watched the warm, soft colors of the blankets ruffled up and wrapped around Brelinka and Sassaska. There locks of Brelinka's brownish hair gently lay on her rough skin, intermixing with Sassaska's black, straight hair, both completely different in textures but both unthinkably brilliant when clashed and placed together.

He saw Sassaska, pale and frosty from her fall, wrapped secure within Brelinka's whole body. Sassaska's slightly blue lips were gently in touch with Brelinka's collar bone. He found it to be so beautiful that he had tears in his eyes.

It was amazing to Nurix how the way they were holding each other as they slept described their passion and love, the beauty that they felt for each other was expressed eloquently without the need for any words to be said.

How the warm, tanned colors from Brelinka's body glowed and persisted in protecting Sassaska from harm. The way Brelinka's arm gently and gracefully hooked around the arc of Sassaska's back. Holding her close. Close enough for Sassaska to feel secure and pleasingly comfortable in her arms.

To Nurix, their love bond was unimaginable and hard to believe that it was kept so casually throughout the trip.

Elana rocked slowly, crouched against the rock wall of the cave and feeling less and less concerned about death strolling in to claim Sassaska. Brelinka had saved her and they were lost in their own little world now.She gave up watching them to watch Nurix. Elana found it amusing, thinking that it was adorable to see the man slave try to study them, to try and discover what it is like to love someone that much.

Elana slowly stood up and watched her step in the dim light, not wanting to trip or step on Sassaska or Brelinka, knowing that their moods would be spoiled terribly.

Nurix began to change his observation and fascination to gaze at Elana walking around them. Elana, rubbing her hands together to keep warm approached Nurix and sat aside from him, holding her hands out near the fire. Her body seemed to tingle as the warm, pleasant heat gently poured over her. She closed her eyes, and breathed slow,. It was in reaction to the sensual and en-drowsying sensation of the fire's heat. She sat silently looking into the fire, running her fingers through her curly red-streaked hair.

She was calm and serene as the rock wall behind her, wrapping her arms around her knees and starting to hum an old folk song.

She looked exhausted. Under fine brownish eyes small dark half-circles had formed. She slowly turned around, looking right back at Nurix. She smiled, showing her manners to him.She sighed silently, so silent that Nurix barely heard any breath come out of her. She crouched there, staring at him. Her head slightly turned to an angle as she continued to look, causing her curls to slide down and shift over her left ear.

Nurix smiled formally as well, thinking that it would make up for him rudely staring at her. He then lowered his eyes immediately, thinking that she was waiting for him to turn.

"My apologies Elana . . . I didn't mean to look at you that long." Elana laughed a little. " No that's alright. I thought that you wanted to say something to me. I don't mind you staring." she said.

" As long as you aren't staring when I'm changing," she finished.

Nurix gave a laugh then stopped himself, reducing his laughter to a grin with a nod. " I'll try to make sure that I won't stare when you change from now on - although it'll be difficult."

She began to sit comfortably with her legs crossed and her chin on her palm. " You make it sound like you can't control yourself when it comes to staring at me changing . . . You seem to observe everything around your environment, why do you ?" she asked, finding a topic to talk about.

Nurix raised a brow. "I . . . I've been doing it since . . . forever. It's something that I've taught myself to do . . . So I catch things which displease my mistress. To understand what's going on without having to ask my mistress. . . to survive . . .

It's also a way for me to learn things, to understand why things are the way they are. I'm the kind of slave that looks at every detail, every groove . . . everything. If you've trained your eye long enough, like I have, you learn that you're able to hear a story from what you see. From the way a person looks, reacts, breaths, walks, talks, acts or sits, you get an idea of the person itself.

You can learn where she came from, how old she is, what her name is, and how much she's suffered . . ."

Elana seemed to get even interested as her pupils largened and focused completely on him. " So you are able to read a person's body language ? Able to read a person's mind ?" she said with such interest in the tone of her voice.

Nurix nodded. " You could say that . . ."

She smiled again and got a little closer. Her expression showed eagerness yet a slight disbelief. Nurix knew that she wanted him to read her.

" Can you tell me what I'm thinking right now ?" she asked.

Nurix smiled. He had already predicted the question.

She stared patiently at him, waiting for him to answer her.

He sighed, looking at the way her body was positioned. Her crossed legs pointed at his direction, her eyes were focused and her hair fallen, and fastened by the back of her ears. He followed her shoulders, down her arms leaning forwards, her hands covering her mouth, covering her smile which her cheeks showed as he stared, causing her eyes to squint briefly.

Her breath seemed to be slow and calm but then she sucked her stomach in, giving him the sign that she was slightly excited, excited that he was telling the truth. He then finished up, seeing herself crouched and leaning head first to his direction showing complete alertness.

" First of all, on the surface, you're thinking 'He can't possibly do this ?', but underneath, where the deep thoughts lie ... You're attentive to me, yet you have assurance in your feelings of being ...superior ... You think that ... what - I need something from you, your friendship perhaps or your protection ... "

Her eyes began to widen, her ears rose a little, causing her hair to cover them as her scalp rose a little as well like a cat getting scared.

Nurix smiled and chuckled a little.

"...and now you're surprised because I'm right..." he finished.

She was impressed, surprised and amazed. He was completely correct in almost every part of her thoughts about him.

She laughed,

"You're right ..." she said. She then raised her brow seductively,

" ... May I try to read you ?" she said slowly, and calmly, wanting to try it, and playfully mock him.

He smiled and nodded.

" Alright ..." she said.

Nurix sat there looking at her, thinking if she was really trying to read him or basically putting on a tease.

She squinted her eyes and turned a little, sensing something about his posture, or at least wanting to give the impression.

"You're ... You're thinking about ... how dumb I look, staring and trying to figure you out ..." she slowly started to laugh a bit.

She couldn't do it, not in the least.

He actually was thinking how naive she looked.

Nurix smiled in surprise. But surprise at the witty remark she made, not at her body reading skills.

" Almost . . . but 'almost' is more than good enough . . ." Nurix said.

" Well, for a beginner I guess Nurix, but . . ." she paused. " Will you teach me how to read body language ?" she asked.

His eyes widened as his scalp moved back in surprise once more. This time, he was truly shocked. Nurix gulped at the sound of her question. He was lost on what to say. He had never been asked such a question, never knew how to reply as well.

" Are you joking, Mistress Elana ?" he asked.

"No . . . I think that it's a useful tool to have . . . It's interesting, don't you think ?" she said.

Nurix sighed and closed his eyes" Elana . . . I . . . I don't even know how I learned it myself . . ." he said.

" But you know enough to give me a few notes, can't you ?" she said.

" I am a slave Elana, I'm conditioned to be able to do that, so that I can protect myself and so I will know what my mistress wants . . . I know how to do this so that you don't have to. It's for your convenience." he said. His voice seemed to rise a little, feeling slightly frustrated upon his feeling of shock. "Besides, you won't have my motivation to learn - which is to stay alive."

Elana moved a little closer with a look of slight apology being expressed."Nurix, have I provoked you in any way ? If it makes you uncomfortable to teach me we don't have to do it "

Nurix sighed again and then shook his head.

"No Elana . . . you haven't provoked me. I've provoked myself with my own logic . . .I feel that I would fail you as a teacher, for I've never thought at all about teaching anyone . . . I wouldn't know where to begin . . ." he said.

" . . . I'll teach myself as you guide me through it. To tell me what certain movements and expressions mean . . . I want you to be my guide Nurix . . ." she said.

Nurix smiled and then gave in. If she was going to try herself, and only want descriptions and definitions, he would be able to give them to her. He agreed to her question.

He nodded mildly, " . . . Alright Elana . . . I'll guide you . . ."

She smiled gently, moving closer to him. She then kissed him on the side of the cheek as she affectionately ran her fingers on the other cheek and slowly pulled away.

It was her way of saying thank you.

Nurix smiled and then kissed her back.

Elana was startled, not expecting it.

Nurix then looked into her eyes.

" Thank you . . ." he said.

She chuckled a little, feeling quite daft.

" You're learning . . ..Yes, Nurix you're learning . . ."

" You teach me . . . And I'll teach you . . ." he said.

She smiled as she nodded.

The story to me seemed to be getting long and rather boring. It was too emotional and sweet. I liked it for a while because there was an interesting beginning, but now I wanted something interesting to happen. I guessed that if I was patient, the Old Man would get there. But I guess that he was saving the best for last.

So I made the best of the remaining story before he was calling it a night.

" Why was it that she was close to him ? I mean the kissing part?" I asked to understand what was going on in the story.

The Old Man laughed.

" The kissing part bothers you ? Why ?"

" Because . . . you just don't do that . . . I don't kiss you to thank you for something, so why do they ?"

The Old Man sighed, "Different civilization, different culture, and different beliefs. The Mistress' did that as a custom. It was a formal and polite thing to do that meant nothing big . . ."

" Then why was it, when Julyo kissed Elana, it was considered an intimate feeling other than a 'formal kiss '?" I asked.

"Oh, you remembered that, did you ? Well there's a big difference in kissing the side of your cheek and placing your tongue into someone's mouth. A formal kiss is on the cheek, the forehead, the side of the head; as long as you don't touch their mouths. Once you do that, you're telling the other person that you want them to be closer with you."

I nodded, finally beginning to understand the gestures in his story.

" Alright Old Man . . ." I said.

" Now; let's get back to the story shall we ?"

I nodded.

"The storm outside the cave seemed to never let up during the past few days. At first, it would appear that it was safe to go out, but then another part of the blizzard would hit and leave them back in the cave. During the nighttime, the cold winds would come in and suck out the heat of the fires, making it extremely uncomfortable. It was chilly, dim, and dark. After the second night, the slaves took one of the tarp tents and hung it over the mouth of the cave, so it acted like a door flap. It worked, keeping in the heat, and keeping out the cold, but the cave started to get stuffy and even darker inside.

Sassaska was getting better, but she was still weak. Weak in body and in spirit.

Three days passed by and the storm was stronger than ever, having no beginning or end to it. The slaves had tied down the tarp, so that it wouldn't flap around as much from the winds.

Sassaska listened, hoping that the sounds of the whistling winds would stop. But they didn't. The more she listened the more her hope sunk deeper and deeper. The horses grew skinnier because the slaves put them on extreme low rations. She knew that the supplies they had: a bit of smoked meat, a few extra bundles of firewood, grain for the horses, and dry clothes, were all going to run out within a few more days..."

Elana, was taking care of the five horses; feeding them their rations, keeping them calm from the cold and grooming their manes. Brelinka had all her weapons out and was sharpening her arrows for her hunting long bow. She was bored and did it to pass the time. She got into the sharpening and then had an idea to modify them without needing many tools. After all, they were in a cave. But she was frequently disturbed by the strong winds speeding past and blowing the tarp off the door and distracting her from her from her work. So she got the women slaves to try and tie it down more securely.

Taboo and Nurix worked quickly, fighting to tie and fasten the tarp over the mouth of the cave in such a way to be sure it wouldn't be blown off every few hours. Still, the winds coming in seemed to be concentrating on blowing the tarp away, which made it harder to complete the task.

"Quickly Nurix, hold it at the corner !" Taboo said, wrestling the wildly blown tarp to a previously nailed-in peg.

The wind forced in some of the outside snow, pushing back the corner of the tarp which wasn't fastened down yet.

As Nurix forced with all his might to place the remaining corner on the lower peg, He slipped on the snow which was forming into ice when it encountered the heat inside. He lost his grip on the tarp, which began flapping all over and letting in even more snow.

Nurix struggled to stand up, slipping and sliding in the snow.

" Men, you're all too week to do anything . . ." Taboo said, shaking her head in dissatisfaction at Nurix's puny efforts. Taboo easily pushed him out of her way as she grabbed the last corner and fastened it down. Nurix watched her fix it in place. To her it seemed easy. She didn't struggle at all. She knelt down, pulled the corner towards her, and then tied the string around the lower peg.

The wind inside the cave stopped immediately, there was no more in coming now. There was only the emotionless cold, greedily eating up the stuffy heat from the fire now.

Taboo stood up and ran her fingers through her sticky, locked up hair in relief. She sighed, slowly walking toward the dim firelight.

Nurix got up, walking towards the tarp which was now stretched tight, like the top of a drum. He slowly placed his hand on it, feeling the wind beating a mad tune upon it, trying to force itself in. The tarp was cold and rough to his touch. It was an amazing piece of work. If it had been just him even with five or ten other male slaves, putting up the tarp would have been utterly impossible in the storm. But here it was, tight, strong, and keeping the storm outside, all because of the casual work of one woman, and a pretty average woman at that.

Nurix was in awe of the power of what one woman could do, trying to measure their strength in how many men would equal the strength of one woman. He thought it would have to be at least eight, if not ten.

His hand, still on the tarp moved from side to side feeling the tautness, the pull, then his touching stopped. He backed up, feeling the cold air rushing in underneath the bottom of the tarp and seeing the gap between the top of the tarp and the cave ceiling. By accident or perhaps by design, fresh air rushed in at the bottom and the smoke was drawn out through the gap at the top. It was ingenious, but not that efficient, as the air inside was still stuffy, smoky and thick.

"What are you looking at, man ?" asked an irritated voice from the back of him.

Nurix slowly turned around,

There was Taboo, who had not gone to the slave's hearth after all, but had been motionless in the dark, not caring a single bit where she was.

"I'm feeling the tarp."

" Yes . . . I could see that. I want to know why, you daft little man."

Nurix didn't know what to say. He didn't know if she would understand his amazement if he told her.

She waited for his answer.

Nurix, thought quickly for another excuse to give her but couldn't. He felt his thoughts, about how many times were women stronger than men, were his and his alone. He didn't think that it was any of her business, but he still had to give an answer.

"I . . . Just; like the feeling of tarp . . . It's like being inside a drum." he said, making it up off the top of his head.

Taboo raised a brow. She felt his excuse was peculiar, but let it go because he was a man. She thought that he didn't know any better; because he was a man.

" You're a strange little man, Nurix . . ." she said as she stood up and started to the slave's hearth further back in the cave. "But I like you for it. And the touch of a man would not be unwelcome some time, if you have the urge." she said as she walked into the light.

Nurix sighed with relief, thankful that she didn't want to go further with her sexual thoughts. He knew that women, once they got sex on their minds, often couldn't be stopped. And with their vastly superior strength could take what they wanted anytime - especially from a slave boy who had no woman-protector/wife.

Rhyme, who was cutting the dried meats and separating them into groups stopped working and started to giggle a little as Taboo joined her and Nurix wasn't sure whether Taboo had told her of her sexual offer to Nurix or whether it was just Rhyme, being dumb again.

In any case, Nurix felt that he had to do something to keep himself busy and out of Taboo's sight. The close quarters and the boredom could inflame Taboo's passion and she might do more than just talk about it. Once women got a thought in their minds, they usually couldn't get it out unless they acted upon it.

So he went and sat alone near the Mistress' dimmening fire. He picked up a long branch of dry wood from the bundle placed near the fire but then just looked at the fire, watching it dancing on the charcoaled wood and slowly dying.

He broke off a piece from the tip of the branch and threw it in to keep the fire going.

The fire moved it's thriving hunger to the twig, immediately engulfing it and sucking its life out, changing it into a shrivelled carcass of what it once was and then consuming even that.

Nurix broke off another piece and threw it into the flame. The fire continued to grow making itself full once again. Nurix then placed the rest of the branch along side of the others, giving its entire soul to the fast, furious life of the flame.

It seemed like a philosophy of life. Live fast and brightly, giving off heat and light all in a rush. Or stay in the cold and dark, slowly drying up over the decades - burning giving up life still, but tiny bit by tiny bit.

Nurix continued to watch the flame-dance, fascinated by it. The fire's seductive motion ate up his worries and thoughts and burned right into his mind. Even though the wind howled outside, the horses made their sounds to each other, Brelinka ground out sharpening sounds and the slaves whispered together, Nurix heard nothing but silence as he stared at the fire, mesmerized as if he was in a trance all together. Nothing seemed to exist but him and the fire.

Yet, for some reason, Nurix heard Sassaska's weak voice, barely above the sound of a breath, as she tried to reach for the cup of water which had been placed near the fire to warm it.

Nurix saw her trying to reach for it, as she slowly tried to sit up, extending her arms, and reaching for it as she wettened her chapped and dry lips. Nurix felt sorry for her, and slowly picked up the cup and stretched out to gently place it in her hands.

Sassaska's eyes were focused on the cup, and she gulped with the urge to slake her thirst and quickly drunk the warm snow water, swallowing every last drop. She slowly wiped her mouth with her hand, and placed the cup on the ground right next to her.

She looked up to Nurix and nodded.

She stared at him with an expression of gratitude but still the feeling of prideful superiority could be seen in the pupils of her eyes.

" . . . Thank you Nurix . . ." she said.

Nurix knelt down, to sit. He looked back at her and nodded.

" How are you feeling?" he asked.

Sassaska was surprised. She expected him to walk away or look down at her presence, like a typical slave. She wasn't expecting him to talk to her, nor did she want him to.

" I'm fine . . .Thank you for asking . . . Slave . . ." she said, trying to make him go away.

She waited for him to leave to help the other slaves or go and chat with Elana like he usually did, but he didn't. He just sat there, staring at her.

"Shouldn't you be with Elana ?" she asked.

" If Elana want's me, she'll call me to her. Besides, you've finished your cup. I' m waiting for you to give it to me." he said.

Sassaska looked at the cup. She picked it up.

Nurix reached his hand over to her.

She was about to hand it to him but then held it for a little longer.

" You're not looking down. Why is that ?" she asked.

" I have no need to, I already know I'm a slave. Why would I have to keep reminding myself ?"

" Because you're a man." she said.

" Yes, I know . . . I am a man and a slave, I should bow doubly low when I am talked to, I should not make eye contact and I shouldn't be asking questions, especially of a woman. Why is it that way ? Does anyone even know ? So I've learned to do without all of the ritualistics and just serve. " he said in return.

" Why ? You know that you'd get beaten for doing such things in most houses." she said.

Nurix raised a brow. " And, in most of the houses where I was owned, I have been. But why should anyone care ? When was the last time a person cared what a slave did ? And anyway, even when I obey all the rules, I'm often beaten too."

She looked at him, thinking that he was being smart with her. But she liked it, she chuckled a little. Perhaps this shaking up of her thoughts was what she was supposed to learn on this journey.

She knew that Elana had something to do with this slaves attitude. She remembered that for the past week they had spent a lot of time together.

Even when they were in the cave, they were always talking. She shook her head in amazement.

" What has that girl, Elana, been teaching you ?" she asked. "Or what is it that you are teaching us ?" she finished.

Nurix grinned at her, shaking his head slowly as he put his finger on his mouth giving a shushing expression.

She nodded, as she finally handed him her cup. She then looked down, feeling her doubts come back to her.

" I guess that it doesn't matter," she stopped herself before going on to say what she felt. Then her smile began to lower.

Nurix glimpsed her face growing dimmer with her weakness. He read a lot of things on her face, so many complex emotions, tensions and worries but he only had to read her eyes to understand her main feeling.

She showed that she was not confident that they would all make it out alive. He could read that she felt that this storm was the rage from the God Marsolla, perhaps because of her defection from Priestess to Empress. Perhaps because of her cheating death and escaping it. Now her companions would suffer for her bad leadership and the betrayal of her God.

Nurix began to feel sorry for her, for being so lost of hope.

Nurix grabbed her cup and stood up.

" Get better soon Mistress Sassaska, We have put our lives in your hand. Don't die . . . Yet . . ." he said as he turned and walked to the leather canteen, near the supplies. He poured some of the melted snow water into the cup, walking back to her and bending down to place it near her.

She slowly lay down once more, beginning to feel herself spin. She faced Nurix's hand still holding onto the cup and looked up at his eyes.

" Just . . .get through this, We need you, We're going to see the rest of the journey through . . . All of us." he said.

" Thank you . . ." she said as she began relax, the ordinary words having an extraordinary effect on her, restoring her confidence and letting her put her thoughts of inadequacy to rest so she could sleep again.

Nurix stood up once again, but this time to leave her to sleep.

She closed her eyes and began to doze off.

He didn't know what to do now.

The only thing he knew what to do was go to the other side of the fire and stare right into the fire once more, so he did . . .

The days went on and everyone waited for the storm to end. The bear meat was running slim. It drove the slaves to try and kill one of the horses for meat, but Brelinka stopped them before they could. They were almost out of sticks to burn in the fire. They only had one bundle left, not enough to feed two hearths. The rest were burned away from the long, previous nights.

Because there was only enough for one hearth, the slaves had to sleep near their Mistresses. For Nurix, it wasn't a problem that bothered him, since he was used to it now.

Everything seemed to be happening as predicted, but most of the time, everyone tried to not think of it. They only waited for the storm to end.

Sassaska had gained her strength back and was able to walk. When she could, she used some of the charcoal from the fire and kept a tally on how long had it been.

To her surprise, it grew and seemed to be a long time. Brelinka's use for the time ran out. She had sharpened, tightened, and modified not only her weapons but everyone else's, resulting in nothing else for her to do except stare at the cave's ceiling and hover around Sassaska.

Taboo and Rhyme always had things to do, but to them, the tasks began to feel more ridiculous than actually helpful to anyone, even themselves.

The only ones who didn't seem to be bored and hopeless were Nurix and Elana.

The more they stayed in the cave, it seemed, the closer they became. Until, they were almost unseparable.

Elana was now skinnier and so was Nurix, but their spirits weren't as weak as their bodies. They continued to hope that the storm would end, while everyone else seemed to want to die.

" Elana, what is it ?" he asked.

Elana looked to the tattered up tarp, flapping from holes worn and ripped out by the constant winds. Snow was now blowing in and piles of it was peeking though the sides of the mouth of the cave.

Nurix looked to her and saw her face." You're beginning to feel the same thing as the others aren't you?" Nurix said.

She slowly turned her face. "I still feel that . . . we'll make it out alive. So what made you say that ?" she asked.

Nurix smiled. "Sometimes your face naturally shows the truth . . . the feelings hidden deep down inside without the need to express them at all. These things are written plain for anyone who can read." he said.

She ran her fingers through her hair, then rested her face on her palms as she looked to Nurix. " I see that you're beginning to think the same thing aren't you . . ." she said, as she sighed.

Nurix nodded as he looked to the tarp. His stomach growled because of hunger.

It had been a day since he ate, but he restrained today, in fear that he wouldn't have any left for the next day.

" I won't try to deny it." he said.

" What if it's better . . . better with Marsolla ?" Elana asked, feeling his hunger.

Nurix sighed, "You shouldn't think of such things as death . . . Sometimes the thinking can make it come true." he said.

Elana slowly turned herself around, crawling to get closer to the fire, which was barely alive at all.

She took out one of the sharpened arrows, sloppily left right beside the fire and cut off a lock of her hair, to get a quick burst of light.

Nurix saw that she used it to look closely at him.

He looked to the dim light of grey which came in around the tarp as the faint noise of the howling wind whispered in, pushing the stretched-out tarp over the mouth of the cave. The sounds of the strong wind began to get softer and softer and softer, until there was no sound at all. Only the sound of the tarp being pushed by the morphed, gentle wind was heard.

Nurix's eyes widened. He watched even more as the winds that pushed, got weaker and weaker, and weaker.

" I think that the wind's dying." he said, feeling strongly with his belief. He turned his head to Elana, trying to keep the tiny, finger sized flame from burning out.

She only gave a glimpse to him. " Nurix, please. The storm does it all the time. We were fooled once and it nearly killed us out there. None of us are going to be fooled again."

Nurix sighed. He understood what she meant.

Every time they thought that the storm was over, the storm would hit again, almost like it had a mind of its own. It was as if it had only one purpose in living, to tease and challenge all who opposed it's strength, acting excruciatingly harder on the ones who flee. 'Like a demon from the spirit of Marsolla, hunting the lost, to claim as their allies.' Sassaska used to say in her sleep as she fondled the beads on her hand.

But to Nurix, he felt that he couldn't suffer from the curse like everyone around him was. He knew that there was going to be a way out. He just needed a sign to prove him right. Nurix sat there, staring at the wind beginning to pick up once more.

Brelinka came out of the deeper caverns of the cave. She was looking for other things to burn in the flame, trying to sustain the remaining wood and supplies they had to last them longer. But, even with her energy and good intentions, she was having the look of nothingness.

She had nothing except her weapons. Her bow and her arrows stripped off her spare warrior- saddle from her skinny horse. She was feeling cold herself and, since she believed herself much tougher than the others, she imagined how cold they were feeling.

She looked to Elana, shivering as she cut another lock of her hair to keep the fire going, even though the smell was terrible and the hair only fueled a brief spark.

Brelinka took out an arrow and broke off the beautifully wavy barbed head. She threw the arrow head to the floor and took the wood, gently placing it near the small flame, which now began to die.

Nurix looked up at her, sitting, and shivering as he swallowed what little saliva he had left in his mouth.

She stood reflecting her gaze back to Nurix. She was expressionless but still, instinctively showed her obvious prejudice at him. Like an obedient cat, staring patiently at something, Nurix understood that she didn't mean it.

It was because he was getting close to Elana.

She then sighed, changing her expression of her face, but still keeping it in her eyes as she remained locked on him.

" Nurix . . . I hear that were almost out of meat rations . . . Is that true, slave ?" she asked sternly.

Nurix nodded, watching her slowly sit down, holding another arrow, getting ready to break off the head.

" There's not enough food at all . . . We're also running out of wheat and hay to feed the horses . . .." Nurix said silently, as he stared at the tarp, moving with the wind.

She slowly crouched down, sitting next to Elana, who was trying to keep warm on the tiny flame. She sat close to her, throwing her arm over Elana's shoulders, covering her with her dirty, dingy, greyish blue cloak.

She rested her head on Elana's temple. She then started to rub her hands with Elana's. She then kissed her on the top of her head, holding her.

Elana leaned herself onto her. Shivering and silent.

" I guess that it has come to this . . ." she sighed and closed her eyes.

"Tell the other slaves lying around to kill my horse. There'd be enough for the other horses to survive . . .. This way . . .. All of us will live a little longer . . .."

Nurix nodded once again.

" . . .I will . . .." he said.

Nurix, then looked to the tarp, feeling like he was hoping for something, some sign, some kind of significance telling everyone that the storm was truly over.

Something . . . A ghost, anything.

Then something did happen.

Nurix looked and watched as the tarp stopped moving and now swung on a side as it's stretch-torn corners from the pegs lay fallen. He looked out and saw the brilliant color of white, so powerful that he had to squint his eyes to see anything at all.

He slowly got up, feeling the blood rushing to his long, stiffened legs. He wondered to himself if this was the sign he was hoping for, the miracle that was going to save them.

He struggled to stand, feeling the thousands of needles pricking him as he moved his legs, staggering not to fall. He quickly placed his hands on the cold granite wall of the cave for control, feeling its rough texture as he continued on to the tarp. The closer he got, the brighter it was.

Then his eyes raised in joy.

Sassaska, slowly rose in her sleep, woken from the bright lights of the snow outside. Her teeth chattered as she tried to stare with her blurred vision.

Then as it began to clear, she too began to look with a grin of satisfaction on her.

Brelinka, almost about to snap the arrow in two, slowly held it in her hand as she turned around.

Nurix was about to undo the two top fastened corners of the tarp. As he reached over to take them down, he felt himself excited to unravel the world that they had survived to see.

Suddenly a ferocious force of a gigantic paw tore through the tarp. Nurix jumped in fright, feeling his whole body tremble. His hair stood up as he fell to the floor and struggled to run.

A frightful growl echoed into the cave, causing Brelinka to stand with chills running into her.

Suddenly the tarp fell onto the beast's head and it rolled around in confusion, and shredded the canvas to pieces with a huge roar.

Then the beast was revealed to everyone. It was a grey furred snow bear, if anything even bigger than the one Brelinka had shot a couple of weeks before.

It was furious and struggling to claw at Nurix's legs.

Elana immediately rolled and grabbed the spear lying near Brelinka. Sassaska shakily stood up and armed herself with another spear.

The bear, clawing it's way in and ferociously fighting to get in, growled once more.

It was hungry.

Elana and Sassaska jabbed the bear, trying to keep it busy so that Nurix could get out of the way.

Brelinka stood there, staring into it's eyes, as she slowly bent down to grab her bow.

She slowly drew it, placing the arrow that she was about to snap into it, and aimed. Her eyes were wide, her instincts, wild . . . She too, was hungry.

She raised her head.

" . . .Meat . . ..Meat . . Meat . . " she began to chant.

Nurix watched her face. Her hair raising, her breathing slow and her on-going chant mesmerizing. Her jaw was loose and moving forwards, like a feline hunter watching a baby gazelle with desires.

She then shot the arrow.

Meant to pierce armor, it went right through the bear's chest and came out the other side, hitting the cave ceiling and causing a large rock to fall bang the bear on the nose.

The bear moaned and whipped it's head back, hitting the side of it on the cave wall and tore off half an ear.

The Bear suddenly realized that it had, for the first time in its life, encountered an even more fierce predator than itself. It whimpered struggling to back out, it's fur sprayed with blood, it's nose and ear bloodied and broken, it's heart, even now, spilling it's life blood onto the snow.

The bear was in pain and wanted no more of it. But then, as it struggled to escape, Nurix watched all the women, even the slaves slowly come to it as if it was a religious ceremony.

Brelinka now throwing her bow down and grabbing a spear, walking to it with the other mistresses, and even the slaves Rhyme and Taboo grabbed the small daggers they had for grinding things. They all walked to it like a pack of wild, hungry dire wolves, all growling, and all beginning to chant what Brelinka had started:

" . . ..Meat . . Meat . . Meat . . Meat . . ..".

The bear immediately stumbled, whimpering, out of the cave, terrified and hysterical and already dead.

Nurix felt that the bear was frightened enough, but the women were only getting started. They continued to chant all together, in harmony with Rhyme's hyena-like laugh. They ran out of the cave right after it.Nurix's eyes widened in shock. He had to follow them to see what was going on.

As he ran out, feeling the freshness of the air, he slipped and landed in the soft, fluffy snow. He huffed and puffed as he watched the women growl and yell as they surrounded the poor, 15 foot bear. Until recently, King of the Mountain. Now the bear, looked as if it was about to cry as it tried to scare the women, throwing it's forearms and shooting them to the women. But the women only backed and forthed and moved towards it slowly.

Suddenly, as Elana distracted it with a jab, Brelinka jumped up onto it's back and stabbed with all her might. The bear gave a ferocious howl of pain as it reacted by standing on it's hind legs, throwing Brelinka off.

Nurix felt the bear's pain and was about to cry with it. But at the same time he was fascinated by the show, so obsessed he had to continue to stare.

When the bear stood up, Elana ran and stuck her spear into the belly. The sound of the spear splitting and bursting, made Nurix's stomach turn in disgust as he watched Elana pull the spear out, splattering gore over the pure white snow.

Sassaska then jumped from the side chopping her spear and digging the wavy blades right to it's neck, satisfied as the tendons of the mighty bear snapped.

The bear finally fell then, paralyzed from Sassaska's blow to the neck. But it's head was still alive and it rolled and snapped, determined to take its attackers with it.

Sassaska used the spear's sharp point and severed the bear's nerve cord deeper at the back of its neck and the bear, showing itself in agony, slumped, its head now as frozen as the rest of its body.

It didn't move, it didn't cringe, it didn't cry any more . . . it couldn't. The only thing moving, the only clue that it was still in existence were it's eyes.

It stared to Nurix, watching him as the women continued to cut and chop and feed on him.

Nurix then read his eyes as he had read so many human eyes before. He was shocked, feeling compassion for the bear, feeling sadness, feeling sorry. For what he read was very little, but powerful. The bear was simply saying "I'm sorry . . ."

Nurix gulped, holding his tears as the bear then closed it's tearfilled eyes.

The women, panting and backing away from its carcass didn't look like women at all to Nurix.

Elana's eyes were still locked on the bear as she stabbed with her spear, her mouth was covered in blood and her hands still were twitching from adrenaline. They all looked like that, like wild animals, all stained with blood and liking it.

Their nostrils and their mouths wide open with the stench of blood from their clothes and hands.

Brelinka sighed and brushed her blood clotted hair. She looked to all the women, all covered in blood; all dirty, and thirsty for more.

Nurix watched, crawling closer, wanting to know what was going on between the women, but the women were expressionless, faceless. They showed no emotion at all. They didn't feel the horror, they didn't feel the pain and the cruelty.

Nothing was felt, nothing but excitement.

As the other women turned to her, Brelinka pulled out the remnants of her spear. Her breathing got harder, her mouth laid open in rage, her eyes filled with strength, hunger, and furiosity.

She quickly threw her hand up into the air, holding her bloodied spear, dripping dark droplets down her arm.

She then gave a howl, a howl so loud that it knocked the snow off the distant trees. The other women watched her in honor as she did it again. It was her kill. She had the right.

Then they all began to howl. Their cry of victory, and they wanted it to be heard to the world.

No longer were they weak, no longer were they hungry, no longer were they challenged by the demons of the Marsollan cold. They had taken the challenge and had beaten the wind . . .

Taboo and Rhyme, who had been in close with their mistresses stabbing and chanting, immediately started to skin the bear, knowing that it was a task that would come up later on.

Taboo cut it's paws and stripped its head of flesh, while Rhyme giggled and worked, pulling the skin from the bear. As they did this Nurix watched morbidly, still shocked and traumatized by the killing of the bear.

The women, on the other hand, were satisfied from that kill. That day, before they started their Journey once more, they started a fire outside, using half of their remaining emergency bundle of sticks. They fed on the bear, not caring that the meat was a little cold or rare, to them it was a blessing that had come .

At that moment, there was happiness and hope. They were no longer helpless, or sad, waiting for death to come and take them. They had brought death to death itself.

So there they all sat, feasting on the stiff, wet rare meat and slaking their thirst by scooping the fluffy white snow and melting it in their mouths.

They all were starving, feeding, cutting off bits of bear, and filling their wet, greasy mouths - even the two slaves as they worked. All except Nurix, who was sitting huddled up, staring at the headless, pawless, lumpy, bloody, remnants of what was once the body of a grand 15 foot bear.

He couldn't feed, he felt too guilty, too scared, and too disgusted to eat, so he chose not to. Instead he sat there, feeling the warmth of the fire in the mid afternoon.

He closed his eyes, but still couldn't escape the scene. He heard fingers pulling and tearing wet meat, endless chewing, and the mouthful laugh of Rhyme. In a way, hearing it was worse than looking at it, for the mind made them all more depraved and barbaric than they really were.

Everyone ate and ate and ate, continually stuffing their thin, pale happy faces with more and more.

One of the women threw him a chunk of meat, thinking, poor little man that he was, he might be too shy or too timid to come to the bear and rip off his own share.

The huge chunk of meat landed with a wet thud at his feet and the sound shocked him into opening his eyes.

Nurix stared at his chunk of bear belly. It was soft, fatty, fleshy, rare, and it made his mouth water, but he just couldn't bring himself to grab it and wolf it down like the others. He couldn't force his mind and senses to fantasize its texture and flavor. All he saw was the living bear, with it's sad look. It was like trying to eat a close relative.

He tried to block himself from thinking about it in this way. He wanted to eat, his mind wanted him to, it wanted him to give into his cravings for food. His body certainly wanted him to - he was salivating and swallowing almost unconsciously. Yet there was something that is stronger than body, stronger than mind and stronger than any other force in the universe - and that force was spirit.

To Nurix's spirit, his mind and body were becoming as feelingless as the others. He didn't see any regret or doubt in the women's eyes. All he saw was happy little faces being fed.

But his could not be among them. He wouldn't eat it, after what he had seen and read from the dying bear's face. Even if it meant him going the whole day without eating, which was dangerous for him at this point.

Elana, who was stuffed after her seventh serving, sighed in satisfaction. Her grin on her dirty face and her relaxed eyes, told Nurix that she was happy, warmer and full.

Elana, covering her mouth with a handful of snow, then wiping it with her sleeve glimpsed to Nurix, who was staring at her, then staring at the meat lying on the pink stained snow and sighing.

He cringed his teeth, licking his lips then stopping himself as he shut his eyes tightly and shook his head in disapproval.

Elana moved a bit closer to him. She glanced at the meat, seeing that it wasn't steaming anymore, verifying that it had been lying there on the snow for a long time.

" Is there something wrong Nurix ?" she asked softly, feeling worried for him.

Nurix sighed and grinned but didn't look at her.

" Why haven't you eaten it yet ?" she asked.

Nurix closed his eyes, trying to hide his desperation for feeding with rejection.

" I'm . . . fine, do you want my piece?" he said quickly as his stomach began to tighten and urge for it. He held his belly, thinking that his hunger was going to drive his stomach to digest itself.

Elana sensed something wrong with him.

She moved closer and gently patted his back as she turned to see his face. She stared at his long, thin face. His mouth trembled with hunger, yet his eyes to Elana seemed strong, holding back his desire to eat. To her it was a mystery why, and she slowly reached for the meat.

"Nurix . . . You haven't eaten . . . . you look ill . . ." she said.

" I'm fine . . . Please, don't worry for me."

" What is wrong Nurix ?" she said sternly, wanting an answer and seeing him growing weaker.

Nurix stared into her eyes. His eyes started to water and become a little red." What are my eyes showing, Elana? What is it that you read in my face?"

"Well ? What are my eyes showing. I must know" he said sadly.
Elana shook her head, she wanted to know what was going on,
but disproved of his childish behavior. She felt that he was going into
dementia, hallucinating from the cold, thin air and the lack of nutri-
tion.
" Alright . . .Alright . . . . I'm reading you . . . ." she sighed, running
her eyes down his face, not noticing the detail of his expressions.
" I've read your face . . . It says nothing. Now please Nurix, eat
something." she said.She became concerned. She looked at the meat
on the cold snow. She slowly picked it up, passing it to Nurix. Nurix
forced it away. He took it out of her hand and put it back on the ground
again. Now, he was getting furious at Elana.
"What did you see ?" he asked suspiciously.
Elana sighed." You're hungry, and you're holding back . . ." she
said, thinking that she answered the question. She then picked up the
meat quicker and passed it to him once more, resulting in the same
thing; Nurix again put it down and refused to eat.
Elana slowly moved away from him a bit, so that she was facing
him completely without the need to turn her head. She then stared at
him, crossed legged and slightly tilting her head, like a curious pet cat.
She grinned apologetically.
" Why are you acting this way ?"she asked calmly.
Nurix immediately sensed a sharp pain flash in both sides of his
head. Suddenly, the world seemed to spin and rock in a fluid motion.
He was getting dizzy. Nurix scrunched his eyes, quickly resting
his forehead on his palms. He began to mutter.
Elana didn't understand what was going on. "Why was he acting
this way ? What reason would make him too proud to eat ?" she thought
to herself. It couldn't be hard work or anything he ate. For the whole
day, she knew that Nurix had eaten nothing and had done nothing,
nothing except watch the killing of the bear.
"The bear . . ." she whispered to herself.
She didn't notice at the time because she had thought nothing of
it, but she realized now that watching the death of the bear must have
been gory for him, especially if he had read it's face.
Elana quickly moved up to him once more, slowly lifting his head
" Nurix, does this have anything to do with the bear ?" she asked.

" The bear, this place, the cold. All of this has something to do with me - but the bear most of all. I know it sounds daft but I feel that I can't eat, mainly because of the bear." he finally said.

Elana chuckled a little. But then sighed, trying not to humiliate him with her thoughts of his behavior.

" You watched us kill the bear . . . It must of been very traumatic for you . . ." she said.

" I did more than watch . . ." he said with a miserable sigh, "I read what he was saying when you were busy mutilating it." he finished.

" What did it say to you ?"

" It said that it was scared . . . That it was sorry for entering our cave, and that it wanted to be left alone . . . You killed it . . .. You killed it when it was scared, not when it was putting up a fight, or hungry, but when it was afraid . . . How is that honorable ? Why do we have the right to eat it ?"

Elana sighed. She looked at the meat now cold and moist with the pink stained snow under it. She picked it up, feeling it begin to sag in her hand.

"You know you're right . . . We did kill it . . . But I think you're wrong about it's motives. We killed it for protection. All of us knew, even you . . that that bear was hungry as well as angry, it smelled us, and it wanted us." She slowly turned to Nurix again. "And if you remember, it almost got you . . ." she finished sternly.

Nurix nodded, remembering the giant, dense paw tearing right through the tarp. He remembered being so frightened from it and rolling and running as fast as he could.

Elana, stroked the side of his cheek with her thumb. Nurix let her stroke him.

" . . . The bear wanted to eat you. Do you think that he would have taken the time to read your face ?" she asked logically.

Nurix gave a pathetic grin from slight amusement.

" No . . . I guess that the bear would have taken my life without any remorse . . ."

" . . .The bear was trying to kill you, and now it's dead. Killed before it could get to you." Elana said.

"You're right, the bear has lost to us. It paid the price for trying to get us." Nurix admitted.

Elana sighed as she shook her head. "The bear didn't lose yet . . . He's still trying to kill you . . . Kill you with your own conscience."

" What ?"

"When the bear looked at you and gave you the haunting expression, it gave you something else. It didn't show you pain, agony, or anything else. It told you that it wasn't going to lose to you. It was going to kill you . . . . Since it failed at trying to kill you physically, it now is trying to kill you mentally . . . If you refuse to eat the meat . . . you'll die, and the bear would win . . ."

" But the bear showed me it's soul."

Elana stopped him before he could go on. " The bear is just an animal . . . It doesn't have the same kind of feelings as we do . . ." she explained.

Nurix didn't understand what she meant.

" How can you say that animals don't have feelings ?" he asked.

"Animal's have feelings, just not the same as we do ."

" Yes. That part's right. Not the same as we do. All an animal is concerned for is survival; when to eat, when to sleep, when to mate, when to fight, and when to run. It's feelings are underneath all of that. Besides, when that bear was letting you read his face ? Well that bear was already dead. Brelinka killed it with her first arrow through it's heart. It just took a long time to die. It could not have gotten away or survived no matter how honorable we wanted to be."

Nurix sighed, knowing that he was not going to get anywhere with the debate. He still had some guilt about eating the meat. But the only thing that Elana explained to him clearly was that the bear wanted to kill him, and it was succeeding.

The more Nurix restrained himself, the more he became weaker. He began to stare at the meat now, finally giving into his hunger for it.

"I am hungry," he admitted as he slowly reached over to pick it up and eat it.

Elana immediately grabbed it from him before he could handle it. Nurix was puzzled.

Elana smiled and stuck the cold piece of meat on a stick and slowly moved it into the fire. " The meat was out in the cold too long. If you eat it, you'll use a lot of your body heat to warm it up when you eat it." she said. "And that will weaken you further."

Nurix nodded, not caring for any reason to eat anymore.

" Maybe from now on, you should stay out of the way, near the hearth inside. You'll be safer there." Elana said as she roasted the meat.

" No, I want to be part of the hunting . . .I'll help. Carry your weapons and things like that . . ." he said eagerly. His feelings for the bear had seemed to disappear in front of her. She smiled with interest at what he was saying.

" Will you be quick in handling the weapons?" she asked.

" Yes, I can draw weapons for you quickly . . ."

Elana sighed,

"I don't know, why is it that you want to come all of a sudden ?" she asked, swaying the meat in the silky fire.

" I want to observe the kill . . . It's fascinating, I want to read your faces and I want to read the faces of the animals you hunt . . ." He said, staring at the fire.

Elana became curious,

" How is it fascinating to you ?"

" When you hunt, you seem to change personalities . . . Like you are possessed . . ." he said.

Elana gazed in interest to what he was saying, understanding what he meant.

"When I watched you kill that bear, you acted like you were a demon. Your eyes seemed to change, your mouth opened like a hungry dire wolf. And then when you kill . . . It was graceful yet powerful . . . almost too powerful and it intrigues me." he said.

Elana smiled. She looked at the meat, hearing it sizzling up. She moved it to Nurix. The meat that was once soft and reddish pink was now steaming blackish brown, suddenly soft and sweet smelling.

She ripped it off the stick and handed it to Nurix.

Nurix held it in his palm and gulped.

"Now eat it . . . please." she said.

Nurix smelled the meat. The savory smell gave a nice overwhelming sense of satisfaction. He slowly opened his watering mouth. He put the first piece in, his tongue sensing the texture and taste, filling his stomach with digestive juices all waiting for their share of the food.

He immediately started to bite the chunk off and chew slowly and deliberately.

The sensation of chewing pleased his hunger for it was now satisfied with the meat he long refused to eat. As he swallowed he could feel the meat go down his throat, entering his stomach. He then ate more, and more of the chunk he held in his hand.

As he chewed, he began to smile and chuckle with relief, feeling the guilt for the bear disappear as he continued to eat.

He mouth began to get tired but he didn't stop, he couldn't stop, for his hunger grew with every piece he chewed.

Elana was also relieved.

Nurix swallowed his last bit of the meat, then sighed and gazed at Elana.

" How was it ?" she asked.

Nurix smiled, " The meat was good. The taste is still in my mouth . . . I can't get rid of it." he said.

Elana sighed as well. " Thank you . . ." she said.

Nurix looked at her with a confused look. Only when he read her face, did he begin to understand what she was thanking him for.

She was thanking him for eating the meat . . . She was thanking him for not dying.

Nurix then grinned pleasantly, " you're welcome . . ."

" Nurix finally understood something. He learned that when it came to dangerous animals, there was no time for compassion or for saving, or for anything else. He learned that in the wild it is more the survival of the fittest than the survival of the nicest." the Old Man said. "And that's something you can apply to everything, whether you're out in the wilderness or not."

I nodded sleepily.

" Later, that day, they packed their things, including the bones and the preserved skin of the bear. They took out the horses, who hadn't seen daylight for a long time. They then saddled up and made their journey down from the mountains.

Now they were entering the foot hills and heading for the town of Ques . . ." he said, looking at me closely.

And that's the last thing I remember. I fell asleep and I don't know how much I missed.

The next day, out at sea, as the crew sat around on deck during the evening meal, I didn't have to bother the Old Man to continue. Someone else did it for me. The whole crew was hooked now.

" Ha, I've never heard of a tale such as this." one of the crew said.

" Yes, I know. Old Man, how is it that you remember such a story like this ?" another one asked.

The Old Man seemed to be out of words to say, " Well Um, I guess that a story that has women in it always stays in your memory."

Suddenly, everyone started to laugh at his remark.

I sat down, amused myself at his comment.

The Old Man seemed to be in a blur, " Why, what was so funny ?" he asked.

" Just the way you said it Old Man, it was hilarious." I said as I calmed myself down.

The Old Man chuckled a little. " Ending with that note, I guess that we should start to sleep tonight instead of talking," he said.

The crew groaned, wanting him to continue with the story.

And, never one to refuse the chance to shine in front of an audience, the Old Man sighed again and closed his eyes.

"Alright . . . .. well, they had just made it down from the high mountains and there they entered a heavy forest. They had travelled for days, stopping at a great lake in the foothills which was miles long, to wash their things and to let their skinny horses feed, rest and recover from their long and agonizing journey from the mountains."

After four more days of travelling, they had made it out of the mountains altogether, not losing a single horse, although, the horses at this time were now extremely skinny compared to when they started out.

They were also all overly packed with whatever the three mistresses could find going down the mountains: extra branches to use for fire, small furry long-eared Jack hares, and extra bags of smoothened bones and smoked meat from the bear and all other animals they found along the way. Although none said it aloud, they had been badly frightened and had no intention of being caught without enough supplies again.

It was not until the fourth day that they had escaped from the clutches of the cold, rigid mountains, to see the golden sun set over the barren foothills. For the first time in weeks they saw small brown-grassed flat meadows in natural clearings in the forest.

The fifth day was quiet as they travelled along the skinny, straight rocky road in front of them. The heavy forest had pretty well disappeared and they were in a country of low hills, like waves in the ocean, as far as the eye could see.

There were heavy clouds, though, and it was dim in the thinly grown grass and shrubs they were travelling through. Only small animals and birds lived in them and most of the time you couldn't see or hear them at all.

The vast meadow of short grass and brush plants went far into the horizon, like a painting where the scenery seems to grow misty around the vanishing point. It wasn't quite a desert, and wasn't quite the plains. Further on, there were more rolling foothills and a few more solitary mountains, but the country was not as rigorous as the region they had just travelled through.

These were low, brownish dirty-looking hills, covered in dry plants and little vegetation. The same went for the mountain ahead except for the ice cap on the top of it, but, as they had found out for themselves, that was usually typical for mountains all over.

It was a peaceful place, because there was no other human life. But they were certain that coming up, there would be a lot. In fact they expected to encounter human civilization within a couple of week's travel, where there was thought to be some sort of town. That was what Sassaska remembered for sure before she had lost the map. Hopefully that was true.

The five horses had gotten tired and now walked briskly after a long extensive gallop a few miles back. Nurix rested himself on Elana's back, staring at the vast scenery of short grass and shrubs. Although it made it a little difficult to control the horse, Elana didn't seem to mind much that he was leaning on her.

Sassaska lagged a little behind because she was reading a little literature from the remaining scrolls.

She was telling the rest of them information which might be useful for them in some way or another. The reality of it all, she was doing it out of sheer boredom as well.

" Listen to this . . ." said Sassaska, trying to read as she bobbed up and down because of the horse. " . . . the Buushu have no real religion, and don't even share the legends, customs or anything we believe in . . . No stable belief in Marsolla, No written tales of any sort. Only an unspoken belief in a deity Goddess Tierra." she finished.

" So we all don't have to worry about that 'stepping on the first step' junk here right?" Elana said jokingly

Brelinka slowly turned and gave a quick glimpse at her.

"Yes, the Buushu are a nomadic kind of people. They don't have time to set up a proper religion. They have something else which separates them from us Arkaitons and from the Makaiton Clans.

They have the Code of the Warrior, which they start to learn at a very young age." Brelinka said.

Elana turned to Brelinka,

" Wait a minute. I was raised Buushu guard. I don't see the Code of the Warrior making that much difference. The Arkaitons have a Warrior Code Book, same as the Makaitons. How are Buushu any different from them ?" she asked.

" No. You were raised by a Buushu and have been honored in being allowed to wear the Buushu braid. But you were not raised in the full Buushu way. Their code book tells them that if they are in battle and are seriously wounded, they are not allowed to be helped by anyone. That example out of the many I know, should give you an idea about them."

"Sure, I know all about that. But it's just a rule of thumb, not to get bogged down with wounded. It takes a handful of warriors to take care of one wounded woman - and you dilute your force that way."

"No, Elana, that's the logical rationale for it, but it's much more than that. As a General, I had to study the strategies of every tribe and what makes them employ those strategies. With the Buushu it's all to do with them being nomadic. There is no permanent place of rest for them. They lose women, men and children left and right, through sickness and accidents and have to keep leaving them everywhere. The tribe can't wait, because they follow animal migrations and if they stop, the entire tribe may die. So everyone must be able to depend only on herself to recover and catch up. It's a harsh life, but it breeds an independent spirit. Buushu never ask for help. And never give it . . . Everyone knows that . . ." she replied with a smear.

Sassaska kept reading on, feeling that what Brelinka said was true. She just wanted some written document to back her up.

She then gasped, " . . . Ooo . . . well, this time you're wrong . . . There are only few groups of Buushu that are truly nomadic. The more you go on, the more you'll find that they're farmers and hunters. The Nomadic ones are usually groups of hired mercenaries, guards, even training Instructors on their long journeys back and forth. Thus, they give the appearance that they are still nomadic."

"That's not entirely true." said Elana. "They still have the Grand Round. I've been invited to go quite a few times."

"I don't see anything about that here ." said Sassaska.

"It's like a reconnection. You join a bunch of friends or family or even strangers, and go on a year -long migration, living in the old way and travelling all around the ancient Buushu routes, all over the country. You learn to survive and fight and work with others. I've always wanted to go."

" So wait . . . In their code book, do Buushu have some sort of martial art ?" Sassaska asked. "Do they teach it secretly in this Grand Round ?"

Brelinka shook her head. " Not that I know of. They don't have any sort of inner power either. What you see is what you get. Just physical force and willpower - trained to the limit and enhanced."

Sassaska shuffled the paper a little more. " Well it says here that . . . Um . . . Oh yes, that they believe in the releasing of their strength . . ." she said. "What's that ?"

" I've heard that said, but I never knew what it meant. But it seems to support my point. The Buushu have something in common with the Arkaitons.

Our Martial arts are based on controlling our inner demons and releasing them when the time comes . . . In hunting and so on . . ." Elana said. "Like we did with the bear."

Sassaska nodded her head, almost agreeing with her, but Brelinka though, didn't agree.

" No . . . Buushu only believe in the physical. In the here and now. No magic, no supernatural stuff. Except for Tierra, for some reason.

Just what works right now. They believe in some sort of drink to give them the power they need for super-human martial situation .They believe in getting drunk . . ." she said.

Sassaska then unrolled a little more of the scroll. "Hold on there's more . . . by the serum of a drink, a strong alcoholic wheat barley which is brewed for warriors only . . . You're right. They're drunks." Sassaska said as she began to roll up her scroll.

Brelinka watched her roll it up and put it back into her saddlebag.

" What, that was it ?" Brelinka asked.

Sassaska looked at her. " Yes, that's all she wrote . . ." she said.

"It's not so simple.

It is a whisky, yes But the alcohol is only necessary to lower the inhibitions and get the solution into the blood quickly. Along with the whisky there are many secret herbs and potions, which strengthen the muscles, take away any sensation of pain, increase the endurance and speed and focus the will. This drink, rather than making you into a drunk, makes you into a superwoman. I know. I've tried it."

The other two women were stunned by this revelation and no one spoke for quite a while as they digested it.

They travelled for as many hours in the day that they had light, stopping for a little rest and to relieve themselves only when necessary. Even then, they wouldn't want to waste another minute, and jumped right back on their horses, and continued on.

Nurix watched from his position, still resting his head on Elana's back, holding her firm waist and staring to his right and left at the passing, and ever so changing scenery, as they traveled for a few more days, stopping to set up camp and then eat the latest thing they caught while they were on the road. The days, as they did up in the mountains, soon ran into one another and turned into to a couple of weeks in travelling. But they got closer to country that seemed to be better and better.

But all Nurix could think about was the scenery. To him it seemed that seconds only went by as the region changed at his very eyes. From rocky to smooth, from cold to hot, from dirt and short shrubs to tall and grand evergreens to tall grasses, it continued to change. He began to feel himself change, too, as they went on. His hair grew longer, his vision grew a little weaker, and his curiosity grew smaller. He felt that he was growing and getting wiser while everyone else around him didn't seem to age at all .

After the third week of traveling, they were winding their way through the last few hills between them and the great plains. They were travelling single file down a beautiful little valley with the hills close by on each side.

Sassaska, who had read almost every scroll she had by this time was now only concerned in finding the town. She was sick from their trek now and wanted to see some sort of civilization. A town, a hut, a mud shelter, anything that would show a small sign of some sort of culture.

They journeyed on as the last rays of the setting sun turned everything to gold, looking for a good place to camp for the night.

Brelinka, who was travelling in front, suddenly slowed their horses down. Sassaska and Elana were both puzzled as to why they had done so and rode up front beside Brelinka to find out what was going on.

Slowly, Nurix sat up in awe and stared.

Taboo and Rhyme slowed the supply horses that they were riding and came to a stop, staring in amazement too.

Right in front of them, eating away on the branches of the trees, were giant, eighteen foot beasts. From head to toe, they were covered in brownish red wool. Their tusks were long, and curving.

Immediately, the animal closest to them growled and twisted its head to the side, entangling it's grand tusks to snap off the large arm of the tree it was feeding on.

" Mammoth . . ." Nurix said in shock.

He'd only heard of these creatures, but he had never seen them up close before.

The Mammoth didn't notice them, or it just didn't seem to care that they watched it. The mammoth then snorted through it's wooly trunk, and brought it up to its forehead, waving it's small ears.

" Where there are mammoth herds, there must be a Mammoth Herder . . ." said Elana.

She wanted to move closer. but then Brelinka immediately grabbed her reins. "No . . . Don't judge them so quickly, just because they seem friendly. We don't know if they are wild herds or tamed herds. And even if tamed, they may be war mammoths. You never know what people might do with mammoth this far north. And, to tell you the truth, I don't want to find out." she whispered.

" . . .Well, from the looks of them, they seem friendly . . . If they were wild, then that big one would have bluff-charged us instead of raising it's trunk at us." she whispered back to Brelinka.

" Damn. There's not enough room to go around them and trying to herd them somewhere they don't want to go might be dangerous. I think the only thing to do is to go back the way we came a few miles and camp there and wait until they leave. They probably don't go up much further than this, since I didn't notice too many trees back there - so there'd be nothing for them to eat."

"I hate to stop . . . " Sassaska started to say.

Suddenly, a long, loud sound of vibrating pulses was heard followed by a large cry from one of the mammoths.

Elana jumped in surprise.

Nurix raised his head a little, to peek over Elana's shoulder, seeing a woman dressed in simple white cloth and straight brown pants, playing what seemed to be a large windy tusk which was hollowed out so thinly that it was able to project strange vibration sounds when she blew into it

She was riding on top of a stubbier, shorter, denser, stronger, and uglier - looking Mammoth. It's head, seemed to have some sort of a contraption made to hold the tusk horn and used as a controlling mechanism. Large, thick leather straps ran down it's bulky, fuzzy forehead and then split into two separate straps fitting comfortably around the eyes and going down to the tusks.

The three of them and the slaves kept quiet.

Suddenly the woman on the mammoth blew into the horn once more, making the odd, strange-sounding noise, echoing louder than the first.

Then all of the wandering Mammoths started to move away and headed to her.

As the large one slowly started to move with the other dozens in the far distance, Sassaska looked to them both, " Well at least we know that they're domesticated." she said.

" Should we go down there and say hello ?" Brelinka asked.

" I guess that would be the proper thing to do, wouldn't it ?" Sassaska replied. "Since we're going that way anyways."

Elana and Brelinka slowly kicked the sides of their horses. The horses grunted, but gave in and started to move. Sassaska and the slaves stayed there for a few minutes.

Sassaska looked at them with a grin. " Well, girls, I guess that we should go with them shouldn't we ?" she said. "Even though those things scare the hell out of me."

Taboo, looked the large beasts in fear, but Rhyme didn't seem to care, she immediately let loose a wild burst of laughter, and kicked her horse forward

Taboo then looked to Sassaska.

" Alright mistress, you're right . . . Let's go . . ." she said.

Sassaska laughed as she slowly got moving. The slave followed behind her.

The woman on the stubby mammoth was about to give another blow into her horn, but she caught a glimpse of Sassaska, Brelinka, Elana, and the two slaves lagging behind.

Her first thought was that they were hunters, wanting to poach one of the mammoths for it's fur and meat and bones. She slowly reached for the spear locked onto the side of the box saddle she was sitting in. She drew it, but she held it down, so they couldn't see it.

The three women and the slaves stopped, seeing that the mammoth-girl was surrounded by her mammoth herd, many of whom had now turned and were facing back down the valley toward the newcomers.

The travellers halted in front of her. Sassaska was smiling, happy to see a new human face.

" Excuse me herder, we want to know . . . "

" Are you hunters ? Because if you are, I'm sorry . . . You're going to have to kill me before you can get your greedy little hands on one of my mammoths." the herder interrupted.

Sassaska stopped speaking, not knowing what to say. She closed her mouth and looked at Brelinka. Brelinka shrugged, not knowing what to do. Sassaska then sighed and looked up once more.

" . . .We're not hunters or poachers; we're travellers, friends sent from the Empress herself." Sassaska shouted.

The woman looked at the six of them. She saw that they were slightly dirty, carrying many skins and bones. She then looked at Nurix sitting there, looking at all the mammoths.

She slowly unbuckled the strap of her spear,

" You're lying ?" she shouted back at Sassaska.

" No . . ." Sassaska shouted, drawing her saddle bag up to show her scrolls and letter of safe passage.

Suddenly, the herder, thinking that she was being attacked, immediately stood up on the her large box saddle, pulled out her spear and held it over her head, aiming to kill.

Sassaska slowly moved her hands up, holding the saddle bag.

" What's in the bag ?" the herder shouted.

Brelinka quickly darted her horse in front of Sassaska, her own explosive spear in her hands, in a warrior's ready position. Elana, with her Buushu training had been even faster. She'd had her spear out before the herder and made it to a standing position, although she almost knocked Nurix off in the process.

"Don't worry . . . " said Sassaska, now wedged between Brelinka and Elana. "We mean you no harm . . .. Just . . . let me show you some written proof from the Empress herself."

"Wouldn't matter . . ." the mammoth-girl interrupted, wrinkling her nose and sniffling briskly. " . . . Never learned to read text . . . Too poor . . . and not much use up here." she said.

Sassaska stopped trying to look for the right scroll from her saddle bag. She slowly placed the saddle bag down over the neck of the horse.

" . . . All we want to know is how far is the next settlement. If you tell us that, we'll be out of your hair . . ." Sassaska shouted.

"You don't seem the pouching type . . .you all would of tried to kill me by now." she said as she began to lower her spear. Still she was aiming it as she brought it down, in case they tried to kill her when she was vulnerable.

"That's because we're not!" shouted Brelinka.

Suddenly the woman, startled from Brelinka's shout nervously lifted her spear once more, shivering it.

"Oh, God !" whispered Brelinka shaking her head in irritation. She slowly moved her horse away from Sassaska, making herself the main target although she was sensing that there would be no danger.

Elana looked up at the girl, seeing the way she was holding her spear, and the way she nervously shook.

If they were poachers, this kind of nervous, but dutiful girl would have been difficult to deal with. She would be very unpredictable and, with her high position and her control of the mammoth herds, she would be almost impossible to defeat.

Nurix looked up at the girl standing on her mammoth and then his eyes widened in amazement. He slowly bent over to Elana's ear.

"She's just a little child, probably 13 or 14 at the most. She's pretty scared too." he whispered.

Elana's interest then grew a little, she slowly moved her horse around Sassaska and closer, staring into the eyes of the herder.

Elana grinned, about to laugh. " How silly is this ? We're trying to negotiate with a child . . ." she thought.

She smiled, and backed her horse a little watching the child go on trying to decide if they were really game poachers.

Elana watched Sassaska slowly moving her horse forwards

" . . . I'm telling you, back away poacher . . ." the girl shouted.

Sassaska nodded her head, and slowly moved back.

" Please ma'am, we are not poachers, we just want directions to the closest town from here." Sassaska said.

They went on arguing and Brelinka felt that they weren't getting anywhere. She didn't want to kill the child, but she would if any harm was threatened to Sassaska or Elana. With her experience, she could spear the herder from the position she had moved into - and do so before the girl could make a move.

Sassaska and the girl were still shouting at each other.

Suddenly, Brelinka interrupted them both. " What can we do to prove to you that we're not poachers ?" she shouted.

Both Sassaska and the woman standing on her mammoth became quiet immediately after she said that.

The woman paused and said nothing.

" Well ? I'm waiting for your answer, girl." she scalded.

" I could ask you what animal I'm riding on . . . You wouldn't know that if you were a real traveller. But if you were a real poacher, you'd purposely lie to me so that you'd convince me that you're not. I don't know."

Brelinka then shook her head with a slight smile and slowly moved her horse closer and closer to her.

" Stop right there or I'll . . . I'll kill your horse." the girl shouted on top of the Mammoth.

" Fine, I'll make it easier for you to hit it . . ."Brelinka said, slowly stopping her horse and getting off it and continuing to walk closer to her.

The girl got nervous, her eyes widened, as Brelinka got closer and closer, until she was leaning on the woolly belly of the Mammoth.

The herd-girl shivered nervously, pointing the wavy head of the spear towards Brelinka,

Brelinka then slowly backed away and held out her arms.

" Well, you didn't kill my horse, but I think that you were waiting to kill me, weren't you ?" Brelinka shouted calm and sarcastically.

The girl ,standing on the mammoth ,nodded frantically.

" Yes, that was completely the case . . . I'm warning you now, step back or you get it . . ."

Sassaska got scared, thinking that Brelinka was provoking her to the point of killing. " Quit it Bree, what are you trying to prove ?"

Brelinka gave a quick stare, " Oh, nothing . . . I'm trying to get killed . . ." she said as she winked at Sassaska.

She then faced the nervous girl, who getting extremely jumpy.

" After all, I'm just a poacher who could have killed you, killed one of your mammoths and ran off instead of trying to talk my way out of all this. . ." Brelinka said, staring calmly at the girl, expecting nothing to happen to her.

The girl breathed heavily and deeply, not knowing what to do.

Brelinka waited for an answer.

" Well ?" she furiously shouted.

The girl, now shivering, slowly let her spear down. "Alright, you've all proven your point . . . You're not poachers." she said sorrowfully.

Brelinka gave a smile of relief and gently let her arms drop to her sides.

Sassaska, who was also relieved, came off her horse and approached Brelinka.

Brelinka turned her head and gave a grin of relief and victory towards Sassaska.

Sassaska only raised her brow with a small frown beginning to form on her face as she patted Brelinka on her shoulder and pulled her close to her ear.

" . . . What were you doing, you could of gotten yourself killed .." Sassaska whispered.

Brelinka gave a small laugh, "I stopped her from causing any sort of damage . . . Didn't you know that my horse was at stake ?" she said jokingly.

Sassaska only sighed through her nose at Brelinka's joke and looked up to the girl on the mammoth.

"Are you really from the Empress ?" the girl asked. "Do you, want

me to point you to the next town ?" she said apologetically, not knowing what to say at this time but feeling that she had to do something.

Sassaska nodded, " Yes, we are - and that would be very nice . . ."
she said, answering both questions.

The girl sighed, " Alright . . . Get on your horses . . . I'll guide you
and your friends as I take the herd out to graze out further on." she
said.

Sassaska nodded once more. " . . . Thank you . . ." she said.

The girl regretfully nodded.

" . . . What's your name ?" Brelinka asked.

The girl looked down at her as she made her way to her woolly
hoofed horse.

" Danoise; my name's Danoise," the girl said.

Brelinka then grabbed the reins of the horse and slowly flung them
over it's head, " Well Danoise, I want to know something . . . How old
are you ? " she asked.

Danoise gave no answer as she slowly sat down on the large squarish saddle on the mammoth's neck and reached to pick up the oddly
lengthened reins.

As she was about to get the mammoth going, Brelinka asked once
more " . . . Well, how old are you ?"

Danoise ignored it again and then changed the subject.

" Keep heading east on the dirt trail . . . until it turns into a real
road. Then go if you go South East, you'll reach a town by the name of
Ques." she said.

Brelinka didn't understand why Danoise didn't want to answer
her question. Danoise's ignorance only made Brelinka more persistent.
Brelinka had a feeling that she was very young because of the way she
acted. The way she made a quick judgement of poachers, instead of
asking the kind of mature, calm questions that Brelinka and the others
expected.

Brelinka was about to ask one more time but Sassaska shook her
head, expressing not to go further into the question.

They waited patiently for the girl to start moving. The girl then
jerked the reins, pulling the tusks upwards a little. The Mammoth gave
a laborous cry then started to move.

She turned around, " Well come on . . ." she shouted.

Everyone started to trot behind the mammoth as the herd began to catch sight and started to move, joining the procession.

The travellers were moving slow, so was the herd; but they all stared in awe as they watched the thickly packed, reddish brown, woolly beasts, the size of small houses encircle them and stomp gently, almost wanting the women to stare at them.

As one went by, Nurix stared at it.

The sheer size amazed him. The animal's eye focused on Nurix, probably in surprise as well. Nurix watched as it slowed down. Only it's beautiful, winding tusks appeared next to him. Nurix's amazement drove him, and he wanted to touch it, to see what it felt like. Yet, he was scared that he was doing something that no one wanted him to do.

"What if Danoise turned around and saw me doing this ? Would she stop the herd and refuse to take us to town ?" he thought.

Elana quickly turned for a glimpse at Nurix.

" My God Marsolla, look at the size of these beasts ? They look as if they were from some sort of a fantasy tale ." said Nurix.

"Amazing creatures aren't they. They're ugly but they're powerful, and we depend on them for almost everything: Their bones for jewelry and ceremonial weapons, their fur to strengthen and help insulate heat in a tarp tent and sleeping skins and their meat for food. There are smaller ones which are specially bred for war . . . But what they've lost in height over the years, they gained in width. The true Battle Mammoth is now much like the one Danoise is riding. We call them Mastodons, but on the battle field, they are known as the Line Breakers. " she said.

" How do large animals such as these get tamed and bred into useful war machines or domesticated into a source of food ? Even a calf from one of these is probably the size of a horse.

It's too impossible to imagine someone sitting and placing these things in a gated fence. They could probably break through stone walls if they had to."

" I don't know how long it took to tame them originally, but all I do know that they were dying. They couldn't find food in the ice and women started feeding them and leading them to newly melted lands where there was food to find.

This was hundreds of years ago now, but since then, they have all been born into captivity - except for the wild herds. Now they trust us, and we trust them." she said.

Nurix stared at the tusk in amazement, then brought himself to grab a hold of the curly tip.

Suddenly, the mammoth raised it's head ferociously and growled a loud, unearthly cry.

Elana's horse was slightly spooked and jumped. So did Nurix. His eyes widened and he quickly grabbed onto Elana's waist with all his might. His breathing was quickened a bit.

Elana giggled a little in amusement. "Getting a little cocky aren't we now ?" she said.

Nurix slowly loosened his grip around her waist, still tingly from fright. " I . . .I'm sorry; I didn't think it would care . . ." he said as his breathing slowed a bit. " . . . Well, I've learned my lesson . . ." he finished.

" If there's anything that I've learned over the years, it's that no one ever learns their lesson. They just learn to let their fear control them." she said.

"Well then, I've lost control of my fear then . . . Either way, I'll never touch the tusks of a beast like that as long as I live." Nurix said.

"Cute . . ." said Elana.

The Old Man stopped talking. Probably just catching his breath, but then the crew got anxious to hear a bit more.

" Well Old Man . . . then what . . ." one man asked.

The Old Man looked at him, and was about to say something. As he opened his mouth, the crew leaned a little, thinking that he was going to tell another part to the story.

He then closed his mouth and sighed.

" I think that the Old Man's tired . . ." I said, thinking that was the case for his silence.

" Actually I was going to ask if any of you have any questions?. You were all rather quiet during the story . . ." he then turned to me with a slight expression on his face.

" Other than someone I know . . ." he finished.

"Well, I have a question, Old Man." said one of them.

The Old Man turned around and looked at him. "Spit it out, son."

" Well, I was thinking. You are always saying about these women who were stronger than us . . .Were they . . . muscular and manly look-ing ?"

The crew seemed to cringe as they got an image of what he was talking about.

The Old Man laughed.

"No, no, no, they were strong. I'll give you that, but they were far from muscular looking. They had denser muscles, more tight and quicker in reflex, but they were no larger than women's muscles today. They also had the extra layer of fat, making their skin and body soft to the touch. They were slightly taller than women today. But only by two or three inches.

Their bodies were slender and their legs were long. Their complexions and textures varied and were very diversed. Ranging from black eyes to light brown. Their hair ranged from flat black and straight to curly reddish brown. Skin colors from the palest of snow to the darkest tan of dawn. They were all truly beautiful. And that was what made them the greatest warriors. Their movements and their fighting methods were also elegant and balanced like them. They were like great cats, powerful and graceful at the same time. You would love them if you saw them, but the problem was that they loved each other as well." the Old Man said.

" Who ever said that was a problem in the first place ?" another said.

Suddenly the crew broke into a perverted laughter,; all of them making the picture in their heads and morphing it into their fantasies.

The Old Man chuckled a bit as well.

"What about these giant mammoths you talk of ? Why don't they exist anymore ? What happened to them ?"

" Well they still do exist. And over here in the colonies too. You just haven't gone north far enough to where it's always as cold as ice. But the great herds of Atlantis are no more. Some strange sickness went though them, many years after the time I'm taking about, and nearly wiped them all out."

Sisko then sat up once more, still in his sleepy haze.

" I've travelled as far as the Ice would take me. When I was a boy, I remember seeing these animals, these beasts you mention in your story. But you're wrong Old Man. They exist down south, where it's warm. But they are not woolly or larger than giant houses fit for a king, nor do they have as long and as curly a tusk as you talk of."

Everyone was then silent, so was I .

The Old Man gave a small chuckle to himself as he looked to all the faces.

His small smear to one side of his face went around, everyone looked at him, hesitating for what he was about to say next.

" If there was one thing I've learned from the tales of Atlantis, it's that the young grow to be ignorant and the old regret losing that brave ignorance" he said.

Sisko raised a brow in curiosity, " What, Old Man ?" he asked.

" I know the beasts of which you speak." said the Old Man. They are called elephants, and are smaller cousins. They have no hair, only a bare skin. And they live in the hot lands of Africa and India. But these poor cousins are not the beasts I speak of. The great mammoth of legend. They do exist young man, much like Atlantis exists, you've just got to open your eyes and go deeper. For then you'll find them . . . Besides, how far north or how many exist today is irrelevant. I am here to tell the tale of Atlantis, not to tell the tale of mammoths." the Old Man said wisely. "They are only a minor detail."

Sisko thought a bit about what the Old Man had said, but the only part he understood was when the Old Man told him that he was telling a story about Atlantis instead of a story of Mammoths. He then agreed to shut up, not wanting to get into a heated argument with the Old Man.

"Alright Old Man, just go on with the story . . ."

"You're sure you don't want to tell it. Sisko ?" the Old man asked with a grin.

"Okay. I'm sorry. I won't dispute the facts again."

"The Old Man nodded, pleased that the lesson had been taught so easily. Then he resumed:

As the women followed Danoise and her herd of mammoths through the soft, bush-blistered hills; the sounds of distant women singing a vigorating chant seemed to echo through the air.

Brelinka trotted her horse alongside Danoise's pet mammoth, scouting and charting in her mind where they were heading and where they had been. Partly because she was good at it, and partly because she was bored.

" How much farther until we reach town ?" asked Brelinka.

" A few more miles along this route of long grass and you should be able to get the glimpse of the workers laboring in the fields." Danoise said briskly.

They carried on for a little longer until Danoise came to a halt. She immediately stood up and blew into her giant horn three times, signalling a halt to the other mammoths. All the mammoths groaned as they stopped, huffing and seeming to catch their breath.

Sassaska watched the giant beasts stop in perfect discipline.

" Listen, the sound is stronger !" shouted Elana, who was slowly creeping her horse towards the labor song of the peasants.

Danoise pointed further on in front of her.

"There, Keep heading that way and you'll hit Ques."

Brelinka looked up at her.

" Won't you show us around ?"

"If you are truly Arkaiton then you'll easily get in . . ." she said in a prejudiced tone.

" What do you mean ?" Asked Brelinka.

"You have the face marks of a Makaiton."

"I was Governor of Makaitia and earned the right to wear them." said Brelinka.

" Well I hope you don't get into trouble in Ques, then. The whole town is made up of Arkaiton merchants and dealers. And since they are Arkaiton, they seem to be curiously partial to their own kind."

" That's unusual,"

" No it isn't. Out here where the Empire's rules and regulations barely scratch life ? Out here, anyone can do what ever they want . . . and get away with it, if they have the force to back it up." Danoise said. "And that means that poor Buushu like us suffer for it."

" But they are Arkaiton ?" Brelinka asked.

" Yes. And that is the problem. This is as far as I go . . . I can't leave the herd for too long. I am responsible. Now you and your friends will have to make it there on your own."

Sassaska approached Brelinka on her horse, curious to why the herd had stopped. She looked at Brelinka's face, then up to Danoise.

"What's going on ?" she asked.

Danoise sighed, ignoring her question.

" She's not taking us any further. The town is down the way, we just have to follow the road and the sounds of the peasants singing in the fields . . .. Isn't that right Danoise ?" Brelinka said, focusing onto her eyes.

Sassaska watched as the intensity between Brelinka and Danoise seemed to boil, even though they didn't say anything to each other that would of caused it.

" Well then, I guess that this is good bye." Sassaska said to try and break the tension between them. "Thank you for you help. We appreciate it."

" Yes . . . This is good bye." Danoise said, as she slowly pulled the reigns of the mammoth to the side, signalling it to turn around.

As Elana and the two slaves slowly got out of her way, they watched her made the mammoth move faster. She was irritated from the tone of her voice.

"By the way, warrior, you asked for my age . . .." she shouted, not wanting to turn around.

Brelinka turned her horse around.

" Well, how old are you ?"

" I'm 15 years of age." she shouted back.

" Funny, from the way you were acting, I expected you to be much younger than that . . " she said slowly sniggering to herself.

"And so we leave our heroines, covered in mammoth dung and on their way to civilization" said the Old Man, yawning.

" But what about the town of Ques. Can't we get there before we go to sleep ?"

" If I tell you that part now, you'll all forget." the Old Man said.

"No we won't!"

" We've got good memories, Old Man."

"Silence !" shouted the Old Man.

Suddenly the crew, not expecting the Old Man to shout, quieted down.

" Rule number one: when I say that I am tired, I mean that I'm tired. Is that clear ?" he said.

Everyone was quiet. They then looked at each other and nodded like scared little children.

The Old Man calmed down a little.

" Good, well then, I've got to get to sleep. We've got a long day tomorrow." the Old Man said as he got comfortable on the deck floor.

" Oh, well, I guess we can wait until tomorrow." said one crewman.

" Tomorrow,; that's not a long time away" said another.

" SHUT UP ALL OF YOU !" shouted Likooshas from down below.

Everyone immediately went quiet and closed their eyes, now focusing in falling asleep.

I slowly laid down myself, staring at the many stars above me, wondering about the story. For some reason, the more and more I listened to the story, it seemed more of a story that the Old Man lived through rather than one he learned just through hearing.

It was the detail, the love for certain characters that I sensed, and his knowledge of everything that this one said to that one as well as all the everyday things about Atlantis.

He seemed to know more than any other man who'd ever claimed to know about Atlantis. Yet he never claimed to be from that legendary place. And he talked of it so passionately like he loved Atlantis so much that he didn't want anyone, except whoever he thought worthy, to go there.

The clues were all in the story and my new goal now was to find out who the Old Man really was.

For days we sailed, crossing the two Peaks and refusing to look back, in fear that we would regret what we were doing. The newly made sails flapped full of air as the boat sped quicker than ever before, without the rowing of the crew.

This was different than what the men knew. The waves were bigger and constantly rippled, unlike the smoother and softer waters they were used to sailing in. The ocean that they sailed was foreign to everyone except the Old Man; but to him, it was like an old friend which he had wanted to leave. He knew everything: how to sail faster, how to navigate during the day, and during the night, and a lot more that would only confuse an experienced sailer of the inland sea. The men knew nothing out here; all they did now, was use the strong wind to their advantage.

Likooshas was almost always on deck now, straining to look west, hoping to see land; hoping the land would be Atlantis.

The Old Man walked up to him and patted him on the back.

" Don't hurt yourself, old boy, Atlantis is much further away. I can guarantee you that." he said.

" But if it sunk, then there should be some sort of mountain or peak sticking out of the water."

The Old Man kept himself from chuckling.

" You actually believe that it sunk ?" the Old Man asked.

Likooshas turned around. "All the stories say so. ' Past the pillars of the inland sea, lay the swallowed peaks of Atlantis' tears." he said, rephrasing an old child's tale he once heard.

"So what are you planning to do when you spot the peaks - dive for the treasures ?" the Old Man asked.

"Something will be left. The survivors would have climbed up on the peaks with their treasures, then died there. We'll just sail in, pick it all up and go home." the pirate said, nodding. "After all, we're nearly a week out from the Pillars. No one has ever sailed this far before. It has to be around here somewhere."

" Likooshas, believe me when I say this - Atlantis did not sink - no matter how many stories you have heard. It is as big as half the planet. And it is farther than any other place known to the world you came from.

We sail on an endless ocean that entraps it from everyone else. Where it is, will take us several weeks to get to. So I don't believe we'll be seeing it soon," the Old Man said.

"Old Man, I thank you for taking us on this mission, but never ever correct me in public or even think that my beliefs are less than yours. You are old and you could be going mad."

The Old Man stared at him with a look that felt sorry for him. He pitied his ignorance to understand the truth of anything.

Nonetheless, the Old Man started to laugh and slapped him on the back once more." I often think that myself, so you may be right. Just keep looking Likooshas. Just keep looking" he said.

The Old Man then staggered down the rocking deck, almost tripping as waves splashed onto it. One man, pulling to gain control of the sail, saw him almost fall and quickly grabbed his arm. The Old Man got control of himself and continued on.

He approached the man who was sitting down and controlling the wooden rudder. " We're off a bit." he said. "Keep heading the boat away from the sun in the morning and toward the sun in the after-noon. and we'll keep the wind and we'll be heading the right way," the Old Man said.

" Huh?" said the rudder man.

The Old Man started to talk a little louder.

" We're heading too far north. We need to turn a hair south or we'll lose the wind and be taken somewhere else on the current !"

" Alright Old Man, so I'll turn the rudder mildly, right ?" the rudder man asked.

The Old Man nodded.

The rudder man got up to make himself more comfortable and accidentally swung the rudder hard to one side. The boat suddenly surfed on a wave and then crashed down in the trough with a giant force. Everyone tumbled around, but then got control of themselves once more.

The Old Man looked to the rudder man.

" Aren't you glad we fastened the hull a bit stronger ?" he said with a smear of relief.

The Rudder man only nodded, feeling tense and stiffened with fear from the incoming waves. The whole crew, whatever they had been doing before, were now huddled in fear, wishing to go home or at least wishing not to die out in the cold and lonely clutches of the vengeful Sea Gods.

The Old Man, who was calm and serene, only turned to gaze at the rippling, rough waves in the far distance and shook his head slowly, as if he was saying 'No, I won't die yet,' to the wind.

As the Old Man looked out at the sea, I held onto a piece of tied down roping, staring in awe at the grayer skies and the wind's incredible strength in forcing the waves at us with no remorse, like a sulking god who didn't want us to be out here.

Another scary part of it all was that we were miles away, far outside the Peaks. Usually, when you sailed, there was always the comforting thought that you were seldom out of sight of land. If anything happened, you could usually swim to shore. If you could swim. But that wasn't the case now.

I watched Likooshas stare at the waves, hoping to see land, thinking in his obsessed little mind that there had to be land close by. There always had been before. The reality that the Old Man had pointed out to him was that Atlantis was further away than anyone had ever dreamed. Likooshas was just afraid to believe it.

It was evening a couple of days later and, to my relief, the wind and waves had finally died down.

Most of the crew were below deck, breathing the hot, stenching stuffy and uncirculated air as they slept. The Old Man had stopped telling the story for a while. He was too tired.

In the old days, when the rudderman got tired or night fell, we would just tie off the rudder and let the boat go its own way. But the Old Man changed all that. He said that there should always be some-one controlling the rudder at all times or the boat would be lost, so the Old Man chose himself to be the night rudderman so he could read the stars and keep us on course. But he had no spare time for the story any more.

If it wasn't too windy or scary, I often stayed out to keep him company. My job on such nights was to keep the controlled fire pot going and to keep a full bucket of water nearby in case the pot was to fall over.

The Old Man seemed to love the slow sounds of the water as he gazed to the stars. He turned the rudder to the left, as he found some particular star to aim at.

I looked out, seeing the moon glow over the waters in the far distant darkness.

" Ah, yes. I bet that you can never get the same feeling when you're in the Inland Sea." the Old Man said as he took a deep breath in of the salt air.

" You mean that feeling of fear ?" I asked.

'That's one way to describe it." he said.

"How many days travel to be exact, is Atlantis ?" I asked, still gleaming aside at the glow of the moon.

" Approximately ? It all depends on whether you or the crew are content in going on. If you all prove that you are determined, then it will be brisk. If you are impatient and irritating to me, than we will get there when you are a blundering Old Man like me." he said with a mild smile.

There was a great pause between both of us. I looked to the sky, seeing the blue clouds and the bright green stars above.

I could see definite constellations and miniature, less obvious ones within them. I sighed as I turned around.

"Old Man, tell me why ignorance will make the trip last so much longer ?"

"It's like Brelinka saw it that way with what Danoise had said. They did not care to wonder what she had meant when she said that only Arkaitons would fit in. If they thought about what she had said, they would've pondered in the high grass for weeks."

"Wait a minute. What's going on ?"

I moved a bit closer, getting a little interested in the story he was jumping into.

" Well boy where did I leave off ? Oh yes. Now, they were down off the mountains and into the plains, heading for the town of Ques.

They were now riding on what appeared to be a faint sign of a dirt road"

The sounds of the singing women got stronger as the travelling six, eager to see civilization after weeks of moving through foothills and mountains, staggered out onto the plains.

As they approached a long field of golden wheat, they were greeted with women working in cutting wheat and singing their long, enchanting hymns.

Elana watched the far distance, seeing the approaching town with better detail every step they got closer. Nurix was passing the time by carefully braiding Elana's soft hair, as he sat behind her on her horse.

As they progressed, the track became more of a road and turned slightly. The golden wheat fields were closer and not separated anymore.

Right then did the singing enrichen and the noises of hammerings and the graining of wheat became more alive than ever.

Along the sides of the road, women swung their wheating tools and took what they cut and stuffed it in bags tied to their sides. The men, had their heads lowered, as they walked through the rows with buckets of water to offer to the women.

As they worked, a few women poked their heads up to see the six travelers trot by. Most of the songs and hymns were going in and around the melody, becoming an endless, seductive noise which never seemed to end. All in time, all in harmony, not a single soul which was off beat as they sung it. It was as if they had sung the song day and night, endlessly trying to get it perfect for passersby to listen to in amazement at their one true achievement. Their song of labor.

" Ru- f- , li'la, he-o lim-ea.. hey,
Grov'sh'le li, nop-nafulia Hey."

It rang across the land in a harmonious tune, refusing to end, refusing to die.

Brelinka slowed her horse along side of Sassaska who seemed interested in their songs and was enjoying the music along with the scenery of the soft gold shine that reflected from the long fields.

Little girls with braids hanging down from their foreheads were playing out in the fields. As they heard the six come down the road they all stopped playing and waved to them, even their parent- peasants wearing leather caps and Buushu trinkets, smiled and gave a glimpse with the pleasantness of welcome in their eyes.

They were farmers, miners, workers, and common folk who were simple and meant no harm. From their clothes the travellers could see that they were evenly divided between Buushu peasants and Arkaiton farmers and all seemed to be getting along quite well, that was the irony of it all - as in Danoise's theory, Buushu were supposedly treated unequally amongst Arkaitons.

They showed no prejudice nor discrimination amongst themselves. Not in the way that Danoise had talked about. Yet the women felt something rather odd about them but couldn't figure out what it was.

Nurix knew what it was.

He watched as the farmers worked and the peasants dug.

The farmers were out in the distance. Out of most of the farmers working, there were always a few standing equally apart from each other, crossed arms, almost itching to move, yet they stood still without joining in with the singing.

Nurix looked closely at one as they passed a few peasants working on the gutter of the road. The stern, strict looking woman locked her squinting eyes onto Nurix. Her Buushu braids fell long, laying on her chest armor over her breasts. Her hand seemed to be gripped onto the handle of her sword; her closed mouth showed no sign of happiness as the other workers sang and seemed happy as they worked. This woman showed no sign of amusement or pride towards anyone. She didn't seem to belong with them at all. She was a loner who's face couldn't be read.

She was an Enforcer.

They had passed women like her and had not even noticed what they were.

Nurix only realized after studying one of them and felt astonished. He then began to understand what Danoise meant when she said that the Arkaitons took a liking to Arkaiton only. The Buushu workers were utterly the slaves out in the fields.

The town's giant walls were made of perfectly rounded mud bricks which supported the ten-foot encagement. Along the walls were oval towers built with arrow holders hanging on the edge of all of them. One bow-woman was posted in each of them staring out and looking for distant travelers .

One of the bow-women immediately rang a bell and alerted everyone inside that end of the large town as they saw the six approach the town doors which were wide open with peasants going in and out as they pleased. They seemed to be no threat to the two rough looking guards who stood on each side of the door.

One guard was a Buushu woman, obvious because of her shortly cut hair except for the two clan braids which fell from the back of her head. Wearing a rusty and overly dented Arkaiton chest armor with rib-like decor. This model went around the plate and wrapped around her chest to her back, making it look like the rib cage of a woman, yet she wore only one large shoulder pad which looked as if it had layers to it. It's edge tip cupped outwards as it's curved side touched her neck.

She wore a brownish cloth which was worked with deer skin. They only covered her legs over her knees while a long stretch of deer-skin perfectly cut covered her groin and extended down to her shins. Her boots were typical ones that you would find on a soldier, but they were covered by a stiffened leather which wrapped around her calfs, so that the only part of her long legs showing were her knees. She was no doubt a warrior belonging to one of the Buushu Clans, working as a Mercenary.

The other woman was Arkaiton. Nurix could tell because she had the symbol of the Arkaiton spear tattooed on both sides of her nose. Her tribe was obvious, even though they both wore the same type of armor. She wore a red top with a tightened knot on the back.

It was used by Arkaiton warriors to keep their long hair back during battle.

She wore no shoulder pads, but had the long, thin, steel-like shield tied to her left hand, while with the other hand she held her long Buushu-made spear.

Nurix watched them, noticing that they did not talk amongst themselves. They stayed a certain distance away from each other without ever acknowledging the natural discrimination that they had for each other. But Nurix knew that they were both warriors, warriors who had been taught different codes to battle. The two guards' cultures had nothing in common in their teachings, except for one thing: if there was a threat or a battle, they would both fight alongside each other. Not because they were paid to do it, not because they cared for each other, they would fight along side each other because it was in their teachings, and it would be the all for the preservation of the greater good of their town, which they were paid to protect.

But until then, they would rarely talk with one another. Nurix knew, their whole life was shown merely to him by a single sneer from the quick glimpse of one to the other.

As the six slowed down their trotting, the two guards focused onto them. The Arkaiton woman tightening her grip on her spear, the Buushu woman breathed deeply as she slowly reached for her sword.

Sassaska immediately signalled for everyone to stop. Brelinka stopped right next to her while Elana and the slaves stopped twenty feet away from the rears of their horses.

" They look like they're a couple of stubborn fools as well." Brelinka snarled silently to Sassaska.

" Hopefully these stubborn fools can read." she said as she began to dismount from her horse and grab a hold of the scroll packed tightly inside her saddle bag.

Brelinka did the same, slowly unmounting her spear as well.

Sassaska turned her head, looking at Brelinka, was curious what Brelinka was doing.

Brelinka slowly walked up to Sassaska, gently touching her back with her hand. Brelinka then moved her lips closely to Sassaska's right ear, "Just in case they are hostile. If they're as bad as Danoise was, then they will be twice as dangerous.

After all, they're warriors like Elana and me."

Sassaska looked at her eyes and was slightly bewildered by her comment.

" You were always the paranoid one, Brelinka."

She turned her face and slowly undrew her scroll from her pocket.

Brelinka held her spear tightly as she rested it erect on her shoulder.

" Hello travellers, State your business or start packing and head back the way you came."

Sassaska stopped, Brelinka with her.

" We've come from Atlantis' capital.

We've travelled far from Lina and . . ."

" We've got enough traders and merchants from both the east and the west" the Arkaiton guard interrupted.

Sassaska paused for a moment.

" We are expeditioneers, not traders."

" Well ,keep expeditioneering that way ! As I said before, we're full of your kind." The Arkaiton woman snapped at her.

Sassaska started to sound a little irritated. "We've been sent by Grand Empress Ameraldia, herself, to travel through this part of the country as our journey continues further east."

" From the Empress you say ?" The Arkaiton woman started to chuckle a little.

The Buushu woman began a mild under-powering smile.

".. Out here ? The next thing you're going to tell me is that you're the next woman to take the thrown as soon as the old witch dies" the Arkaiton Guard finished.

Brelinka started to chuckle a little. Sassaska smiled a little at her ending comment.

Sassaska slowly approached the Arkaiton guard. The Buushu woman saw her and slowly walked up to her, followed by the Arkaiton guard.

Sassaska unrolled the scroll in front of them, the Arkaiton snatched it from her and started to run down the page. As she did, she took quick glances at Sassaska.

She started to have a mild look of apology. She read on, unrolling the scroll a little more.

the scroll a little more.

Suddenly, her eyes came to a screeching stop.

Her eyes slowly came off the paper and stared at Sassaska and she moved the paper towards her.

" What's that word ?" she said as she pointed to it.

" Enlightened" Sassaska said.

The Arkaiton nodded and then took the page back and went on reading. She rolled up the scroll after she had finished reading it. She handed it back and slowly bowed her head in Sassaska's presence.

"I'm sorry for my stubbornness, Heir Sassaska." she said.

The Buushu guards eyes widened a bit as she heard what her Arkaiton colleague said.

The Arkaiton immediately turned around.

" Well, what are you standing around for ? Go and tell the Governess of the arrival of Sassaska, Empress-elect." she snapped at the Buushu woman.

The Buushu woman immediately changed her surprise to a sigh as she started to walk to the Governor's' town house.

Elana and Nurix slowly dismounted from their horse and stretched..

Elana approached Brelinka and Brelinka turned around to see her little sister.

" So what's going on? Are they giving up and letting us in or what ?" Elana asked.

Brelinka had a tiny smile on her face as she began to lean her shoulder on her. " Well, I think they just found out who Sassaska is." Brelinka said.

Nurix said nothing as he watched from his distance, next to the horse. He was no longer interested at the Arkaiton guard paying her respects in grovels to Sassaska. Instead he turned around and looked back at the peasant workers, hearing the faint sound of their song.

But no longer was the song as strong as it once was. Now it seemed to be a little more silent than he ever imagined. Then he heard why.

In the far distance, he could hear the faintest cry of pain over and over again. He could tell that they were mild whimpers of agony and humiliation.

Nurix began to hear quick slaps of some sort of tool, but the work song made it so muddled up that he couldn't tell what it was

But the sounds of agony after every mild muddle of a noise began to make logical sense to him. It was one of the women being whipped out on the fields. That was why the songs were lowered a bit and that was why there were the cries.

Nurix began to see with the workers out on the field, with the enforcers not joining in with their songs, with the silent Buushu guard in the presence of the Arkaitons that all the Buushu peasants, all of the workers, most likely Buushu, and the enforcers, most likely Buushu, were utterly slaves. Utterly slaves, indentured workers sent to labor for sustainment of their property or to pay off a debt that was forced upon them by the taxes of the Governor.

Everyone had a story which, if you were Buushu, seemed to have to be paid off and repented by these work fields.

As for Nurix, he didn't want to think of the many lives out there. He didn't want to get involved with something that might have been started long ago out in the foothills, in the middle of nowhere. Something that concluded in this sad work that needed to be done.

He didn't want to get involved, so he didn't think of the reasons and blocked them off. All he could do at that moment was stare back at the long line of sweating labor women working as they sung. But not wanting to see the little voices of agony or the thoughts of how they got there.

All he did was listen to the songs and ignored the distant shadow of a woman being whipped for a crime that was minor or that she might not have committed.

I looked to the Old Man who seemed to become a little quiet as he told the story.

" So the Buushu were used as a slave clan ? I thought that they were warriors and considered the best of the best." I said, wanting to change the subject from the story to a single point.

" The Buushu were everything, ranging from your greatest heroes in history to your greatest foes of legends. They were mostly warriors, but where there are warriors, there must be a lower class of peasants and workers to keep it all together." he said as he looked into the fire from the pot.

" You mean there were different kinds of Buushu that wandered the land of Atlantis ?"

He sighed as I said that, giving the expression that he had answered the question more than once. " Depending where you were. There were classes of peasants who were believers in the Buushu cultures yet they never ever fought nor would they of been any good at it, if they had.

Then there are the others who were the warriors, sometimes nomadic, sometimes stable. It all depended on whatever their prophets said was needed to be done."

" Profits, like prophets in business ? What do you mean?" I said, beginning to get intrigued by the Buushu culture as he explained it to me.

He gave a chuckle at my naiveness.

"Well boy, you know how the Arkaitons and Makaitons believed in a God called Marsolla ?"

I nodded at him,

" Well the Buushu had mixed beliefs about that. Some, which were closer to the borders were believers of the God Marsolla. They believed in Prophets - not business profits, but future-seeing prophets - who were usually drugged priestesses in peasant temples made to tell the good and bad seasons to farm. Although, most would claim that Buushu were not believers in the supernatural, it was quite the contrary.

The other Buushu who were warriors, had a more mysterious Prophet called the Amoza, coming from a different deity which was claimed to be closer to us than Marsolla would ever be. It claimed to be the mind of the world we live on and as we know it. This great Goddess was named Tierra."

" What was so special about these Amoza women?" I asked.

" Their Goddess spoke to them. It was a direct communication, mind to mind, and the Amoza distributed the word of God to every one else. Tierra would only speak to one at a time, so there was only one supreme Amoza woman for every generation until she died and then another one was selected by Tierra. Usually three warriors were chosen to venture to find the next Amoza who Tierra chose to be worthy."

I nodded and was interested in what he said.

A culture with a completely different belief system than the two main players.

" Wow, this's getting complex for a tale, Old Man" I said, watching him begin to snigger to himself, "But you haven't thrown me into chaos yet Old Man, I'm persistent and it'll take more than a change in beliefs to throw me off." I finished.

He hadn't lost me. I was only feeling a little irritated by his constant strain of obscurity in the story. Either that or I was a chauvinist who believed in the down play of all women.

" Well, I'm glad that I haven't lost you. I'm beginning to fear that I might lose myself as I go along with the story." he said jokingly.

I smiled and nodded, wanting him to go on with the story.

He stared into my face and read my expression, oddly like I imagined Nurix would have done when he was reading someone. But the connection would be too weird for him to come right out and tell me that he was Nurix right away.

" Alright, I guess that you want the show to go on don't you ?" he said as he breathed through his nose and slightly snorted at me.

" Go on with the story Old Man." I said.

"The story, oh yes. As I remember, I was talking about The Buushu, right ?" he said making sure we were on the right track.

I nodded, beginning to imagine some of the Buushu women he talked about.

" The beauty about them was that you either became intrigued by them or you became disgusted by them. They were the were considered very rich characters.

Sometimes tragic heroes sometimes triumphant heroes. With all respect to them, they were all rebellious bitches, peasant and warrior. Most of the guards and paid Buushu soldiers refused to discard their cultural war dress, war paint, distinct tattoos, when they were told to. Usually they wore the armor issued to them, but they wore it in a way where it made them stand out like sore thumbs.

Most strategic Arkaitons disliked them for that.

Some wore the whole outfit but wore the calf coverings. Some wore the top portion yet wore their warrior flaps and gear, and worst of all, they refused to cut their braids. A comment to do so was considered an insult among insults. It was like me telling you to wear women's incense and walk naked around the villages of your home. It was humiliation to the worst of its nature."

" Wait !" I said, alerting him to stop his talking for a moment.

" If the Buushu were rebellious then how could they function as an army ? Why were they considered great warriors if they were so picky at things ?"

The Old Man smiled at my question.

" Ha, that was the good part. You ask me that question and expect an answer from me. But to answer that question, I'll ask you a question," he said jollily as he clapped his hands together.

I waited, wanting to hear his question.

" Are you afraid of death ?"

" Why, yes I am afraid of death" I answered, wondering about the question.

"If you were sent into war and you witnessed the death of most of your friends and family and you were over-pumped with fear and anxiety, would you want to die with your friends ?" he asked.

I thought for a moment, imagining if all of my family died in front of me.

I began to think about it. I knew the answer I wanted to give, which was that I would want to go down fighting, but I also knew that if I was drenched in fear, I would do everything in my power to get out of it. I would run, run as far away from the ones thriving to hurt me. It was because I was a coward.

" Yes Old Man, I would run away from them." I said. " But what does that have to do with the Buushu ?" I finished.

" The Buushu. They were a culture who respected and applauded death. They didn't picture it as a tragedy of any sort. They pictured it as the ultimate achievement in their lives. As if their life was complete enough for their Goddess to decide in taking their souls to the vast heavens.

That was why they were the best warriors.

They knew no limits when it came to fear and cowardice, they fought ruthlessly, almost able to fight any sort of martial art that provoked them. They were afraid of nothing, they fought to the death. Even then, it was thought that their spirit kept on fighting even though their bodies were dead. But the biggest reason why they were the most used in combat was because they were cheap to buy." the Old Man said, catching his breath.

" So they were arrogant. Was there any honor in them ?"

The Old Man raised one brow,

" Honor ? They had honor, believe me when I tell you this They were very respectful of their beliefs and cultures. They were also closely bonded with one another.

They were the ones who philosophized that 'whiskey is thick, but companionship and your way of life is thicker'

They were very rude as well. Rude, as arrogant is what I mean." the Old Man said.

Suddenly the boat was struck with a large wave, giving it a mighty shake.

I immediately grabbed a hold of something sturdy next to me. The Old Man only shook his head as if he was expecting worse from the ocean. His focus then immediately changed as he focused back to me. " Are you alright, boy ?" he asked.

I slowly crossed my legs once more and sat on the deck floor. I nodded to him.

" Well, Old Man. Go on with the story" I said.

" Ah yes, the story. This part, I am about to tell you will give you an example of the Buushu. It'll show you what I was talking about." he said, nodding his head happily as he shook his pointed finger at me.

I was getting more and more impatient.

" Fine. Like I said, go on with the story !" I said, feeling that he was playing with me by not getting to the point.

The Old Man only grinned. " Uhhh, well." he sighed.

" Within a few minutes of the guards realizing that Sassaska was the next heir to the throne, their whole perception changed completely. Not only did they let them into the city, but the Governor." he paused trying to remember the name or to make one up, " Governor Vivesk greeted them, and assured them a luxurious stay at her town. She let them stay at her monastery house which was quite large. It was like the rest, had totems that were for ritualistic praying, a garden to meditate in, religious scrolls to study, and last of all, the main attraction for most traveling Arkaitons, was a bath house. It was built over a hot spring, so the water was always warm and soothing.

In fact, If I remember the story correctly, that was where Vivesk accepted to meet them. They were to get dressed in the bath clothing given to them by the male servant, slaves.

The six were to stay for six days there at Ques, to recuperate from their long journey and to resupply themselves with much needed rations, arrows, an oil lamp for the night time, and last, clean clothes.

Vivesk offered most of these much needed supplies and assured them that they didn't have to pay.. Obvious diplomacy, to kiss up to the heir of the throne, it was. But appreciated nonetheless.

Elana walked into her room with Nurix trailing right behind her and carrying two saddle bags, one spear, and a bundle of skins and clothes.

The room was very bright all around. The light, cloth-like sheets which acted as a ceiling, projected the brightness of the sun like a magnifying glass.

The whole house was made of wood, lots and lots of wood. Thus, giving the sweet, pleasant smell of pine to where there was no escape.The bed was large, big enough for two women sitting a foot apart from each other to lie and talk. Its mattress was made with smooth, soft hey, so finely woven that it had no sprout ends sticking out of odd angles. Over that was a large thin blanket which was to wrap around it, to make the slumber even more sensual than it already was.

Nurix found the incense of the pine pleasant. He gave a mild smile as he paused for a small breath. Then he went to the corner next to the bed and slowly placed the luggage he carried on the wooden and stone floor.

Elana, stretched her arms out a little, then gave a slight sigh as she unknotted her dirty, dingy cloak, which by this time smelled of mud and horse manure.

She slowly threw it over a finely carved chair which faced the window covered in a see-through silk to keep out bugs and other types of critters.

Nurix slowly looked around, watching Elana sit on the same chair and slowly begin to take off her worn-down boots so that she could massage her blistered and cramped up feet. Nurix slowly saw the light from the screen-covered window gleam its golden sunlight onto the small particles of dust gently floating fluidly through the air and over Elana's red streaked hair. Her braided hair showed art through every wave of it's curls as it fell in locks down to her back.

He smiled, and then his serenity was interrupted with the worksongs of the Buushu and Arkaiton farmers outside in the fields. The song they sang put Nurix in a trance.

He slowly began to approach the window. As he did, he paused, and looked out at the view.

To his astonishment, what he watched was the whole town. Small wood huts and homes all connected by dirt roads evenly flattened out for horses and carriages.

All around, the town was quite beautiful.

Nurix slowly leaned his hand on the chair where Elana was sitting, unbuckling the strap from her other boot.

He looked on at the town. There totem poles carved in with the finest accuracy to depict women's faces and animals. Most of these faces looked outwards in the direction of the sun..

There was the large wooden wall made with many a tree and tons of clay to harden and fortify the inside of it. The wall was indestructible.

The watch towers were oval and rugged. None of the bark was shaved off the trunks of the logs. The watchwomen lay there in hammocks, peacefully rocking back and forth as their faces looked to the plains.

Horses from the town pulling merchant's carriages left and came as fluidly as whiskey in a drunkards glass. It was questionable why they had guards as there seemed to be no threat at all.

He looked further on, outside of the walls.

He began to hear the song of the workwomen once more. The enjoyable beats which there seemed to be no end to. The laborers out in the fields clanked and chopped as they sang, giving an eerie backbeat to their symphony. Like a giant orchestra followed by a chorus of Altos and Sopranos singing in harmony.

Elana cooed with relief as she started to rub her sore feet. "Um" she moaned as she rubbed her toes, "What's the scenery like out there?" she soothingly asked.

Nurix turned, " It's quite beautiful and rather peaceful out there, Elana. The air is crisp, the noise is silent except for the songs. This town seems to be very religious."

" Why's that ?" she asked.

" There are a lot of totem poles facing west."

" Oh ?" she said. "Totem poles are symbols for different things: luck, honor, death, birth. It all depends on who you talk to," she finished.

" They're all facing west. What do you think that means ?" Nurix asked.

Elana sighed, rubbing the side of her neck, trying to un-densen her stiffened muscles.

Nurix gently placed his hands on her shoulders, getting under her warm hair and slowly started to rub the sides of her neck.

She smiled and cooed as he slowly massaged her taut muscles, feeling her warm curls brush on the backs of his hands; Elana slowly moved her neck to one side. Nurix smiled and continued his massaging.

He smiled serenely as he continued.

" Ba- shuu, -kin' ifo, mo-na- Hey-" came the mild song outside. It was part of the lyrics from the work song.

The attention of Nurix changed.

He glimpsed out of the brightly lit sill, seeing smoke beginning in the huts.

The music seemed closer, then he saw the reason why.

The workers were coming back from their labor.

" Go and seal the gates !" came a yell from one of the guards posted in the watch towers.

Nurix began to watch the detail of the women, all tired and sweating from the hard day's work.

They still sang coming back. The men came into the city with the women. Nurix could tell the men from the women. The men were bulkier in their build, hairier, fowler, and they never lifted their faces in front of the women.

Nurix watched as the last few workers carrying their long, wavy sickles in front of them and their giant pick axes across their shoulders. Some of them had braids, Buushu-looking braids sticking out of the head caps that they wore to keep the sun off.

Some wore no tops, to perspire without discomfort when they worked cutting wheat, but most wore a strap to hold and keep their breasts from getting into the way of their swinging and working.

Elana began to feel Nurix's touch get lighter and lighter. His rubbing then came to a sudden halt.

Elana, slowly stood up and walked around the chair. She felt curious about Nurix's fascination at the workers coming back to their tiny huts and beginning to cook their long deserved meals.

She slowly wrapped her arms around his chest and rested her head on his shoulder. Nurix felt the pressure of her chin giving a sensational feeling as it lay pressing his collar bone. He did not react to her.

Elana moved her eyes and gazed at the many, many workers being checked by the enforcers and guards who guided them in.

" Is this what your focus is so fascinated by ? Indentured servants?" asked Elana.

Nurix said nothing as he watched the male slaves slump and slouch as they followed some of the worker women with their heads lowered. They had no emotions, they were utterly machines used for convenience. He watched for any of them to start talking but none of them ever did.

Nurix lowered his eyes. He gave a silent sigh wanting it to only be heard by himself.He felt afraid and confused. He wondered about his life and existence. He wondered why he was a slave who was so lucky. He began to think about the outdoor slaves: Rhyme and Taboo, who were brought into slavery by war code and tamed to be Sassaska and Brelinka's pets. He was bought by Elana, who wanted to be his friend.The many other slaves in the monastery where Nurix grew up were never given the opportunity to be taught to read, write, or even speak for that matter. He was chosen to be taught all these things.

And lastly, male slaves in general were mostly mute, never looked up, were usually disliked by women, and usually used only for procreation.

Whereas Nurix was encouraged to speak, to debate and to help his mistress.

He had everything that slaves dreamed about: the ability to read and write, the ability to talk and socialize with the mistresses, and most obvious, the chance to live and to take place in an adventure, which was usually a fantasy told to unfortunate children.

Nurix at that moment chuckled in compassion and gently grabbed Elana's hand resting by his sides.

" They never seem to talk" Nurix said.

" Who ?" asked Elana.

" The male slaves down there. I pity them"

Elana began to understand his feelings and gave a respectful pause of silence for Nurix. "I know. It is a sad thing for them, but they were raised that way. To be obedient," she sighed.

Nurix didn't comment her on what she had said. He was mildly insulted, for he was born under the same caste.

" I am sorry, I didn't mean to be rude, Nurix."

Nurix smiled and slightly turned his head, feeling the tickling curls of her hair press onto his now thickening beard.

" It wasn't rude" he said silently.

He closed his eyes, and kissed her on the side of her tempo. "Thank you. Thank you for choosing me" he whispered to her.

Elana's heart filled with joy as Nurix said that. She gave a quick kiss back to him.

She began to feel herself getting a little warm. She was filled with mixed emotions at that moment. She was worried for a long time with the guilt of being the Mistress to Nurix. She wanted to make him feel a bit more free, but still the guilt kept her from completely feeling glad for herself. She knew that what she was doing to him was actually more detrimental to him, for she was letting him be a little too free. Although, this was what she wanted, she still believed that Nurix was a slave and could be nothing more than a slave to her. Not only that, but there would be a time when she would have to restrict Nurix's freedom behavior once she was much older. She was an Atlantean woman, and letting such a slave believe in such things was immature. But she wasn't at that point in her life yet, she was in no position to crush him yet, not at the moment. She smiled and closed her eyes.

She was glad, glad for Nurix, that he was happy with her. Happy in the momen. As they stared outwards at the gates closing up and the mist of the smoke from the other houses begin to rise, they both held each other tighter and closer together.

Then the mood was spoiled

"Hek-Hmm" cleared a purposely phlegm filled throat.

Elana sighed irritatedly as she slowly turned her face. Nurix sighed as well feeling the same irritant as Elana. Except he didn't feel like turning around.

Elana saw a skinny, short pasty-looking man who was dressed in a tunic with sandals. His hair was straight black and so were his eyes. He had no beard and no mustache, and he seemed to show absolutely no signs of muscle tone at all.

In his hands he carried a silk-based robe and a pair of white cloths to wrap around calfs, as well as thinly made sandals.

" Yes ?" asked Elana.

The male slave gave a mild smear as he spoke.

"Good day Mistress. My name is Ekler, one of the many loyal concubines of the Governor Vivesk. She has sent me to give you these garments.

Nurix slowly glimpsed at him once more, taking a long hard look at him.

Elana walked over to this new character who had interrupted them. She looked at the clothes and wondered what they were for.

Ekler, who was still grinning, stared into her eyes.

Elana avoided his chances to look at her. Elana saw him, and immediately decided that he was not to be liked. Ekler was insulted that Elana avoided eye contact with him, so as he handed the clothes to Elana, he snottily turned his head, and began to look at his nails on his right hand.

" Well the Governor isn't going to be at the Bath houses for long. Get a move on and get changed. I'm not going to be patient for long," he snapped at her, waving his hand to the changing room to the left. Elana kept still, seemingly not amused at his remark.

Nurix was somewhat in awe with his remark to Elana.

Elana's eyes widened a little with surprise. She did not expect Ekler to snap at her like that.

" Excuse me ?" Elana asked.

Nurix slowly walked up closer to them with his arms crossed, feeling a little anxious to see how this conversation would end.

Ekler raised one brow and sighed. He expressed both his arms and pointed at the heap of clothings, then pointed to her and waved his hands to the changing room.

Nurix expected him to immediately grovel and plead for forgiveness to Elana. Something that Nurix would do if he was being rowdy, but instead he sighed once more and finished his sentence.

"Yes. Now, you must get changed so that we can go to the bath house to meet the Governor. What is so difficult to understand about that, young woman ?" he asked.

Elana was irritated by him, the same irritance that she would have gotten from a little girl accusing her of being a demon. She was more amazed that a man like him was not killed and buried in a ditch already.

Elana slowly grabbed the clothing and paused to look at him for a moment.

She shook her head " You're certainly a brave little man, I'll give you that," she said. Then she slowly made her way to get herself changed.

The room was now silent with Nurix and Ekler. Ekler slowly looked around. He then looked at Nurix. Nurix had his eyes locked on him ever since he had entered the room.

" So are you her slave ?" he asked.

Nurix only blinked with a mild nod.

He felt that he had no need talking to him. After all, he felt that he was irritating as well.

Ekler looked him up and down.

" You're a talkative fellow aren't you." he said sarcastically.

Nurix only answered with raising both his brows and lowering them. For some reason, he began to feel that the absence of speech in front of Ekler rather amusing.

" At least you've got some sort of dignity in you." he said.

" What do you mean?" Nurix asked.

Ekler looked at his rugged cloths wrapped thickly around his legs and decaying boots.

As soon as Nurix had said a word, he looked up at him.
" So it talks," he said. " Well, you don't look like the type."
" Such prejudice coming from another slave" Nurix said.
He seemed to get a little provoked as Nurix said 'Slave'
His mouth opened in slight disgust to the word. " You call me a
slave, boy ? I am the Concubine to the Governor. There's a big difference between the two, you know?"
    Nurix chuckled a little. "You know as well as I do, that men are
not liked in the world of women. All men are slaves, they just have
fancier titles for themselves. Like yourself for instance: you are a concubine. You are to serve whomever you were given to," said Nurix.
    Ekler gave a confident smear, feeling that he was much more su-
perior than Nurix.
    " I assure you, slave, that I am not one of your kind. I was raised
by the great Guva family. I have a great long history of elegance bred
into me while you don't" he argued.
    " Once a man is married off, or sold or given into slavery, he is no
longer part of the family line." Nurix said as he got comfortable in a
chair close to him. " I am sorry, my fellow man, but your family line is
worthless in the defence to my allegation against you." he paused for a
bit. "- You- Are- A- Natural-Born- Slave-" Nurix said, stretching the
last sentence
    " You are a man" Ekler answered.
    Nurix smiled.
    " I am aware of that Ekler. So are you."
    Ekler became furious, " What is the point of this argument ?" he
snorted at Nurix.
    "I'm sorry." Nurix apologized expressionlessly.
    " You should be, you dirty-looking vermin. I just hope that you
don't start relieving yourself in the room once Visitor Elana leaves with
me to the bath houses."
    " Why, am I staying here ?" Asked Nurix.
    "The Governor sent for Elana. Not Elana and her slave." he said.
He began to focus on his nails once more.
    Nurix sensed that he didn't want to be in the argument any longer.
    " What takes women so long to dress ?" Ekler said to himself as
he started to pace.

"One of those great mysteries that will never be answered." Nurix said amusingly.

Ekler stopped pacing and faced him with a sour look on his face. " I never asked you." he said and went back into his pacing frenzy. "Slave." he snapped below his breath.

Nurix shook his head, feeling uninterested to pursue it.

Nurix felt that his bickerings with Ekler was to pass the time. But, like other things, he found it interesting: getting into an argument with another male slave. Not only a slave, but a spoiled slave who apparently was raised like a little prince from a rich family. The typical slave in denial.

Nurix watched as Ekler went back to pacing. He began to feel himself uplifted as he tried to analyze the fragments of body language, eye motion, tone of voice, and utter expressions that Ekler was giving off, not realizing he could be read like a book.

Nurix felt uplifted because it gave him a fact that he had never known to exist in the world ruled by women: that there were some women who tolerated snotty, complaining little men.

Nurix had always assumed that men like Ekler were brutally beaten to be tamed by their wives or mistresses. Or strangled to death and thrown in a ditch somewhere amongst the wilderness-infested roads.

Elana slowly came out. Her dingy, odor-filled clothes were gone and she was now wearing the garments which had been handed to her. She slowly walked into the room. Ekler stopped pacing and looked her up and down. Nurix did the same.

She was extravagant.

The white cotton robe looked like a priceless religious dress worn by priestesses during ceremonies, rituals, or blessings. Her thighs were revealed by the slits to the side of the dress, giving the full beauty of her long legs and anatomy in startling glimpses as she moved.

Even the sandals she wore made her exceptionally attractive in Nurix's eyes.

She seemed less of a warrior when she was dressed this way. In other words, she seemed a lot softer and smoother and much less dangerous.

Ekler and Nurix both gasped, to her unexpected beauty.

Yes, even the world-weary Ekler was struck by her transformation but he quickly changed his astonishment back to his sarcastic, angry nature. " Well it took you long enough for you to look like that." he said.

Elana smiled, taking that as a compliment. She slowly looked at Nurix who was in turn still gazing in awe at her. " Well, I'm not going like this without you." she said.

Immediately, Ekler walked and looked up at Elana.

"No, no. I will not take that-"

Elana's eyes lowered into a slight concern at Ekler.

Ekler corrected himself, thinking that Elana would do something to him. "Him ? Into the Bathhouse ? No, He's far too scruffy-looking."

Elana sighed and ignored him. " Nurix, will you escort me there?"

Nurix slowly stood up. He smiled and nodded. " Yes, Lady Elana. It would be my honor. I'll certainly escort you there." he said.

Ekler, sensing his objective had lost its focus in front of Elana quickly came into her range of sight once more.

" No, I was given specific orders from my wife to bring you to meet her. I was given no instructions to bring along your pet boy with us."

Elana laughed, " Pet Boy ?" she repeated obscurely.

Nurix slowly came up to Elana.

Elana gazed at him, raising a brow to the words stuck in her head.

Nurix then looked at Ekler's frustrated face.

Elana smiled and looked to Nurix's eager face. Nurix wanted to go with her, but felt a little offended with the term 'Pet boy'.

" Boy Pet, will you escort me to the bathhouse now ?" she asked in a gentle tone as she formally lowered her head and held out her hand.

She was teasing Ekler in front of him. Nurix only did what he thought was right. He smiled and formally gripped her wrist, waiting for her to wind her fingers around his.

"I'd be honored to escort you down Lady Elana." he said, joining into the amusement and taking it further.

Elana kissed him. Kissed him directly onto the lips, not in the formal way that she usually did.

Ekler gave up in explaining.

He was too fed up and seemed to have lost his patience. He sighed and rolled his eyes up and gritted his teeth.

"Sometimes I wonder why women do such strange things?" Ekler mumbled to himself.

Nurix was still embraced in the kiss. He was quite surprised, wondering how far Elana wanted to take this amusement. But it was obvious that the kiss was not part of the joke, merely Elana going a little too far, but in a direction she certainly wanted to go. Nonetheless, Nurix immediately stopped her. His heart beat fast and he was confused to why she would do such a thing.

Elana gasped and understood that she went too far.

Ekler started tapping his feet on the ground chronically fast. Fed up and thinking them more and more childish as they went on.

"Well, we should go now. You know before the Great Empress dies?" he said sarcastically.

Elana's eyes opened and slowly, she began to pull away from Nurix.

Nurix slowly closed his mouth and cleared his throat to the comment

Elana's smile changed to her serene look, partially effected by the comment, both of them still holding each other's wrists.

Ekler sensed a slight tension as he mentioned it, but he felt that they deserved it. After all, they had teased him when he wanted them to listen to him.

Because of his snottiness and complaining nature, because of the argument between Nurix and him, because of the time that he arrived compared to the predicted time that was told for them all to be at the bath house, because of all of these things. Ekler felt no curiosity towards the tension built at what he had said. What he was concerned about now was getting to the Bath house before anything else irritating was to happen.

"Lets go. Now!" he said frustratedly as he briskly started to walk to the outside but forgetting to step over the giant block in front of the wooden door frame. He tripped and fell.

Elana and Nurix cringed as they heard him violently hit the floor .He slowly got up, dusting himself, not noticing that his nose was broken and that blood was slowly trickling down.

Then the pain kicked in.

"Ahh !" Ekler screamed as he felt his face and saw the blood beginning to stain his fingers.

Suddenly, seeing the blood, Ekler fainted.

Nurix and Elana stood there for a few seconds, looking at his collapsed body and holding themselves from laughing.

"We should help him up ?" asked a rather relaxed Nurix.

Elana only smoothly and slowly shook her head as she said. " He looks so comfortable in that position on the floor. I don't think that we should disturb him." she said.

Nurix turned and looked at Elana with a strange remarkful expression on his face.

Elana's cheery eyes held her amusement inside, but could not contain it, then finally it burst out, sprouting out as laughter.

Nurix then agreed in his mind that it was rather amusing as well, and felt himself beginning to give off little, tiny laughs alongside Elana as they patiently sat down and waited for their guide to recover.

Quite a few minutes went by before Ekler, the Concubine, came to. After he awoke, he felt a sharp ringing in his head, then saw the blood on his fingers. His eyes widened with fright. He was the kind of person who couldn't stomach the sight of blood.

Nurix got up, went over and slowly knelt down and checked if Ekler was alright.

" How are you ? You tripped on the first step," Nurix said.

Ekler slowly stood up, a little disgruntled from his fall. " Huh, the first step ! They should ban those foolish luck charmers. People can die from those sorts of things !" he said, rubbing the side of his head.

Nurix slowly got up at the same speed as Ekler.

As the concubine got up, the pain of the acceleration made his realigned nose throb with every pulse.

"Ooh, I know that it's going to leave a mark for a long time." Ekler whispered painfully, trying to touch his nose but backing off because of the agonizing pain.

Elana touched Nurix by the shoulder as she came closer to see how Ekler was.

Elana cringed to the sight of his blood stained face and his over swollen nose which was red and blue all over.

It was a hideous thing to see.

After a few more seconds of assurance to Ekler that his nose didn't look as bad as it truly was, Ekler started to get back into his objective mode. He realized the time from the dimmening lights, a trick that most people were taught to know, and knew that they were at the most, an hour late.

He became jumpy and snappy once more.

"Well then, enough about me, let's get a move on ! We're late for the appointment already." he said with a slight crack in his voice.

He walked up to Nurix and moved him out of the way. Nurix slowly lowered his head and backed out. He knew that Ekler was only doing it because he needed an assurance of power and authority to make up for his foolishness in tripping over the first step in the door way. Ekler took a sniff as he walked by and shook his head in disgust.

He slowly turned his head, gently touching his nose, trying to close the nostrils but being revoked with pain from his nose.

Nurix was curious and felt a little insulted by Ekler's gesture.

As far as Nurix was concerned, there was no smell at all. He found nothing displeasing about the way he smelled. Neither did anyone else up to this point.

"What's that smell?" Ekler asked.

"Huh ?" Nurix asked, hoping that Ekler scenting the air and getting closer to him was only merely a coincidence.

" Please don't tell me that you have been wearing the same clothes for half a year."

Nurix sighed.

" Well I don't smell anything. It must be you." Nurix said, defending himself.

Elana sniffed the air and also sensed nothing.

Ekler, once again, wanted to become offensive. Nurix could see it in his eyes. But Ekler was too antsy at the moment. His main concern was to get them to their destination. He now truly didn't have time to discuss hygiene.

"Out of all the concubines in the Governor's house why was I the man that had to come and talk to these barbarians ?" he mumbled to himself as he started for the door, this time watching where he walked a little more carefully.

Finally, Elana and Nurix were on their way to the bathhouse.

As they walked through the roads, they saw the large woolly hoofed-horses packed up with all sorts of utilities. There were very few mammoths around, standing bravely amongst the houses and dry bark trees but the few that were on the roads they roamed stumbly and sluggishly, hauling heavy-duty material behind them. Their long, curved tusks were yellowed and blackened near the tips showing that they had had experience in labor. The Guards made sure of that, piloting the great blind folded beasts left and right. Where did they put these mammoths when they were done work ? It looked like that they just left them outside, for there was no gated encagement for them.

In fact, most of the town was sketchy and vaguely put together. The houses and huts seemed temporarily-built for the evening, yet they had the feel of being there for much longer.

The roads were not tended to. There were no marks of stomping or scraping to pack the ground or to keep the long grass growing between the cracks. Mostly, there were weeds growing in patches around the sides and wheat itself growing down the middle of it.

When looked in more detail, the town was only half fixed and half tended. Even some of its defences were deteriorating. The only parts that seemed to be overly well done were the houses for travelers, the priestesses monastery and the totems, which were all over the place. It was a town which was not meant for permanent residence. It was more of a rest stop for travelling merchants, and it was now apparent that this town depended strictly on the money of merchants.

The one building which seemed to be the most extravagant out of all the rest of the houses and was even nicer than the monastery was the Bath House.

The grand doorway was graced with two beautiful sculptures of Marsollan warriors taking the form of a women. They were engraved into the long thirty foot totem carved from the finest wood. The steps were symmetrical to one another, even the first step leading into the building, was the same size, unlike the first steps in the other houses all around town.

There were no doors, but the entrance had a miniature pool of water right when you went over the first step which was built into the doorway.

The room was painted white and the atmosphere was mildly dingy, but mostly moist and damp inside. The lights were incredibly dim with only a few candles to light the vast hallways. The floor everywhere was inches deep in warm water. Here and there in the fog were huddled figures - people kneeling and muttering in the midst of prayer whispers and hymns. Some were on rocks and many just knelt in the water. Some were meditating in thin cloth robes while some were entirely naked, only wearing the many religious beads given to them to sustain their faith in Marsolla. There were also few stone statues inside, most of which couldn't be seen in the fog.

Ekler expressed that Elana and Nurix had to be silent, to not say a word but to look down at the dark, wet floor and avoid eye contact with the praying figures for fear that their mumbling meditations would be interrupted.

They walked for a few minutes, looking down the vast hall. Their feet were engulfed in the water from the pool. The whole hallway consisted in sitting rocks and an endless pool. As they approached the main bathing room, Ekler strutted a little more faster trying to get into one room, then waiting for them to follow behind him.

As they came in, Ekler slid the paper thin door to close it. The room was now a lobby with another door just waiting to be opened by the hands of Ekler.

Nurix moved a little closer to the eager door, hearing mild laughter and conversation going on in the next room. As Ekler briskly moved Nurix aside. He opened the inner door, waiting for that very moment, wanting to offer its great surprise. Hoping to get some attention.

Fortunately, as the door swished open, there was a surprise.

There, right in front of them, was a vast room with white-washed walls and the aroma of perfumes in the air.

The sounds of conversation that Nurix heard, immediately stopped as they walked into the obviously brighter room. There was the small hot spring with women slaves working, keeping the hearth in the chimney, which was big enough to cook a whole horse, burning brightly. There were many men slaves kneeling down around the perimeter of the spring, looking down to the water while Sassaska and Brelinka sat listening as a stocky woman with brown curls chatted cheerfully.

That was before Elana and the two men entered the room, of course.

Elana slowly started walking to the spring. Nurix was right behind her, looking around the room with slight amazement. His expression was in awe, giving a stupefying look at the sheer size of the room.

Suddenly, Ekler gave him a sharp nudge in the chest. The nudge definitely received his attention.

" Keep your shoulders loose and look down !" Ekler whispered as he himself performed his own given instructions.

Nurix slowly looked down, holding his ribs in pain from the nudge.

"Well, well, well. You finally decided to show up three hours late" Brelinka said as Elana stopped in front of the spring.

Elana looked at the three women, wearing their simple garments which proved very revealing as they became utterly transparent in the hot spring.

" So this is the adorable little Elana. She's not as young looking as you." the stocky woman said, shoe-shining Brelinka.

Elana gave a brief smile.

"Yes, I am Elana." She said. She then bowed her head.

"And you must be Governor Vivesk."

The woman gave one nod with a joyful grin.

Ekler slowly knelt down and put his hands on his thighs as he began to look at the water.

Nurix stood there for a few moments, embarrassed and unsure on what he should be doing.

Ekler gave an intended throat clearing which was heard by the other women.

Nurix looked at Ekler's position and slowly did the same. As he slowly knelt down on his knees, a sharp soreness of cold pain engulfed his knees as soon as it had touched the tiled floor.

" I am honored to meet you Elana." Governor Vivesk said. "Please, the air is cold. Join us inside the spring." she finished.

Elana gave a polite smile, taking off her sandals and slowly moving them aside with her foot.

She stepped into the water, the warmth of which pleased her immediately.

She quickly became comfortable in it and seated herself on the imbedded, smoothened sitting stones under the water.

" So did you run into any trouble with my Concubine ?" the Governor asked as she looked over at Ekler's emotionless face, and crooked, swollen nose.

Elana also noticed his nose but seemed to be comfortable with it. Vivesk slowly looked at Elana.

" I see that he has been hurt. By your hands ?" she asked.

" I apologize." Elana said.

Vivesk sighed, " Well, what can I say, I am rather relieved that you, know how to discipline slaves as well as I do. The only complaint that I do have is that you seem to feel sorry for him. For only breaking his nose, I mean."

Elana raised a brow. " You mean breaking a concubine's nose is not enough ?" she asked.

Vivesk gave a laugh, thinking that her question was rather naive. " Why no. I usually result to neutering them." she said casually.

Nurix gulped when he heard the sound 'neuter' and slowly moved a few inches away.

Brelinka and Sassaska were a little overwhelmed with what she had said.

" Neuter them?" asked Sassaska.

The Governor nodded.

" Yes. I take one of their testicles out when they act up. If they do it again, I take out the other one. I've learned that if you do it at a younger age, your male slave will always be happy and loyal, like a little child." she said.

Elana kept quiet, feeling too embarrassed to join in with the conversation. Instead, she looked around at the other slaves who sat around. They were all men, and all rather plump and soft looking. They seemed young, but they had no masculine appearance at all.

Almost all of them had no facial hair. They never seemed to talk much, probably because their voices were squeaky from the operation.

" I don't mean to question your tactics here Governor, but what about reproduction ?" asked Brelinka.

The Governor raised a curious brow." Reproduction ? There will always be whole men in Atlantis my friends.

Besides, I already had four children. All of which were boys."

" Neutered, I presume ?" Elana asked.

Vivesk gave a glimpse towards Elana. " But of course. I even did the neutering myself. It's really an act of love. Something every mother of a boy should do. It really makes their lives simple and cheerful. It takes away all those dark urges that men seem to always have. And it keeps them beautiful for their whole lives. "

Brelinka nodded.

"Besides, " the Governor continued, " You can't expect me to spend all of my fortune on educating my sons to become obedient husbands? It's much cheaper to make them superior servants to sell off to Buushu Council members, or to promising rich Arkaiton Governors who have to go off to other cities. You, yourself were sent off to Makaitia as a governor, didn't you say ? And wouldn't you have loved to have a good Arkaiton boy around, who knew how to cook, how to do all the things you were used to ?"

Brelinka nodded again, not trusting herself to say anything.

" Who were the fathers ?" asked Sassaska.

" Ekler, my most obedient concubine was the planter for my children. He was the only one that never acted up. He was my most trusted Concubine. But . . ."

She looked over to Ekler.

". . .I see that he has been giving you some trouble, so I shall perform the dissection on him - tonight - and show you how it's done" she finished.

Elana heard Ekler gasp in shock at what his mistress had said. Immediately Elana started trying to defend him.

"No that's alright, he wasn't disobedient. He simply tripped. It was an accident. He's learned his lesson."

" No, really, I've been thinking of having him fixed for a long time. And now, if you say he's become clumsy, well, what better reason ? Doing the operation is rather simple. Come along and watch. You should learn the technique. It takes your problems away instantly when you do it."

" No, I think he is obedient enough. He's given you many years of true service." assured Elana.

" Truly, the procedure is rather simple.

Use a contraption called the Scrotum Scooper . . ."

"I think he really has been through enough for one night." argued Elana politely.

" . . . And you slide it under the skin. Twist and pull and . . ."

" I get the point." ended Elana seeing that it was hopeless to talk the Governor out of it.

The Governor noticed that she was upsetting her guests so she agreed to stop talking about the surgical procedure for neutering male slaves. "Anyway, let's change the subject, shall we?" Vivesk said.

" So I see from the beads you wear, that you were once a priestess. Or still are one? " asked Vivesk.

" Yes, I was the Grand High Priestess of Marsolla at the High Council in Lina, but I am now heir to the throne. I can no longer give all my time and my whole soul to the study and practice of Marsolla." she said, nervously rolling her fingers on the beads wrapped around her hand.

" But if you are heir, then, why aren't you at Lina, preparing to be crowned ?"

" The wise Empress Asmereldia is a good ruler and believes that I should see and experience what I am going to rule before I actually take the crown. She feels that I will understand my purpose as leader of the Empire a lot better if I do this."

" A tour of Arkaiton territory, I could understand. That's thinking for the best of our kind. But why are you traveling out this far ? You are almost off limits from the Arkaiton region. You are at the border leading into Buushu territory. There's nothing else out there to explore except the Buushu Plain and the Makaiton lands. If you should ask me, the Buushu and the Makaitons shouldn't be considered equals in territory observation. Besides, they're always having their silent little war. It never ends." Vivesk said.

" There are feud battles which go on between the Buushu and the Makaitons ?"

" Oh, yes, of course. Those two have been foes since the beginning. Out here, when the Buushu go through their Grand Round migrations, they usually do it to retrain themselves, then end the Round by attacking the Makaiton border states."

" You know of this ?"

" And the Governor before me."

" Why hasn't there been any notification sent to Lina ?" Sassaska asked.

" There have been many notes and messages sent to Lina. I feel the question should be: why didn't anyone care?"

" Alright," Sassaska agreed. " then that's the question I'll ask: why didn't anyone care ?" she asked.

Vivesk only sighed. " Listen, child, if you are going to be the leader of this grand empire, you must understand the traditions of the old." she said. " You know the poem 'Cycle of War ?'" Vivesk asked.

"It goes:

War brings death,
Death brings anger,
Anger brings revenge,
 Revenge brings strategy,
Strategy brings War."

she finished.

"Yes, I am familiar with it." Sassaska said.

"When a Clan goes into war, you let them fight their own battles, or else you step onto their dignity. Most Arkaitons in the Empire think the same way I do. At least I am thankful for that. The way most of us think is that we shouldn't risk the lives of our brave warriors in a war which had gone on for at least a hundred years. If the Buushu and the Makaiton have a strangle hold over each other, it's fine with me. I want them to kill each other off so that there's more land for our kind to stretch our legs." Vivesk said.

Sassaska nodded, partially agreeing to what she had just said. But she felt so naive about not knowing about the war between the Makaiton and the Buushu. She had always believed that there truly was peace within the Empire.

She truly believed that the Empress cared for all. That was probably the reason why the Empress wanted Sassaska to go on this journey, so that she would be able to see these things and be a better leader than the old Empress had been.

" What was the cause of this hundred -year war ?" Brelinka asked, curious. As a former Governor of Makaitia she certainly knew that the war existed, but had never wodnered why until now.

" Oh, I don't know. The Makaitons probably felt disgusted by the Buushu or something like that. One story is that once there were only Arkaiton and Makaiton, explaining why the two cultures are similar. Then the Buushu moved up from the south and drove a wedge between the two groups. But that's only a theory. There are no facts to back it up.

Not too many Buushu know why they fight either. You could ask any of my Buushu soldiers and they would tell you different reasons: They are fighting for their rightful land, They are fighting because the Makaitons plan to take over the Empire. They are fighting because the Makaitons have more meat than the Buushu, I can tell you a lot more of the things I've heard which sound more and more ridiculous." she said. "There is even talk that the Buushu and Makaitons will unite to overthrow the Arkaitons and seize power - and the fighting is the conservatives fighting the young hotheads who support this plan."

" So you truly feel nothing ? You feel nothing for the many Buushu or Makaitons who have died without any knowledge of what they were fighting for ?" asked Sassaska.

" Sassaska, child. I am in control only of a little trade-stop town in the middle of nowhere. It isn't meant for political philosophy. It is a place where Arkaitons send their prisoners to do labor. It is a place that grows golden wheat to feed travellers and their horses. It is also a place for merchants to rest a while on their way to somewhere else. but that is it.

I am paid enough to keep the town running. I only keep the peace between my merchants, farmers, and nomads. That's it. The running of the empire I leave to such as you."

"But you, yourself, you don't care?" asked Sassaska.

"No. I don't care. Because I have no moral reasons to. I cannot concern myself with things outside my area of expertise. Just as I cannot afford to care about every hungry child crying in the streets of Lina. Or in the slave pens of the great houses. You have to focus your energies on the area you live in. You have to live in the real world.

Look at the big picture. The Buushu are mainly groups of nomadic clans, some still nomadic, most not. Many Buushu thrive on what they hunt, on what they grow. Are they different to us, the Buushu ? I don't know. And I don't care.

The Makaitons are groups of spooks who worship fallen Marsollan animals. They are like a hermit society which only let their merchants leave in and out of their buffer zones. Even the officials of the Empire - as you well know Brelinka - are not free to travel that country. Why ? I don't know. And I don't care.

All I know, and all anyone else knows, is that they are at war. They have continued to fight for decades. Why ? I don't know. And I don't care." she said. "I, and those who came before me, have notified those in Lina about this. They don't seem to care either. And you, Brelinka, when you were Governor in Makaitia, did you not know of this war ? Did you not report it ? Was nothing at all done about your reports ?"

Brelinka nodded. It was true.

An overweight male slave came up to the spring, holding four cups and a leather-skinned bottle filled with a special grain whiskey. The three of them could tell because of the strong smell of alcohol.

" Excuse me Governor, here is the drink you asked for." came a squeaky voice from the male slave.

The Governor smiled and passed the cups around.

" Oh, yes. I forgot to tell you that my colony also produces the best rye whisky in the Empire. I ordered a specially brewed batch for all of us to taste."

She looked up to the slave.

"Bobo, pour the whiskey for us." she said, holding out her glass.

Bobo the slave came around and filled up the cups, then left the bottle and started to walk slowly away from them disappearing into the door with the dark patch of shadows in it.

" Tomorrow, I want to take you all to the eating house for the finest food you have ever tasted. There we will continue our talk of useful information."

" We will be looking forward to that." Brelinka said.

" Good, then let us give a toast to the Empire and it's newly chosen leader. May her years on the thrown be the golden years that everyone will remember." she said as she held up her glass.

The other three clashed their cups together.

" To the Empire!" they toasted.

The Old Man pushed the rudder left from where he was sitting. The boat made a sharp turn and the wind started to fill the sails as the boat slowly caught speed and sliced through the rippling, rocking waters.

As the waves began to rock the boat a little more violently, the wood on the hull began to creak, creating the anxiety, at least in me, that the force of the waves would crush the boat right in half.

I took deep breaths feeling that anxiety, that fear that the boat would utterly disintegrate and dissolve us with it.

" Getting scared boy ?" the Old Man said as he handled the rudder a little more carefully.

I only looked ahead, seeing a wave getting larger in front of us. Suddenly it crashed down upon the deck. The icy cold water raced towards the Old Man and I. As the thin layer of water splashed over my feet, soaking my pants, it shocked me. The cold, like a thousand needles poking into dulled nerves, made me stand up quickly.

The boat ran up the large wave and immediately fell as the wave died.

Instantly I was throwing myself onto the damp wood . Splashes came creeping up once more, soaking both me and the Old Man.

He only threw his long grey hair around to get rid of the water trapped in it. It didn't seem to bother him. He seemed to resist the cold sensations of his nerves, he seemed more refreshed as it came unto him.

I could tell that there was a storm brewing up and I felt that the Old Man had led us right into it. The Old Man was crazy, to be deliberately heading us into a storm. What was he trying to prove to us ? I couldn't believe what he was doing.

"What have you gotten us into, Old Man ?" I shouted furiously.

The Old Man only glimpsed at me then ignored me as he started to ride another wave.

I felt the boat begin to rise. Getting scared, I quickly tried to get a hold of something as the boat reached the edge of the wave. I saw larger waves coming up and closed my eyes in fright, in anticipation of the fall. Then it came. The boat flew off the wave and flopped onto the waters. The sound of the wood trying to give out and the ropes straining to hold everything together preyed on my worries.

I tried to stand up, but my body shivered with the sensation of fear all over. I could only face him with my eyes urging to close them in fear rather than show my anger at the Old Man. I was still furious at him.

" Why won't you answer me Old Man ? Why have you taken us into a storm ?" I shouted once more to him.

He gave no answer once more. He seemed focused on the storm building around the boat. The waves became larger and rougher yet the Old Man stayed calm and placid amongst the splashing, stinging salt water.

" Are you as deaf as you are old ?" I shouted, hoping to get a response from the statue trance he was in.

The boat began to sway from left to right . The Old Man was dodging the waves.

I fastened myself to the deck floor, trying not to be thrown around as he swayed the boat. Suddenly there was a rumble. Rain started to drizzle and the stars became covered up. The storm was suddenly upon us and its rage was thirsty for vengeance against us.

The boat then started to sail even faster as the Old Man piloted it madly between the waves. The front bow started to sink, the balance was off and I found myself beginning to fall.

I quickly looked up. A wave was pulling us into its surf. Not any usual wave that would be expected.

The wave was black, ferocious and one hundred feet high. It was the wrath, the vengeance itself, opening its grinning mouth, pulling us in to certain death.

My mouth fell down in awe. I was scared stiff, the chills coming down my back, the cold making my nose run, and the shivers I was creating were powerful enough to wrack the meat form my bones. The back of my hair stood up as the boat sailed at full speed into it.

" You shouldn't show your fear !" the Old Man finally said. "The Gods can smell it. They take great pleasure in our destruction !"

The Old Man had finally broken his silence, but it was almost too late, for the wave was beginning to cup over the boat.

I slowly turned my head, stiff of fright. I expected the Old Man to be the same. I expected him to be sorry for his misfortune.

The last thing I expected of him was to start talking about the story some more.

"Come closer, boy, I'll tell you a bit more of the story."

" What did you say Old Man ?" I shouted back to him.

" You should stay calm. It isn't what it seems !" he shouted. "Let me tell you more of Atlantis, to take your mind off this."

The wind began to whistle and blow fast. I slowly felt my ears begin to ache from the constant cold environment I was trapped in.

" We are going to die because of it !" I shouted, And all you can think about is your story ?"

" It's just a wave ! It's just for show! Its harmless !"

" Like the part of the story you're going to tell me ?" I said.

The Old Man shook his head. " No. The story is not harmless at all. It's the most dangerous thing you will ever face. But this wave ? It's nothing. There are ten thousand of them coming at us right now. All we have to do is sail through the wave ! It'll only take a second." he said. "The story, on the other hand, is something you'll have to struggle through -and it will stay with you as long as you live."

" Don't tell me the rest of the story Old Man ! I don't want it to be the last thing I hear !" I shouted wanting to change the subject.

Immediately, the Old Man turned the rudder briskly, The boat rode inside the tunnel of the wave. I looked up, seeing the beauty of the water wrapping around us and falling into its own demise. Like glass turning into splashes of ice.

But the boat was now sailing upwards.

I quickly grabbed onto a rope. I was scared, feeling myself wanting to fall into the water under me. I screamed off the top of my lungs as hard as possible, feeling my fingers become frail and weak with fright.

" You want the last thing you ever hear to be yourself, screaming like a monkey ? I'll tell you a tale that will make this seem like a sunny day !" he shouted.

I gave no answer, in suspense from the boat's hull now straight and vertical from me. I only wrapped myself around the taut roping and turned my head once more to see the Old Man.

Like an optical illusion, he was fine. He was still sitting perfectly relaxed, controlling the rudder.

I gasped and panted as the boat got going even faster, still riding on what you would imagine as the wall of the wave.

" Alright Old Man, shoot away !" I shouted, scurrying over to hunch beside him, wishing that the boat would return to normal.

"Ha, boy, have I ever told you the three-step Buushu solution to win your way out of any sort of argument or quarrel? No ? Then listen carefully. This is the night for it."

The next day came shining in. Nurix slept on the floor, and awoke with a sore back.

Elana had a pleasant sleep on her bed and felt rather rejubilated from her resting.

Nurix was sore all over and his joints were stiff from the cold. They both got up and started to stretch and get loose. As Elana walked around the room, she stopped to look out of the window sill. The sun shone golden rays down onto the breakfast smoke from the fire holes of the houses below. The smell of enrichened pine filled the air as did the joyful chirp of birds said hello to the morning sky.

Nurix walked to the same window sill, looking out and enjoying the sensations that Elana was pleased about.

She seemed to shine with a cleansed sort of glow.

" Good morning Nurix, how are you ?"

Nurix gave a silent grin. " I'm fine. A little soar but fine." he said.

"Oh, poor slave," she said as she rubbed the top of his head.

Nurix was amused by her teasing.

" You know, you're allowed to sleep in the bed alongside me." she said. " Why is it that you choose to sleep on the floor ?"

" Force of habit." answered Nurix.

Elana gave a slight chuckle.

"Well, I hope sleeping in my bed will become a habit that shall replace it." she said.

Nurix nodded.

" I hope it will as well." he said, looking out of the window, seeing the farmers and slaves begin to leave the compound and go out to the vast fields to continue the harvesting. Once more, their great work song was heard as they started to walk, but because of the early clear morning, it sounded better and purer than the day before.

" There they go again." Nurix said.

" Yes. Well it's the beginning of a new day. I say that we should stop thinking of sad things." Elana said, leaving the sill and getting her clothing garments on.

Nurix instinctively wanted to follow her but he had second thoughts and stayed.

He looked out at the view. There the plains lay golden and in the background were the misty, fading Ice-capped mountains.

They heard a knock at the door and there was Ekler, standing, nonchalantly; obviously sent from the Governor to escort them to the food house as she had promised. He was rather quiet this time as he waited for them.

Nurix slowly turned to look at him and noticed that he seemed afraid, or in pain. Then he looked at Nurix. Both of them saying nothing, both of them staring into one another's eyes, both wondering what the other was thinking.

After Elana was ready, they started walking once again, Ekler doing so with a slight limp.

Most of the scenery to Nurix was very different from the night before. Although it was the same exact town, the environment was extremely different. The sun was out, the echoes of the slave chorus from the fields filled the air, and last, the merchants were up and selling. The whole city changed its personality overnight.

Now, Nurix couldn't see the sad unfixed houses and the badly tended roads. All he saw and heard were merchants selling, servants buying, warriors watching, guards guarding, mammoths slugging, horses trotting, and women talking. This town was no longer the sad little enforcement hell that Nurix had imagined nor did it meet up to the Arkaiton pot of discrimination that Danoise, the mammoth herder, had talked about.

He saw no segregation, no hatred for one another. Everything seemed to fit in place, much like when they had arrived, seeing the slaves, indentured servants, and Buushu farmers working in harmony with one another.

Nurix remembered that where he saw the happy slaves singing their labor song; behind the facade of happy smiling faces; behind the illusion of harmony and peace and behind the golden and beautiful fields; lay the Buushu overseers' evil eyes, watching and hoping for one bad farmer from the crop. Someone to enforce their punishment on, to relieve the pressure which was built up inside of them.

" Watch your step when you go in. The first step in the door way is larger than most people are used to ." came the exhausted voice of Eklar, tamed beyond belief now, although there was no mention made of whether the governor had kept her promise to neuter him.

Nurix stopped and looked at the front of the hut. The food house was noisy and rowdy. Inside echoed the sounds of flutes and stringed instruments with the background sound of an obscure, pulsing vibration of what sounded like a mammoth-tusk horn. All along the sides of the outside wall of the hut were barrels of fruits and vegetables, the carcasses of half-eaten uni-horned sheep, empty and broken bottles of whiskey, and cheaply made stone work tools.

As they came into the hut, Nurix felt that the floor was moister and softer than the outside. It felt this way because it was covered in straw to keep the mud down.

Although the floor was a nice touch, it was the warmth and happy stuffiness of the place that held them captive. The tables were filled with all sorts of merchants and their hired protection; talking, betting and challenging other merchants with their warriors.

The lights were dim and the only opening in the food hut other than the front entrance was the hole in the roof, made for the fire to escape.

Nurix looked around, seeing a lot of Buushu mercenaries, and three Buushu merchants. Nurix could tell because of two of them had long braids coming down the sides of their heads and the other had a head band with the Buushu sun on it. There were also a lot of Arkaiton varieties: merchants, warriors, delegates, and slave concubines.

Nurix began to notice one party in particular which he felt to be unusually familiar. He shifted his gaze and was noticing the notorious Makaiton and not for the first time. He had been owned by a Makaiton merchant for his first ten years - she had bought him directly from his Buushu mother and had later sold him to an Arkaiton and he had been bought and sold quite a few times before ending up at the monastery.

From what he remembered of them, the Makaitons were considered the ones with ghosts.

They believed in the strengths of adopted beasts: Work horses, wolves, rams, sabre-toothed tigers, deer, mammoths, etc. They believed that they could take on the characteristics of their totem beast and fight like it for brief periods. They took drugs to make these spirit transformations take place.

Their beliefs, other than the beliefs of beast strength, were quite similar to the Arkaitons. He had remembered these details about their culture from his first mistress telling him about the greatness of the Makaitons when he was a little child.

The Makaitons wore a lot of dark colors. Some wore armor which did not have any rib-like decor at all. Their armor was shaped to look like the chests of beasts. Locks of hair came out of odd places of their armor plating. Around their boots and shoulder pads, lay brightened wool, knitted onto the fur which over lapped to cover their rusty armor.

Most of them found it fashionable for their boots to have trinkets, even for holster straps. Makaitons loved odd things to make them as warriors more intimidating to their opponents.

Yet, even with the extra buckles and the facial tattoos, they were all very similar if not identical to other warrior Makaiton individuals. Nurix couldn't tell what they were. The Warriors, the Merchants, and their slaves were indistinguishable. Maybe that's why they were called the people with ghosts. They couldn't be seen in their numbers but felt in the minds of their observers.

"Elana !" shouted a voice.

Nurix looked around, he saw Governor Vivesk waving for them with Sassaska and Brelinka sitting aside each other at a table by the wall. There was a vast variety of food on it, and three seats empty and waiting to be claimed.

"Ah, You have arrived at just the right time, my friend." said the Governor

Elana slowly sat down next to Sassaska. " Why is that?" she asked.

Nurix sat near the edge of the table, while Ekler sat right across from him.

"Because Vivesk was about to tell us the theory of why Marsolla never speaks." Brelinka said with a tone of polite amusement.

Elana gave a porcelain smile, disinterested by the topic.

" I never knew you were a philosopher, Governor," Elana said.

Sassaska gave a mild chuckle to herself.

Vivesk nodded. " Yes, I swear. My mother told me that I had a special talent for these kinds of things. She would say that as she left to go and support the family. Ironically, it seemed that she left whenever I was about to talk," she said, joking, "so it may not have been what she really thought. . ."

Then her happy expression changed to a troubled ponder about her past. "hmmm - that woman," she said, lost in thought.

Sassaska felt that she had to say something. She felt that Vivesk was going to become upset.

" Well. Tell us that theory of yours. Why don't you do that ?" she said.

Immediately the Governor's expression changed. Vivesk gave a sigh and then smiled once more. "Alright, I'll tell you my theory.

I believe that Marsolla is a type of animal which died out because of over hunting. It was a very important animal to our people and when that beautiful and useful animal was finally gone, the people felt so bad and so guilty that they began to worship it. First the shape and then just the name. It may have started as a superstitious thing, but because a social thing - to keep the people remembering one important lesson: Never waste anything that can be beneficial."

"You could very well be right" said Sassaska, reaching back into her knowledge form her High Priestess days. "Most people don't know it, but our ancestors used to have statues of Marsolla. I've seen them. They were round and red, like a ball - I don't know what kind of animal that could be. But maybe it's stylized."

"Yes. Maybe it was something that flew. Remember all the tales about how we could fly and do magic in the other place. Maybe if you ate this thing you could fly too."

"You know before I left, I was speaking to the Empress about old rumors and she was saying that there was a Buushu tale about men in the south who could fly."

Maybe the animal still lives down there."

"Ha ! Men that can fly. That would be as unlikely as women who stay home and clean the house."

They all broke into laughter at that.

Nurix tuned out from their discussions of Marsolla and wandered his eyes across the many other tables.

He stopped his eyes on a table which seemed to be most interesting to him; where there was one middle aged Makaiton woman with her back to him with two other young Makaiton women who seemed to have an eager look similar to the curious stare of a cat. They were both intimidating to look at and appeared to be body guards for the older woman.

Across from the three tough-looking Makaiton women was one calm, slender, charming looking Buushu woman.

She was holding onto the neck of a skinny, lumpy glass bottle. Her other hand had large metal rings over her index and middle finger.

The Older Makaiton woman turned and revealed a large tattoo of a wolf over her eye. She noticed Nurix staring at their table. Their eyes met for an instant then she ignored him and turned back to the Buushu woman. Nurix felt that the older woman looked oddly familiar to him, almost too familiar. That was when it hit him; his first mistress in his life was a Makaiton merchant. He had made the connection between the two because of one familiar memory check. His mistress had a tattoo of the head of a wolf around her eye just like the middle aged woman that he was staring at.

He tried to block out the conversation at his table, now concentrating with complete interest on what was being said over there.

The Buushu seemed to be sleepy eyed, resting her pointed chin on her other palm while the other hand still held onto the bottle. Her attention was fixed on the woman with the tattoo as she began to speak:

" Buushu. I see that you have a lot of guts sitting at a table where your enemies outnumber you three to one." the woman with the tattoo said.

The Buushu woman laughed at her comment. "Actually merchant, you are wrong." the Buushu said with a suave expression on her face.

The tattooed woman nodded. "Oh, and what do you mean by that, young child ?"

" We are at a trading post, Merchant. Behind these walls we are not foes, we are all one big happy family. I have no enemies.

Or so the Imperial trading policies state." The Buushu woman said as she slowly undid the top of the bottle and took a sip.

The two women with the cat stares laughed at her comment. The Buushu woman smiled, in retaliation to their laughter. "Even your matched pair of idiots are not my enemies."

The idiots stopped laughing.

"Oh yes, How could we ever forget the 'great Imperial policies?'" said the tattooed woman. "The rules made by an Arkaiton ruler. The same people who thought of the paying your kind less than the average woman. The very same people who let your people, your family members fight to the death every summer during the great migration to our proud Makaiton lands. Maybe it's because you Buushu kind are all daft, believing in your odd Goddess, Tierra. Most of your kind are considered dirty, foul smelling barbarians." she finished.

The Buushu woman slowly sat up and adjusted her chair. Nurix could see that she was provoked a little from this last comment.

The Buushu woman slowly breathed deeply. "Would the Makaitons have done anything better ? Buushu and Makaiton have always been fighting without any resolution towards the war. Your kind are ruthless, demonic monsters who thirst for power but are too stupid to gain and hold it. Your kind are a very secluded culture; probably because you are too ashamed to admit that you all are aroused by the smell, the touch, and the strength of animals."

"Was that a deliberate insult shot at myself ? Or my culture ?" the tattooed woman said.

"Oh, I was just saying what was on my mind. Must be the alcohol truth- talking." The Buushu woman said.

" A Buushu drunk on a fine whiskey, how unusual is that ?" the tattooed woman said sarcastically. " I believe that that is what your entire culture is going to come out to be: a bunch of drunks surviving by the pity of everyone else." she finished.

One of the women with the cat stare started to look at the bottle up and down.

" What kind of a whiskey bottle is that ? Is it something you stole from a travelling merchant's caravan ?" the intimidating woman asked.

The Buushu looked at her and started to exaggerate as she talked, as if she was talking to a little child.

" It's not whisky. It's battle wine.

You see, I am at war with myself. And this, this is not a bottle, this is a weapon !" she said with her expressions overdoing the effect she wanted. "I was at this table first, enjoying myself and then you three animals turned up and started insulting me when I was drinking. Check the house rules - whoever has the table first chooses her guests. I don't choose you three - so leave. Find another table."

The tattooed woman only laughed. " You are truly a mighty warrior, who can only brag behind the protection of Arkaiton rules. What would you do without them ?"

" Oh, not to worry. The Buushu teach that there are always the Three Solutions to fall upon if something strange happens. They always work," the Buushu woman answered, with a smile.

" Well that's good to know. At least you are prepared for everything," The tattooed woman said.

" Have you ever travelled to the Makaiton Buffer zone during the past few summers?" the tattooed woman asked.

" Why no. I am usually busy doing the killing of Makaiton aggressors in the Buushu Plain, well outside of the Buffer zones. Why do you ask ?" the Buushu asked as she took another sip of her wine.

" Oh for no reason. I wanted to know if you counted the many heads and impaled Buushu bodies we had along the mountain sides last summer. What was that ? Two or three hundred ?"

One of the other Makaitons nodded.

The Buushu woman slowly swallowed the burning wine in her mouth, feeling the warmth sink down her belly.

" Oh, that's not so bad." the Buushu woman said.

" Why is that ?" asked one of the cat staring women.

" At least they died in battle, and at least we knew who they were. But let me ask you - when we allow you to come down from the mountains, to collect your dead, did you ever see the many naked bodies left to rot out there ? Their hair cut off and tattoos shaved from their skin? It is always quite a sight to see; bare naked women with no individual marks to tell them apart, only their smell of rotting flesh to tell you what they were: foul, animal molesting slugs." the Buushu said with a bickering chuckle. "The nameless dead ? The thousands of them ? Well I put a great many of them there. "

The Makaiton women became silent, fueled with rage because they all had lost someone they loved dearly in that bloody battle plain. The Buushu knew this and felt very satisfied about what she said.

" Sometimes I wonder why you Buushu are still around. I know that when the Makaitons take the power of the Empire, there will be no room for your kind to exist on this world. I, personally, would make sure of that," the tattooed woman snapped.

"Oh, was that an insult thrown at myself ? Or my culture ?" the Buushu woman said sarcastically, slowly screwing in the top to the Bottle. As she did, the two cat-eyed women stood up and drew daggers. The Tattooed woman growled at her and became furious as she stood up too, " You listen well, once the Arkaiton fall, so will their rules, so will their loyalties, and so will their beliefs. In the end, there will only be Buushu fighting Makaiton. Once all the rules are gone, once all the regulations are broken, once all the governors are chased out, there will be nothing stopping us from starting the genocide of your kind, Buushu, whatever you are. Once everything is gone, once rhyme and reason no longer exist, what will you Buushu resolve to ?"

The Buushu chuckled to herself, crossing her arms but still holding onto the bottleneck.

" I see that you have forgotten this whole conversation. We Buushu are warriors and we will survive by using the three solutions that I've mentioned before."

" Oh yes, the three solutions. What are they ? Explain to me how they will stop the great genocide of your culture, before we kill you here and leave your body for the next party to trip over ?"

The Buushu woman sighed and shook her head. She said nothing as she raised her right brow, gleaming into the eyes of the two thugs that protected the tattooed merchant and were about to kill her.

She slowly unscrewed the top to take a long, smooth guzzle. She then screwed the top back on a little tighter. Her hands were firm as she did so.

"The three solutions before I die ? I think that you three good Makaitons would love to know what they are, right ? You have demanded to know.

And since I am a humble Buushu woman, about to die, I have to obey anyone because I am below everyone. Oh, of course I'll show

Julyo

The two cat-like women hissed at her, the tattooed woman was not amused by her sarcasm.

The Buushu woman grinned.

" Solution number one:" she said.

Suddenly, with lightning reflexes, she used the lumpy bottle to hit one woman on the head , with tremendous force, breaking her skull and killing her instantly. The Buushu, still moving at blinding speed, set the bottle down and grabbed the dagger from the dead woman's lifeless hand.

"Kill one fast and unexpectedly . . .

. . .and solution number two. . ." she said, quickly lunging across the table and stabbing the other woman right in the heart. The other woman was shocked and fell right across the table.

"Kill the rest at leisure, while the shock lasts.

And solution number three . . ."

The Buushu woman gave a quick, hyped laugh as she made her third solution move towards the woman with the tattoo who was caught up in the quickness and suspense from the Buushu's lightning speed and deadly purpose.

The Buushu opened her fist to release two curved spoons which were part of the ring the she wore.

She firmly shot her open hand right into the tattooed woman's nose, pulling up and puncturing her nostrils. The tattooed woman was caught like a fish on a hook, not able to move because of the pain of her nostrils tearing apart from the pressure of the Buushu's curved blades.

All conversation stopped as well as the music. Elana turned around and saw the Buushu woman standing up with the tattooed woman caught in her fingers and struggling to get free from them. Elana recognized the Buushu woman immediately, her eyes widened with surprise as her memory search came to a stop.

The suave, quick, Buushu woman standing in the middle of the room, waiting to finish off the Makaiton was not just another Buushu thug. Although her hair had lengthened a little, she was no longer wearing the uniform that Elana was familiar with, she was still easily recognizable.

The Buushu woman was Julyo.

" Oh my Marsolla," Elana turned to the Governor who seemed to not notice what was going on.

" Shouldn't you call the guards ?"

Vivesk sighed and yawned with boredom.

" Don't worry child. There's no real need to call the guards for help. The problem will be dealt with and over with soon."

" What?" asked a surprised Elana.

Sassaska and Brelinka gave no comment in the matter.

"Child, they're not Arkaitons. Their people have fought for one hundred years and there isn't going to be anything that will change their hatred for one another. That woman standing up is Buushu. They build them tough. Even if she was hurt. She'd be strong enough to lick her wounds and help herself back to her home. It is of none of our concern." the Governor said." One way or another, the problem will take care of itself."

Elana wanted to help, she tried to stand up, to stop the conflict but Brelinka shook her head and gently forced her to sit down with her hand on her shoulder.

" You agree with what she is saying ?"Elana barked.

" It isn't your fight Elana. We are not guards. We are not out to right the wrongs of the world. we are on a mission. You shouldn't interfere with things that you don't understand." Brelinka said calmly. "Who are you to decide which one is right and which one is wrong ?"

Elana shook her head,

" It's you who don't understand ! That's Julyo out there!"

Nurix turned back to the action, knowing that the heated argument at his table would build into a grand debate.

He watched and listened in as he had been doing throughout the meal.

As the Buushu woman strained her eyes and looked into the tortured, bloody face of the tattooed woman, she licked her dry lips.

" Why don't you finish me off, like you did my women ?" the Tattooed woman said with a heightened voice because of her blood filled nostrils.

Julyo turned her head diagonally and continued to look into her frightened eyes.

" Because that's not the third solution"

" Oh ?" the tattooed woman said. " then what the hell is the third solution ?" she asked.

Julyo gave another quick laugh.

" The third solution is to let the last one live. To tell the rest of her kind."

The tattooed woman gave a growl in frustration, feeling the blades slit more of her nostrils every time she squirmed. Still, she fought to break loose nonetheless.

If there was one thing that woman couldn't stand was showing that she was being humiliated by a Buushu girl. That was what kept her struggling.

" What is it that you want me to do ?" snapped the tattooed woman.

"You've . . ." the sharp pain of the blades heightened as she tried to raise her voice. The tattooed woman gulped, trying to speak calmer.

" . . .You've killed my escorts, and now you've cut my nostrils, I am merely a merchant who is no better a warrior than the common slave.

Do you expect me to travel to the next settlement? In Buushu territory without any escorts for protection ?" the woman asked as she shrivelled a bit from the pulsing pain ringing around her sinus and nasal area.

Julyo, sighed. " I expect you to stay here as long as you wish, to forgive, forget, and to laugh. Just not at my table."

Julyo started to look around the room. The many faces stared in shock, but then began to lose interest in the sprawl. As soon as there seemed to be no conflict between the two, all interest had stopped. As the faces began to turn away one by one, Elana and the rest of the people on her table were no longer camouflaged by the numbers of people standing. They were now revealed in full to her.

Julyo was surprised and astonished to see them there, mainly Elana. She had almost forgotten completely about the tattooed woman still held in her grasp.

The woman snorted as the blood trickling down her nostrils began to irritate. Her snorts turned into a pathetic growl of ramblings. " You expect me to sit down, re-establish social commentary ? You expect me to hold no grudge ?"

Her tone began to get a little more powerful but Julyo felt no interest to listen to what she had to say.

She lowered her arm and freed the tattooed woman who shook her nose and rubbed the cuts high on her nose where the blades had come through.

Her eyes still locked with fury at Julyo.

" You could have ripped my nose off Thanks to you, I'll be taking in more air when I sleep, thanks to you !" she rambled, angry for the two new nostrils which Julyo had gifted her with.

Julyo raised a brow at her ramble. "Quit whining. If I'm not mistaken, you had just ordered your goons to kill me. Yet I let you live. You should be kissing me in places nice girls don't talk about."

Both women calmed down, both faceless in expression, both silent. They then slowly sat back down at their blood and corpse-covered table. Julyo gently moved one of the dead woman's arms aside to give them some elbow space.

There, a male servant from the cooking room noticed that their wooden, reddish-stained glasses were empty and came by to fill them up.They paid no attention towards the pouring of their cups.

" Well Buushu, may I get the satisfaction in knowing your name as a consolation ?" the tattooed woman asked.

" My name is Julyo. And yours ?"

" Haven't I told you yet ?" she asked.

"It must of been lost when I was explaining the three step solution to your women," Julyo answered.

The tattooed woman gave a sarcastic, despicable laugh. "Oh yes, I must be getting old for my age. I seem to have lost something then too. Anyway. Buushu, my name is Cru'ce Fix."

"Interesting name ?" Julyo said casually, not caring too much.

Cru'ce gazed around, biting her lower lip to keep her frustration in. " I am sorry if I am not courteous at the moment, but I feel that all your 'diplomatic' skills could have been employed better here.." she snapped politely.

"You seem to keep forgetting that you were going to kill me. So this was simply a social miscalculation on your part. Now, as I was saying before you so rudely interrupted me by having your body guards try to kill me - Get the hell away from my table."

Suddenly the tattooed woman stood up and looked down upon Julyo. "Someday, there will be a vast war. When that day comes, I will be looking for you and I will kill you" she said quietly.

Julyo felt that it was her turn to give her own sarcastic laugh. She did it in a manner where she over exaggerated it to look as if an amusing joke had been told. " Oh darn, and I thought that we were going to get along so well" Julyo said.

Cru'ce only nodded slowly. " I hope, if you don't mind. I feel not well at the moment and a little uncomfortable too, so I am excusing myself now."

" It was nice that we had this interesting conversation"

" Yes, I hope to see you around. Then we could finish our discussion and finally come to an understanding." Cru'ce said with the facial expression of a stalking cat.

Julyo smiled, " I just can't wait"

Ending at that note, Cru'ce briskly walked out of the eating house and made no effort to clean up the mess. Julyo leaned back in her chair and took a sigh of relief that Cru'ce was gone. She then reached for her bottle and held it close to her chest as she sipped it a bit. She slowly turned her face, looking in the direction where Nurix was staring. She felt his eyes and thought to return the favor.

This made Nurix very scared. Julyo didn't care about Nurix though; she had recognized the face of Elana at the same table and wanted to see if she was still there.

Elana on the other hand didn't know what to do.

Nurix slowly patted her arm.

" Elana, Julyo is staring right at us. I think she's looking for you."

Elana gave a glimpse and saw her. Julyo's face lay expressionless. She barely gave a blink or a sign of anxiousness to meet her.

Elana turned around again, gazing at her old friend with the same expression on her face. "She hasn't changed at all during the past few months." whispered Elana. Then she slowly took her eyes off of Julyo.

Nurix swayed, looking at Elana, then changing direction to look at Julyo.

Julyo's clear eyes continued to watch Elana, then she broke away from her and turned her face back to the table. There she took another sip from her bottle.

Brelinka looked at Julyo for a second then turned around to Elana. "Aren't you going to go over and say hello to her ?" she asked

Elana paused.

Nurix could see that Elana was unsure what to do. To him, it seemed that something close had happened to both of them. Something that made both Elana and Julyo ashamed about it. This made him even more interested to meet Julyo, to know what happened.

Elana slowly got up.

" May I accompany you ?" Nurix asked, trying to hide his eager curiosity.

Elana, still quiet, nodded, stroking his chin.

"Please" she said.

Elana slowly turned around, waiting for Nurix to get up. Then they both slowly started to approach the table where Julyo sat alone.

Julyo kept silent and serene as she sipped her beverage, staring at the body lying face down over the table with no thought of panic. Nurix was amazed at her calmness after the quarrel.

Elana slowly took a seat, facing in front of her, the body was blocking the two.

Julyo looked up at her. She put her drink down and began to speak, "Elana, hello" she said.

" Julyo, I see that you are well." Elana said.

Nurix stood up, thinking that it was more convenient to stand than to sit with them.

" Well as you can tell from my reaction I didn't expect to find you here so far away from the monastery at Lina, "Julyo said.

" Yes, well I am glad that we've met each other again." Elana said with a pathetic smile.

" It's been months, I've missed . . . Did you come across any difficulties ?" Julyo asked.

"We did hit the storm when we were crossing the mountains But we survived that." Elana tried to rest her elbows on the table, but the dead body was lying right in front of her.

Julyo saw the inconvenience.

" Oh, sorry; allow me." she said as she gently kicked the body off the table.

Nurix backed up as he saw the body hit the straw-covered floor.

Julyo smiled a bit.

Elana put her elbows on the table.

" Thank you, Julyo" Elana said.

" So why are you at Ques ?" Elana asked, trying to make conversation.

" Because it's along the way, back to my village." she answered. "I was taking my time, hoping to get to Buushu lands in time to catch the Grand Round, then it' back to Lina for me."

" You mean, you're still a guard at the monastery ? I thought you were going home for good."

" Oh, no. I'm there for part time. I stay there and then migrate back home during the long summers for retraining on the Plains. You should join me one year - earn your braid."

" But you stayed at the monastery all the time I was there." Elana said.

" It wasn't because of the inconvenience of going home. It was because I fell for you" she said mildly.

Elana paused, regretting the question.Julyo slowly leaned closer to her.She was quiet as well. Then she sighed.

" So, where is it that you and your group going from here ?" Julyo asked, trying to change the subject.

" Once we've restocked most of our supplies, we'll be heading to the next settlement. I ponder that it will be the Buushu towns and villages, but we're not really sure, because we lost the map."

"Then where ?" Julyo asked.

" Well after we've seen most of the settlements, towns and villages in the Buushu territory, then we'll be moving on to see the Makaiton lands." she gave a slight grin in front of Julyo.

" Then we're going to head back to Lina" Elana finished.

Julyo's curiosity grew.

" Why is it that you're going to such great lengths to visit all of these places ?" she asked.

" For the Empress," Elana said, plain out and simple.

" She wants to study the provinces and update her maps and so on." she finished.

Nurix sensed that she was hiding the truth, thinking that it would cause some unwanted controversy.

" I see." Julyo said.

Nurix could tell that there was nothing really to talk about, but she still wanted to stir up conversation. In the hopes that she could establish something that he couldn't figure out yet. This intrigued his interest even more.

" So what was the year of the map ?" Julyo asked.

" Excuse me ?" Elana asked, clueless to the question.

" The year of the map. That'll determine the accuracy of the pass ways and roads. A lot can change in thirty years." she said.

" I never got a chance to review it personally. We lost it, trying to survive from the storm a while back. Until we find a replacement map, we're probably just going to talk with merchants and accompany their caravans to the next town, although it'll sure slow us down travelling that way." Elana explained, rubbing her hands.

"Then what ?" Julyo asked.

"Well, one problem at a time."

Julyo's right brow rose up with a concern.

" So you don't have a stable plan ?" she asked.

Elana grinned, thinking of a comment.

" Well yes. You see, I had a sure plan on how we were going to continue on with the mission: We have a Priestess, Sassaska, and we were expecting her to talk to Marsolla and for sure" her amusement began to show through,

Julyo gave a stiffened smile.

"Marsolla's going to give us a sign every time to point us to the way." she finished as she started to chuckle with her own comment.

Julyo laughed with her, not noticing her hand gently patting her palm and squeezing it. Suddenly, there was silence between both of them.

"Surely you mean Tierra ?"

Julyo immediately noticed her hand and quickly moved it away.

Elana slowly moved it to her lap.

The pause continued for a moment. Both of them feeling a little uncomfortable about what had happened.

Nurix was in a haze of questions and he didn't understand their reaction towards each other. He didn't understand their past, or what had happened before.

He didn't understand that Julyo once loved Elana dearly and had painfully tried to contain her feelings after an incident which had happened before he met any of them. He didn't understand that Elana pitied Julyo for falling for her, she felt flattered at the time, but at the same time, never had the same feelings to reflect back.

Nurix, couldn't see the complexity of it all. All he saw were two people regretting their accident in touching each other's hands.

Julyo took a silent sigh and breathed silently. She kept no eye contact towards Elana and slowly moved her seat back; she was about to stand up.

"Well, good luck in your journey. I hope to see you soon back at Lina next year." she said as she got up and gathered her bottle and the knives from the dead.

She slowly turned around, nodding her head in front of Elana, "Good bye, Elana" she said.

Nurix watched as she started to walk, feeling that he was about to miss something if she left. Elana kept quiet in front of her but nodded good bye to her.

Elana felt a little uneasy, that she was acting so uncomfortable in front of her old friend. She then began to feel that she wanted her to stay at the table, to talk and converse about what had happened. She also felt that her chance was lost if she said nothing But she sat there, thinking for a few more seconds, pushing herself to call for Julyo once more.

Then she did it: she stood up and, just as Julyo was about to step out of the door, she shouted; " Julyo! wait !"

Julyo slowly turned her face, eyed with curiosity.

"Julyo, come back" Elana said with an eager look. She nervously pressed her teeth on her lower lip and waited for her to come back to the table.

Julyo slowly walked away from the flap door entrance of the food house. She started to re-approach her. Elana's eyes wanting her back, but unsure why.

"I . . " she muttered, nervously trying to say what she felt.

"Yes ?" Julyo had an anxious tone in her voice.

"I think Marsolla has given me a sign. Since we don't have a map, or a replacement that will be coming soon . . . "

" Yes ?" Julyo said slowly stepping a little closer.

" I . . . Well , I believe, that it would be ideal if . . ." she stopped and tried to continue her sentence.

". . . I mean, you are Buushu?"

"Last time I checked." Julyo said a little sarcastically.

"You're supposed to be naturally gifted with direction. . ." said Elana.

Julyo gave a blank, stupifyed look. Elana had lost her through her nervousness.

" What are you implying." Julyo asked.

" Will you be our guide?" she finally blurted.

Julyo was in pause for a few seconds. Her eyes, brightly excited but her fair, magnificent structured face, hardened by the warrior's callous training held her excitement and true feelings at bay.

" You know, I will not stop at certain towns and most of the way, I will be travelling by the trail of the grazing animals."

" Yes, I know."

" There will be Buushu of all kinds, some who will be our friends and others who will be our foes. If you travel with me, I will take you as far as I possibly can, but I will not take you to the borders of the Makaiton provinces." Julyo said.

" It doesn't matter. By then, hopefully, we'll be able to go by ourselves."

Julyo nodded with a grim thought. She seemed uneasy about the provinces of the Makaitons, obviously because of their two cultures being in feud with each other.

" All right, I shall be your guide" she said.

Elana gave a pathetic smile,

" Thank you"

" By the way, I am getting paid for this, right ?"

Elana froze for a second. She didn't know how much she was asking for and was contemplating how much they had. Nonetheless she gave the best answer she could under the circumstances. She only had one thing on her mind. One problem at a time.

" Most definitely" she said with a nod." I will most definitely ask."

It was late morning when I woke up. The sky was grey, remnants from the storm last night. The Old Man was nowhere to be seen and the cold air was crisp and fresh.

A perfect experience to wake up in, especially after a harsh night.

There were a few others slowly arising from the bottom deck, groggy and yawning, they hardly even knew that there was a violent storm. All that was going through their heads at that moment was if there was any beer left. As one man slumberly rocked over to one of the barrels at the side of the ship, he took out the wax cork and took a smell.

" Ahh, that's something to get you up in the morning." he muttered to himself with a little smile of satisfaction as he put a wooden cup under the spout.

I slowly rose, feeling the urge to urinate. I walked to the side of the boat, I started to empty myself outwards, staring at the waves and the grey sky disappearing into the beam of light that lay across. My eye sight was filled with sand, tears that I wept while I was asleep. As I began to rub my eyes, I was astonished to see what was right out in the middle of the distance.

Although the air made it misty to see, I still knew what it was. It was an island. It was large as well as dark looking.

Suddenly, my heart leapt into my throat, my stomach was getting filled with butterflies.

There was land.

Land in the middle of the ocean.

The first thing that ran into my head was that this island was the legendary Atlantis which the Old Man was always talking about. I couldn't contain myself any longer.

My excitement made me start to shout out with laughter for no reason.

" Land ! Land ! There's land !" I began to shout, still peeing.

"It's Atlantis !"

The man who was previously sniffing the barrel, and now drinking a cup of beer slowly stumbled up, wondering why I was acting so strange. Then he too stared in awe as the island lay in front of us, calling us, waiting for us to come to shore.

He was silent while I was yelling with joy.

"My, my, my, boy. I think that pissed us up the real Atlantis" the man said as he patted my shoulder.

I couldn't believe my eyes. Right in front of me was the legendary Island. The lush green of trees, the tall and steep peaks soaring above. It glowed as if it was a paradise, shining and alluring like the fabled world of Marsolla which our ancestors had to leave.

As more people slowly stepped out to fall into awe one at a time, they received instructions by the shock-stricken Likooshas to turn the boat and head towards the shore.

Hearing all of the ruckus, the Old Man, who had gone underboard during the middle of the night, poked his groggy head out of the trap door. He looked around, grumbling and cursing because a bad night's sleep.

The men were happy and filled with enthusiasm as they manned the sails and changed the boats direction.

Those not involved in manning the boat began to sing folk songs aloud. Some of them even began to dance along with the clapping and tapping being played out by fellow crewmates.

" What's going on here ?" the Old Man shouted demanding an explanation. One of them started to approach him and pull him into a happily-performed fisherman's dance.

This only made the Old Man a little more irritated than he already was. " What is the meaning of this ?" he said as the man let go and let the Old Man fall to the deck.

Likooshas, who was staring out, scanning the island with his own vision slowly walked over and knelt down to the Old Man.

" What the hell is going on around here ?" the Old Man sneered. "One minute all of you are asleep and belching, and now after I turn my head around, all of you are jumping in joy."

Likooshas sighed and gave a mild smear on his face.

" I see that you cannot take a celebration well. Although I hate your very soul, I am proud to say that your mission has been fulfilled aboard this ship."

" What are you talking about ?"

We've arrived at Atlantis ? At this moment ? Right off the star-board bow." Likooshas left him to go back and look some more.

I went over to help him up.

"It's Atlantis." I said. "You were right. It really does exist."

The Old Man shook his head. He went and got a cup of beer and sat down with his back against the side of the boat, not even looking at the island.

"Come over here Greko." he said.

I went and sat beside him.

"Let me tell you a story about making assumptions, " he said.

The day had finally come. The actual day of the departure was within three hours of becoming a reality for Kline. Because of the presence of Zex, journalists from every branch of the Empire were at Prox. The idea of a Great Race had fired the imagination of everyone.

Within the air base, a magnificent crowd of one hundred thousand eager citizens had come to watch the launching of eight Be-Quads.

Five hundred Imperial troops stood by to keep order.

And right in front of the open Beetle-like transports lay their cargo: The thirty smartly dressed expeditioneers of Bringington stood in a sharp line in front of them. Kline and his scruffy eight men stood aside from Bringington's and kept their personal feelings to themselves as they noticed the transmissions crew of the Journalists cranking up the generators to broadcast the event through the radio waves.

Kline kept silent from all of his fellow Journalists who wanted to interview him. His heart still held the wound for Ennis and he felt the urge to keep everything confidential.

King Zex stood charmingly in front of the audience. Hearing their cheers, their praises for him, he gave merciful glances at the public in thanks for their loyalties, loving every moment of it.

"My loving Public . . . We stand all as one at the never ending climax of our grand Empire . . . We stand as Sudutans; the most powerful Empire the world has ever known !" Zex paused to let the roars and cheers continue to create their glorious aura.

Then he continued on speaking. " . . .Long ago, our ancestors were approached by the brightness of Marsolla in the coldest of days. He said to us that we must prove our worthiness to him by passing tests that he would set.

Our ancestors stood up to him and told him that we would prove ourselves worthy in our own eyes and that we would make him hesitate before challenging us ever again.

So we dreamed up a power to compete with the God - diamond power. We used it to lift ourselves up from savagery. We used it to explore new lands, to attain new possessions, to elevate our life-style and to understand what our destiny was to be.

Thus we came, thus we saw, and thus we grew !" he roared once more, awaiting the golden halo to come once again. The crowd obliged.

"And now, after thousands of years, we have shown our worthiness to the eyes of Sudutans so that not even the God himself could strike us down from our superiority. For we have become Gods ourselves. The Gods of Sudutan Atlantis."

The audience screamed.

"So now, we face one last obstacle. We, the people who have conquered armies across the seas. We, the people who were able to construct machines to fly. We, the people who can talk across the country with our radio. We, the people at the top of the world, we are faced by only one danger. The danger of losing our Godhood. Losing our civilization. Losing our whole way of life. We need diamonds to power our Godhood. We cannot anymore be held back by petty superstitions about the Northern lands.

As a child, I watched my Father reign true amongst the public and wondered why he was loved . . . He was loved because he tested the beliefs of the world, and succeeded with valiance as did the Emperor before him and the Emperor before him.

The cautious warned us not to cross the western seas for there lay the angry arms of Marsolla, yet we still traveled and conquered. The trembles of the sceptical told us not to fly for we were never supposed to have learned the secrets of the air, yet we did fly to conquer. Ever since the beginning we've broken the rules and defied the old. But now we are left with the greatest superstition that tells us to beware of the North.

Today we challenge Marsolla once more to test our worthiness; whether we as a people can conquer the North, for once we have conquered the North, we have conquered Marsolla !" he lectured, hearing the adoring public honor their heritance of defiance by all doing the same thing.

They began to cheer the name of Zex, saluting him with their hands up in the air.

And Zex bowed.

" So, in return, I give you our challengers of Marsolla . . ." As he turned around, Bringington marched to his left, his men staying back.

Kline slowly walked to Zex's right showing no emotions to the crowd nor to Zex himself.

Yet the crowd didn't seem to care. Zex had attained their cheers to the point which they would cheer at anything.

" Now quiet yourselves to let our challengers step forth to gain your positivity !" he said to the crowd of ten thousand citizens.

Zex immediately grabbed both the hands of Bringington and Kline and rose them high into the air.

" . . . Long live Zex, Long Live Zex . . ." the crowd cheered out loud.

The interviews and ceremonies went on for another two hours, all until the observation balloons were raised up to check the weather for the radius of thirty miles all around. Zex had backed up into one of the observation balloons to watch the take off of the Be-Quads. The Comfort girls of the men had arrived and awaited to fasten themselves within the cargo ships. Dav'inne smiled as he threw his arm around the slender beauty he had bought. The same went for Clubio who already had become intimate with his girl.

Bringington, who was standing in front of the journalists and their broadcasting crews, lectured about his own triumph from rags to riches.

Kline ignored most of the other journalists, awaiting the moment for take off. He sighed, unstrapping his pigskin helmet in an attempt to release the trapped heat from his head.

Dole came by,

"Kline, there has been some last minute changes . . . We've been given a portable radio broadcaster to record our progress . . .

We've also . . ." Dole stopped, noticing that something was wrong with him. Kline turned his head but said nothing. He didn't seem to care about the portable broadcaster.

" . . .Still moping around because of Ennis ?" Dole asked him.

Kline then turned himself all around.

"She was one in a million . . ." Kline said mildly, reaching for his cuca box. "And I'm a one in a million bastard for trading her away for nothing but money and fame."

Dole nodded compassionately.

"I disagree. It was all for the best, my friend. If you didn't give her up to Zex, we would have been jobless. Besides, there's always going to be another vulgar-acting woman out there in the world for you to find. They're quite common, actually," he said.

Kline gave a smile as he rubbed some of the powder into his gums.

Kline closed his eyes, in a blinding flash of peace.

" Sorry, finish what you were saying, Dole . . ."

Dole took out a scrolled map and unrolled it. " See the mountainous glaciers over the Isthmus . . . The height of the mountains added to the pressure of the winds will make it impossible for any of the Be-Quads to go over them. We can travel by Be-Quad about three hundred miles into the Glacier Desert, but that's about the limit. We will be dropped off three quarters of the way across, north of the Glacier Steep, giving us approximately a 10 days to reach the top of the peak and fly down the glacier. Of course, on the other side of the peak, we have no idea what to expect. No one has ever seen it or charted it. How far we'll have to go to find land - or if there is any land over there, we don't know. So we'll have to . . ."

"Wait! To fly down the other side with the Drag Quads and ninety pounds per man, two hundred and ten plus for the two carrying the comfort women, that's insane !" Kline interrupted.

Dole gasped mildly, " What are you talking about, Kline. Gliding down in one hundred mile wind resistance is far safer than taking a chance with a five ton metal and wood cargo Be-Quad. For starters, Be-Quads can only go a distance of one hundred miles at a time - and we don't know what to expect on the other side. Second, Drag-Quads can stay in the air almost as long as the individual can stand to be up there.

And third, with the Drag Quads, not all of us will have to die together."

Kline stuffed his box into a pouch within his thick tanned over cloak and straightened out his expensively linked Vital strap to reduce his nervousness." Alright, so we'll all die separately. But yes, point taken about the mountain climb, but what about Bringington?By making us go this route, and putting this obstacle in front of us, Bringington, with his thirty men and his easy route to the east will make it to the North continent three weeks in advance."

Dole looked over his shoulders at Bringington who was still boasting to the journalists. He pulled Kline tight into a huddle.

"What I have received from my sources is that Bringington plans to fly to one of the outpost Islands and try his luck reaching the Northern Peninsula without the task of going over the glacier. But the fault to his plan is that the outposts are required to inspect all saling ships, fying ships and passengers before letting them off the island. Not only do they have to go through inspections, but they have to sign papers and grants for every inch of equipment they have. Taking roughly two weeks all together.

Bringington knows about the inspection, that is why he will take a hand picked crew to take off on one of his cargo ships while the others would be left behind to fill out reports. But he's going to try and make his way out during the night. That is when he'll be caught and fined. His Be-Quads will be confiscated and he will be stuck on the island until he gets a hold of a boat of some sort."

Kline took a glimpse at Bringington.

" But if he has clearance from the King, then he is untouchable." he commented.

"Not according to my information. Keep in mind, that the Cummundores there would do anything for hard currency. Thus, everything will fall into a complex web of forms and clearances that will bog Bringington down for weeks. Well, we've agreed to pay for a delay of two weeks, anyway."

Kline gave an enthusiastic smile and gave a pat to Dole even though he had no idea about Dole's thinking patterns or how any of these complicated deals would stop Bringington.

"Well then, best that we get a move on." Kline muttered.

The Imperial Sponsors slowly stepped onto the stone take off strip. They motioned for Bringington and Kline to come over. Kline nodded and pushed Dole to the side as he made his way. Bringington called a halt to the questions of the journalists and stepped through the tangle of crew specialists generating their checklists of equipment.

Bringington stood in front of the discussing Sponsors. Kline straightened his standing presence. Both of them gave a respectful nod to each other, then to the Sponsors.

" You both should start loading your craft now. Both parties have been cleared for take off. Once you both have landed at your appointed border post, use the portable transmitters to send word of your arrival. " one of them stated.

Suddenly one of the observation balloons gave off a greenish powder. Everyone looked up at the hazing dust forming into a cloud.

" The air is clear for ascent !" another Sponsor stated.

The main Sponsor looked up at the sky, then back at Bringington and Kline,

" Kline, you will be landing at Critesk Mia, right where the first sheets of glacier meet the line. Bringington, you will be landing at the Juppa outpost.

Both regions will be of equal distance from your designated expedition destinations. Good luck to the both of you . . ." he finished, saluting them as he turned to the observation balloons.

The Sponsors began to back up, giving the signal to the expeditioneers to begin boarding.

Bringington faced Kline with a sly grin. " . . . I hope you enjoy your trip over the Glacierous mountains . . ." he said.

Kline nodded with no emotions in his face at all. "Yes . . . You know, once we cross the border of the Mia divide, you and I will no longer have to feign being friends . . .We will be able to kill each other as previously dreamed . . . Too bad we'll be on opposite corners of the northern world . . ." Kline stated.

Bringington looked to the north, seeing the haze of green dilute itself into the air.

" Well then, if we don't see each other during our expeditions, may the best man win . . . that being me, of course . . ." he said with a mellow tone.

413

They both gave a respectful nod to each other and made their way towards their own Be-Quads.

Both parties then took off and the skies were filled with the clustering Beetle- like bulks, one heading straight north to the Critesk Mia line of descent, while the other six headed for the Outpost Islands. Kline, and his men arrived at the border within two hours of air travel. There they rejoiced in praise for their arrival at Critesk Mia.

The night had been long with the moans of the comfort girls as they performed their duties beautifully to the men.

Kline awaited his turn but began to feel the painful guilt as he slowly envisioned the face of Ennis over one of the women, thus panicking.

He stepped out for a breath of fresh air. There, he stood and gazed at the colossal range of mountain and ice miles away. The great Glacier itself was so massive, rigid, and blank that the coldness of their frost was able to be felt from where Kline was standing, miles away. It was then, in his gaze at the Glacier range, that he realized why the ancients of long ago believed it to be uncrossible. It was then, that the paranoia of Bringington's vengeance began to generate a storm of possibilities within his own mind.

He heard some of the men chasing a girl through the streets and head their cries as they caught her. Before morning they came to him looking for money to pay off her family. They had killed her, just as they had earlier killed another girl near the training area.

Kline, thinking of Ennis, agreed to pay some out of the expedition funds, but told the men that the rest would come out of their share.

Day came as fast as time would allow it to come. Kline, the Expedition Cummundore. Dole, the Sponsor advisor. Clubio, the Imperial advisor. Luca, the long range observer. Dusty, the Aero-specialist. Squirrel the mechanical engineer. Dav'inne, the Medical officer. Vittorio, the scout. Angellina, and Bisu, the Comfort girls, they all stood and held onto the railings within the hold of the noisy Be-Quad as it worked itself up the steep of the mountain. The winds from the peak of the mountain pressured down upon the oval transport. The Imperial pilots looked for a calm place in the windy landscape; a window of opportunity to drop off Kline's team and the supplies and leave without being blown into the mountain.

As the ruggedness of the flight began to cause shakes, Dole began to show signs of nervousness. His hand, holding the railing began to sweat from the friction.

Kline kept himself near the pilots, watching their ascent towards the designated break in the mountain for their safe passage.

Vittorio tightened his woolly jacket, knotting up to keep warm as he felt the coldness seep through from the bronzy metal he leaned against.

Dav'inne breathed soundly, holding his nose high in the air. He had no fears within him, even when the Be-Quad began to fly up a little more horizontally.

Kline looked ahead, through the cockpit and stood at his spot, holding onto the railings, attempting to try to talk with the pilot.

Bisu, one of the comfort women who he had been spooked by the other night, concernedly came closer to him. She had never before been rejected and felt disturbed by his reaction.

"Cummundore," she asked gently.

Kline turned around and gazed at Bisu. He said nothing, still remembering the other night when her face transformed into Ennis. He gasped a little and gave an expression of attention to her.

Bisu moved herself to the side,

"Cummundore Kline, I wanted to talk about the other night . . . You seemed frightened in some way . . . Was it because of me ?" she asked naively.

Kline was about to answer her but felt it necessary to keep his reasons confidential for the time being.

" I was troubled a little by your face that night It reminded me of the face of a dear friend who died recently. And was a little out of breath, maybe from the altitude . . . It was a rather stuffy night . . ." he suggested, lying through his teeth. "Nothing to do with you."

Bisu lowered her eyes. She felt hurt from his remark about her facial features and about the fact that she was not irresistible enough to overcome altitude, stuffiness and any other minor discomfort. She then bowed her head in mild obedience.

Kline discontinued his attention with the woman and pulled himself towards the pilot of the Be-Quad. He stared through the heavy glass , that acted as the main windshield of the pilot.

" How much farther will it be until we reach the landing point ?" Kline asked over the loud noise of the outer wings slicing the air at tremendous speeds. The pilot kept his focus strong on the noises of clicks per speeding rate.

The pilot's eye also fell into deep concentration over the pressure valves unable to balance out evenly. He was almost caught in his own world of mathematics and precision, yet he found it possible to comprehend Kline's question.

The pilot gave a tortured grin, refusing to take his eyes off the mountainous scenery or the measurement meters. " We'll land when ever I can find us a slope that's out of the wind and which does not give too much of a vertical caution." he said, ending his response very abruptly and beginning to descend, with slower pulses of clicks. "Maybe that one right there. Let me check it out."

Kline felt the descent and forced his palm tighter around the wooden sectioner to keep himself from falling.

As the Be-Quad descended, Clubio gripped tightly onto the hand of his comfort girl, Angellina. She smiled at him and respected his grip.

Luca paid no attention to the drop for he had experienced descents many times before as an Imperial Observer. He tugged on his jointed over-brace, made of the same metal links as his darkly corroding Vital.

Dav'inne strapped on his hardened pig skin helmet, hearing the wings coming to a slower hum and a clank.

The Be-quad slowly began to dig it's monstrous legs into the soft snow of the ice cap. As the surface lowly revealed itself to the pilot, he turned to Kline and gave a sigh of relief.

"Well Cummundore, you've made it this far. Now you can set foot upon the Glacious desert . . ." he said as he arose from his electrically heated seat, walking over to help lower the shaft ramp. As he turned the wheel to relieve the pressure in the tubes, the ramp lowered.

At almost the same instant, the cold air of the outside wind filled the compartment with it's briskness. Snow immediately began to rush into the opening.

Dav'inne and Luca immediately stood up, knotting their woolly jackets together to keep out the cold.

The blinding snow lit up the room with its own paleness of color.

Clubio covered his eyes as he glimpsed at the brightness, turning away and lowering his head.

" Quickly, get your supplies out of the ship, before the wing grease freezes and cargo compartment fills with snow !" the pilot shouted, releasing the seven packs of Drag-Quads from the safety nets.

Kline walked up to the conveniently packed Drag-Quads with their utilities strapped and secured. He grabbed the shoulder straps and heaved it onto his back. The others immediately grabbed their own amount of supplies.

Kline staggered to Clubio. Both squinted as they looked upon each other. "Make sure that all of our supplies are taken. Once you get out there, keep close to the team !" he shouted.

Clubio nodded, looking outwards at the snow. " This Expedition of yours . . . It better be worth our risks !" Clubio hesitantly replied, looking out at the blinding desert of snow.

Kline gave a mild smile. " It'll be worth every amount of currency, you can get your common little hands on . . ." he said, patting his strapped up shoulder.

Clubio neglected to reply once more, seeing the hurrying expressions from the pilot whom was worrying as the snow began to melt over the iron floor plates.

Clubio then grabbed a hold of his wingless Drag-Quad with one hand and his woman with the other hand, dragging both outwards into the snow.

Dav'inne quickly packed up the medical utilities and tightened their straps over his Vital hold and his leather chest armor. Vittorio looked around, seeing that there was only one Drag-Quad left along with the bulky, portable transmitter. It's cranks and churns lay visible, making it a very crude and primitive looking piece of machinery.

"Always me with the most to carry," he exhumed in a lowsome sigh. Nonetheless, he strapped on his Drag-Quad pack and fastened the portable transmitter over his belt and Vital strap. Then, tightening the buckle over his helmet, he made his way out into the blizzardly snow. Dole gasped as he stepped out into the thick deep snow, wondering if he was ready to take part in the expedition.

The crew made their way out of the humming Be-Quad.

They quickly threw their supplies into a bundle once they exited the staggering transport.

Kline looked at the pilot, who was beginning to pull up the ramp with a turning wheel. " Good luck to you Cummundore ! May you succeed in the name of Sudutan Atlantis ! We're all rooting for you." he said waving proudly at Kline.

Kline gasped, feeling the need to hold onto his old necklace that he wore to calm him from his insecurity, as the Be-Quad shaft sealed itself shut, leaving them totally cut off from their civilization.

Kline staggered forwards as he witnessed the take off of the Be-Quad, making its way back south, where it was civilized, where it was warm.

For the first two days, the team pushed themselves further up the mountain, only taking breaks to sustain themselves, then pushing on, wading through the deep powdered snow that lay ahead of them.

Snow covered their frosty faces and icicles appeared over their disassembled Drag-Quads. The going was tough, waist deep and almost straight up. But they had trained for this, so it wasn't unexpected. Of course they had also trained to fly and would have preferred to do so, but the height, the wind and the cold made it almost impossible to predict what a vertical flight skip would do. Either the air would be too thin for their wings to pull themselves erectly, resulting in a tumble all the way to the bottom, or the noises of their clanking would cause an avalanche to engulf them within a prison of soft, deadly snow.

Thus they continued to hike up, withstanding the cold and its many tortures. The further they went up, the harder it became to breathe. Even with the growing pressure of the wind speed, they gasped chronically for air.

Kline took a moment to catch his breath. His hands ached and burned as he clenched onto the icy surfaces of the next rock he held. His muscles in his arm throbbed, wishing that he would stop for a moment, but Kline knew he would never see the top if he gave up at that moment.

The team had come to a steep point of the mountain which disallowed the group to hike anymore. Instead they all had to climb with their heavy equipment. For Clubio and Dav'inne, they were burdened with guiding their women, Bisu and Angellina up, too.

Kline turned his head and looked down at Dole, who's facial hairs carried frost flakes and grits of snow. He huffed vapor from his mouth, suffering from the same struggles of Kline.

"Why have we stopped moving ?" Dole asked with a suspended groan.

His fear of falling over kept him from looking up at Kline.

Kline tilted his head vertically, gazing at the ridge of the peak he intended to reach.

"I needed to catch a breath for a moment." Kline answered, tightening his grip as he felt his forearms tensing and his knuckles trembling.

Dole took a breath of sighs.

"Well I hope you don't mind when I bring this to your attention, but we're climbing over a mountain, dangling by our finger tips, risking our lives as well as our dignities so that we can get to the other side.

Now please restrain from taking any offense when I say that we're not doing all of this so that you can stop midway through, to take a nap and a breath. Yes ? Or do you think you can just stop anytime you please ? If that is the case, then I'm going to grab a hold of your boot and pull you off the mountain myself !" Dole said irritatedly.

Kline paused, too tired to remark about Dole's out -of-breath verbal attack.

He began to hurry his climbing by a few steps, regardless of the amount of stress and tension he was building in his muscles.

They climbed further on, almost losing the women and the portable transmitter to exhaustion and the extremities of the wind pressure.

Nonetheless, the crew of ten finally made it over. There they sat in a crescent, facing the northernly direction against the wind, gazing at the endless plain of snowy nightmare in front of them: mountain after mountain, they would likely have to climb before they would even reach a point where they could see if there was any land.

Kline, having pushed himself to the limit for the two days of climbing, felt that he could not endure assembling his Drag-Quad to cut to the next mountain. His shoulders were sore from the cold and he had to rest for a day at the least.

Kline, fell to the softness of the snow, panting with remorse for being so persistent as to make it to the top in so short a time.

" Group . . ." he said, only able to raise one heavy hand.

The others struggled and rolled themselves over, quickly throwing off their heavy burdens.

" We rest here . . .. We rest here tonight." Kline gasped, working to gain air.

Dole rested on his knees, looking at the blinding snow which was causing the surfaces in front of him to glow.

The others were too tired to question Kline's decision to stay the night at the top. Thus they stacked their Drag-Quad splints and interlocked them so that nothing would be lost. From Kline's laying position, he noticed the portable transmitter, strapped to Vittorio. He grabbed a hold of him as he walked by.

" Vittorio . . .Sen-send a message back to home, that we've made it to the peak of the first mountain . . ." Kline heaved.

" But that is nothing worthwhile to record . . ." Vitorrio replied to him.

Kline shook his head.

" Everything we do in this crew his worthwhile to report . . . The fact that none of us have died or fallen so far is worthwhile to report. If we do not let the public know how we are doing, then the public will not care about anything we do at all . . ."

Vittorio did not understand Kline's reasoning and was about to say a counter statement, but Kline forced his grip over his leg.

" Just do as I say, lad . . ." he said.

Vittorio grumbled to himself and then strenuously turned the crank shaft a few times to charge the battery and make the radio operational.

As The group unraveled their personal shelters tucked under the padding of their Drag-Quads, Kline sat up, tightening his jacket and rubbing his hands over his frozen Vital strap and his knee straps. He hoped for the friction of his hands to conduct heat, but what he gained were only numb hands. He clapped them together to regain feeling and then reached for his cuca box, taking only a little bit of it and snuffing a sample from his finger.

Dusty sat aside from him.

He unraveled his tools for his personal shelter. When he was done, he slowly sat down, facing off into the north. He noticed Kline's cuca box and requested for a bit.

Kline nodded and handed him a dash. Dusty wet his finger and gathered the dash to put it over his gums.

Kline then put the box away, feeling weary as he realized how quickly his supply was depleting.

The winds howled and soared as if they were alive with passion.

Kline serenely stared off, wondering about the edge of the ice desert and what would be there, waiting for his crew.

Dusty shook his head, feeling the effects of the drug. " Excited about the flight tomorrow ?" Dusty asked eagerly.

Kline turned his head to him, knowing that Dusty loved to gloat about flying.

Kline sighed apathetically,

"I'm as excited as the rest of you are . . .What do you feel about the descent to the next mountain? I mean as an aero-engineer, what will the mathematics show ?"

Dusty tilted his head.

"Mathematics have nothing to do with this. To a certain extent it does, but most of the time it's the rush of instinct. The descent won't kill you if you're going at a minimum speed, but the wind will brush at you, and make it very uncomfortable all the way to the next mountain." Dusty stated with a smile.He then made his way into his bound-ready shelter, about to seal the flaps behind him.

" But this wind resistance will not take our lives. It's too afraid to do so . . ." he added.

Kline nodded and laid himself on his cloak, keeping his cloths dry.Dusty took another glimpse at the distant, blue-shined mountains. The walls of sheer ice, which were said to be the stunned fists of Marsolla, warning all to keep their distance.

"Why is it you want to go to the North continent again ?" Dusty asked curiously.

"I believe that the north has an attraction to me. The risk I have taken to go this far and the threats of Bringington and of Zex that I had to endure and even this discomfort we're going through now; it has all been worth it.

The North has been my romance ever since I was a child. The Marsollan mythology as well as old folk superstitions designed to scare off the meek, well, they only pulled me here twice as strongly," Kline posed. Then he sighed. "but mainly, it's for the money and the title . . ." he finished.

Dusty grinned, "Ah, yes. The weakness of all Sudutan men. Not the glory, not the war, but the profits !" Dusty then leaned back into his tent.

"You aristrocrats are all the same . . ." he said, chuckling away as he closed up his door flaps.

Kline nodded his head and continued to stare out at the dim clouds over the mountain peaks, seeing the coming fog beginning to encage the camp. He waited for Dusty to be fully enclosed in his temporary shelter before he frowned.

"Crazy, arrogant prick of a man . . ." Kline added under his breath.

The boat sailed towards the island and scrunched up on the beach, interrupting the Old Man's story.

"And that's what happens when you base your opinions on assumptions. Kline assumed that going to the north would be easy - once he had the money. But nothing worthwhile is ever easy. Just like getting to Atlantis . . ,"

Crewmen jumped off to run ropes up the beach and tie them to trees along the shore.

"Atlantis ! I love you !" yelled Likooshas, "And I love you, too, Old man for getting us here to Atlantis,"

Crewmen standing around gave a cheer to this.

The Old Man shook his head," That cannot be Atlantis, we are far from our destination"

Likooshas raised a brow," If you do not believe me, Old Man, then take a look for yourself," he said as he crossed his massive arms, looking onto the shore.

The Old Man slowly arose to his feet and turned around.

"Behold ! Your beloved Atlantis," Likooshas said pointing out to the island and slapping the wooden boatside that he was leaning on.

As the Old Man took a long look, his disbelieving face immediately changed into a slight grin. He slowly turned around to the crew who were continuously singing and dancing.

The Old Man watched them dance and bellow, then turned to Likooshas," Alright. I won't ruin the party. You're right, Pirate. It is Atlantis,"

Likooshas nodded, "Ayyy. I told you so,"

"But it is the farthest flung outpost of Atlantis that ever existed. I recognize it. I would know it anywhere by that snaggly mountain peak - which was known as the last Pillar of Atlantis. The island, it is officially called Guenalopa but it was known as Way Station. It was the main gathering point for merchants and diamond traders, for settlers and soldiers. It used to be one of the busiest places in the empire,"

"Why so busy?" I asked, "It looks pretty unbuilt-up,"

"Atlantis didn't want to have too much impact on the natives. They tried to leave them alone to develop on there own. After all, they only wanted diamonds, not generations of childish sub-humans to be responsible for. The only place they really mingled was at the diamond mines themselves - which is pretty well everywhere you'll find a pyramid of some form or another.

That's why everything came here first - and went on to the mainland in special cargo Be-Quads that could go amazingly long distances. So there wouldn't be one big port that would totally change the native lands. Or could be attacked or closed,"

"If it was so busy, why aren't there ruins ?"

They tried to keep it perfectly natural," the Old Man said," The ships stopped and anchored here, and the people lived aboard until they flew on to the mainland. This was like a resort.

You could live on the beach in a grass hut and go native - and many people made the journey simply to do that, but most were on to the mines. They didn't want to stop for long. But the traffic was very heavy,"

The Old Man's grin faded, "So, if Way Station is deserted, I fear Atlantis is truly lost. Gone forever,"

"Maybe Atlantis still thrives," said Likooshas, "Only this outpost is dead,"

"Would you still be alive if your arm was all green and dead. Not likely. Atlantis is no more,"

Likooshas looked as if he was going to cry. I, as well, was heart stricken, sad that Atlantis was forever out of our reach.

All of the crew including myself began to loose that magic shine and happiness, the energy of joy seemed to just drain out of us..

Likooshas shook his head, closing his eyes hard and banging his fist into the side.

" This is not Atlantis, is it" he said holding back his quick yearning instinct to throw the Old Man off the boat.

"Why no. This is not Atlantis, but it'll do for the moment."

"What do you mean by It'll do ?" Likooshas asked gritting his teeth.

The Old Man began to nod and point at the same time,

" You see that mountain peak there ? That is one of the Pillars of Atlantis !"

" The what of Atlantis ?"

" Nicknamed that because of the series of mountainous islands along this route. Islands used by pioneers and merchants going back and forth continuously through the known world,"

The Old Man ran his right hand through his hair, " You see, this island in particular will be very beneficial, especially to you. I'm glad that we found it. Frankly I thought we were much too far north. Good thing we saw it - otherwise we'd have ended up in the southern ice."

Likooshas looked towards the brightly lit island with a scowl, as if it was the island's fault for not being mainland Atlantis. Although the scene in front of him was soothingly beautiful, he couldn't keep in his furious temper for it ate at him indefinitely, ever since their departure from the Peaks of Hercules.

" What the hell are you talking about, Old Man, why is this island so important to us ?"

"Every ship and every person who passed through here, had to pay a tax. And that tax was in the universal currencies, which were the materials to generate power. There will be a big storehouse of those materials somewhere here and, believe me, you will be very interested in finding those,"

" How old are we talking ?"

" It doesn't matter. They will keep forever,"

Likooshas' eyes widened in surprise. Suddenly he reached over and grabbed the Old Man by the collar of his tunic and pulled him close.

"Look at this place. It's totally deserted. Most of the supplies would of been eaten by rats or decomposed by now ! Don't you see that this island is a waste ?"

" Why, no Likooshas, not at all," the Old Man advocated calmly, making some slow and graceful movement to free himself from Likooshas' grip.

" Atlantis' technology during it's reign was the best in the known world. I can assure you that any supplies we find and the materials I spoke of are still intact,"

" How can you prove that, Old Man ?"

" I can prove it and I will prove it, by finding them and showing them to you. But just think about it - a great civilization wouldn't be titled a great civilization if it had pest problems that they couldn't take care of,"

Likooshas stepped back from the Old Man.

"Alright Old Man. You've convinced me this time,"

" Don't I always ?" the Old Man barked as he snickered to himself.

Likooshas frowned at him and turned around to the crew," Get ready. We're setting camp on the shore," he said powerfully.

The crew, spirits restored and hope of booty renewed, quickly began to smile and sing and get ready for their departure from the boat even remembering to gather a barrel of beer or two to take with them.

Later that night, conversation and controversy went on. The Old Man had talked Likooshas into letting them explore the island the next day.

The Old Man was positive that there was something worthwhile on this island and he guaranteed everyone that it was going to be worth the exploration. Besides, as he so rightly pointed out; where were they going to go anyway ?

I, frankly didn't care. After all, I wanted to hear the story of Atlantis in its prime, not see the remnants of it. I felt that Atlantis was a tale which was not meant to be spoiled by the true facts. The truth that mighty Atlantis has fallen and is no longer the great world power that everyone hears in the legends is a sad ending to a great story, and ruins your vision of it.

Like the legends of great leaders and heroes from
long ago; it's heart breaking to hear the truth about them - that
they were just ordinary people and all the magic has just been built up
around them. That was how I felt.

The Old Man sat down, surprised to see that two to five members of the crew were also sitting patiently, waiting to hear the tale
tonight. The Old Man was astonished. He never knew that many people
were eager to hear the never ending story.

" You all want to hear the tale ?" the Old Man said.

"Yes. Tell us the tale from where you left off," I said.

The Old Man slowly sat comfortably near the fire and stared into
the many silent faces. He had their attention.

"But, you see I cannot go back and tell you all what you have
missed,"

"That's alright, Sisko has already told us everything we've missed
and Greko will tell us anything that Sisko missed.

Go on with the story !" said one very grim sounding man.

All the others began to agree and talk at once.

" Silence !" the Old Man shouted.

Within a second, everyone stopped talking and waited for him to
go on with the story. The Old Man looked slowly at everyone's eager
eyes.

"Alright, alright, I shall go on with the story Under one condition," he said holding out his finger.

"What's that, Old Man ?" I asked.

"Someone please tell me where in Marsolla's name have I left off,"
The crew gave a mild chuckle.

" You're at the part where Kline and his people were ready to
leave," Sisko said as he was huddled up, trying to sleep near the fire
place.

"Um Thank you Sisko," the Old Man said.

"No," I said, "they had left and were up on the mountain in the
snow,"

"Yes, that's true. I remember now. Alright," the Old Man started,
"I shall continue on with the story from there," he said.

Everyone gave a sigh of relief.

It had been a gruesome five-week expedition through the vast white snow and arid thin air, even after they scaled the first peak. They had flown from mountain to mountain, continuously, during the several weeks always finding just one more in front of them. And there was no sign of greenery land at all.

Angellina, the young comfort girl, had died within the first week. Clubio had accidentally dropped her when the first flight to the next mountain took place and she had never really recovered. Somehow, even in all that cold ice and snow, her wounds became infected and Dav'inne, the Medical officer had not been able to kill that infection with the drugs they had brought along. Her health rapidly plummeted and, when she finally died, slowly and in agony, so did the spirits of the whole team.

It was said to be faulty knotting over her strapped belt, a knotting she had done herself, but Kline suspected that it was negligence on Clubio's part. From the look of him after the accident, Kline suspected that Clubio felt guilty, either about tying the knots himself or not checking them thoroughly. Kline said nothing to Clubio though, he kept his thoughts to himself as he did his grief for his own woman, Ennis.

Bisu, Dav'inne's girl had also begun to suffer. She loved to drink and often fell asleep naked, with no coverings, often with her tent door wide open. During the last few weeks, she had suffered greatly from the wrath of the frost. First her hands went numb, her legs became useless, and within a few days after her crippledness, she, too fell severely ill.

Dav'inne stayed close to her, hoping that there would be a chance to save her, but most of the others feared coming near the poor girl. They knew that catching a cold would result in death without the proper alchemy to help it. Thus, Dav'inne took a chance with his life for a woman that could have been replaced just as easily as Angellina.

It was during the third week of silence that Kline approached Dav'inne.

Kline felt that Bisu was slowing down the expedition, and needed to reach a compromise on what to do with her in the next hop. She was dying, that was clear. And just like Angellina's, it promised to be a long, agonizing death.

Already, their food rations, Drag-Quad lubrication, and patience were seeping away. Kline was not going to risk stopping in this hostile climate for days or maybe weeks with this burden who was needing more and more heavy medical attention every second and was heading for death anyway.

Kline was in the big tent with the others. He rubbed his hands to keep warm, leaving his leg and arm braces loosely tied on so that he could move around in comfort but still not lose too much heat. His beard grew heavy for he had no time to waste shaving, especially in the frosty temperatures where he too could possibly be grasped with a cold.

As Squirrel made another daily transmission concerning their whereabouts and day to day gossip, Luca sat upright, examining his worn down Drag-Quad, taking out his oil can, re-lubricating the friction roughened ball joints anchored within the unit's powerhouse.

Kline gave a sigh, unraveling his dampened box of cuca and realizing that it was more than half empty. He grumbled, realizing that the last few dabs were hardly worth the trouble. He placed it back into his overwoollen, lama jacket. He was becoming more irritable as the days went on without his precious cuca.

The lack of the drug even seemed to play tricks on his mind.

Dav'inne finally came out of his set up shelter and entered the main tent. He blew over his hands and then rubbed his arms and stopped to sit and talk with Squirrel at the transmitter.

Kline treated him with caution that he might carry sickness, and moved even further way across the tent..

Dav'inne noticed him, and he scooted over, on his hands and knees to address him.

"Good evening, Cummundore. How is everything ?" Dav'inne asked briskly.

Kline nodded his head,

" Congratulations. Squirrel says our expedition is leading. We have nearly two weeks travelling time ahead of Bringington's party at the outpost Island. He has trouble getting the permits . . ,"

Kline stopped him there, hearing horrible coughs and moans coming from Dav'inne's shelter. Dav'inne, on the other hand, took no notice to Bisu. He seemed used to the fact she was suffering.

"She seems to be getting worse, " said Kline.

"Yes. If I'm any judge, she'll be dead in a few days or a week at most,"

Kline slowly moved closer to Dav'inne," Yes, that was something I wanted to talk to you about. As you know, the mountain range is still before us. We don't know how far the ice and the mountains extend. We don't know whether there is any land open at all up there. And we've already passed the halfway point. With our present supplies, we could never make it back. So we have to push on and find open land. . The problem lies with Bisu,"

"How so?" asked Dav'inne.

It is very unfortunate that such a pleasant young girl would cost us an extra week's ration, constant attention, and the possibility of infecting someone else. Especially if she's going to die anyway,"

Both men turned and gazed in the direction of Dav'inne's shelter.

" Yes, I know. She's been a handful to keep alive during the past week. I am very sceptical about her being fit enough to travel along with us as we make the next flight. But, nonetheless," Dav'inne paused as he became aware to Kline's attention.

" Cummundore, I understand the importance of the expedition as well as the high expectations which not only the King, but also Marsolla has burdened upon us. I've talked to Bisu about her situation and she has insisted that we leave her behind, but I am not at the liberty to leave her alone in the cold.

I am not going to ignore her, especially when I was the one who insisted she come."

"You risk a lot for this woman, but you must think for the whole Expedition now. Much as you may want to risk yourself, you have no right to risk the entire expedition.

Do you realize by your selfishness in trying to stay with this dying woman, Bringington might get to the north and back already ? Because of your quest to sit with this woman as she dies, you risk the health of all the rest of us," Kline uttered.

Dav'inne's mouth fell open. He felt stung by Kline's accusations.

" Please, Cummundore, do not accuse me of trying to save my conscience. I felt that sitting with her at this time was the most selfless thing anyone could do to another person. And I strongly do not believe that Bringington could be as fast as us.

You may be the leader of this expedition, but I am still the Medical Officer. I can tell you about morals as well as the conscience of the human mind. I know the physical and mental problems of every single one of you. Just as I know my own obligations and duties.

For example, I can see that you suffer from cuca withdrawal, a very dangerous kind that could result in madness. I can see that Dusty suffers from brain damage, that Clubio suffers from Murder Madness, and that Luca suffers from sweet blood. I myself, suffer from selflessness.

I remind you once more, and then never again; I know about Ennis. I am not the selfish one here," Dav'inne argued.

Kline picked at his unshaven chin, continuously thinking about Bringington and his possibly taking the lead in this race.

"Then prove to me that you are not selfish. Put Bisu out of her misery," Kline said, patting Dav'inne on the shoulder encouragingly as he pointed in the direction of the shelter where she lay dying.

Dav'inne looked down, "I can't do this. I already told you, Cummundore. Not with this woman, and not now when it's the comfort girl who needs the comfort,"

"Dav'inne. I don't know if you realize what Bisu has become during the last few weeks but what she is now is a paralyzed, disease-ridden hag.

She is in horrible pain, which you cannot relieve and which will not go away until she dies. The best comfort you can offer her is to put her to a restful sleep,"

Dav'inne shook his head, " But she might recover. Maybe she will cure herself. Miracles do happen. Something can happen. I have been exposed to her and I'm not ill in the least."

Kline calmed him down by putting a hand on his shoulder ," You told me herself, she's as good as dead here. And you know that nothing can save her. So don't prolong her suffering. Help her now. The sooner the better. You know it is the right thing to do,"

Dav'inne threw Kline's hand away from his shoulder.

" I am a Medical Officer, and I cannot cause anyone to die. It's not right !" he raised his voice.

Immediately, the others turned their heads in curiosity.

Kline raised a brow," Will you feel better if I went in with you to finish her off, or would you rather I do it myself ?" he sighed.

Dav'inne stood in shock. He had never seen a man so focused on killing a woman in his whole existence as a Medic. His eyes raised in surprise. Kline's question seemed very unexpected to be asked at the time.

"Are you mad, sir ?" Dav'inne asked.

"Yes or no ?" Kline replied.

There was an absence of sound between the both of them for a few moments; Kline becoming frustrated by Dav'inne's over-reacting conscience and Dav'inne overwhelmed with Kline's practical way of solving problems.

Both stared off at each other awaiting an answer suitable for one another's beliefs. Then Dav'inne opened the flap to the tent and pointed the way to his shelter.

"After you," he said softly.

The nest day was hot and mirky as the Old Man, Likooshas, and I searched for the long lost outpost vault. It had been a wild goose chase for more than an hour.

The rest of the men had spread out, looking for any kind of artifact on the island, but the Old Man insisted that we accompany him in an unlikely direction.

Likooshas and I were truly positive that he was lying about his familiarity with the island and was just too proud to announce it to anyone. After a little bit longer, climbing hills, following long grass-invaded foot trails, and crawling into deep patches of jungle, the Old Man was huffing and puffing like a tired old bull. But he wouldn't quit. We went on for another two hours, climbing further on up the mountain and sweating like pigs.

The Old Man was positive that the main control outpost - the Governor's fortress, whatever it was, was high on the shoulder of the mountain, looking out at the view of the bay.

"It's not practical to have it so high. Everything would have to be carried all the way up from the beach," said Likooshas.

The Old Man smiled, still huffing and puffing and pointed up to a nearby bird's nest in a tree, "It makes perfect sense," he said, "when you can fly,"

He was eager to go on, but Likooshas and I had other plans. We had taken a break and both of us were sitting down on rock stumps at the edge of the mountain.

The Old Man, although tired and swarmed with flies as well, was pacing slowly with his hands on his waist. He stopped and bent over as he fought to catch his breath.

As soon as he caught it well enough to talk, he turned to Likooshas and glimpsed at me," I hope you both are ready to see the greatest view you've ever seen in your lives," he said.

Likooshas snorted at him and turned to look at the rocks and boulders on the bottom bed of the mountain.

" I didn't come here to look at a spectacular view, Old Man," Likooshas said, wiping the sweat from his brow," I came here to see the outpost. I came to take the treasures, or whatever the hell you say we will find there," he finished.

The Old Man slowly crouched down to give his legs a rest.

"Don't think like that, pirate," the Old Man said.

Likooshas slowly turned to him.

" The out post, Old Man There will be things of value to us, to the crew," he said.

The Old Man grinned, "I can tell you right now," the Old Man started, "That the view will be a lot more valuable than what you'll find inside the outpost,"

Likooshas slowly got up, "Hopefully, that is not the case," he said.
The Old Man slowly got up, too. He faced me, handing out his arm to help me up. He pulled me up quickly and then slowly looked up at the mountain.

" Well then, let's get started, shall we ?" he said.

I groaned, looking at the steep, rocky trail which seemed endless. By the time we had arrived up at the shoulder - a large flat area right before the real steep peak began, the sun was already at the top, meaning that by the time we got back to the camp, it would be night.

As I fell on the flat, high grassed flat peak, cursed with the severe exhaustion from the climb, hearing the pestering flies and insects hovering and crawling all over myself, I tried to look up and see where Likooshas and the Old Man were. The heat was battering down on me, keeping me moist and soggy from my dripping sweat as I struggled to stand up on my weakened legs.

I panted as I looked around, feeling the veins on the side of my head beat heavily.

As I stood there, I felt the drift of a powerful wind passing myself. I slowly turned my head to the direction of the wind, closing my eyes as the wind, cool and crisp, began to evaporate my sweat and cool me down. I breathed in the air, gasping it, swallowing it, filling my lungs with the coolness of the wind.

Then I opened my eyes.

I was in shock from what I was seeing. It was what the Old Man told us all the way up, the thing that would be even more incredible than the old Atlantean treasures we all were so eager to see.

What I witnessed in front of me was the most breath-taking view I had ever seen. I was stunned.

Descending cliffs covered in hazy grass, the fluctuating heights of shrubs and trees, so full and brightly rich with shades of green. The scenery of the horizon of grey just above the beautiful grand blue ocean which we had traveled through. The sharp blue sky with puffy white clouds. And far, far below, the brilliant half-moon of bright sand. It was like being a god.

The contrast of green, blue and the reflection of the sun, so clear, so pure, so untouched by shadows and darkness. It was like a glimpse of a perfect world

Even as I followed my eyes along the shore line, seeing the white water beating onto the yellow, gritty sand, I heard the soft sound of the birds as hundreds of them began to take off all at once, far below me like an orchestrated performance by the mighty hand of Marsolla himself.

I slowly smiled, feeling the life that was being presented to me. My haziness and drowsiness seemed to disappear, for my mind was no longer thinking of it. My mind, my senses and my joy were all turned to a symphony in all positive notes, being played by the wind as it traveled so cool and crisp over me.

I laughed out loud and as I slowly lowered myself, straight back, onto the ground, letting the long grass pat my shoulders, and the soft bed of grass slowly sink a bit, like the luxurious bed of a king.

The Old Man appeared, towering over me.

"You were right," I said, "The view is like heaven,"

"You'll never forget it as long as you live," he said, "I certainly never have,"

"Where's Likooshas ?" I asked.

"We found the vault. I told him where to go in there to look for what he wants,"

"Really ? Let's go," I said, sitting up

"No, let him rummage around in there like a mad bear until he finds his treasures. Let's just sit here, you and I, and enjoy the view for a while,"

"Well if that's the case, why not tell me what happened to Bisu,"

"Poor little Bisu," he said, "Terrible things are done which mostly start with only the best of intentions. This is what happened to Bisu:

Both Kline and Dav'inne stepped into the moist and damp shelter, oil lamps darkened for the weary Bisu.

Kline slowly stepped closer to Bisu, who seemed to be sound asleep. Her eyes had dark blue sacs around her sockets. Her hair lay tangled from the many days of being neglected. Her wet body, was wrapped tightly with the warm blankets but even that didn't hide her smell. The scent of a woman who hadn't washed in over a week which held both the repelling and the erotic elements hand in hand, coupled with the indefinable but unmistakable whiff of impending death.

Dav'inne shook his head gently as he hovered above her. He knelt down to reach her head and mumbled a few Marsollan prayers to her.

"I can't believe that we're going through with this . . ," he moaned as he unraveled his Bankra blade from it's wet holster. Patches of mist began to appear on the surface of the weapon as it was exposed to the warmer temperature of the room.

As Dav'inne backed his hand with the blade, over his head, preparing to make the fatal chop, Bisu's eyes opened up and stared into Kline's face. Dav'inne froze in suspense, unsure on what to do.

Kline smiled. "Hello, my dear, how has your sleep been ?" he asked.

Bisu blinked, swallowing spit to moisten her irritated throat.

Dav'inne breathed deeply and nervously, keeping himself from weeping. Bisu moved her head as she turned her wondering eyes to Dav'inne, holding the shivering Bankra Blade, curve down aiming for her neck.

Her dreary reaction speed seemed careless. She gave a mild yet pleasant sigh as she breathed in the cold, blistering air.

"Why has Dav'inne raised his Blade above me ?" Bisu asked naively.

Kline came a little closer, gesturing to Dav'inne to keep the blade raised. " Don't mind our dear doctor, Bisu. He is only doing what he thinks is right,"

Bisu said nothing to question him. She seemed to hold to a code of obedience around the men, especially within the presence of Kline. She would not question them or make a scene. She was taught well by her father.

Kline reached slowly for her hand. He could tell that she was trembling and wanted to comfort her till her death.

" You see young girl, we have been too selfish with you. We all love you and want you to stay with us as long as possible. So we have been ignoring your pain and misery. We did the same with Angellina, remember. And she was in agony for days and days. We're just too selfish. So after you have comforted us so well, we want to comfort you. Because we all love you," Kline smoothly stated in a caring manner.He was always good at trying to ease people into a blissful aura of hope.

She shook her head as she broke into tears and her wheezing erupted into a painful cough. She felt devastated by Kline's statement.

" I am so sorry, Cummundore Kline. Can you please forgive me for what I have done, getting sick and being such a burden?"

Kline caringly brushed her forehead with his free hand.

He stroked her hair gently and then rested his palm over the burning hot surface of her head.

" You needn't worry about a thing Bisu, because I promise you that you will be forgiven. And remembered. And always loved,"

Bisu cried a little more, now squeezing Kline's hand in fright. She was scared of death.

"Was it because I was not attractive to Marsolla, or to the men, or to you?" she asked with a plead, "Is that why I got sick?"

Kline gave a pleasant chuckle. His voice became quieter as he comforted her a little more," Now be still. You were the most attractive woman to us all. Everybody liked you even more than Angellina.

And by the cloth of the evening I promise you that you will be rewarded by Marsolla by showing us your selfless act to save the rest of us," Kline cooed, stroking her once more and squeezing her hand.

Bisu turned her head to the side.

" Nighttime promises disappear with the moon. They're only good for the moment, the time, but not the instant after," she said softly.

Kline paused. What she had said was almost exactly to the words of Ennis, the night he paid for her for the first time.

Kline began to tremble at the thought of her coming back to haunt him for his betrayal.

Bisu turned herself towards him, But then, in his cuca-deprived mind, her sweet young face began to change form to resemble that of a sickly apparition of a dead and bloodied Ennis, seeking revenge.

Kline's eyes widened in fear as he tried to let go of her. But her grip over him was strong. Kline began to stagger up, pulling Bisu harder.

Dav'inne tried to calm him down. The cuca withdrawal was really beginning to take its toll on him. Bisu cried more and more as her fear overpowered her pain.

"Snap out of it, Kline !" Dav'inne shouted, but it was no use. Kline was in another world well outside the gates of his sanity.

Dav'inne lowered his blade and rushed to pull Kline apart from Bisu.

Kline noticed the Bankra blade lowered in the Medic's clenched fists. He lunged over Dav'inne, knocked the sword away. He scrambled after it and fastened his grip over the frosty Bankra blade, then sliced madly at Bisu's wrist several times.

Dav'inne screamed in surprise, watching Bisu fall into shock.

Kline tried to pull the curve of the blade out to chop once more but it refused to come out of her wrist. The blade had entangled itself with the bone and tendons of her hand. The more he tried to pull it out, the more Bisu screamed in agony.

Dav'inne felt sick to the stomach as he watched Kline's arms become even more bloody while they both stood with the smell of spurting blood and raw meat engulfing the frosty cold.

" Kline, let go of the blade before you cause anymore problems !" he shouted reaching for the sword.

Kline was frightened to death, still trying to pull the curve of the Bankra out of her hand. His hands trembled as blood sprayed brightly over the handle of the blade.

Immediately Dav'inne smacked Kline from the blade, grabbed the bloodily slick handle and pivoted the Bankra to sever her hand completely. Then he rolled it around his hand and sliced once, expertly at the direction of her neck.

Blood fountained.

Her screaming came to a stop as her eyes faintly shut. Dav'inne panted and threw the Blade down onto the floor. He turned to Kline who was huddled into a ball and rocking back and forth.

Dav'inne furiously grabbed the bloodstained Kline by the shoulders and pulled him up, checking Kline's eyes with his red-coated hands.

" The next time you want to lend moral support, make sure that you don't hallucinate !"he shouted at him with pants of exhaustion. " You idiot,"

His body was at an alert state of reaction.

Kline looked at him and calmed his juttery nerves down. He turned his head, noticing that the woman was hardly Ennis at all. It was young Bisu, instead who was bleeding to death from the slit across her throat and from the stump of a missing hand.

Blood trickled down with the salt of tears as she turned herself over slowly and fell into eternal sleep.

Dav'inne brushed his hands against his chilled Vital strap in the hopes of reducing the hardened blood from his palms.

" Such a mess !" he grumbled, now covering Bisu's face with the covers.

Kline gave a nod to him, loosening his collar knot," You have done well, Dav'inne. We will all prosper because of your selflessness,"

Dav'inne said nothing, waiting for Kline to leave his shelter. Kline tidied himself up as he stepped out of the shelter.

The men of the expedition were absent of thought once they had seen the sad little cadaver of young Bisu, laying on the greyish white permafrost. Her blood turned black and her eyes glazed over. What scared them the most was the expression of her face. The distress and the sorrow. Her slit neck, now dry and ruffled with the stains of clotted blood all over. It was a shock that such a young woman of beauty would be so easily turned into an abstract figure of abominality.

Once she was looked at tenderly by them all, and tears were shed, Kline wrapped her in a blanket with the help of Dole and Clubio, and threw her off the mountain as they packed up to make their next leap.

"That's horrible, " I said, "They just treat her like garbage,"

"Men have always treated women like garbage. It is the one thing we will all have to pay for when we finally see out god face to face, the Old Man said, "Come on down and see what we've found. Likooshas should be done throwing stuff around by now,"

He got up and disappeared down the hill.

I quickly stood up, feeling dizzy suddenly and looking down at where I was sitting. Then I realized something: the Old Man was nowhere to be seen.

I walked around, looking for his footprints, some sort of sign that would point to the direction of his location.

" Likooshas ?" I shouted. I waited for a reply only hearing my echo come back.

" Old Man ?" I shouted, only receiving the same thing.

I continued to look around in the high grass, thinking that they were lying down somewhere.

Then I fell.

I tripped and started to roll down a steep slope covered in thorny shrubs and bushes. I knew this because I felt every bump and scratch of them as I kept rolling until a giant boulder broke my fall. I slowly got up, tired and sore, and fully shook up.

I groaned as I rubbed my neck to get rid of the pain.

" So you finally decided to show up did you?" came the voice of the Old Man.

I slowly turned around and saw him standing right in front of the mouth of a cave.

" The outpost vault is in there ?" I asked bluntly, thinking that the cave didn't reflect Atlantis' greatness and power.

" This is the storehouse," the Old Man said, holding a peculiar and odd looking torch in his hands.

" A cave ?" I said.

The Old Man only sighed with annoyance.

" Likooshas said the same thing. Funny how you pirates all think alike,"

The Old Man started to walk out and lead me out further for me to receive a far clearer look.

Then I realized what I was seeing.

It was an oval-like structure, very large, smoothened all around, and decorated with faint scratches. Scratches of writing which I couldn't make out even if I tried.

The structure was partly engulfed by decades of landslides. That alone probably explained why the fall was so steep.

" It's a lovely piece of work," I said with a little sarcasm.

Personally, I saw no beauty in a dirt ridden structure which probably wasn't completely intact. It was a ruin, a relic of the old. That was probably why I didn't see anything beautiful about it: I was young and it was old, like I had just said. And no matter what anybody says, opposites don't attract.

The Old Man started back into the cave.

Come on, you'll want to see what we found," he said, holding his torch proudly as he insisted I come with him.

I slowly followed him into the structure.

" Well," I started, " What did you find? Anything of value?" I asked eagerly.

The Old Man only smiled, "You might think of it as worthwhile," he said with a little laughter.

" Then why are you laughing ?" I asked him curiously.

" Oh, I don't know. I guess that I have a dark comedic mind," he said, "I am laughing at the faces you and Likooshas are going to make when you see the trash we'll find in the oval supply room that lays in front of us."

As he led me through a partially collapsed hallway, he slowly but forcefully pushed the door of a room open.

" Did you find him ?" came a voice.

It was Likooshas who was looking up at several web-infested, dirt-attracted cans and barrels which were unopened and still in place on the shelves.

"Yes I did. He was lying around in the grass, dreaming again," said the Old Man, "Did you find your treasure yet ?"

"Nothing that looks treasurous to me so far,"

"You might want to try those sealed little barrels with the curly marks on them," the Old Man suggested.

As I whiffed the air, I sensed the aroma of granite and cluttered dust. It smelled fresh and irritating to the nose. I quickly covered my mouth, so that I would keep myself from sneezing and choking to death.

I looked around in the dark room. The Old Man had found another odd-looking torch and lit it for me. The flame seemed to burn without a wick and without consuming the stick that held it. Perhaps there was oil cunningly concealed inside.

I nodded to him, showing that I was grateful for his assistance.

I looked around in the oval room. The windows were blasted in with ancient mud, and remnants of glass lay all over the place.

Everyone was silent as we each investigated something of our own interest.

The Old Man looked around and picked up a few scrolls, reading fragments of them. He also wiped the dust off certain contraptions, then he began to fiddle around with the knobs on these strange things.

Likooshas was interested in what was in the cans and barrels. He sniffed around, looking for dusty bottles of whiskey or rum. As he looked, he came across a bottle of clear glass. It was revealing a dark substance inside of it, all the fillings lay very thick and condensed at the bottom of the bottle while the watery, clear fluid floated on the top. He quickly grabbed the bottle and stuffed it in his knapsack and continued on foraging through the old supplies.

I walked around, looking at all the books that lay fallen down and torn up to pieces. I slowly bent down, seeing a beautifully cased book. I had never seen one of them before, only hearing about them enticed my excitedness to hold one of these things.

I held it and felt the texture of the spine.

I slowly dusted off the packed mud on top of it. The words written on it were very abstract. Not that I could have even understood to read my own language, let alone whatever this one was.

I opened to the first page, looked in and tried to make out the scratchings that were made inside. As soon as I gave up and turned to the next page, I saw a very detailed picture of an exotic flower. That was when I immediately realized that the book that I was holding, caressing and pretty well worshipping, was upside down.

As I turned the book around, I looked at the picture some more. I looked at more pages, noticing many pictures of flowers, plants and grass. Some were familiar to me and most of the others were very foreign.

I noticed the written explanations on the sides, pointing to the pictures, (not that it actually helped make me understand, going by the fact that I couldn't even read).

I flipped around, noticing the same things as I went along: More plants, flowers, sea weed and greenery. Then it began to get really interesting.

I stopped at a picture of a strange animal. It was a side portrait of the most ugliest animal that I have ever seen.

The picture showed a skinless animal, drawn out with all of it's muscle structure and bones visible. At it's front lay a long trunk, like a large tail extending outwards.

There were lines pointing to the organs, limbs and muscles. It must of been a diagram of some sort which helped to guide a person to tell all the insides of an animal.

I turned the page, hoping to see more pictures and I saw four side profiles there. All of them had trunks and seemed very closely related to one another.

I took a guess that it meant that they were all similar types of animal in some way. The first picture showed a beast with two tusks sticking out of it. It's ears were large and bent to the side so that they were visible. Another picture below it showed a similar face except the ears were a bit smaller and it's cranium seemed to bulge out a lot more. It showed no sort of tusk at all.

To me this was very interesting.

From the Old Man, these beasts were called Mammoths , yet both of them did not appear to carry magnificent tusks or fur at all. They seemed like pigs with long noses. That was all.

I continued looking down at the last two portraits.

As soon as I looked, my question was answered:

The first picture revealed a beast with small ears, barely visible by the sketching. It's hair was thick and covered the eyes and hump and even on the lobe on the top of it's scalp.

And last, it's curly tusks peeked out, large and heavy looking. It was the most ugliest out of the ones that I had seen so far.

The last picture showed a beast which seemed to look a lot more pig-like and a little more primitive. It's trunk was small, it had four odd tusks coming out of it's mouth. It's ears were round and it's forehead was sloped in. I was unsure what this one was.

The same as the first two, it left me with questions : were these mammoths as well or separate species ? I thought.

I stared at the pictures and tried to make sense of the written diagrams along side of the profiles. I slowly closed the book, leaving my finger between the pages like a paper mark. I started to approach the Old Man, hoping that he could tell me about these animal profiles and what they were.

He was still fiddling with the contraption. It looked like he was able to read the symbols. I watched him as he grabbed the squarish machine and persisted on disassembling it. For another few minutes, he plugged recoiled wires, weaved strange strands of metal around cylinders, and then seemed to give off a glow of happiness as he came close to whatever he was trying to do.

Suddenly there was a crash, followed by the sound of metals and stones pouring onto the stone floor.

The Old Man slowly put the box down and walked over to see if Likooshas had killed himself.

" Likooshas ?" he said," Are you alright ?"

I quickly ran over, nervous that he was injured as well but then, as I approached them, I saw that Likooshas' eyes were in awe. He stared at the fallen barrel and the cargo it held.

As I looked down, I was in awe as well for what cargo lay on the floor were piles of solid gold strips and uncut diamonds.

The Old Man was the only one who didn't seem very surprised.

Likooshas, a little happy and amazed, quickly turned over another barrel. More jewels, crystals, diamonds, and gold strips poured out.

Likooshas looked up at me.

" We've found treasure," he muttered, "We've really found the treasure of Atlantis !" he said a little louder as he started to laugh.

"See," said the Old Man, "I told you there'd be some valuable stuff here."

Likooshas paid him no attention and started bringing down all the barrels he could find and smashing them open like a madman, muttering and laughing to himself. This was his life's dream, after decades of petty robberies and sad little murders. This was his moment.

"Come with me," the Old Man said, leading me out of the room and into the hallway, "Let him smash everything open. It's too noisy in there to concentrate. Let me tell you some more of the story."

"Sounds good to me," I said, clutching my book, with my finger still inside, marking the page.

"Without the women to slow them down, Kline's expeditioneers flew for two more days and nights across the ice and snow, stopping only for quick meals and for quick re-lubrications of their Drag-quads. When darkness came they landed like a flock of raggedy birds, set up their tents and then were gone again at first light. But still there was no land in sight."

The mist of the stormy weather worked itself against the motley seven as they flew harder against their natural boundaries.

Kline breathed furiously, feeling the early effects of thinning oxygen from the high altitude and the discomfort of his sweat freezing over his thickening beard. His legs and arms ached and pulsed from the cold braces , which cut off his circulation after hours in the air. It was getting difficult to shift his tired body to navigate himself.

The clanking of his Drag-Quad became more jagged and scratchy, meaning that his lubricant within the joints were burning away quickly and would have to be replaced soon.

Kline squinted as he felt the wind seep through his glass goggles filling his eyes with tears..

It was then that Luca Beard, flew beautifully past Kline. His long and narrow wings, measured for his weight and size, beat with the clicking precision of five hundred beats per second and made him resemble a dragon fly, the master of flight.

Kline tried to get his attention.

Luca's monocular periscope had been extended for hours now and he was looking through it constantly, so he didn't notice Kline. Luca's search for the perfect mountain stopping place was still under way. The crew had to land some time soon. Their wings needed repairs and they all needed rest and food.

Kline's fingers became numb trying to wave at Luca.. He flexed his joints and caused friction over the pipe-like handles of his Drag-Quad's pressure valve and speed monitors, making a clanking noise, but Luca still didn't notice. Kline tried for a few moments more to gain his attention and finally, by accident, Luca turned, gazing at him with the monocular periscope.

" What do you see ?" Kline shouted,

But it was no use. The beating of their overworked, mechanical wings were too loud for anything to be heard. Kline then resorted to sign language.

" Any landing places ?"

Luca shook his head.

Clubio came buzzing over, staying close to Kline. His hair had been greased with the lubricant oil and thus had hardened the full height of his frilly Mowhawk and it was acting as a minor air rudder. He was only able to see the others with the rolling of his eyes or through his peripheral vision.

He made several hand signals trying to tell Kline that the thunderstorms were about to erupt.

Dusty flew fifty feet below and began pulling up at a ferocious angle. His hair was almost enclosed within his pig skin helmet and his hands were crossed across his chest, trying to keep his body stable from the speed he was pushing himself to go.

Luca immediately slowed himself by a large factor. His search for a flat surface to land had come to a pleasing finish. Just under the tip of the mountain peeping through the damp mists of water vapor, was a large, flat area.

"Dusty, inspect !" came Kline's hand signals into the air as he slowed down too, seeing the grin of the hovering Luca's face.

Dusty, who had caught the message through his peripheral vision, decided to show off and quickly shut down his engines and began to fall straight down. He widened himself as he dove, trying to keep himself facing the ground.

Kline came to a stop, finally getting used to setting his wings on hover mode. There he caught his breath and untensened his shoulders and watched in awe as Dusty fell like a rock, dropping into the misty clouds and disappearing.

Squirrel slowly came to a halt, then Dole and Vittorio, as well as Dav'inne. They all watched the spot where Dusty had dropped into the clouds.

Far below Dusty felt his cheek bones ache from the numbing hurricane of rushing air. He breathed deeply, making sure not to lose his breath. Under the clouds, he began to notice details on the darkly shaded mountain top. It was then that he felt the pressures of the wind pushing him away from the flat area he had come down to inspect.

Quickly, feeling that he was about to lop-side, he reached for his generator cord.

As he straightened out his other arm, he forced his legs to keep stable for the wind was pushing them upwards. He knew if he turned on the wing blades while his legs were up, they'd be severed on the beating wings. He yanked the cord, hearing the generator working, then dying.

As he noticed the ground coming up much too quickly, he gave another pull, now sweating all over in terror. Nothing. He yanked it for the third time, feeling a jerk from a sudden reflex of the wings, yet there was nothing after that.

"Fly Hard, Die Hard . . ," he thought as he took a breath to relax himself, resisting the impulse to think about death. After all, he was a young man.

He closed his eyes tightly and, by feel, changed a switch intake to full capacity. He pulled the cord and with a roar that startled him, the Drag-Quad became operational, pushing Dusty up at the maximum speed and working overtime to reverse his rapid fall. He strained every muscle in his body to keep still as he navigated himself towards the flat of the mountain. His body shook from the clanking of the wings, and his back and chest burned from the sudden change in direction.

Dusty held his breath as he tried to slow himself down.

His trajectory wasn't correctly planned out, thus he had to stop, hover and then land instead of making a clean run down. His pressure valve lowered as he slowed the beats of the wing blades and hovered a few feet off the ground.

Clubio awaited a signal from Dusty, yet nothing came through.

Squirrel, wearily looked around, feeling the wind current becoming stronger.

He also worried for the safety of Dusty. Being an engineer and expert himself, he felt that Dusty's careless drop through the mist was a dangerous stunt that could overstrain his Drag-Quad.

A slight opening in the clouds allowed Luca to catch sight of Dusty going for the landing.

" Dusty's testing the land !" Luca gestured through his fingering.

Luca pushed up his monocular, and slowly moved himself closer to rest of the fluttering band.

" We can land with a slower trajectory I believe," Clubio signaled.

Luca glimpsed at his pressure valve.

"The wind current is becoming more violent. I recommend that we land soon," he signed.

" We should drop down. It's the fastest way !" gestured Vittorio.

" Dropping might burnout the lubes in our wing joints !" Squirrel concernedly fisted.

The group gestured at each other for a few moments, until Kline turned down his beats to minimum speed, slowly dropping down in the sky.

Suddenly there came a loud explosion.

The others stopped their sign language for a moment and piloted themselves apart from each other to gain a better look around.

"Could that have been Dusty," Luca wondered.

Immediately, everyone cut their beating power and dropped rather quickly towards the mountain flat. As they got under the clouds they began to notice smoke drifting upwards from a small figure in the distance. The figure was Dusty, face down in the snow. His wing joints had burned off all of the lubrication oil, and seized up the Drag-Quad, tearing the power house right in half.

He looked to be seriously injured.

Dav'inne, seeing Dusty trying to push himself up, hurried towards the flat. Squirrel shook his head in disappointment, realizing that he was correct about dropping and starting up the Drag-Quad in cold weather.

The crew finally landed, quickly shutting off their engines, loosening their braces, and throwing off their heavy equipment to help Dusty up.

Dav'inne slid over to him, seeing that the shrapnel of his power-house was still steaming. As he moved the boiling pieces away, he noticed Dusty's jacket cut up from the breaking wings.

"Dusty, can you hear me ?" he shouted at him.

Dusty screamed in agony.

"I can't feel my arms or my legs !" he moaned, beginning to drop tears over his numb cheeks.

Dav'inne quickly turned him over and called Vittorio to assist him. " Here, boy. Keep talking to him. Dusty might have damaged his back in his landing !" he explained. Vittorio glimpsed the bleeding cuts all over the back side of his jacket and gasped. The others ran up to help Dusty.

" Keep still Dusty, Dav'inne's going to figure what's wrong with you."

Dusty's eyes rolled up. His suffering had brought him into shock. Vittorio kept talking to him.

Clubio crouched himself down. "What kind of help do you need, Dav'inne?" he immediately asked.

Dav'inne sighed ,"Get my medical equipment and get the big tent up. His injuries seem more serious than a few cuts and bruises."

As the crew worked steadily to set up camp and help with Dusty's injuries, Kline backed himself away.

His head pounded and he felt short of breath. The withdrawal from cuca still continued to eat at him. Quickly he clenched his fists to fight the pulsing urges. He breathed deeply, walking further to the edge of the flat of the mountain without anyone noticing.

It was then that he began to smell a scent which he hadn't enjoyed for twenty seven years. The long lost but familiar aroma took his mind off the withdrawal and he followed the scent through the thinning mist. The smell which he always dreamed of experiencing once again finally came to him. It was then when he looked over the edge, facing north that he felt the warmth of the setting western sun.

It was then that his eyes widened in happiness. For over the mountain ridge there wasn't any more jagged ranges or blizzard storms in the distance. What he saw and what he smelled instead were the tops of rounded evergreen trees and shrubs.

What he had finally found was the Continent of the North.

The myths and legends of the ancients, the fantasies of Sudutan scholars, and the daydreams of children were finally proven true and, even better, there was no one to ruin it. There was no Bringington to stop him, there was no threat of Sponsorship rejection, and there was no pressure. What there was, was the waving green scenery of endless trees moving in the gentle breezes, so different from the harsh winds of the upper altitudes. What there was, was a great flock of birds being stirred up from their nests to flutter into the sky.

What there really was for Kline, was a feeling that, finally, he had come home.

The crashing noises stopped, and so did the Old Man's story. We got up and went back into the storeroom to find Likooshas. He was giggly now, and I felt that way as well, for right in front of us lay great mounds of treasure. Atlantis treasure. Gold and diamonds, jewels and crystals of all sorts - the most valuable things in the known world.

The Old Man sighed at our celebrative spirits.

" Greko, could you hand me a few of those gold strips and some of those small diamonds ?" he said; "that is, if Likooshas won't bite your fingers off,"

I nodded, grabbing some gems and stuffing them in my pockets while handing him his gold and diamonds.

He took a hold of them and then seemed to be estimating something in his head.

"Calculating your share ?" Likooshas said as he opened his knapsack and filled it up with all sorts of the treasures from the floor.

The Old Man gave a smile. " Not quite," he replied.

He then turned to me. " Greko," he started. Then he noticed me carrying the book.

" Yes ?" I asked.

" There's something interesting I want to show you," he mentioned as he beganto walk. I followed him as he went back to the contraption that now lay in pieces. He immediately started to fiddle around with it again. I crouched down as I watched him work.

"I caught a glimpse at that book you're holding. Can you show me the title ?"he asked.

I nodded and then gave him the book. He looked at it and read the symbols on the front out loud . " No Man's Land: Recorded Documents: Volume II."

He showed a mild interest towards it and began flipping through. " I am amazed at you, Greko. Of the hundreds of books in here, you have found one of the few which has the recorded historical documents on the Northern Continent," he said.

" This is the same story of North Atlantis ?" I asked.

The Old Man only looked at me with a glimmer in his stare.

"It is a valuable, and worthwhile document to have, young lad. The Sudutan Expeditioneers charted everything up there, once they found out that there was no ice barrier, that is," he said.

" Everything is accurate ?" I asked.

" Everything except the women of course. They mention warrior women as a myth, a folk tale, made to scare off travellers. There are no listings of the Makaitons, Buushu, Arkaitons," he said as he flipped through it. "And do you want to know the reason, boy ?"

I nodded.

" Because most of the men who came close enough to study those women ended up dead" he said with a grin.

I was astonished at it. I began to flip around in it too, honored to hold the document in my very hand. I then remembered to flip open to the page where I saw the mammoths.

" Can you tell me if these are the great mammoths you once mentioned ?" I said eagerly as I showed it to him.

He smiled as he looked at the pictures. "Ah, yes. They've classified all the species of Mammoths that exist in the world," he said. He looked at the pictured and then said; "Here, let me show you something," and he pointed at the hairy mammoths.

"These are the mammoths I mentioned. This one," he pointed to the scruffy looking one with only one hump on it's head, "it roamed most of the known world. They were wild and not as powerful. Ranging from 10-14 feet, these animals were anything but scary,"

He moved his fingers down to a larger picture of z grotesque mammoth head. It was short-haired, bulkier, and meaner-looking.

"This one is an Atlantean Mammoth. These beasts were bred for war, bred to be ruthless. They were 18 to 20 feet tall, and able to run through a hut, if they felt like it. Their skin was rough and thick, almost impenetrable to average spears, and they had a very low tolerance kind of temper. Excellent for war,"

I looked at it with amazement. Then he closed it up. "The rest of them, I shall tell you about later on when I feel that it is necessary," he said with a smile as he handed my book back to me.

I grabbed it and held it close, so that I wouldn't lose it.

He continued on, fiddling around with the contraption. I remained silent, as he did." You know, it's interesting how this culture worked," he muttered, thinking that I was listening to him.

"What do you mean ?" I said.

He glimpsed at me and then continued to look at the machine as he took the gold strips and placed them like cables around it.

"Well," he stopped as he wrapped the strips around another cylinder," Most of us, today, in the known world look at gold, silver, and precious stones as something of value" he said, reaching for another strip.

"Go on," I said.

" But back in the days of Sudutan Atlantis, Not the North continent might I remind you, but Sudutan Atlantis; gold, silver, gems and diamonds were looked at as being of value but value in a different sense. You see, the whole civilization was powered, fueled, and energized by these resources," he said, now reaching for the diamond.

"But how could that be ?" I said," If that were the case, then how could they stay so great for so many years ?" I asked. "There couldn't be that many diamonds or that much gold."

He held the diamond tight in his grip.

"You see, back then, there were a lot more diamonds, gold, and silver. Once they used up all of their own, Atlantis had to expand its Empire, not to control land or people, but simply to look for other places that contained these elements. They knew that if the resources ran out, then their civilization would collapse,"He paused.

" Now, if you believe the tales of great inventions and wonderful things are all simply a collection of child's tales, then watch this," he said.

He slowly placed the diamond between two thin metal plates.

There came a silent hum.

Immediately, the hum got louder and the diamond began to glow.

Suddenly, bright lights began to flicker on and off in the room and then stayed on, lighting up the whole place like magic.

I nearly fainted.

Likooshas did.

The Old Man sat on a table and nodded, admiring the lights. I sat down beside him, still clutching my book.

"The stories you've been telling, "I asked; "are they all here in this book ?"

"No. Kline was the first to officially discover the Northern lands, but many others followed and took notes and made observations. That's what your book is. Like a textbook for people to study,"

"So it won't have in here whether Dusty lived or died?"

"No, but while we wait for Likooshas to recover, if you want to sit a minute, I'll tell you about Dusty,"

I sat.

" If you remember, they were sitting on a flat part of the mountain. Dusty was hurt and Kline had found the open lands,"

During the nighttime, Dav'inne, Clubio, and Vittorio helped to mend the broken bones of Dusty. From his accident, he suffered a left leg snap down the femur and a right arm fracture within his radius. They had bent the bones back into place, sealing the wounds with staple pegs and splinting with pieces of tentpole. They wrapped everything with the clean cloth bandages to keep everything in place. Luckily, Dusty's Drag-Quad braces were still intact, so they used them as casts for him to continually wear until his breaks got better.

His Drag-Quad pack though, was broken beyond repair. All four wings were shattered and severed from the actual ball joints within the engine.

The six picks of the power house were unable to be found for they , being hot, had buried themselves in the snow when they flew off. Squirrel gave up trying to repair the unit once he saw no possible way to find the six picks as well as the diamond.

Most of his supplies didn't survive the explosion either. His shelter was burned and his food rations were flattened and ripped open when he landed. The only equipment which he still had intact were his Bankra blade and his short range rifle. Even his ammunition was lost. Dav'inne used bits from his other shelter poles to make a crutch for him.

Once Kline had shown them the mystery forest on the edge of the flat, however, their grief and pity for Dusty immediately disappeared. Vittorio stopped talking to Dusty to make an excited transmission back to Prox announcing their discovery.

They had just made history. There would be great rejoicing in Prox. Bringington would be crazy with jealousy.

Luca was immediately sent to scout the land regions from the air, to plan out the next resting stop. Also to look for areas where there had been volcanoes or where there was hard stone, in the hopes of finding diamonds. Once he had come back with a positive location, Kline immediately called for Vittorio and Dole to go there with Luca. They had to carry Dusty and set up camp.

Kline wanted the rest of the crew - Squirrel, Dav'inne and Clubio to accompany him on foot so they could get a first look at the land.

For hours, Kline and his group explored through the thick bushes of forest. They created smooth pathways, using Squirrel's Drag Quad to cut through.

Squirrel had modified his Quad to walk with it. He wore it backward and strolled slowly, so that the wings would act as cutters and chop through nearly anything. Clubio tied a rope around his waist so that he was able to lean far forward without the risk of falling over and to keep him on the ground if he accidentally took off.

Clubio kept himself on guard as he held on tightly to Squirrel's rope. His eyes wandered about as they hiked onwards. The paranoia within kept him on the edge, for he'd never been in thick forest before. His time as an Imperial professional had only sent him to thin sheets of jungle and mainly desert terrain. The humidity here, where the ice was melting, made him uncomfortable.

Never before had he imagined that such greenery could exist or that trees could grow to such huge dimensions.

Kline began to grow impatient as they walked on without any sight of the others who had flown on ahead to make camp in the wilderness. The humidity of the air and the moistness of the soil made it even more irritating for him, especially when he had to carry the Drag Quad and his other equipment.

His cuca withdrawal also increased his intolerance for everything, by far.

Dav'inne, the Medical Officer seemed to be the only one of the group who liked the hiking and the exploration. He loved the colors and smells occurring all around him. So he strolled with his forty pounds of Drag Quad heaved on his back lightly, his loosened braces and his extended barrel projectile air gun resting across his shoulders as he stopped to look at plants and collect samples of things that were new to him.

" It is amazing that such beauty had escaped the eyes of us for so long," he muttered with an enlightened smile.

Clubio gazed wearily at him.

" I've never seen such thick forest in my life time. It makes chills go down my spine," he muttered.

"That's because your mother caressed you too long and fed you with her milk until you were a man !" Squirrel amusingly shouted over his Drag-Quad.

Clubio gave a piercing stare and quickly let go of the rope tied around his waist.

Squirrel almost toppled over. His bottom pair of wings dug themselves into the soft soil sloshing it all over. Squirrel got the message to keep quiet. Kline paid no attention to their chatterings as they moved onwards.

It was then that he was hit with a sore ache in his head. He slowed himself to regain his senses. As he rubbed his eyes, the vision of Ennis returned to him for a brief moment. His eyes grew fearful. He breathed deeply, now feeling the suspicion of her apparition all around him.

He became more observant as they continued on through the thick patch, trying not to think much of it.

But as the sky grew dim, her voice began to echo through his head," Will you be back to take me tomorrow ?" the voice continued to chant.

He had taken her to the north after all. She was with him everywhere. He came to a stop in his tracks, noticing that his shin covers as well as his knee guards were dirt ridden and smelly.

He shook his head and the chantings seeped away. But her apparition came once more, for a short length away, he saw her figure staring right into his eyes. Kline was shock-filled, for her stare was emotionless, her hair brightened and her skin tanned and beautifully clean as the first day he ever saw her.

But most horrific of all were her eyes. They were dark, catlike and never blinking as she seemed to come closer over the shrubs and grass, gliding smoothly.

This was what kept Kline in a paused trance, the same way that he imagined an animal to be frozen in fear as it noticed the stalking predator. That was where Kline's perceptions began to change. Suddenly he realized it wasn't Ennis's ghost he was watching. This figure approaching him wasn't the ghost of misfortune. As it got closer, it became more obvious that it was not a woman at all.

Clubio's eyes widened as he tugged on Squirrel's rope to stop him. He armed himself with his rifle and crouched down.

" Jaguar !" he shouted.

Kline hit the dirt.

Clubio aimed his foresight at the body of the gigantic beast and fired, but much to his surprise it didn't drop dead. He had missed.

Clubio immediately shook his rifle jaggedly so that the air pump would fill quickly. Squirrel shut off his Drag Quad, trying to reach his rifle holster.

Dav'inne quickly pulled his gun off his shoulders, and speedily unfastened his Drag Quad, slowly side tracking towards Kline.

"I've got you, you poor excuse for a rug," Dav'inne whispered quietly, slowly moving with the Jaguar.

Clubio's air pump was full, and he pushed his magazine further up into the chamber. He aimed, pulled the trigger and missed yet again.

" She's a crafty one ain't she !" Squirrel shouted, now ready to fire.

Dav'inne continued to chase after the spooked animal, which now was going through a complex network of trees.

As Kline tried to break away from the trance, he began to notice that this was no ordinary cat. It had spots, as a jaguar would, but its base was far more prominent and powerful. So was its face, for its eyes were larger and its muzzle thinner than most. And last, it carried two large sabre-like fangs a trait unknown in jaguars.

Kline watched the animal stray away from him, now running for its life from Squirrel, Clubio and Dav'inne.

Another shot was made by Squirrel, who was taking slow steps in fear of falling over. This one missed too.

Dav'inne came towards Kline, Helped him up and then continued to hunt the animal.

Clubio came towards him and pulled him by the hair.

" What is a jaguar doing hunting people like prey ?" he said with enraged eyes. His fear ran up and down his whole body. Kline could feel the shivering of Clubio's fingers through his grasp.

" I tell you Clubio, that that animal is no Jaguar. It is a beast which has never before been seen in Sudutan Atlantis. That is a curious and hungry specimen attempting to taste a hypothesis: whether or not I was edible,"

Squirrel and Dav'inne had chased the animal out of the woods and got it out onto their pathway. Dav'inne fired first, hitting the animal right in the neck.

It lunged back in pain yet it did not bleed.

"Strange, it's not dead ," Dav'inne said in a baffled manner.

Immediately, the animal became even more fierce, now showing the whites of its teeth, carefully approaching the two.

Squirrel then opened a shot at its head. Once again, it flew back but was without a scratch.

The animal began to charge towards them now, no longer giving them the respect of a hunted prey.

Dav'inne and Squirrel grew tense. They started to stroll backwards, one step faster than the last. Squirrel then unfastened his Drag Quad, then the transmitter, then his supplies, knowing that it was going to add more dead weight to him as he walked back.

" Is your air pump filled to maximum yet ?" Dav'inne asked.

Squirrel nodded in mild terror.

" Both of us are going to shoot it at the same time. Slowly raise your gun and fire when I say so,"

Squirrel nodded at him quickly, pushing up the tin magazine.

Both raised their rifles, still walking backwards. Both aimed, awaiting for a moment to fire.

"Fire !" Dav'inne said slowly.

Squirrel trembled and could not aim with his gun. His hands shook.

"Fire! Damn you !" Dav'inne shouted, startling Squirrel as well as the animal.

Both fired almost simultaneously.

The animal quickly shifted its body. The pellets definitely hit it directly, this time breaking skin.

"What kind of an animal doesn't die after four shots !" Squirrel horrifically shouted out loud.

The animal growled angrily. It was annoyed rather than hurt by the nuisance of the pellets and now was going to kill these irritating trespassers.

It immediately pounced.

Dav'inne and Squirrel threw down their weapons and staggered to get out of its way.

The animal snapped at Dav'inne, who was briskly crawling away.

Kline screamed and hopped away, trying to balance out his Drag Quad.

The animal lost interest in Dav'inne and began to come after Kline as it had originally planned to. Clubio noticed the animal speeding in his direction. He shivered as he pulled the generator start for his Drag Quad. As the wings beat faster Clubio crouched down into the ground, using his wings to act as a defense. The slicing wings rocked Clubio from side to side. The animal slowed down, curious about him. It lunged at Clubio, resulting in severe cuts all over its front legs.

The animal cried in immense agony, as the wounds bled pulsingly.

By then Dav'inne, Squirrel and Kline, had drawn their Bankra blades and gathered around the moaning animal.

All of them breathed deeply, controlling their fear and grinned as they noticed the animal gaze at them all with bafflement.

" I believe that I need a new rug" Kline stated.

"All of them chopped and sliced at the densely muscled animal until they knew that it was dead. They wouldn't stop, not for a second. Even when its reflexes stopping jumping and it lay still, they sliced and slit until there was nothing left to stab," the Old Man ended with a smile.

The lights suddenly went out.

The Old Man's eyes widened in amazement as he reached out to the contraption to try and get it working again.

" You know, because of a simple diamond like this, and a few strands of gold wire, Atlantis was able to do almost everything. Men were able to fly. They rode horseless chariots. They had lights like these, and the common use of many labor-saving appliances," he said.

The lights began to brighten again, giving off a cool glow of bluish yellow.

"They were masters of efficiency, the Sudutans. Ingenious isn't it ?" he said.

Suddenly, the lights flickered off again, the humming quieted, and the Old Man's face lessened in awe as he watched the diamond stop glowing.

"Of course, that was the problem. When you come to depend on such things and then the power goes off - well, life as you know it is over,"

There was now only the torches, which were very dim in comparison.

" But then again, like our ancient stories of the Marsolla: all great empires, no matter how remarkable, eventually have to fall to the hand of misfortune,"

I looked at the glow flickering and coming to a stop. I was baffled by its magic powers, making all of the humming lights come on all at once. I slowly turned to the Old Man, who at this point was fiddling with the magic contraption once more.

" Why are the lights going off ? Is the magic in the diamond not strong enough ?"

I asked.

The Old Man sighed, "Huh, magic. That's a new one" he mumbled to himself," You could say that the magic, in general, in this box is old and stubborn. Like me. There's nothing wrong with the diamond itself" he mentioned, "just in the systems that carries the power from it,"

He tinkered a little more and then plucked off the uncut diamond. Gritting his teeth with a little frustration, he turns the contraption around. I saw several eaten-through string wrappings with gold strands coiled around them. All of them seemed to connect to more gold wires that disappeared into the table. And maybe went to the lights and doors. That was when I realized that the magic in the diamond was channeled and sent to make the lights and doors work.

I slowly reached over to one of the roping wires and stretched to touch it.

Suddenly, the Old Man slapped my hand.

I looked up at him.

" Don't touch the wires, you'll electrocute yourself!" the Old Man said as he fine-tuned the contraption.

" I just wanted to see the magic go through towards the lights and things," I explained.

" Well, I am sorry to tell you that this magic is like thunder. Controlled thunder, might I add," he pointed to the wires on the back.

" These wires, you see? They carry the power like veins that carry blood around your body., to the certain areas in which it is needed."

I still really didn't understand how it worked.

" It really isn't magic, if you ask me," the Old Man said.

"Oh, but it is magic," I defended.

" I guess," he said, ," If you understand how it works, than there is no magic, but if you don't have any understanding of it, then magic it is."

I looked at him with a puzzled look," So it isn't magic ?"

He replaced the eaten-through strips and slowly got ready to place the diamond back on the sharp stands.

" Well that's up to you. Do you understand what I am doing? How the energy from this diamond is taken out ? Why the gold is needed for wiring ?" he continued as he began the descent of the diamond to the grippers inside the contraption.

" No," I said simply.

He smiled at me.

" Well then boy, then this is magic, " he said.

Immediately, the diamond began to revolve. The hummings became a little smoother than the last time, and this time there were frequent spots and strains of red, focused light.

The lights came on again, and stay glowing.

The Old Man's face was lit up and glowing along with the whole room. He was happy with his successes. The room got brighter and shone with a bluish-yellow all around. The Old Man then placed the top over the contraption so that there would be no dust that would clog up the parts.

The Old Man slowly stood up and walked over to a heavy looking door, made of iron. Parts of it were rust eaten, but if it was as old as I thought it was, it was remarkably well preserved.

I was still crouched down, marking a place in my book with a scrap of blue-stained string.

He looked back at me," Well come on boy, let's open up this door!"

I slowly stood up and went to the rust-eaten door. The features of this 5 by 10 foot door were grotesque. My brow went up.

" And how are we supposed to open this door up ?" I asked.

" We are going to find the knob and turn it," he said somewhat amusing himself.

I paused,. "All right Old Man, you're on your own on this one," I said.

He looked around at the door, looking for some sort of a switch. When he found a handle, he turned it a few times. There was a powering sound that followed afterwards, then a jamming and cramming noise after that.

The Old Man slowly walked back.

He saw that the door had moved an inch open and was trying to labor itself more open, but the rust clumps kept it from doing it.

" What's wrong ?" I asked.

"The doors and hinges are rusted tight. I don't believe that this door will come open this way,"

" Then what are we going to do ?" I asked, hoping that he would give up his crusade and leave me to stare at my book.

" We are going to have to turn to the second plan," he said as he walked over to a fallen shelve case with a dry, wooden pole sticking out of the side. He ripped the pole out from the decomposing supply shelf and walked back to the door. He wedged the piece of wood into the opening and began to use it as a lever.

The door groaned and screeched as it received help from the Old Man. Dust flakes and big chunks of red rust fell off and still the door struggled to open. Finally, the door knocked off enough of the rust for it to turn ruggedly and, still screeching, it lurched open a foot or so.

The room lay partially exposed to the lights from the outside, yet no light ever shone in. Like a portal leading to another dimension, the room gave off no scent or interest to me. Only eeriness.

The Old Man slowly reached his hand into the room and felt around the other side of the wall to see if there were any switches to make the lights glow inside the room. He found them and turned them on. The Old Man was excited at first, waiting as the lights warmed up and slowly brightened.

" Most people who came through here would stay on their ships until their holiday was over or until they flew on to their destination. But a select few would be invited ashore. This is one of the many quarters that Governor's special guests would rest in. It looks like the only one left. Most of the others around here are collapsed and packed with mud.

Judging from the sealed door on this one, it's been a while since this whole place was touched by the hands of man.

But these rooms were always loaded with treasures, to impress the guests about the Governor's wealth. There might be some very interesting stuff in here - much better stuff than those table scraps that Likooshas is lying in," he said.

The lights continued to brighten and the more they did, the more the Old Man showed excitement and anticipation in his eyes. When the lights finally glowed brightest, the Old Man took the pole and levered the door open some more, until there was enough space for him to slip in.

"Wait here a moment, boy," he said, "Let me check it out."

In a heart-beat he had slipped back out again, gasping in shock.

" What is it Old Man ?" I asked, " Are there any treasures that are unexpected ?"

He stood in front of the door, his mood totally changed.

"Don't come in boy. Not yet," he said with fright in his tone, "Let's wait for Likooshas to wake up. He'll decide if this is something for your eyes or not - since he seems to be your legal guardian."

Likooshas was still in a swoon, lying amongst his treasures of diamonds and gold. He been shocked into a faint when the lights went on, but I suspected he was just tired from the climb and was now having a snooze. I didn't really care. More time for me to examine my book.

"None of the stories of the women are in here at all ?" I asked, frowning and holding the book up.

"No," he said, shaking his head. He was still bothered by whatever he had seen inside, "At the point this book was put together, the King didn't want anyone to know that there was a whole civilization up here. He wanted a diamond rush. He wanted people to come up and look for diamonds and gold and maybe settle up here - thus increasing not only his wealth but his territories too. Besides, no one really took the women seriously or believed the rumors of their great strength."

"It sounds like nobody told the Atlanteans anything," I said, still flipping through the book and looking at the pictures.

"The people of the Sud, they didn't want to know anything," the Old Man said. "They were comfortable and well fed. There was no end of entertainment.

So what if the lights went off a bit early every day ? That was sort of romantic, in a way. And romance was a big thing. It was like a game people played. There were even holidays to celebrate romance, a special day when you were supposed to confess your secret love for someone. It was called "I've never told you this before, but..." Day,"

"You're making that up."

"I swear. Romance was an industry. Everybody kept score. But it was toying with a very powerful emotion and it could turn out to be very dangerous."

"How could love hurt you ?"

"It's something that can happen to any kind of human being. Even you, young Greko. Even in the strange women's culture to the North. Since your book has no women stories, let me tell you one. It'll help me get calm again.

This is about Elana and Nurix. They're still in Ques. After the crucial supplies were refurbished, their clothes and boots renewed and the horses made healthily plump, everyone was ready to go on with the journey."

Although everyone was eager to leave, Elana wanted to take one last look around at civilization before they went into Buushu country and left cities behind for a while.

Sassaska and Brelinka were still talking with the Governor about the conditions they could expect to find and Julyo was finding out last minute information on the trail ahead, so Elana was granted a few hours to take a stroll, under the condition that she wouldn't buy anything too large to take with them. She tended to be an impulse buyer and often ended up with large, more or less, useless things that had to be carried along for sentimental reasons. Nurix and Julyo were good examples of that, Brelinka had joked with her.

So, she told herself, she was just going for a look. She took Nurix with her to wander the streets; which were over-filled with life. Nurix, at this time, was proudly strutting alongside in his new garments and shiny buckled boots, like a dog on a new leash.

The clean, new clothing felt nice on his skin, unlike his original scratchy fabric that he had worn for years in the monastery. Instead, he now wore a dark waterproof worker's cloak which was tailored to his liking.

His boots no longer bore dirty, grimy brown rag-bandages tied around to keep them from falling apart. Today, he wore brand new boots and nice things and he was glad for it.

Elana, on the other hand, was the same scruffy companion that she always was, even in new clothes, although she was few pounds heavier from the food and drink she ate during their visit at Ques.

As they slowly strode through the market streets, Elana's arm wrapped around Nurix's. They looked at all of the merchandise that was being sold, ranging from perfumes, fairy tales, and fine clothes to poison, artillery mammoths and mastodons, and last of all, slaves. All of which they both had seen before.

There was nothing that caught Elana's eye that was of interest, partly because she had no wants and partly because she had no money.

Nurix looked at the tables and booths of merchant women, trying to sell their things to Elana. He paid no attention, knowing that no merchant would ever try to sell anything to a slave.

It was later that Elana found a booth where there were not too many people eager to buy things. There on the table lay exotic weapons, beautifully designed, with curves and animal-like features to enhance their deadly nature. What soldier could resist?

Elana slowly approached the booth, seeing no merchant. She looked, with interest at the products on display. There were necklaces with the lockets showing strange beast-like faces on them. There were knife handles which resembled tales. Almost everything on the display table showed some sort of animalistic design on it. There was even a some kind of single war-glove, the top of it was encrusted with metal plates and gold lining ran down the fingers and came up to a connecting point at the wrist. It resembled a fist of a skeleton. Elana slowly picked it up and looked at it's complex design. She felt the thickness of the finger sleeves and noticed that they were rather stiff.

Nurix looked at the other items on display. He felt an odd familiarity with the designs, thinking that at one point in his life, he had seen them and even held them in his hands. He slowly reached over and touched the handle of one of the knives. He felt it's bumps and detail, trying to remember the familiarity.

Then a familiar voice broke into his day dream.

" I see that you all are fascinated by my merchandise,"

It was a voice from his past.

Elana was startled and accidently dropped the glove onto the table. Suddenly, great thin knives came out of the sides and tips of the finger sleeves like the claws from a sabre toothed cat. From the springy activation of the glove, the black cloth on the display table was slashed.

Nurix looked up at the Merchant. He was surprised to find that it was the woman with the Tattoo of a wolf across the side of her eye. Now to add to that facial art, there were two long, thin scars on the sides of her nostrils. It was Cruce'Fix, his former mistress.

"Oh, pardon my mistake, merchant" Elana began as she looked up at her face," I shall pay for the damages done to your cloth,"

" That is alright. It was my fault for startling you. My apologies, my dear," she said.

Nurix nervously put the knife down on the table and moved back, almost behind Elana.

Cruce' slowly rested her hands on the table and gave a smile," So, do you see anything that appeals to you ?" she said as she glimpsed at Nurix and then back at Elana.

Nurix froze and, for one reason or another, was slightly terrified by this encounter with his old mistress.

"Um . . . I'm still just looking around" Elana said, not knowing what else to say. She still looked at the glove with the metal claws sticking out of the finger tips.

Cruce'Fix noticed her gaze and slowly picked up the glove," Ah, I see that you have found my lion's paw," she said as she stroked the top of the glove, making the blades immediately recede back into the tips.

"Yes, it is very elegant. Very decorative," Elana said.

" Yes, it is," Cruce' started, "But very dangerous too. This is the weapon of choice for many famous Makaiton warriors: like Helena, the Sabre Toothed Daughter; Grifyo, the Dog Heart; Cruptile, the Predator Girl," she reminisced.

"Hand crafted by warriors for warriors. Y ou can't ask for a better weapon in this day and age," she finished.

" Fascinating," Elana said," But I can tell you that, sadly, I am not really interested in buying weaponry at the moment,"

Elana slowly picked up a silver, well-detailed necklace.

471

She looked at it's magnificence and beauty.

" The style of this art, however, is intriguing," said Elana, "What does the etching symbolize?"

" The image here tells the tale of dire, the wolf. This is a medallion for good luck," Cruce'said, "Those who wear it are protected by the spirit of the Great Dire Wolf, the King of the Dark Forest,"

" I see that you Makaitons are culturally fascinated by creatures of nature,"

" As much as you Arkaiton warriors obsess to try and harness the inner demon in everyone," Cruce' said, "Marsolla's demon of legend. The killing machine that will not stop."

Elana was surprised to find that the merchant knew about Arkaiton beliefs in such detail.

" Why, I am surprised to see that you know of my cultural beliefs,"

" It would be an insult not to know the cultures of all the women of the empire," Cruce' said charmingly.

Elana gave a slight smile, obviously a little charmed by her.

" Besides, all warriors must know their friends well. And their enemies better, " Cruce' said.

" I take a guess that you are more of a warrior than a merchant" Elana said.

She laughed mightily," Here's some cultural details you can learn: all Makaiton women are taken at the age of ten to be trained until the age of sixteen. In a way, we are more of a warrior race than any other clan nation throughout the Empire."

" Even the dirty, primitive Buushu culture cannot be compared, warrior wise, to our culture," Cruce' said.

" Their warriors are the toughest, though," Elana said.

" I disagree. They fight independently, with arrogance, barely any armor, most times with stone weapons, and, always, they fight without honor," Cruce' said.

"Not true," said Elana.

" I once thought I could make a grand alliance with the Buushu and accomplish great things. But there is no-one to ally with. There is no organization. They are all like individual animals, all fighting for themselves. Where, then, is their nobility ?" asked Cruce'.

" They fight to the death," Elana said plain out. " The Buushu have honor just as much as any other clan nation: Arkaiton, and even Makaiton," she finished.

Cruce broke into laughter, " Oh, you Arkaitons are all the same. You all want to be the diplomats. And I respect that about your clan culture. You, yourself are obviously Arkaiton, yet wear a Buushu braid. It is diplomacy, nothing more. You should also carry a Makaiton weapon or wear the totem tattoo on your face. Then you would be all things to all people in the empire, " she said. "Of course, for myself, I have no diplomacy. I don't think a nice Arkaiton girl like you should disgrace yourself by wearing a Buushu braid. You should not support them. The Buushu are a damned mongrel nation," she finished. "They cannot be trusted with any responsibility. One just assaulted me yesterday in a food house. And no-one came to my aid. She killed my two companions by trickery, and yet she is free to walk the city. We give these Buushu far too much respect. They are sub-human."

Elana slowly let the necklace dribble back onto the table cloth.

There was a pause of silence for a second. Elana was astonished about the sheer prejudice and nationalism spoken against the Buushu everywhere she turned.

No one cared about them, even her sister and friend. She couldn't even reason with herself why she was the only one who felt strongly for the Buushu. The only answer she could come up with was that she had been raised by a Buushu bodyguard, whom she loved dearly and Julyo, her closest companion was Buushu. Nonetheless, Elana kept her feelings inside. After all, she was only conversing with a market-day merchant and couldn't be bothered to stir up any trouble.

"Luckily, in this great Empire," she said, "Everyone is free to have their own opinion. No matter how strange."

Cruce'Fix shrugged and looked over, seeing Nurix patiently waiting, but trying to avoid making eye contact with her. She found him very familiar. She knew that she had seen that face, yet she couldn't recall where.

"Nice looking slave you have there," she said, changing the subject. "Is he well trained enough to handle a little man-weapon, to protect himself. I have some good ones. ?"

Elana was a little relieved, but Nurix gulped.

" His name is Nurix. He was once a slave in the mountain monastery near the great Ice capped mountains, " Elana said, slowly stroking his hair. Nurix was still silent.

"He's very smart and very obedient."

Cruce' nodded. She gazed at him, looking him up and down.

" I recognize him," She said with a mild smile. "I think I sold him to that monastery."

Then she reached over to his shoulder. The force of the grip caused a pinning pain in his collar bone. She slowly pulled him closer and quickly turned him around.

Elana stepped closer and grabbed Cruce's hand whenshe heard Nurix's shocked breath from the pressure of Cruce's fingers pressing down." What are you doing ?" Elana said, feeling annoyed and plucking Cruce's hand away. Nurix, a little frightened, slowly stepped a few feet back from her.

" I'm sorry, I just had to see something," she apologized.

" What did you have to see ? If he bruised easily ?" Elana snapped.

" I wanted to see if he had the tattoo on the back of his neck. Like the one I remembered.

Elana then turned around to check him. She felt around his collar and on his shoulders like a concerned mother for her injured daughter.

" Are you alright ?" she said softly.

Nurix nodded." Yes, I-I'm fine. I know that she . . ." he stopped for a second, turning to see Cruce'. " I know that she meant no harm After all, she was my former master," he finished.

Elana gently pushed aside Nurix's hair covering the back of his neck.

There lay an oval green tattoo on his neck.

Cruce' looked over and saw it as well.

"See ? High-caste Buushu," nodded Cruce'. "Ahhh. So it is you, Six Piece."

Nurix stood silent, staring into her cat-like, stalking gaze. He simply nodded.

Cruce' looked him up and down."You've grown quite a bit, Six Piece. I see that you are no longer a skinny little runt like you used to be," she said, trying to make herself sound polite and jokey in front of Elana. "Somebody's been feeding you well."

Nurix made no answer. He breathed slowly through his nostrils as he nodded slowly.

Cruce' gave a vicious grin. "You were always the silent one whenever you were nervous or something. I do remember that from you," she said.

Nurix took a deep breath. " Yes, some things about me haven't changed. And some things about you have not changed either," he said quietly.

Cruce' paused. " Why ? What hasn't changed about me ?" she asked curiously.

Nurix looked at the weapons and warrior jewelry laying on the table. He slowly touched the knife once more. As he touched it, long suppressed childhood pictures of duels, swords and knives clashing came to his mind. He saw images of women warriors alive and dead, all grinning in satisfaction. He remembered nightmarish things, things like Cruce' firmly pulling innocent male slaves and farmers aside to test swords, spears, arrows, and other things on. And her customers, drinking and laughing about it all.

He didn't remember who the victims were or what they looked like. All he could picture in his mind was the end result. Hacked up bodies. Children looking betrayed as they were hacked to bits, to test the heft of a sword or the sharpness of a mechanical claw. Looks of sadness, almost like the bear had given him on the mountain. Maybe that's why it affected him so much. He blinked slow, trying to rinse his eyes from the memories that clouded his mind.

He looked to the side of her face, seeing the tattoo of the wolf over her eye socket and running along her cheek and forehead.

" You still make and sell weapons," he replied with a touch of harshness.

She smiled and stared at him. Then she nodded to him. "I see that you remember things well," she said.

" Yes," he replied. " So how many children have you tested these ones on. ? How innocent people had to die to fill this table ?" he hissed.

Cruce' blushed.

Elana immediately tried to stop Nurix but Nurix continued on, resisting her.

" Fifty ? Sixty ? One hundred ?"

Elana tried one more time, " Nurix, please stop it," she pressed.

" I remember the sales parties?" Nurix said. "Do you remember saying 'Watch how sharp this is - I can cut this child right in half?' Do you remember saying 'But with this you get more weight. This will cut a child in half lengthways?' Or how about making pyramids? Building them from the severed heads of Buushu children. Has that all stayed the same, you monster?".

His tone seemed to become louder and louder with every word. The more he continued, the more Elana tried to stop him, and the more Cruce' became silent and embarrassed.

"The souls of how many lost Buushu children lie right here on this table ?" he shouted.

Cruce' gasped .

Elana gently squeezed his arm, and trying to forcefully persuade him to stop, yet he still went on, pushing her away.

" How many bodies do you stand on back there to meet the eyes of normal people . . . "

Finally, Elana slapped him on the mouth.

She didn't know her own strength and it knocked him back several steps and opened a cut on his lip, which bled freely.

Nurix looked at her in shock. She had hit him, something he never thought she would do. Nurix was frozen from pain, from astonishment, and most of all, he was frozen from a broken heart.

Likooshas moaned and snorted and broke the spell.

"See Greko. Learn this lesson well. It's never our enemies who hurt us. It's always our friends and our lovers. Nurix finally felt he was safe and could open up and shout out his true feelings - and who hit him ? Not his cruel old mistress Cruce'. No. It was his sweet young mistress. And it hurt all the more, not because it broke the skin, but because it broke the heart.

The Old Man sighed and ran his hands over his face. "On second thought, Greko, maybe you should take a look in there. That's the mess that love leaves. It is a sight that you will likely remember as long as you remember the beautiful scenery outside."

I got up and went to the partly opened door and saw what he was so shocked about.

Right in front of me lay four skeletons. Two men dressed in rugged, brownish pants with a long, chewed up strap across their shoulders were in the middle of the room on the floor. One lay on top of the other, as if they killed each other while struggling mightily together.. Beside them, looked like a skeleton of a woman stabbed in the chest with a very thin blade, which was stil there and sticking out of her rotted clothes. The beautiful dress that she wore, mainly fabricated in very thin, silky panels, with inlaid jewels and pearls, now lay in dirt, covered in mud clumps, and eaten in parts by time and small creatures who had managed to get into the room. Close to her was another man, his head severed and lying close to his body.

The smell of evil and the draftless sound of emptiness completed the hair raising feeling of eeriness.

" What happened here ?" I muttered as my heart pounded frantically,

The Old Man came up behind me and stood there, silent, and only blinked at my presence.

" This is romance, gone wrong, boy" he finally said.

I looked at the bodies, frozen in my own tracks, and unwilling to move.

"Love," he said. "Fallen out of the sky."

I stared at him, feeling close to trembling at the sight. It was a little disturbing yet fascinating for I had never seen true remains of people before. I could not bring myself to say anything.

The Old Man sighed, stroking his white hair back and heading for a place to sit inside the room. As he slowly walked closer to the bodies, he accidently kicked the remnants of a hand off one of the bodies. He almost tripped, then apologetically, he looked for the hand and placed it back in the position where it originally lay.

"Pardon me" the Old Man muttered quietly to the offended body.

I moved a little closer and slowly crouched down to take a long, examination of them. I wondered about the bodies. The two men lay there, together, the ends of their bones gnawed off by rodents, fragments torn from the dried tendons and now as small as little shells. The woman and the man laid there too. They all were now prisoners of the scene, frozen and forced to tell their tale over and over to whomever looked upon them. Their sorrow, their grief, their anger and their endings. It was all reflected just by their positions.

The Old Man felt my eyes sailing across the bodies, sensing my fascination, and in return respecting it.

"How did this happen?" I wondered.

He grimly smiled, sustaining his silence for a while, then he began to move. He walked over the male skeleton that was on top of the other one. It was lop- sided half on and half off the bottom skeleton and lay face down in the dirt on the floor.

He looked into the puncture hole in the skeleton's back that was visible because of the worn out uniform that the skeleton wore, bore the horrific hole.

" This man was shot by a pressure cannon," he muttered to himself.

I looked at the body. The man must had been in agonizing pain when he was killed. So painful that his expression was still frozen in a skeleton form of horror.

" What's a pressure cannon ?" I asked looking up at the Old Man. The Old Man turned to me.

" Have you ever seen a blow-gun ?"

"A hollow tube with a poisoned dart in it ?

"Exactly. You blow in one end and the dart flies out the other. This is the same, but the tube is smaller, the dart is smaller, and instead of blowing in the end with your mouth, you have a machine to do it - so you get a much bigger breath. The end result is a projectile weapon that can be held and fired by anyone that wants to, man, woman or child."

" This man was shot with the er, 'projectile' ?" I asked. "Why ?"

I watched as the Old Man put all the pieces together and made up a story on the spot

The Old Man gazed across towards the other two skeletons. The woman and the beheaded man.

"Look what you have here, " he said. "Three men and one woman. A sure recipe for disaster. The woman might have been with one of the men. Or might have been the woman of a man who wasn't here. Maybe away somewhere, or dead. It doesn't matter. A woman in such a situation is like a drug, and soon all the men are addicted, whether they want to be or not. It is the nature of men. She probably didn't realize the silent tornado she was causing, and may have thought that they were just all good friends, talking and having fun.

Maybe they were at one time.

Imagine how this came about. They are assigned here. They get to know each other. Then something happens. The ships don't come any more. The Be Quads don't come any more. They are stuck here, for life. There is no way off the island.

Suddenly friends are not so friendly anymore.

The only treasure left on the island is the woman, and all the men want to own her. Yet she is committed to her man - whichever one he is - or even more likely - he's not even one of them.

If he were, there would likely be children, but I see no evidence of children having been here. So it's probable that her man isn't even here. Maybe he went on to look for diamonds or study the natives. Suddenly, civilization is gone. No ships. No flights.

They may have been alright for a few months or a year or two. But the drug of the woman just being around them would never let them rest.

From the way these are arranged here, this is what I think really happened.

This man - the headless one - kept his feeling bottled up. One day he couldn't stand it any longer. He got the woman in here and tried to force his attentions upon her. She rejected him, being faithful to her man. So the headless guy went crazy and killed her with a dagger. If he couldn't have her, no one would have her.

Attracted by her screams, this one - the one with the big hole in him - he came in carrying a sword. See, it's right there, under his hand, and stuck in that other guy. Strange that it's not a Bankra blade, but a straight barbarian sword. Maybe he was from one of the colonies. In any case, maybe he was the man that this woman preferred. Maybe he was just another man who loved her. Anyway, I think he arrived when Headless had just stabbed her. He went crazy and, with his sword, lopped off the head of the murdering bastard. But he was too late. She was dead or dying. Then this other guy came in, carrying his gun - the projectile weapon. Now maybe he was the good friend of the headless guy. Maybe they were more than friends. In any case, he was devastated. The headless guy, his good friend, had been killed. He grabbed the guy with the sword and shot him. But the sword guy hung onto him and fell on him, sticking the gun guy with that sword as he fell.

Suddenly, in just a few seconds, this entire little tribe, they're all dead. And there's not another human sound on this island until we turn up."

I could see it happening that way.

"The Old Man shook his head. "Three men. One woman. The chemical formula for a sure explosion. The unimaginable power of love, trapped in a very small room."

He shook his head. "BOOOOM !"

He looked at me and shrugged, then something caught his eye.

The Old Man exhaled in delight as he slowly reached to grab, what I believed to be, the projectile weapon. It was dark and beautifully crafted. It's barrel was wide, but the metal around it was perfectly preserved. As was the air tank which it was connected to. Unlike the previous owner, the projectile weapon was well intact, showing very few signs of rust.

" Could that happen to us ?" I asked.

The Old Man turned to me.

" I beg your pardon ?" he said as he studied the projectile machine a little more, then put it in his pocket. I paid no real attention or concern for his curiosity for the projectile thing. Instead, I rephrased the question with a little more evaluation.

" Likooshas' men, Us. Will it happen to us if we're away from civilization for too long ?" I asked once more.

The Old Man gave no answer but a sigh and a grim smile.

I slowly got up, expecting an answer.

" Well, will it ?" I asked.

" Do you want it to happen ?" he asked me.

" Not particularly.," I answered.

" Well, don't worry. It won't happen to your scruffy crew. It can't. This kind of tragedy only happens when you have women among the company and we have no women. Men of all types can live in harmony, in almost unendurable conditions, for decades. It is only the scent of a woman which will drive men mad and make them kill one another. And the woman may not even know what destruction she has caused. They are very dangerous creatures. So learn a lesson here and remember the old Atlantean Bachelor's slogan: No women - no trouble," he said.

I laughed at that one.

"Now" he began, changing the subject a bit. "Let's close up this tomb and let these poor souls rest in peace."

I nodded, looking back at the remains, convinced now that their fate could never happen to us.

As we slowly worked the corroded door closed, the tortured sounds of the metal woke up Likooshas and, after picking up as much loot as he could carry, he staggered over to us right at the second we got the door shut.

He was curious to find out what was inside the room.

" What's in that room? Anything more beneficial?" he asked with greed in his eye.

I looked at the Old Man, unsure as to what to say.

The Old Man looked at the ridiculously over packed, Likooshas, keeping himself from laughing.

" Just some romantic stuff. Nothing worth looting," the Old Man said plainly.

Likooshas nodded, staring at the Old Man closely, looking to see if he was lying. Then he turned to me. I kept silent and tried to stay expressionless. It paid off.

He sighed. " Well If there's nothing else to take from here now, then we should be heading back," he said. "We'll get the crew up here tomorrow to bring down more."

The Old Man smiled, wearily. "I agree. Atlantis is dead. Let's carry her bones away and scatter them far and wide, so she can never be put back together again."

We walked in silence for a while, after that gloomy pronouncement, but I didn't feel the loss that he did. And I was irrepressible.

"Remember when we were back on the beach fixing the boat?" I asked.

"Hmmm," he said, not paying me much attention.

"Well, one night you gave me a big whack on the head too - just like Elana gave to Nurix. But I don't hate you for it. How come he's such a whiner. I thought he was a tough guy who had been bought and sold and slapped around a lot. How come, all of a sudden, his heart is broken and he's pouting?"

"Greko, you're a still a kid. You expect grown-ups to treat you unfairly and kick you around. And when they do, you think nothing of it. But later, when you're a man, betrayals and unfairness will pierce your heart much more sharply. And betrayal by the woman you love and trust, will hurt more than a sword thrust to the heart."

"He really loved her?"

"They loved each other. Although neither knew it yet nor would admit it even if they had. But, as we walk down the mountain, just listen to this and you'll see what I mean:"

***

Cruce' looked up at Elana, a little surprised herself.

There was a long pause between them. Cruce' continued to gaze at Nurix's troubled face, then turned to Elana, but could still only speculate as to what had happened between them.

Elana sighed, not sure herself and trying to get out of the situation as fast as possible. She was extremely flushed with frustration and embarrassment. She couldn't bear to continue talking.

" I'm terribly sorry Cruce', but I feel that my slave has caused a lot more trouble than I wanted him to," she said slowly patting Nurix on the back and then wrapping her arm around his.

Cruce' smiled pathetically,

" That's fine" she started, "It is always nice to be reminded of the past once in a while. Isn't that right Nurix?"

Nurix was still in shock and was resistant to say anything at all.

Elana felt a little humiliated by Nurix's behavior. She also felt embarrassed about her own behavior and wanted to get away, but didn't know how to part.

" Anyway, I believe that I have wasted enough of your valuable time, merchant, with this idle chit chat, I have to be going," she said as she briskly started to walk, pulling Nurix along with her.

Cruce' smiled but did not wave back to them as they slowly disappeared into the crowd.

Elana continued to walk, Nurix was pulled along by her brisk steps like a reluctant dog on a strong leash. She leaned her head to the side to Nurix as she walked.

" I am surprised at you, why were you behaving so rudely in front of your former mistress ? That was unmanly-like," she scolded.

Nurix gave no answer. He kept silent and ignored her. He only looked at her sadly and turned around, letting her guide him through the streets.

Elana didn't like it.

She knew that Nurix was angry at her for hitting him, but she felt that it had been the right thing to do, for he was acting up.

Nurix looked down for a minute and then turned around as he matched her fast walk.

" So you feel that I should be a pet ? Property ? Told what to do ?" Nurix said, walking at her pace and refusing to make eye contact to her as he talked.

Elana glimpsed and took a hard look at his emotionless face as he walked in pace with her.

She turned around. " Why are you taking this measure so harshly. It wasn't like I damaged you, or threatened your life in some way, like that High Priestess did in the monastery or that merchant did when you were young ?" she asked with a mellow tone.

Elana accidently bumped into a passerby who had stopped in front of her. Elana smiled and apologized. The passerby smiled and thanked her for apologizing to her and continued on her way.

Elana started to walk again. She glimpsed at Nurix once more, hoping for him to say something.

He gave no comment.

" I understand that I hurt you Nurix but you must accept the fact that you are a man. And not jut any man. You are my man. And not just my man, Nurix. You are my slave."

" What is your point," he said abruptly in the middle of her lecture.

" My point is that you must behave in the manner expected of you," she said.

Nurix showed no expression even though he couldn't believe what she was saying.

Elana continued on. " You can't expect to act bold and aggressive, like a woman. It embarrasses me. Like I don't know how to keep you under control or like , even worse, you're controlling me. Everyone expects you to be silent and polite when asked to be, told when and when not to speak, and shown to be presentable in front of company, Nurix. If you are not, I suffer for it."

Immediately, he stopped walking with her. He turned his face and looked deeply into her eyes. He tried to read them with his special power, tried to see what she wanted, truly.

He read concern, embarrassment, humiliation, and confusion. He read her emotions, and read that she felt like a naive person, not a woman, but a girl who could not control her slave, a foolish girl who lacked responsibility, a very childish girl with a feeble mind.

It was her paranoia, what she felt others thought of her, fearing that even he, a lowly slave, felt this way about her.

He read that she hated it, that she wanted to show everyone that she really was a woman, an honorable, tough, capable Arkaiton woman. She wanted people to think of her differently than how she felt when Brelinka looked at her, as a baby needing constant care.

He also read that she was sorry for what she had done, that she wanted to apologize to him, that she felt wrong for telling him to behave.

At that moment, Nurix gasped and looked down. He began to understand her reasons for acting this way and in his mind, he finally gave in, releasing any grudge that he felt for her. But he still refused to smile and continued to remain emotionless and quiet.

Elana turned her face, feeling negative about him and wanted to know why he had stopped. She didn't know that he had read her mind, through her body. That he had read every thought shown by the expressions of her face, her body and soul. She didn't know that he was the only one in the world who could even begin to understand a little bit about why she was acting this way.

All she wanted to know right at that moment was why he had stopped, and hoped he would continue walking on their peaceful stroll without her having to use physical force on him again.

Then it hit her, why he had stopped. She sighed with a little relief, it wasn't that he was still mad at her, and it wasn't even because he wanted to tell her that he hated what she had done and what she wanted him to do for the rest of his life while he was with her.

He had stopped in front of the gates of the monastery where they were staying. He had stopped because the gate was closed in front of them and he was standing there; emotionless, attentive, and waiting to serve her, just as she had demanded he do.

She sighed a little and closed her eyes. She then looked up at the gates and realized that he waited for her command to open the gates.

"Nurix, please open the gates," she said with a little sting of authority in her voice.

Nurix slowly knocked on the gate. Two guards, wearing Buushu head bands, came out and stared at them, then opened the gate for them.

Both Elana and Nurix stood there, staring at each other until the gate was open.

Nurix slowly bowed his head and politely awaited for her to go in first. Elana smiled and slowly stroked the long bushy hair on Nurix's scalp as she walked by him and began to stroll inside.

For the rest of the day, Nurix never said a word. He helped as they packed up the woolly-hoofed horses, and a saddle was put on the last pack horse, for Nurix, for the first time, was going to be riding on a separate horse instead of riding with Elana. As the day continued on. Nurix seemed to grow even more distant from Elana and she seemed to grow more literal and negative in front of Nurix.

Although the others wondered for her peculiar change in character, it wasn't all that strange as this was the way all mistresses behaved toward male slaves.

What they didn't know was that it was all an act. A secret pact that both of them had made, silently, standing near that gate as they waited for it to be opened.

They agreed to act in the way that Elana wanted it to be played out: Nurix played the humble, obedient slave and Elana was the strong, dominant and superior mistress. The act hid their true motives, which were to eagerly await a stopping point, when they would be able to sleep, where both of them would be alone, secluded from the world where they would be able to stop the act and be themselves. Where they would be able to talk, to kiss, to be companions as they once were before. Where they would be able to lay together, sweetly, staring at each other without saying a word, without expressing a feeling, just locked and embraced, eyes focussed only on each other, both seeing a long future together.

I was so shocked, that I tripped and fell right on my face on the hill.

I got up and ran to catch up with the Old Man who hadn't even stopped.

"You old bastard !" I said. "You tell me all this stuff about how love is so dangerous and 'No woman-No trouble' slogans and then you spring this on me. A happy ending ? A love story ? That's not fair!"

"That's the real world," he said, then said no more.

By the time we made it down the mountain, the sun had set and the moon had risen and my anger at this turn in the story had all leaked out.

The rest of the crew were mellow as they all sat near the fire with a plump warthog roasting away. We slowly plunked down our loot and they became positively joyous, passing the gold and diamonds around and running their fingers through piles of it.

We let them fool with the treasure and moved towards the magnificent smell of the hog.

"Ah, the Old Man," said one crewman. " Just in time to enlighten us with another tale of Atlantis," he said as he grinned, one hand full of treasure and the other clutching a big piece of the pig.

" As long as it's a story about the warrior women.

We all want to sleep spectacularly tonight, if you know what we mean, Old Man," another said as the crew broke into a kind of perverted laughter.

Likooshas briskly moved towards someone who had a piece of pork.

"Rip me off a piece!" he demanded. Immediately receiving what he wanted.

The Old Man slowly sat down, receiving a cup of drink and a piece of pork, both bribes to get him to tell a story. The Old Man was silent for a while, only listening to the chatter, the flute playing, and the perverse jokes that went on.

" Come on, Old Man, throw us another tale of the women. We want to hear some more," one the crew moaned.

The Old Man took a bite out of his chunk of meat and then a long drink from his cup. He gave a sigh of relief and seemed a little sounder.

He looked to the crew, feeling that they were as eager as anyone to hear the story. So he gave in.

" All right, I'll tell you the story" he said as he turned around to a crewman already heading to sleep.

He poked the man.

" Sisko, where did I leave off ?" the Old Man asked joyously.

The sleepy Sisko only mumbled, as he tried to get comfortable for sleep once more.

" You were at the part where Elana gets into a fight with Nurix and hits him, but they make up and agree to act normal in public."

The Old Man was impressed. "How did you know that. I just told that to Greko up on the mountain ?"

"I dreamed it. Alright. Now can I go back to sleep ?" he asked.

" You may sleep now," the Old Man said. "Dream up the rest and tell me how it all comes out."

Immediately, Sisko turned around and pulled his blanket over his head.

The Old Man smiled and gave a good laugh.

The men praised him more. In their minds, women riding on woolly-hoofed horses, holding spears, fighting and hunting animals was rather erotic. But in the mind of the Old Man, it was much, much different.

"Alright then, here's a part of the women's story that you really won't like at all . . ."

They were all ready to leave. □They were just waiting on Sassaska to finish her meeting with the Governor about the state of the Empire.

Nurix had even managed to get up on his pack horse, although no-one was sure about how long he'd stay on there once they got moving. Julyo was back, with her horse, brimming with all the latest information on the trail ahead. The women slaves were also on their pack horses, talking lazily.

Brelinka had resorted to leaning against the outside of the Governor's house, sharpening her weapons again.

Suddenly, she heard the noises of horses galloping up the main road. She looked up and saw a sight she would never have believed : a full Delegation of the Clans. An Arkaiton woman, dressed in full battle armor, galloping up the road. It was almost a thing of the past. Arkaitons ran the Empire. They didn't go to war. They had no need of armor. And yet . . .

The armored woman's mask-helmet showed a howling demon while the rest of her body armor mimicked a skeletal structure that looked like some sort of stylized death machine. The Makaiton woman who accompanied her wore a full lion-skin cape with a sabre-toothed lion skull grafted into her helmet. She was an Imperial Honor Guard with fluttering banners that signified they were on an important mission for the Empress.

And right in the middle of them was a nicely dressed young woman with a long clan braid, wearing a cap-like helmet. She was a highly decorated Buushu Warrior Chieftain who, it would turn out, had been brought along to escort them to Oxna, in Buushu country, if necessary.

Brelinka stood up in awe, seeing the bright colors of yellow and red coming towards her. She was puzzled why they were out here at the border of Buushu territory. The horses slowed themselves in front of the Governor's Mansion, as the women looked around at the dirt and squalor of the primitive town.

The armored woman slowed and came to a stop, getting off her warhorse and walked towards Brelinka.

"Yes ?" Brelinka asked, holding her just-sharpened weapon ready

The woman looked Brelinka in the eyes as she unraveled a small scroll. " Are you one of Sassaska Batushna Gurshey's company ?" the woman asked.

Brelinka sighed and said, " Yes, I am."

The armored woman nodded and then waved her hand to call the Makaiton and the Buushu over. They came off their horses and stood close by.

" Can you take us to her ?" asked the armored woman.

Brelinka frowned at them, too surprised to be tolerable.

"What is this all about ?"

The Imperials looked at each other and refused to answer her question.

"Direct us to Sassaska, please ?" the woman asked again.

Brelinka closed her eyes." I am her protector. I will not take you to her until you tell me what has happened," she snapped at them.

The Banner Carrier undrew her mask and looked at the other two. They all nodded.

"Empress Asmereldia has died. Sassaska, The Chosen One is now Empress. The Council has pronounced her Empress-elect, but she must travel to Lina immediately, to be crowned at the Official Coronation. It is the only way to ensure the succession. Now will you please take us to her ?" the Banner Carrier explained.

Brelinka couldn't believe what she was hearing. Asmereldia was dead. Her friend and lover, Sask, was now Her Highness Empress Sassaska and had absolute power over all of the known world. But Sassaska was in no condition to lead an Empire.

She was still a girl in many ways, Brelinka knew. She still had self-doubts and was often confused, since her near-death and her long illness in the snowy mountains.

But it wasn't up to Brelinka at all. It was all pre-ordained. And, perhaps, all those who had power thrust upon them were not ready. Never ready for such a thing. Maybe all leaders just muddled through, doing the best they could do. Brelinka herself, as a General, had often felt that way before a battle, but she loved the action and high stakes. She was never more alive, although she hadn't realized this until she alone was in command of her first big battle. She hoped it would be the same for Sassaska.

Meanwhile, the Honor Guard wanted Sassaska. So Brelinka escorted them into the building and informed the guards that she had to interrupt the conference.

The guards, know Brelinka, let her in.

The Governor and Sassaska were sitting on two comfortable chairs in the large room, leaning towards each other, deep in conversation.

They both looked up, startled, as the group rushed in.

The Banner Carrier began the official notification:

"The Empress is dead ! The Empress is born. Long live Empress Sassaska !"

All three of the newcomers dropped to one knee and bowed their heads.

Brelinka did too, but with a huge grin.

"Empress," Governor Vivesk said softly, bowing her head deeply from her chair.

Much to Brelinka's surprise, Sassaska did not miss a beat.

"Arise !" she commanded. " Governor, please extend your hospitality to my delegation. Feed them, let them rest and take care of their horses. We ride for Lina at sunrise tomorrow."

Perhaps , Brelinka thought, there was an invisible transfer of power, of confidence and of grace under pressure that somehow passed directly form old leader to new leader, through the hands of these messengers, or perhaps through the power of the words they uttered. But there was no question in Brelinka's mind anymore:

Sassaska was indeed Empress !

She left Sassaska and the Governor to speak with the delegation and went outside to tell the others of the change in plan.

The whole group was already mounted, even Elana. All assumed that they were about to leave any moment.

"Change of plan. Get down and come over here," Brelinak commanded.

When they had tied their horses and congregated around her, Brelinka said; "Those flashy messengers came to say that Asmereldia is dead. Our Sassaska is now Empress of Atlantis!"

"Long may she live'" they all said, automatically. Then all broke into huge smiles of amazement and disbelief.

"Unpack and rest up in the Governor's house. We leave for Lina at first light tomorrow."

It was such a remarkable idea, to see their travelling companion crowned Empress, that even Julyo to go back to Lina for the coronation.

The next morning, the party left, taking the low road across the plain so they could reach Lina in less than two weeks, where Sassaska would be crowned Empress of Atlantis, First Lady of the Arkaitons, High Mistress of the Makaitons and Queen of the Buushu.

The journey was over.

The rule of Empress Sassaska had begun.

"Wow !" I said. "That's amazing. What a surprise. "

"Why won't we like it, Old Man ?" one of the crew asked.' I get to sleep with an Empress tonight. What's not to like about that ?"

The crew laughed and even Likooshas took time out from arranging and e-re-arranging his treasure to throw out a smile.

The Old Man grinned and chewed on his piece of pork, shaking his head and holding up his other hand to signal that we had to wait while he chewed.

"You won't like it," he said, wiping his lips on the floppy sleeve of the crewman net to him, "because that's the end of the women's story. There is no more. And the end of my story too. I'm going to bed. Sleep with the Empress, lads, and enjoy yourself. That's the last you'll hear of her."

The crew groaned, but not too loudly or for too long. After all, they had meat and beer.

The next morning, Likooshas organized the whole crew to go back up tot he vault and bring down more treasure. The Old Man didn't want to go and Likooshas told me to stay and guard the treasure that he had brought down last night.

After they left, I gathered all the treasure up and put it in one pile, then sat around eating cold pork and enjoying myself.

The Old Man wandered away and poked around the beach for a while, looking for things from his past. He finally came back and cut a few hunks off the pig.

He came over and sat beside me, nibbling on the meat. "Sorry, Greko, to end the women's story like I did last night, but what can I do? That's the way it happened."

"That's alright. To tell you the truth, the women are pretty boring. They really don't do much. I'm sort of glad to be done with them. All that lovey dovey stuff and feelings and kissings and broken hearts. Yecchhhh." I spit out a big piece of meat for effect.

"Well, I lied, you know," the Old Man winked at me. "There is one more part to the story of the warrior women of Atlantis."

"More kissy wissy stuff?" I asked, raising an eyebrow.

"Nope. This is the story you've really been waiting for. The story of when the warrior women meet the Sudutan men. The first Battle of the Sexes!"

My hair rose as he mentioned this. Now Sudutan would clash with Buushu, Makaiton, or Arkaiton. Technology against brute strength. Man against woman.

I could not wait for him to tell me what would happen . . .

After three weeks went by in the camp in the north, Kline had expanded his scouting to a forty mile radius. He also kept Vittorio in continual correspondence with Sudutan Atlantis on the radio, to be sure that their fame was kept fueled.

Dusty gained better health within a week. His leg had swelled down and his arm stiffened up enough for Dav'inne to release the staples from his clean cuts. Their routines were simple during the week, for their search for diamonds was proving inconclusive. Basically they just ate, sat around, hunted occasionally and went on short, fun fights looking for diamonds.

It was a golden period of time. Soon, since diamonds were the main point of the quest, Kline would have to shift his camp to another location and they would all have to work much harder. In the meantime, however, this was paradise for them.

Until the woman arrived., that is.

As Kline sat high on the branches of a tree, sitting on his new sabre-fanged jaguar skin rug, with its many cuts and slashes, he wrote in his personal journal, recording what he had seen and encountered through the week. The morning was quiet and pleasantly spent on recreation.

Clubio had gotten the short straw and went on another routine search, by Drag Quad, for diamond possibilities. He was not expecting to find anything, but he did enjoy it as an excuse to explore further on.

Luca sat on a rock next to his shelter facing Dusty with a game set up. They had been playing for hours without break.

Dav'inne had been asleep throughout the day for there was no need to be working at the moment.

Vittorio aided Squirrel in cleaning out the fur and slivers entangled in his Drag Quad from his venture looking for diamonds the previous day and landing in the forest at likely spots.

The whole time seemed placid, all until Clubio came back in a flurry of wings and shouts.

" I've found diamonds !" Clubio continually shouted out.

Kline slowly sat up from his crouched position in the tree, alert to the sound of diamonds.

" Finally, an excuse to return home !" Kline muttered to himself, slowly closing his journal up and placing his pen through the binding.

Clubio fluttered to a stop, panting from his rush as he quickly unfastened himself from the braces of the Drag Quad.

" Marsolla give way, I've found diamonds! And a whole rushing lot of them!" Clubio shouted.

Vittorio stood up with a smile.

Squirrel only sighed as he saw the way Clubio dropped his Drag Quad with his wings, forcing themselves back, on top of the power house.

Luca stood and rushed up to Clubio, "You hound, you ! Diamonds in the rough !" he said happily.

Kline gave a smile from his tree top.

The others patted him and cheered him. For the day, Clubio was their hero. Clubio then spotted Kline in the tree and slowly stormed up to the trunk, "Ha! So it is true ! Diamonds in the North Continent ! We will be rich, Cummundore ! Rich, I say ! And famous too !" he happily shouted directly towards Kline. "They're just lying around for anyone to pick up. No mining needed yet !"

Kline shook his head in disbelief. "Well done, Clubio, very well done !"

I've got four bags full, "Clubio said, pulling ut one leather bag and tossing it up to Kline.

"You've done it, man," he said. "You've found our ticket back home!"

Kline looked in the bag at the large rough diamonds inside, and poured a few into his hand.

Then, grinning, he re-opened his journal and began to write once more.

Clubio smiled with happiness as the others gave a toast in his honor.

" By this time, next month, Zex will be kissing our asses !" he said arrogantly, holding up another bulky bag filled with uncut diamonds. They all cheered , but then stopped suddenly. They were listening to the faint, haunting sound of feminine humming coming from the forest.

One by one, the men became silent. They all turned their attention to the sound.

" What's that ?" Dusty asked curiously, grabbing his crutch to get up.

Luca slowly stood upon his rock stump and looked around. "Sounds like a woman, doesn't it?"

The faint humming continued on and made the men even more eager to find it.

Since the death of Bisu and Angellina, the men had become more rowdy than usual, desperately trying to contain their sexual hunger. But the sound of the woman in the woods had awakened their dormant urges once and for all.

It was then that the woman slowly came out of the thickness of the forest, humming and curious.

Some of the others ran behind the shrubs and the bushes surrounding their camp site, so that they could head her off if she tried to get away. But she made no such effort.

Kline slowly grabbed a hold of a tree limb and helped himself upright as the woman's features became easier to see. Even his urges were strong, making his heart beat and his mouth water.

As she came, he noticed her clothing first, because he had never seen it's like. On her feet were simple leather boots going up her thin calfs, wrapped with tightened cloth and wool to keep them from falling apart. Her legs were concealed by finely tailored pants, loose and easy to take off. On top she had a loose blouse with a heavy leather vest on top. Most of her was concealed, most likely to keep safe from the cold breezes. This was a slight disappointment, after going so long without seeing a woman, but what parts of her skin were revealed showed unbroken, smoothness.It was evenly tanned like the leather she wore and perfect like the tailory of her stitches.

Her face showed sereneness and confidence and her hair, a wavy thickness of brownish red, reflected her true beauty. She also had a strange single braid hanging down the side of her head with many decorations in it.

Clubio and the men watched her as she stepped into their camp. She seemed bewildered for the moment, wandering about the shelters and looking at the equipment resting all over the ground.

" Hello there . . ," Dusty said. He sat on a tree stump, easing his leg to keep it from aching. The woman turned around and gazed at him. It was obvious that she had never seen a Sudutan Atlantean till this day.

"Beska ?" she asked him.

Dusty leaned in, asking her to repeat what she had said.

Kline, in his tree, found the word slightly familiar.

By now, the men were slowly revealing themselves from the bushes. They slowly approached her with smiles and perverted laughter.

Her mouth was silent for a moment as she witnessed the bulk of them come out.

Dole stepped out, tipping his pigskin helmet to her. "What are you doing out in the woods, my pretty ?"

Clubio then appeared, then Luca, Squirrel and Dav'inne, and finally Vittorio.

Her eyes widened, but the sight of all the men seemed to cause her more irritation than fear.

" Look, she's never seen a man before ! Must be in heaven, isn't she?" Clubio said excitedly. "Ahh -look at her. Like a lamb to the slaughter."

The crew laughed too much, trying to overcome their tensions.

She continued to gaze, standing perfectly still as the men came closer to inspect her body.

"Been gok, feema of your Thrist, Mistress ?" she said.

The men laughed, for they had no concept about what she said.

All except Kline. The accented tongue of the woman seemed to say a verse which triggered a remembrance from the deepest section of his memory. He frowned as he tried to figure out the familiarities of the words mentioned.

Suddenly it hit him - it was the old language. The way they all spoke 1000 years ago. Kline had studied the olden form of speech for years to do his research work, but he had never heard it spoken.

"Men-things, " she had said, using the insulting term; "Where goes your Mistress ?"

Maybe he had it wrong, Kline thought. It seemed a silly thing to say, under the circumstances. But it was definitely the old language. Kline was delighted. Here was another treasure of his first expedition. He had discovered not only that there were people in the North but that they were somehow related to the Sudutans. 1000 years ago or more. They must have broken away from civilization and settled here surrounded by ice. Kline thought he would be really famous now. He would go down in history for this discovery, whether he found a full throat of diamonds or not. Kline was in heaven, imagining his fame.

"She speaks nonsense" Luca said timidly, reaching for her hair to gain a feel.

The woman still stood still, sighing in annoyance.

"Maybe she's an idiot," Vittorio quickly stated, crouching down to touch her thighs.

It was then that Dole, slowly reached for her arm, slowly making her undraw the basket in which she carried freshly picked flowers and herbs

He pulled it close to his chest, putting all of his acts of charm into action. "You don't screw her brain" he said with a laugh, noticing two metal rounded blades around oval rings over the index and the fore finger of the hand that held the basket.

"Tusave n'aowa must'y Ikno Streys," she said to them with soothing concern, pulling her basket gently out of Dole's grip.

"You poor men look terrible - are you lost or are you strays ?" she had said. Kline was understanding every word now.

Vittorio, crouching down beside her, began to forcefully grab on to her firm leg and rub his head over her firm, dense thigh. Her skin was soft, yet something seemed unusual about her. It was as if her inner muscles were like stone.

"There she goes with that gibberish again.," he mentioned, nervously placing his lips to taste the texture of the cloth entanglements.

She lowered her glances to him with a look of pity in her eyes.

That was when things went for the bad turn.

Clubio foolishly undrew his Bankra, turning the straightened blade and gesturing with it.. " I like my women quiet- no matter what language they speak !" he said, smacking Dole out of his way "Let me cut her tongue out first to shut her up," he said.

She still stayed calm, now gaining a smile. She muttered a few more words in an arrogant tone which Kline translated as; "Your Mistress allows you to carry weapons ?" she asked arrogantly. "I'll have her up on charges."

Clubio swayed his head.

Dole slowly walked up to the woman once more, looking her in the eyes.

"Careful there Clubio- her tongue is sharp . . ," he said.

The others laughed.

The woman looked at him curiously. She was a smallish woman and Clubio towered over her, even though he was one of the shortest of the men. He held the sword low in one hand and reached down with the other and grabbed her by the neck.

"You dare touch me, uninvited, man ?" she said contemptuously as she took his outstretched arm and, within a second, she had speedily snapped it in two.

Clubio roared like a wounded bear and tried to ram her with the sword. She knocked it away like it was held by a child. Clubio pulled his dagger and tried to stab her with it. She caught his arm easily, and put her other hand on the back of his neck. Then she turned the knife inward and slowly, as he watched in horror, she forced his own hand to push the knife between his own ribs and into his heart. Blood spurted. She held him up off the ground by the back of the neck, as one would hold a dead rabbit, and turned, displaying his dying to the circle.

"Never get above yourselves," she said. "The price, as you can see, is death !"

Dole backed in shock. " She's a murderer !"he shouted.

Immediately, Squirrel ran for his blade, Vittorio, still hanging on to her leg, tried to trip her, and Dusty stood up with his crutch.

The rest all jumped on top of her all at once. Vittorio heaved again, but couldn't budge her. She dropped Clubio, but kept the dagger.

She used one hand to easily free Vittorio's arm and twisted it behind his back. With her other hand she drove the dagger into his back, below the hand, and his arm was pinned behind him, held there by the dagger between his ribs. He tried to bite her leg, and, annoyed now, she reached her grasp over his neck and with a casual twist, turned his head against her thigh, breaking his neck and eventually ripping his head right off his body.

Squirrel lunged at her with his sword, and she ripped his arm clean off, then threw him towards the transmitter He landed on it with a thump and both were suddenly beyond repair. Dav'inne rammed at her and she hit him with Squirrel's arm so hard he was stunned. She then grabbed his arms and forced his body right into the rigid wings of one of the Drag-Quads on a stand. He was sliced to death within seconds.

Dusty hobbled behind her and hit her over the head with his crutch.

She turned and smiled, then picked Dusty up by the neck with one hand. As he squirmed, trying to hit her with the cast on his broken arm, she rammed her straightened fingers right into his chest through flesh and bone and crushed his heart with her bare hands, right in front of his eyes.

Luca shouted at her, and when she turned, shot her right in the chest with his air gun. The splintered pellet dropped off her breast, but before it hit the ground, she had leapt the ten feet between them and picked him right off the ground and threw him, gun and all, twenty feet in the air, to stove his head in on the trunk of the tree where Kline still hid.

Kline was in a quiet panic up there. What he at first thought was some trick or art of self defense on the woman's part, he now saw was a terrible strength. The strength of ten strong men in the body of one small woman. Like a full grown man fighting with toddlers.

All that was left now was Dole. He trembled in shock.

He was frozen in grief, seeing his dead companions all around him. So when the woman walked up to him, he made no move to escape or fight.

"I think you've made your point, my dear," he said, trying to be nonchalant and to force up a sickly smile.

She stood before him silently and made a fist, which clinged the blades on her ring out again. She casually reached down and hooked them into his scrotum right through his clothes. He yelled loudly, making birds fly in the distance.

Her two fingers curved and jerked, pulling out his penis and testicles with one fearsome yank and shaking the bloody mess off the blades and onto the ground with a quick toss.

The color of dark red began to seep through what remained of Dole's pants. He began to grow pale and he fell face down into the dirt.

Kline now feared this woman completely. She had awesome power and no mercy at all. He stayed silent up in the tree, making sure not to gain her attention in any way, but to no avail. She walked over to the Drag Quads, which were all up on stands for lubrication. She picked one of the heavy packs up with each hand and smashed them together, then threw the tangled mess onto another Drag Quad. The one with Dav'inne impaled on it, she left as it was.

Kline held his breath, beginning to cry in terror as she then walked closer to his tree.

She looked up at him with her terrible gaze. She pointed to Clubio, the first she had killed, and held up her arm with one finger raised. She swept her arm around at all the others she had killed, and held up her arm with two fingers raised. She then pointed at Kline, cowering up his tree. She then raised three fingers, then simply shook her head, wiped her hands together and continued on her way, humming again, as if she had just paused to step on a few ants.

As for Kline, he held his breath until he was sure that she was well and truly gone, all the time wondering if this had been a real woman, of the ghost of Ennis, seeking a bloody revenge.

"Wow. Now that's a story, Old Man." I said, excited now. "I liked the part where she ripped off his arm and whacked the other guy with it. And the part where she ripped the guy's head right off. Ewwww."

"Somehow I knew you'd like that part, boy."

"She was Buushu, right. With the braid ?"

"Kline mentioned the braid briefly in his journals, but I don't think that's enough to go on. All women wear braids sometimes," the Old Man shrugged.

"No. There's more. Remember ? She did the Three Solutions, too, right ? With her arm up showing the numbers of fingers ? And that's a Buushu thing, isn't it ?"

"You know, Greko, I never connected that before, but you're absolutely right. She might have been Buushu."

"No 'might of been' about it - she must of been," I said. "Remember the Empress and Sassaska were talking about the Buushu being the ones in the South with all the old stories of magic men who fly ?"

"I like the way you think, Greko. The three solutions. And the stories of encounters with the Sud. Of course. You're right. Thank you. About the only emotion I really enjoy any more is a good surprise, and you've surprised me with your attention to detail. Let me go and walk this off and think about it."

He got up and wandered around the beach, going into the shallow water and collecting a huge basket of clams, then cooking them up in a huge pot, with a thick savory sauce he made from water, beer and bits of plants and leaves.

I went back to doing my serious guard duty, which involved a lot of eating and napping in the sun.

In the late afternoon, the crew came back, each and every one loaded down like a pack horse with barrels and barrels of treasure. Enough to make us all rich for the rest of our lives.

It was one of the best times, ever.

We sat around the fire, running our fingers through the treasure, eating the Old Man's clams and dreaming of our futures as wealthy men.

"Make this the very best night of our lives, Old Man. Tell us more of the story," said one of the crew.

"The story ?" the Old Man said. "I've told a big part of it to Greko over the last couple of days. He can tell you what you missed. "

"It's not the same. You can tell a tale like no-one else. Just go on with the story from where you left off. Greko can fill in the missing parts tomorrow."

The Old Man sighed and put his head in his hands for a moment. "You're right. There's probably been no better time since our journey began, to tell this part of the story. It's about lifelong friendship, just like we have here tonight. Just to keep you updated, a lone woman walked into Kline's camp, and, when she was attacked by the expeditioneers, she killed every one but him. "

"Whoa !" said one of the crew.

" Now, listen up," the Old Man scolded.

The woman left the untidy stack of death that she'd created in the camp and had continued on her way, humming and untroubled.

Kline had finally started breathing again. But he still remained high atop the tree, in fear of seeing the woman come back to finish her work. He stayed up there, nervously writing down every key event he could remember from the few seconds which turned his celebrating expeditioneers into steaming piles of dead meat.. It was the only thing he could think to do to keep his focus from falling into chaos.

As he wrote everything that he had seen and remembered, and in the writing, changed it forever from what really happened, he began to ponder the woman in more depth.

" How could such a woman exist ?" he asked himself, finally thinking with the instincts as a scribe - a way of thinking he had been trained in and had practiced for years.

" If an unarmed woman, just out for a stroll in the woods, was able to kill seven armed fighting men with her bare hands, not to mention, destroy communications back to the Sudutan lands, as well as smashing up three of the Drag-Quads, then what would the men of the Sud ever be able to do against the men of the North?" he thought.

If the women were like this, how awesome would the men be ?

Kline tried to continue writing his report of the incident before he forgot all the details, but his thoughts kept straying away from what had happened and over to how it could have happened. How could a woman be so strong?

Then, it hit him, and he began to review his notes of everything he'd seen up here in the North so far.

The trees seemed much bigger up here than they did in the South. And the sabre-toothed cat had taken three shots from a rifle and a lot of happy chopping and stabbing to kill. Even the bugs seemed to take an extra slap to squash.

Maybe everything up here was bigger sand stronger. Possibly something in the water or the air or the food created super strength. Perhaps something in the melting ice. Maybe an unknown germ or virus, locked up in the ice for millions of years, was released up here and acted upon every living thing.

He decided to use logic and began writing down what he knew.

One: every living thing seemed stronger up here.

Two: Therefore people were also stronger

Three: The strong woman didn't know we were from the South

Four: Yet she didn't seem fearful alone, among a group of men

Five: She spoke to men contemptuously and fearlessly

Six: She did not seem surprised to be able to fight men easily

It was leading to one inescapable conclusion: She was much stronger than any men she had ever met. Possibly all women up here were much stronger than their men. Possibly the entire society is controlled by strong women, with the weak men playing a secondary role.

Could it be ?

The woman's language was the key. He flipped back through his notes to check. And he was right. The first thing that she said to the men before she savagely slaughtered them:

" Are you strays ? Where is your Mistress ?"

Then: "Your Mistress allows you to carry weapons? I'll have her up on charges."

And then: You dare touch me uninvited, man?"

And when she'd killed Clubio and held him up like a lesson: "Never get above yourselves, the penalty is death !"

The woman showed a natural dominance with her words and her tone. She was used to talking to men as if they were bad children or disobedient dogs. Meaning that women are naturally superior within the north continent he decided and wrote that conclusion in his journal.

Kline grinned and nodded. He sensed that he was on the right track to discovering the woman puzzle.

He was about to write down another point when he heard the sound of the faint plea from the ground.

Kline ceased his writing and listened.

" Help me," came the tortured voice from the ground once more.

Kline leaned out to look at the remnants of his men. All he saw was great splashes of blood and gore, crazy entanglements of limbs, organs and odd pieces of skin, and in the midst of all this butchery, a hand flopped up and down.

" Kline . . . You monkey of a man, come down here before I turn you in for high tree - son !" shouted the voice drunkardly, laughing a bit and then coughing weakly.

Kline remained silent, surprised that some one had actually survived the encounter. But it was not just anyone, for the man who'd survived the wrath of the woman was Dole; who, ironically, was one of the worst sexists and one of the most flagrant abusers of women to ever walk the face of the known world.

"Dole, My Gods !" Kline said. "I'm so glad to hear you."

Kline made his way down from the tree, crafty, so as not to make any noises as he did so. "Dole, keep your voice down ! She could come back !" Kline urgently whispered.

Dole slowly dragged himself to turn over and sit up against one of the overturned Drag-Quads.

"Don't worry, Kline. She is done with us and gone. Much as I myself am."

His pants, soaked through from the removal of his genitals, still oozed and bubbled with blood.

He breathed shallowly to sustain whatever energy he contained.

" Besides, that woman knows better than to come back. She's in fear now. She knows I'll give her a good raping, to get revenge for having my genitals ripped off!" he joked, slowly drifting into drowsiness.

Kline quickly stepped closer to him, crouching down to his knees.

Dole continued to bleed badly though his dirty trousers. His side laces, made thick and crusty by the clotting of his excess blood, were so wet they were dripping. Dole then leaned forward, panting from his loss of breath.

" Dole, you're really bleeding severely . . ," Kline said morbidly, grabbing up Dav'inne's Medical kit from next to the Medical Officer's body.

He could see nothing inside that would stop the bleeding..

Dole tipped his head, looking at his own puddle of trickling blood.

" You're the master of the obvious, Kline," Dole said sarcastically getting paler as his life leaked away.

Kline slowly leaned himself towards Dole. " There's nothing in the medical kit and nothing I can think to stop the bleeding either," Kline sighed. "Can you think of anything ?"

Dole turned his head away as the pain of his nerves in his groin tingled and stung.

" It's nothing that a good whiff of whiskey wouldn't fix . . .," he said, trying to break the mood.

Kline still felt it necessary to try to protect his friend. " Dole, I'm not sure whiskey would be healthy for you right now," he said.

Dole sighed. " Kline, wake up ! I'm dying. And there's nothing you or I or anyone else can do about it. So, believe me, whiskey won't hurt anything. It's funny though, if you had asked me this morning whether I would like to die with a woman's hand on my crotch, I would have said 'absolutely, what a way to go!' But this is a bit different from the fantasy. That bitch. A good feel is one thing, but this, I believe, was overkill," Dole said, gazing at his missing sex organs. He snickered to himself at his own joke and coughed weakly at the exertion.

" Dole . . ," Kline laughed with him to ease his transition from life to death. " You must admit, that was quite a grab," Kline mentioned, feeling his pity seep through his face. He found some whiskey and poured a bit into a wooden cup.

Dole laid his head back against the Drag Quad and sipped it.

" And we weren't even properly introduced. Damn, what a woman, eh? And you missed it all by sitting up in a furry little tree . . . by the way, did you hear my tree-son joke, Kline ?" Dole asked.

Kline felt his mandible tighten as his heart leaped.

"Yes. I got that. Good one. I . . .I was caught up in my writing, dear friend. But I'm sort of glad, in hindsight, that I wasn't able to take part in the fun . . ," Kline said silently.

Dole kept in his tears, as he grew colder. " Oh, I know. That was why . . . I kept quiet. I didn't want to call for you in case she noticed you up there."

Kline breathed a sigh of relief.

" And I thank you for that, Dole," he said. "But you know something . . . she did know I was up there.

She walked over and looked up at me. Scared the hell out of me. Then she gave me some rude three finger salute and walked away. And I haven't been able to breathe since.

Dole smiled. " So what was it that you were writing about ? Your hatred for Bringington once more ?" he asked.

Kline ruffled himself to get more comfortable beside Dole. "No . . . It was the official report about this crew. How we bonded and how we withstood all forces to make it this far. How we fought weather and wild animals and finally found the diamonds. I thought we'd all be able to get old and rich and famous together in Prox, getting together for reunions and bragging. We're still going to be more famous than any other people in the world, Dole. I'll make sure of that. I'll make damn sure that everyone's name is mentioned in the report and that everyone gets all the credit they deserve. What a story it'll be, too. First the diamonds, then the land, and then the woman . . ,"

" Oh, yes. Never forget the woman. You'd hurt her feelings if you left her out. Make her the whole basis of your report . . . Strange how she looked so similar to Ennis, isn't it ?" he said, now fading away and getting closer to his transition.

Kline breathed deeply, trying to ignore the thought of Ennis. She'd already caused enough trouble in his life.

Kline gasped eagerly, trying to listen to Dole's last words.

" I . . .I'll not only put her in the report, but I'll publish it in the next paper when I go back to Prox, and make her the only woman who ever put her hand on your crotch and lived to tell about it. We'll get a fortune for a juicy story like that," he said.

Dole gave a mild smile as he gazed upwards. " That was your problem ever since the beginning, Kline . . . You pretend that greed and pleasure are the only things that motivate you, but it's like you've used rough paint to cover up something beautiful. "

Kline rose a curious brow from his sympathy. " Where did this come from ? I've done what I wanted all along, since . . ."

Dole then shushed him weakly. " Kline, I'm dying. When I am finally dead, you can argue with me as long as you want. Just not now."

Kline closed up his mouth and nodded.

" Even though you try not to show it, you cry for the loss of that barbarian girl . . ," Dole said.

Kline shook his head, " You are mistaken my friend . . ."

"Dead men make no mistakes, Kline . . ," Dole gasped.

Kline smiled and shook his head to make Dole feel easier.

"I traded that girl for fame. Once I'm famous, there will be no end of girls," Kline said.

" Fame. Look how far fame has taken us both ? I've lost my balls and you've lost your mind . . . Although we suffer sad ends, we'll still get our fame and be remembered for something. But it won't do us much good, this fame - we'll be dead," Dole stated.

Kline gasped, as Dole closed his eyes.

" I wish I was born a Sudutan farmer, instead of an . . " he sighed, and was suddenly gone.

Kline lowered his head and began to hum a song Dole had loved, feeling his heart slowly breaking.

Kline finally shed tears, for the first time in his life, as his one and only friend ceased to be.

"And that's the last you'll ever hear of Atlantis from me, " the Old Man said.

"Is that really all? Is the story over? That's not much of an ending!" one of the crewmen said.

"You think this has all been some sort of bedtime story for little children ? Something I made up for amusement ? Let me tall you a secret. The things I have been telling you, they are about real people living real lives. I do not tell stories. I tell histories of real lives. And sadly, in real life, things sometimes just end. There is no great climax. There is no final fight with the enemy. Good does not triumph over evil. Things just go on for a while and then they stop, Dead. Just as one day, you, yourself will stop. And that stop cannot be delayed because there is no fulfillment or not enough satisfaction. It will happen when it happens. And that's all there is to it.

Just like it happened in these tales of Atlantis. Sassaska became Empress. Kline's expeditioneers all died. And Likooshas' Atlantis has been proven to exist no more.

The story is over.

I don't want to talk about it anymore.

But who cares ? We've found the treasure we came for. We'll all be rich now."

The Old Man got up and went to lie down away from the fire. I went over and sat beside him.

After a while, I whispered; "Is that really all you know about Atlantis, Old Man?"

"Hah !" he said with a huff and turned over to go to sleep. " I have not even told half of what I know!"

The End. (Sort of)

(See next page)

511

The Old Man lied through his teeth.

And not for the first time, either.

The story of Atlantis wasn't over. Far from it.
We all do continue with our journeys.
. . . and you just won't believe what happens to everybody !

> \- Greko, the kid.
> Cabin boy and book pitchman

Watch for Book Two in Neil's Atlantis trilogy:

No Man's Land
The Men of the Sud.

Coming soon from Noggin

For advance-release, signed 1st editions,
send $15 to:

Atlantis: Book Two

Noggin Publishing
Galactic Headquarters
289 South Robertson Blvd
PMB Penthouse 880
Beverly Hills CA 90211

or visit out website:

www.nogginshop.com

Neil Thompsett, at only 17, has already written and published three novels as well as writing and directing two short films. He has also restored a 1947 Indian Chief and passed the Mensa test. All in spite of having a serious learning disability. Yet he is still a geeky teenager, worried about girls, teachers and pimples - in that order. In fact, in spite of his successes and accomplishments, he is still such a nice guy that, if you write him a letter, he will probably write you back.